*Praise for*

# Heidi Swain

'A summer delight!' **Sarah Morgan**

'Sweet and lovely. I guarantee you will fall in love
with Heidi's wonderful world' **Milly Johnson**

'A little slice of joy' *Heat*

'So full of sunshine you almost feel
the rays' *Woman's Weekly*

'The queen of feel-good' *Woman & Home*

'A true comfort read and the perfect treat to
alleviate all the stress!' **Veronica Henry**

'A story that captures your heart' **Chrissie Barlow**

'Sparkling and romantic' *My Weekly*

'A delightfully sunny read with added
intrigue and secrets' **Bella Osborne**

'A wonderfully uplifting story with a picturesque
setting you'll wish you could visit' *Culturefly*

*Also by Heidi Swain*

The Cherry Tree Café

Summer at Skylark Farm

Mince Pies and Mistletoe at the Christmas Market

Coming Home to Cuckoo Cottage

Sleigh Rides and Silver Bells at the Christmas Fair

Sunshine and Sweet Peas in Nightingale Square

Snowflakes and Cinnamon Swirls
at the Winter Wonderland

Poppy's Recipe for Life

The Christmas Wish List

The Secret Seaside Escape

The Winter Garden

A Taste of Home

Underneath the Christmas Tree

The Summer Fair

A Christmas Celebration

The Book-Lovers' Retreat

That Festive Feeling

# Heidi Swain

# The Holiday Escape

**SIMON &
SCHUSTER**

London · New York · Sydney · Toronto · New Delhi

First published in Great Britain by Simon & Schuster UK Ltd, 2024

1 3 5 7 9 10 8 6 4 2

Simon & Schuster UK Ltd
1st Floor
222 Gray's Inn Road
London WC1X 8HB

Simon & Schuster: Celebrating 100 Years of Publishing in 2024

Simon & Schuster Australia, Sydney
Simon & Schuster India, New Delhi

www.simonandschuster.co.uk
www.simonandschuster.com.au
www.simonandschuster.co.in

A CIP catalogue record for this book
is available from the British Library

Paperback ISBN: 978-1-3985-1957-2
eBook ISBN: 978-1-3985-1958-9
Audio ISBN: 978-1-3985-1959-6

Typeset in Bembo by M Rules
Printed and Bound in the UK using 100% Renewable
Electricity at CPI Group (UK) Ltd

MIX
Paper | Supporting
responsible forestry
FSC® C171272

*For my dear friend and soul sister,*
*Sue Baker*

# Chapter 1

It wasn't so much that I was *ready* to take another trip, more that the scales had now tipped me into *over-ready*. I had reached home – or to be more precise, my parent's home – saturation point, and was craving the sanctuary of a few days escape before I said or did something I would doubtless end up regretting.

Thanks to a hectic winter and early spring schedule spent further updating Hollyhock Cottage, it had been months since my last getaway and now, right at the end of March I was poised to take some much-needed time out to refresh and reset before the start of yet another busy season living and working in Kittiwake Cove.

I was so desperate to leave the Dorset coast and all its associations behind that I would have happily settled for any destination, but as luck would have it, I was off to a city I loved, Barcelona, courtesy of a cheap flight and a cracking deal on accommodation due to a last-minute cancellation.

Just as it always did, my heart picked up the pace as I stepped into the airport and immediately headed for the restroom, where I would walk in dressed casually and for comfort, and come out transformed into the sleek, sophisticated European city-dweller I longingly wished I was.

My phone pinged with a WhatsApp notification just as I finished repacking my bags post-makeover and I pulled it out of my pocket. I knew who the message would be from and, down to the last letter, what they would have typed.

> Hey Ally! All absolutely fine here, so don't worry
> about a thing. Eat, drink, sleep – or not ;-) – repeat
> and we'll see you in a week! F x

Even though I had the message memorised from my previous trips, it still made me smile and I felt a huge rush of love and gratitude for my best friend, Flora. If it weren't for her stepping up and taking my place at home this week, I wouldn't be heading off to Spain on a sanity saver. I'd be back at the cottage with my dad, turning myself inside out and pretending that I was happy with the life I was living.

One that I had fully embraced and was immersed in, rather than one I still felt bound to go along with as a result of an emotional tangle of deep-seated obligation, anxiety and fear. I let out a long breath as my eyes began to prickle and my throat tightened.

'No,' I told myself, swallowing hard. 'You're not doing that, Ally. Not today.'

I gathered up my bags, pulled back my shoulders and stepped out onto the busy concourse. It was time to find my gate.

Having taken my fair share of cheap flights during the last few years, I knew the best strategy, for me at least, was to keep my head down, my earbuds in (even though there wasn't necessarily anything playing through them) and not become embroiled in tedious small talk.

It was a lesson I'd learned the hard way on a flight to Rome where I'd been stuck next to the ultimate manspreader – not ideal in the cheap seats – who insisted on loudly and inaccurately mansplaining every topic he thought he was an expert on and none of which I could have escaped being subjected to, as I was trapped in the seat next to the window.

The thought of attempting to squeeze past him had been enough to put me off trying and I'd been booking the aisle option ever since, even though I would have much preferred the seat with a view.

'Excuse me, young man,' said a voice beside me, 'would you mind putting my bag in the overhead locker? I can't quite reach it.'

'Of course, sister,' came the kind response, which was followed by some close proximity shuffling. 'No problem at all.'

My curiosity was piqued, not only by the deliciously deep voice of the man in question, but also by his use of the word, sister. My guess was they weren't related, so what was that about? I couldn't take a sly peek because the guy was now putting the bag in the locker directly above my head, potentially putting me in danger of a face to crotch situation, which I had no desire to risk.

After further shuffling, I felt a light tap on my shoulder and glanced up into the face of a serenely smiling elderly nun. That explained the sister reference. I pulled out my earbuds and smiled back.

'I'm just along here with you, dear,' she said, nodding at the window seat.

'And I'm in the middle,' added the nun's young man, who was tall enough to easily look over the top of her head.

In less than a second, I had taken in dark blonde hair, a smattering of stubble and beautiful beguiling green eyes, however, it was the stunning smile that caused the biggest flutter in my chest and the heat to spread up my neck and across my face.

'Of course.' I swallowed, rushing to stand up.

As I moved into the aisle, I could practically feel Flora's elbow nudging me in the ribs and see her wide-eyed expression and excitedly raised eyebrows. We'd been friends practically since birth, so she would know this guy was exactly my type, but it was far too early in the trip to be thinking about hookups and hot sex. I hadn't even decided what I was going to call myself yet, so unexpected in-flight entertainment would not be a sensible indulgence.

That was the other thing about my overseas adventures. I didn't just dress like someone else; I actually became someone else. Name, career, the whole shebang. I adopted a completely made-up persona. I was never Ally. I was never someone who lived by the seaside. And I certainly never shared a house with my dad.

Once the plane touched down and my passport had been checked and put away again, that was the moment I started to truly live my dream life. My quick change in the airport loos always got the ball rolling, my en-route planning supplied the finer details and by the time I reached my accommodation, I was immersed in my fantasy life. More often than not, I role-played the life I had thought would become my reality after I'd received my MA in Spanish and history. The life I would have embraced, had Mum's heart not prematurely given out.

I took a deep breath and banished further thoughts of Mum, as the guy with the seat next to mine inched into place. He smelt crisp, cool and citrus fresh. Definitely good enough to eat. Clearly, my head had got the memo that it was too early to be thinking about hook-ups and hot sex, but my previously dormant libido had eagerly turned a blind eye to it.

Having given him a few seconds to get comfy, or as comfy as he was going to be with his knees practically squished into the rear of the seat in front of him, I slipped back into place and surreptitiously glanced at his left hand. Not that the absence of a ring indicated someone wasn't already spoken for, but it was generally considered a starting point.

Perhaps I *should* throw caution to the wind and dive straight in. A little flight flirtation couldn't really hurt, could it? I wondered how Sister whatshername would react to that going on right next to her . . .

'Pear drop?' she asked, with uncanny timing, as her hand reached inside her capacious handbag and pulled out a rustling paper bag. 'If I'm focused on one of these, I find my ears don't pop half as much on take off.'

'Thanks,' said the guy, his fingers quickly dipping in to the bag and coming out with a whole handful. 'I'm a bit of a nervous flier, so any distraction is welcome.'

He didn't look nervous, but his smile had faltered and there was a slight tremble in his voice.

'Oh, don't you worry,' our travel companion said soothingly, 'we're in good hands.'

'Well, that's a relief.' He swallowed.

'I'm Sister Lucia, by the way,' she added.

'And I'm Logan.'

'Pleased to be travelling with you, Logan,' she said. She patted his arm and leant forward to look at me. 'And what about you, my dear?' she asked, offering me the bag of boiled sweets.

'Oh,' I said. 'No, thank you. My ears are usually fine.'

'And what's your name?' she further enquired.

I knew from past experience that I didn't have time to hesitate. It definitely looked suss if you had to stop and think what your name was.

'Flora,' I said, blurting out the first name I thought of. 'I'm Flora.'

I hoped I wasn't blotting my copybook by lying to a nun. Given that I was only going to be in her presence for the duration of my flight, I supposed I could just as easily have been Ally, but old habits die hard. No pun intended.

'Oh, how lovely,' Sister Lucia exclaimed. 'Perhaps after Flora, the patron saint of the abandoned, who teaches us how to forgive after betrayal?'

The real Flora, my best friend Flora that is, had only been betrayed once and she'd certainly never forgiven.

'I don't think so.' I smiled, sitting back in my seat.

'Perhaps after the Roman goddess of springtime and flowers?' Logan suggested, his smile growing wider again. 'That was her name, wasn't it?'

'Oh yes,' I said, returning his smile with my own and despite the fact I had absolutely no idea, 'that sounds more like it.'

'Don't underestimate the value of forgiveness,' Sister Lucia was quick to sagely say. 'It can be as beautiful as any flower or sunny spring.'

Logan turned to look at me, his green eyes meeting mine. They locked for a moment. He was even better looking close up. I found his knowledge of Roman goddesses rather alluring, too. Logan had hit the jackpot. He had both brains and beauty. I knew, given the opportunity, I'd forgive him anything.

'And what about the origins of your name?' Sister Lucia asked, when neither of us responded. 'Do you know the meaning behind yours, Logan?'

He looked away again and the spell was broken.

'Little hollow,' he said. 'It's Scottish.'

'Is it a family name?' Sister Lucia asked. 'You don't sound Scottish.'

'No,' he shrugged. 'My mum just liked the sound of it.'

I was rather keen on the sound of it, too.

Sister Lucia held Logan's hand and said comforting things while the plane gathered speed along the runway and took off. I would have been more than willing to reassure him too, but thought it was probably only a kindly nun, or someone in the medical profession, who could get away with physically comforting a stranger without coming off as potentially predatory.

'You can take your belt off now,' I did however say to him, a couple of minutes after we'd been given the all-clear.

'It's okay,' he said, looking a little green. 'I think I'll leave it as it is. After all, we'll be putting them back on again before we know it, won't we?'

I didn't remind him that it was a two-hour flight.

'Here,' nudged Sister Lucia. 'Have some more of these. Are you sure you don't want one, Flora?'

'No,' I said, 'but thank you again. I take it you haven't flown much before, Logan?'

I had completely abandoned my no small talk policy by this point. It was the first time I'd ever had such an appealing plane companion and having found Sister Lucia so easy going, I decided I was going to make the most of it. I ignored the disapproving voice in my head telling me that if it had just been me and her, I would still be wearing my earbuds.

'Oh, I have,' Logan said, 'and every time I think it will be less terrifying than the last, but it never is. Not that you didn't help, Sister,' he hastily added. 'My ears are loads better for a start,' he carried on, opening and closing his lovely mouth and stretching his jaw. 'No popping at all.'

Sister Lucia looked thrilled.

'So,' she asked, 'what are you both travelling to Barcelona for?'

I could hardly tell her the truth, that I was planning to have a few days away from my real-life while pretending to be someone else, could I? I daresay she wasn't that broad-minded.

'A quick holiday,' said Logan, giving me time to consider my options, 'and hopefully some R and R. I'm escaping a mundane UK city, for a beautiful Spanish one. I've got a huge and potentially complicated work project looming on the horizon, so I'm planning to relax and recharge ahead of a few full-on months.'

I was tempted to tell him that sounded similar to the reason behind the timing of my visit, as in the few full-on months, but changed my mind at the last minute.

'I know the weather in Spain won't be all that warm,' Logan carried on, 'but I've never visited Barcelona before and

I thought it might be the ideal opportunity to catch some of the sights ahead of the crowds arriving.'

Knowing the city as well as I did, I thought that was a wonderful idea, but he'd obviously not checked the calendar.

'What about you?' Logan asked Sister Lucia.

'Oh, I'm visiting friends,' she told us. 'I haven't seen them for years, so it's going to be a real treat. We're celebrating Easter together. I'm travelling later than I originally planned though, so I've missed quite a lot, but that couldn't be helped. And I have to tell you, my dear, you're going to find a lot more tourists in the city than you might be expecting.'

'Oh,' said Logan, sounding deflated, 'I didn't realise.'

'Easter is very big in Barcelona,' I chipped in. 'Holy Week is especially busy, but it should be a little quieter after the weekend,' I added, wanting to cheer him up again.

'You sound like an expert,' Sister Lucia smiled, leaning even further forward to properly look at me.

'I wouldn't say I'm an expert,' I unguardedly told her, 'but I lived in the city for a year while I was a student, so I'm quite familiar with the place.'

'There,' she said, clapping her hands together. 'I knew you two had been allocated seats next to each other for a reason.' That sounded like something the real Flora would say. 'Flora here can be your guide, Logan. How perfect is that?'

My mouth opened and closed, but I was too shocked to force out a single word.

'I'm sure Flora has plans of her own,' Logan said in response to his neighbour's obvious excitement.

I didn't respond to either of them, not because I was taken aback by Sister Lucia's suggestion, but more because I was reeling from the fact that I'd got so swept along I'd broken the most important of my getaway rules.

Along with limping over the fake name hurdle, I'd now let my guard drop so low; I'd revealed something genuine about myself. It wasn't the end of the world, only a minor detail that could be applied to any number of language and history students, but I needed to rein the truth-telling in. What was the point in making up my own game if I didn't stick to the rules when playing it?

'I'm sure she could squeeze you in for a day or two to tour the city,' Sister Lucia persisted, giving Logan an encouraging nudge. 'What are your plans for the week?' she then directly asked me. 'Are you going to be in the city on holiday, too, Flora?'

'Um,' I said, as a prickle of sweat irritated the back of my neck and I further regretted my decision to participate in the conversation. 'Well . . .'

'It's fine,' said Logan, turning pink and assuming my hesitation was the result of not wanting to see more of him once we'd touched down. 'Of course, you have plans. If you're on holiday yourself then I'm sure you have things you want to do. And even if you're not, why would you want to be tethered to a stranger you'd just met on a plane?'

He sounded so embarrassed; I could have throttled Sister Lucia. She blinked at me, her expression innocent and hopeful, although, I was in no way convinced that she was the former.

'I'm not really on holiday,' I said, wanting to make Logan feel better and reaching for the most common, and hopefully convincing, story I'd used on previous trips. 'I'm flying out because I have a job interview on Thursday.'

'Oh, wow.' Logan swallowed, his Adam's apple bobbing. 'Well, in that case, you really are going to be busy. Good luck. I hope you get it.'

Was it my imagination, or was there a hint of disappointment in the tone of his kind words?

'However,' I then found myself saying, 'if we do happen to be staying in a similar part of the city, then other than for a while on Thursday, I can be all yours.'

I felt my face flush as I realised how I'd put it.

'There now,' said Sister Lucia, sounding satisfied. 'How perfect is that?'

Logan looked at me and smiled again and I realised that, even though, as he had pointed out, he was a total stranger I'd only just met on a plane, the thought of showing him around the city, was a wonderful one.

Perhaps this was going to be one of those getaways that did include someone else and all that entailed. It wasn't always the case. I often went it alone, but my instinct was telling me that on this occasion, the addition of Logan could make my few days away even more ... satisfying.

'You'll have to let me know where you're staying,' I said breathlessly, hoping it was going to be near to me.

'I'll find the address now,' he responded, matching the action to the words.

His hotel turned out to be a mere stone's throw from the apartment I'd booked and that conveniently guaranteed that we could see Sister Lucia's suggestion through. When I pointed out to her that we were staying almost on the same street, it actually felt as though some cosmic force – God according to her – really was trying to push us together.

'This is meant to be, you two.' She beamed beatifically at us both. 'You can even share a taxi from the airport.'

'I suppose we could, couldn't we?' Logan agreed. 'And then maybe meet for dinner later?'

'All right,' I approved happily. 'I know just the place.'

My holiday escape had already taken off in an unexpected direction, but I was more than willing to follow its lead.

# Chapter 2

Just as I had known it would be, Barcelona was bustling, but the weather was unseasonably kind and the company utterly charming. Logan, on solid ground, proved to be every bit as lovely as he had been in the air and it was a total treat to show him the sights, both popular and relatively unknown, and take him to admire my favourite sea views, much-loved museums and preferred tapas restaurants.

We'd spent far more time together than we'd originally planned on the taxi trip from the airport and his fascination with everything and wide-eyed excitement had made me admire it all with fresh eyes, too. His new passion for the city further reignited my already established one and had me wishing I really could embrace the career as a historical conservator in a European city I still dreamed of.

And talking of passion . . .

'After today, I think I'm going to have to give you a new name,' he lazily smiled, pouring us both our third glass of txakoli while a waiter set down a platter loaded with traditional tapas dishes.

It had been a day all about the inimitable Antoni Gaudí.

We had taken a walking tour in the sunshine, which incorporated six sites of his exquisite architecture and I was feeling
every bit as inspired and delighted by what I'd seen as Logan
was. However, his unexpected reference to my name pulled
me up short.

After we had landed at the airport, I had stuck to my story –
that I had a job interview lined up for a position working in a
museum. That I was a passionate historical conservator who had
lived in Italy and France as well as Spain and that my life was
immersed in art, European culture, wonderful food and delicious wine . . . basically my dream life. The one I was supposed
to be living. However, as time slipped by, I'd barely mentioned
it further and had practically forgotten my deception.

And Logan hadn't said much about his life beyond Barcelona
either. I could tell that, living entirely in the moment, we both
wanted to keep the week in a perfect bubble and that had been
fine by me. Our time together was furnishing me with something wonderful to think about, an idyllic mental escape if you
like, for when I was feeling stifled by life back in Kittiwake
Cove. It would be the ideal go to when the walls of Hollyhock
Cottage closed in and my worries about Dad were driving me
to distraction.

'So.' I swallowed, as I felt a prickle of unease slide up my
spine, 'why do you want to give me a different name? Have you
decided I'm not a Flora after all?'

I tried to sound blasé, but I wasn't sure I succeeded. The
possibility of being found out was the one drawback of a getaway which involved attachments that ended up lasting longer
than just one night – and having my ruse exposed was the last
thing I wanted.

This time around, I realised I had relaxed a little too much, but my time with Logan felt completely different to anything I had experienced before, and despite the fact that, so far, we hadn't shared so much as a kiss.

'Oh no,' he grinned, looking blissed out and even more gorgeous than ever, 'you're definitely a Flora. Only now you're more of a freckle Flora.'

I instinctively put my hands up to cover my face. It didn't take much for the smattering that covered my nose, forehead and cheeks to increase exponentially and an afternoon of bright spring Spanish sunshine had certainly helped them along.

'Oh don't.' I grimaced, feeling unbearably self-conscious. It was an emotion I was unfortunately familiar with courtesy of my despised freckles. 'They're the worst.'

I let my head fall forward so my long dark hair, which was simply parted in the middle now I'd released it from the knot it had been tied up in, covered my face. I strove to avoid all mention of the blemishes that adorned my entire body and had been the cause of much teasing and taunting when I was growing up. Logan had hit a nerve. I knew he hadn't meant to, but the way my skin looked had always been a sore point for me.

'You don't mean that,' he said, moving to sit next to me.

'I bloody do.' I blushed. 'I hate them and I swear they're breeding.'

'You've got fecund freckles,' he said and I could hear the smile in his tone, but it wasn't teasing. More like he was pleased with his alliterative observation. After so much Txakoli I had to concede, it wasn't a bad effort. 'Will you look at me, Flora?' he requested, more seriously.

I didn't move and he lifted my chin with the tips of his fingers. He was sitting much closer than I had realised.

'You're beautiful,' he said, his voice thick in his throat as his eyes roamed over my face. 'Absolutely stunning.'

Up until that moment, I had convinced myself that we were going to stay in the friend zone, but happily there was no mistaking the seductive emphasis behind Logan's words. His proximity, gentle touch and when I looked up, massively dilated pupils, which were then just inches from mine, all suggested that we were shifting to somewhere far more intimate – and I didn't mind that at all.

'You're fabulous,' he whispered, the feel of his breath making my skin tingle. 'Every inch of you.'

'You haven't seen every inch of me,' I breathed, leaning closer in.

'Well,' he said. 'I can imagine.'

'Perhaps,' I said provocatively, lacing my fingers through his and resting my other hand on his thigh, which was pressed close to mine, 'after tonight, you won't have to imagine.'

'In that case,' he whispered, sending a pulsating wave of pure desire rippling through me, 'I'm very much looking forward to tonight.'

His mouth caught mine as he shifted to look at me again and the kiss that followed was intense, stirring and charged with more heat than a Spanish sun in August. It was the ultimate first kiss and one I had been happy to wait for.

'Flora,' Logan huskily gasped and I flinched.

I didn't think I was going to be able to cope with hearing him calling out my best friend's name and I had every intention of making him call out.

'How about,' I therefore suggested, 'for tonight, you call me Freckle?'

After that, the tapas disappeared in record time, every bite and swallow accompanied by a loaded look.

'My place or yours?' Logan asked once we'd hastily paid the restaurant bill.

'Yours,' I said, perhaps a little too keenly, so added, 'it's got room service.'

This was another getaway rule. I never invited anyone back to where I was staying, just in case I'd left something lying about that might reveal my true identity. I always put my safety first though and never headed off to an unknown or out-of-the-way place.

'And air-con,' I added for good measure. 'My apartment hasn't got air-con.'

'It's the beginning of April,' said Logan, with a glance up at the sky. 'I don't think we need to worry about overheating.'

'Oh well,' I said, stopping dead on the road. 'If that's your attitude, then I think I'll pass.'

He threw back his head and laughed. The sound made me laugh, too.

'I let myself walk right into that one, didn't I?' He grinned, shaking his head. 'In that case, I amend my previous comment to, you're right, Freckle. We're definitely going to need that air-con.'

'That's more like it,' I said, tugging at his shirt sleeve and pulling him along.

And he wasn't wrong. By the end of the night the temperature in the room had soared and we lay breathless on top of the creased and crumpled bed, waiting for the slowly permeating cool air to bring us back down to earth.

'I was right,' said Logan, lightly running a finger along the length of my collarbone, then tantalisingly tracking south. 'I knew I would be.'

'Right about what?' I asked, my breath hitching as his hand slid slowly over the contours of my body.

My nipples hardened as his fingers lightly brushed them on their trip to trace a circle around my belly button. His touch was feather light and had me yearning for a firmer connection.

'You,' he said thickly.

'What about me?' I gasped as he slowly caressed the top of my thigh and the spark of desire burst further into flame.

I'd had plenty of sex, and my fair share of good sex too, but being in bed with Logan had taken my experience to an entirely new level. Being with him lit me up in a way that felt wholly different. It was more than sex. There was a connection, something deep and meaningful. It was contradictorily both wonderful and inconvenient.

I knew it was imperative that I classed my time with him as nothing more significant than a holiday fling. Deep and mean-ingful moments definitely need not apply. The second our time was up, I would be packing him into the memory box to only bring out in future low moments, and yet . . .

'Every inch of you is beautiful,' he said, his fingers continu-ing their tantalising journey.

'I'm still not entirely convinced you've explored every inch,' I said, moving to straddle him and pin his arms above his head, 'but we've got plenty of time.'

During the next twenty-four hours, we made good use of both the room service and the climate control, but gained no further knowledge of stunning Barcelona. We were completely engrossed in each other and, as Logan continued his intimate exploration of my entire body, I completely forgot about my made-up interview.

'Do you think you should go back to your apartment tonight?' he asked, after a day spent in the bed, the bath and under the power shower, the until then unknown delights of which he had enthusiastically educated me in.

I turned to face him, my hair fanned out to dry across the pillow.

'Oh,' I said, taken aback. 'I guess I could. I mean, I have paid to stay there for the week, haven't I?'

I didn't much like the way my head and heart responded to the thought of time away from him. Perhaps it was a good thing that he was pulling back. Although I couldn't help wishing that I had been the one to suggest it.

'I was thinking more about giving you some space to prepare for your interview tomorrow.' Logan frowned.

'Oh my God,' I said, as I quickly sat up. 'The interview. I completely forgot.'

My reaction, was entirely unrehearsed. It had completely slipped my mind that I'd previously cited the pretend interview as my reason for being in the city and I wondered what would have happened had he not mentioned it. Would I ever have remembered?

'Well,' he said, as he luxuriously stretched out in the bed, 'I knew I was good, but I had no idea I was good enough to wipe your memory.'

I biffed him with the pillow and he laughed.

'You're Flora, by the way,' he reminded me. 'Also known as Freckle.'

'I have to go,' I said, jumping up, gathering my randomly

discarded clothes together and pulling them on. 'I'll call you tomorrow. After my interview.'

His bringing it up was the ultimate wake-up call. It was a shock to realise that I had become so intensely immersed in our fling that my brain had turned it into a genuine romantic getaway. The way my mood had dipped when he'd suggested I should leave was proof enough that that was what had happened and I realised I was in very real danger of leaving Spain with a broken heart as well as happy memories.

'Or I could come to yours?' he proposed.

I pretended I hadn't heard him.

'Have you seen my other shoe?' I asked.

A quick glance in the mirror took me completely by surprise. Gone was the city sophisticate, in spite of the outfit I had now impatiently tugged back on, and in her place was Ally. Plain old, Ally. What on earth had Logan seen in her? And more to the point, what was she doing gatecrashing my getaway? She was supposed to be in the UK, hiding out in the airport loos until I picked her up again.

'There,' said Logan, pointing at the hotel door, behind which my other shoe was wedged. 'And don't forget your jacket,' he added, standing up and reaching for it.

I took a moment to drink him in. Broad, toned, still tanned in spite of the season, and deliciously rumpled from endless hours making love, having sex and making me feel ... it was hardly any wonder I'd forgotten myself, was it?

'I'll call you here tomorrow night,' I told him, taking a step away as he took one towards me. If I let him touch me again, then I would never leave. 'We'll head out to a bar to either celebrate or commiserate.'

'It will be to celebrate,' he insisted. 'I've got a good feeling and hang on, let me give you my number.'

So far, I'd avoided swapping numbers by changing the subject whenever he headed towards it. I'd called him via the hotel to confirm the details of our initial plan, but in light of recent events, I supposed we were a bit beyond going through reception. It wasn't an issue I'd encountered before because my previous liaisons had all had a much shorter lifespan.

'No time,' I said, as I pretended to check a watch I wasn't wearing. 'I need to go otherwise I'll never be ready for tomorrow. I really want this job,' I added for good measure.

'The one you'd completely forgotten about?' Logan teased.

'Well,' I said, reaching for the door, 'I've remembered it now.'

As I stumbled along the corridor to the lift that would carry me away from him, I couldn't shake off the feeling that I felt far more affected by the thought of never seeing him again than I should have done.

# Chapter 3

Having turned entirely back into Dorset-dwelling Ally at the airport, then endured the tedious mostly motorway trip from London carrying an extremely heavy heart, I discovered I was more than ready to negotiate the last stretch of road that led to Kittiwake Cove.

It was entirely unexpected to feel a hankering to be heading back to the home I had never felt was my own, but I put the unique emotion down to a combination of relief that I'd managed to get through the week without being found out, in spite of the fact that my guard had dropped so low it had been invisible, and the hope that my return would scrub out some of the feelings of shame I felt for abandoning Logan. Throwing myself into life back at Hollyhock Cottage would, with any luck, help me. Not completely forget, because I didn't believe I deserved to, but feel a little less impacted by what I had done.

After every one of my previous getaways, I had arrived back in the cove buzzing and raring to go, full of zip and brimming with energy for at least the first few weeks. I would invariably find myself feeling so buoyed by what I'd experienced, I would be able to power through my return and the start of the working season, but this time around, those endorphin-enhanced emotions hadn't shown up.

Rather than enjoying the refreshed spring in my step, I felt weighed down with the excess emotional baggage I'd dragged through Spanish customs and back on to the plane. It was predominantly guilt, but there was a hefty dollop of selfish bitterness thrown in for good measure, too. I felt miserable to have missed the opportunity to make the most of my last couple of days away, even though the situation was entirely of my own making.

Having realised I was in way over my head with Logan, I hadn't called him again after leaving his hotel. The time of my fake interview had come and gone, the afternoon had stretched into night and I had stayed holed up in my apartment, only occasionally peeping out of the shutters to surreptitiously watch the world go by.

I knew it was highly unlikely that I would run into him if I ventured out, but I hadn't dared risk it. Instead, I stayed inside with a novel for company while the sun shone and every other person in the city fell in love. Okay, so that was an exaggeration, but at the time, it was how I felt. I refused to allow myself to dwell on how Logan was feeling.

'Nearly home sweet home,' I sardonically said, as I drove around the outskirts of the large traditional seaside town of Shellcombe and headed for classier Kittiwake Cove.

I tried to keep my eyes focused on the road ahead rather than the glittering sea, which was mesmerising when viewed from the elevated clifftop position the road enjoyed. Not the safest of distractions when you were in the driving seat.

Shellcombe was the town I had grown up in. It was a couple

of miles along the coast from the cove and was all seagulls, ice creams and chips, family holidays and noisy arcades. In complete contrast, Kittiwake Cove was much quieter and, sheltered by a sweeping curve of coastline, had the smaller but prettier of the two beaches. With no public car park, it was never overrun with tourists and offered a more sedate seaside experience than the gaudy delights available in Shellcombe.

There were rockpools teeming with life at the base of the cove cliffs and the sheltered setting boasted excellent swimming and kayaking opportunities. In terms of local businesses there was The Ship, an ancient pub with a restaurant attached, an independent café, smokehouse and a row of traditional fisherman's cottages, all now tastefully renovated for the holiday let market.

And there was impressive Hollyhock Cottage, too, of course. Set above and away from the other businesses, it was Georgian, double fronted and boasted a huge garden, which grew an abundance of the flowers it was named after. The place was far too large to merit being called a cottage, but that was its name and it was the house my parents had inherited from their wealthy employer, Beatrice Baxter, the year I graduated from university.

Mum had been Beatrice's personal assistant for years and then, as her employer's health deteriorated in old age, she became her carer. It was a job envied by no one, as the woman had a fearsome reputation, but over the years, Mum had come to love her like a mother. Dad had worked for Beatrice too and was responsible for taking care of the garden and grounds.

My parents had been fiercely loyal to the lady who had no one else, travelling from Shellcombe every day to care for her and her home, even during my holidays from school. This had caused untold arguments when I had been too young to stay home alone because I was forced to tag along with them. Not only did Beatrice terrify me, there was little for me to do at the cottage and as I shifted into the tween and then early teen years, I frequently let Mum and Dad know how much I resented having to go with them.

'I'm so bored,' became the moaning mantra I adopted during the long summer breaks. And so consumed by my sulky fug, as I got older, I had never fallen in love with the cottage or found my place in it.

It wasn't until Beatrice died that I realised that she had loved Mum and Dad as much as they did her. They mourned her passing deeply and had been incredibly shocked to discover that their loyalty, friendship and unwavering care had been rewarded with the biggest gift she could have bestowed upon them. She had left them Hollyhock Cottage, the most desirable property in the area. By then, I had left my hormone-fuelled teen years behind and was thrilled for them, especially as I knew I would never have to make the house that I had never warmed to my home. However, Beatrice's generosity did come with certain conditions . . .

I hadn't even made it through the open front door before the harried voice of one of those conditions shrieked a welcome. Of sorts.

'We thought you were lost at sea!' it piercingly belted out. 'We thought you were lost! Lost! Lost!'

'Good morning, Kasuku,' I politely responded. 'As you can see, I am not lost, but here again, safe and sound.'

'Geoff! Geoff! Geoff!'

I would have liked a moment to catch my breath, but Kasuku, the ancient and often stroppy African grey parrot, whose eternal care had been the most significant condition of Beatrice's legacy, was keen to alert my father to the fact that I wasn't lost at sea, after all.

'You old rascal,' I muttered.

'You old—'

'Thank you, Kasuku,' Dad cut in, rushing in from the garden, carrying with him a trug full of spring greenery and his familiar earthy scent. 'Ally, my darling girl.'

He dumped the trug on the huge pine table and pulled me into his arms. He squeezed me tight and I hugged him back. I really was here then. It was time to pick up the reins and smilingly soldier on. As fleetingly keen as I had been to arrive back, I knew the season ahead was going to be all the harder with only the memory of a failed holiday to fall back on.

'You should have let me know you were arriving so early,' Dad said, releasing me just enough to kiss my cheek and look at my face. 'You had decent weather then?' He grinned.

He was referring to the abundant freckle outbreak, but I wished he wouldn't. My conscience didn't need further pricking. After everything Logan had said, I was going to struggle to look in a mirror without regretting him until at least late autumn.

'I did,' I said, resisting the urge to ask Dad if he had been all right on his own. 'It was really warm.'

With Flora on-site, he hadn't really been alone and I knew he would fret if my questioning let slip that him once fleetingly saying that he sometimes felt a little lonely was something that still played on my mind. It was one of my biggest concerns about him that I kept to myself and which kept me firmly anchored in place.

'You had more luck than we did here then,' Dad said, letting me go and filling the sink with water to wash his earth-encrusted hands. 'Easter weekend was rotten.'

'Rotten, stinky eggs!' bawled Kasuku and Dad laughed.

'How much longer do you reckon he's got?' I asked, nodding at the cage.

Kasuku looked at me, cocked his head and raised one leg. I just knew that was the parrot equivalent of flipping the bird and resisted the urge to stick out my tongue in response. I knew from previous experience that a reaction like that could set him off squawking in retaliation for days. His vocabulary never ceased to amaze me, though and it gave us all a fascinating insight into the sometimes guarded character of Beatrice Baxter because it could only have been her who taught him most of the guff he came out with.

'Oh, he'll easily outlive the pair of us,' Dad chuckled.

I saw his back stiffen and knew he was remembering that was what Mum always used to say. It broke my heart that the parrot had outlived her.

'Flora said that if you message her when you're back, she'll meet you on the beach whenever you're ready,' Dad told me, his voice a little huskier than before. 'The usual place.'

The usual place was the place we had headed to, to share our secrets since we'd finally been deemed old enough to cycle from Shellcombe to the Cove on our own. Once we'd found it, it had never occurred to either of us that we could have carried on talking in my house, on the beach in Shellcombe or even on the bike journey.

If there was important info to impart, the sheltered rocks were, from then on, the place to do it. The irony wasn't lost on me that, during the holidays, I had to be dragged kicking and screaming to the cottage every day, but given a taste of freedom, I had been more than willing to cycle to the cove with Flora – often in all weathers.

'I hope she's all right,' I said, tossing Dad a towel to dry his hands on. 'I know she was dreading Freddie moving out.'

'She was,' Dad confirmed. 'I wouldn't like to be in her shoes, stuck living in a house with parents like that. Not that I blame Freddie for going.'

'Of course not.'

'You know what,' Dad carried on, 'if I didn't know better, I would have said Flora and her twin brother were changelings. They're nothing like the other three.'

'Thank goodness.' I shuddered, thinking of the contrast between Flora and Freddie and their older brothers. 'You'd certainly never put them together in a line up, would you?'

'You would not,' Dad agreed. 'Though I daresay those three rogues have been in a few of those. Now, how about a bit of breakfast for the weary traveller?'

'Toast! Toast! Toast!' yelled Kasuku.

I was weary all right.

It was bordering on cold with a mean-spirited breeze whipping my hair around my face when I left the house a short while later and headed along the path through the garden that led down to the beach. I inched my scarf higher, wishing I'd worn a hat. Before I opened the waist-high rickety wooden gate, I took in the view and breathed in the sharp, salt-laden air. The sun was still dancing across the surface of the sea making it sparkle. I couldn't deny it was certainly a picturesque spot, but it would never truly be mine.

I turned to look back at the house and acknowledged that it had been a relief to find Dad looking so hale and hearty (one of Mum's favourite expressions) and in such good spirits. My hands aside, I knew Flora's were the best he could have been left in, but that didn't stop the fear that his mental health might suffer in my absence, or that he might have incurred some illness or injury, fighting its way in during the return leg of my journey.

'Ally!'

I turned around again and spotted Flora waving like a loon on the sand below.

'Hurry up!' she bawled as I waved back.

'You got here quick,' I said, rushing to give her a hug.

'I had a back wind.' She laughed; her cheeks flushed from the journey as she nodded over to where she'd left her bicycle.

Arm in arm, we headed right to the edge of the cove and then squeezed our way between the rocks to our secret spot. It was little more than a wide ledge really, but it was surrounded by boulders on three sides, with a flatter one conveniently positioned across the top, which stopped the worst of the weather finding its way in. Depending on the time of year, that could be either searing sun, rain or wind and, occasionally, all three. On windy days, we always hoped the stony balancing act was less precarious than it looked.

'You've had a haircut,' I gasped, as Flora pulled back the hood of her coat.

'I did most of it myself,' she said, shaking out her hair, which was now styled in shoulder-length choppy layers.

Flora's hair was almost black and raven glossy.

'Most of it?' I frowned.

'It just needed tidying up,' she shrugged and I guessed her effort had been a disaster. I would have loved to have seen that. 'I thought I'd save a few quid by having a go at it myself, but it didn't work out. I could do yours if you like. I daresay it's easier snipping someone else's locks.'

'Uh, that would be a no,' I said, leaning back.

'Fair enough,' she said with a smile.

My hair had been long and straight for as long as I could remember and I had no desire to change it.

'I love your bangs,' I said in an American accent, reaching across to rough them up.

'Yes,' she said, batting my hand away and teasing it all out with her gloved fingers. 'I like the fringe, too, but never mind my hair. I want the goss. How did the getaway go? How many hook-ups? How much hot sex? You know I live vicariously through your trips away, so come on, spill your guts.'

I scrunched further down between the rocks where the ledge was wide enough for us to sit more comfortably.

'Come on,' she nudged. 'What are you waiting for? We'll get piles at this rate. My arse is already numb.'

I knew that to a certain extent she was humouring me about living vicariously through my getaways because, unlike me, Flora had never had any desire to leave the area. She loved her patch of the Dorset coast and I can't deny I sometimes envied her ability to be so settled and genuinely satisfied with her lot. Not that she had settled in the negative sense. She'd created the life she wanted to live. An honest life that followed her heart, in spite of the bullshit her parents and three brothers inflicted on her.

That didn't apply to Freddie, of course. He was every bit as wonderful as his sister. He'd just moved into the tiniest flat and if he could have squeezed Flora in with him, he would have taken her, but it hadn't been an option in his minuscule one bedroomed abode.

'Well.' I swallowed, unsure as to how much I wanted to reveal about what had happened during my time away. 'Barcelona was beautiful—'

'Boring. I've heard that before,' Flora impatiently cut in, in a singsong tone. 'Next!'

'Okay,' I relented. 'There was a hook-up. Just the one mind you. You know I'd never go with more than one guy at a time.'

She wrinkled her nose at that.

'Do you mean, you'd only go with one guy per getaway or that you wouldn't be up for a—'

'You know exactly what I mean, Flora margarine.'

'All right, Freckles. There's no need to hit below the belt.'

We grinned at each other and giggled, revelling in our shared history.

'And the sex was really hot,' I further confided, feeling more relaxed as a result of the childish nickname exchange.

'Wow,' Flora sighed. 'Any pics?'

I gave her a look.

'Of the guy, not the sex,' she squealed, putting up her hands.

'No,' I said. 'No photos.'

'What about a name then?'

'Miguel,' I said, the lie tripping easily off my tongue because I'd already pre-empted that I'd need one.

'Miguel,' Flora dreamily repeated. 'From here on known as, Miguel the Magnificent.'

'He was magnificent.' I smiled.

'Dark blonde?' she guessed. 'Gorgeous eyes and a stand-out smile.'

She was describing Logan to a T.

'Yep.' I swallowed. 'That's the fella. Now, tell me all about Freddie's new place and how you're getting on at home without him there to act as your parental buffer.'

'No way,' she said, 'I want more details.'

'You're incorrigible,' I tutted, just as a message from Dad opportunely popped up on my mobile. I hadn't realised our nook was a signal hotspot. 'Dad says will you stay and eat with us? He's doing a roast.'

'Hell yeah,' she said, leaning painfully on me as she pulled herself up. 'How can I resist? Last one off the beach has to carry my bike up the path.'

With a head start, I had no chance of catching her up.

# Chapter 4

As well as being a bona fide green-fingered genius, Dad was also a virtuoso in the kitchen. When he'd left school, he had wanted to follow a career in catering, but his father knew someone who was looking to take on an apprentice gardener and shoved him in that direction instead. In spite of his naturally green fingers, Dad had never really warmed to the role when it was forced on him, although he'd later come to love it, and when he and Mum inherited Hollyhock Cottage and Mum came up with the exciting plans for the future of the place, he took the opportunity to retrain.

Now, he was both a happy gardener and an accomplished cook. The look of the laden kitchen table and irresistible smells that greeted Flora and I after our trip to the beach confirmed that he exceeded at both. It was his dream career combination as he now grew, harvested, baked and cooked the most delicious food to feed not only us, but also the guests who came to stay with us throughout the spring to late summer season.

'So,' I said, once I'd washed my hands and was sat at the table. Flora was already piling crispy roast potatoes on to her plate and Dad was carving a plump and succulent chicken. 'How are the bookings looking?'

I would have preferred to put off talking about work a little longer, but with guests set to arrive in just a few days, I knew from past experience that it made more sense to be ready for action a while before the first weekend got underway.

'Even better than this time last year,' Dad told me, sounding thrilled. 'We're practically fully booked for the entire season. Breast or leg, Flora?'

'Decisions, decisions,' she grinned. 'Can I have both, please?'

'Glutton,' I tutted, as Dad acquiesced and deftly popped two succulent slices of breast on to her plate along with one of the legs.

'Thank you, Geoff.' She beamed, before covering the lot in gravy.

'Hey!' I yelped, grabbing the boat. 'Don't hog all the gravy.'

'Tut, tut!' scolded Kasuku.

'And we've had an enquiry about hosting another workshop,' Dad carried on, ignoring our squabble. 'From an author who lives literally just over the border in Devon.'

I scrunched up my nose.

'What's the topic?' Flora asked.

Dad frowned in concentration.

'Nature writing,' he said. 'Or something like that.'

'Isn't that what Fay does?' I asked. 'I'm sure that's one of her specialities.'

'I couldn't remember at the time,' said Dad. 'But you're right. Can you email the chap next week and explain we already have someone local offering the same thing?'

'First thing on Monday,' I nodded. 'We wouldn't want to upset one of our more home-grown tutors, would we?'

'Absolutely not,' said Dad. 'Out of county contributors are

welcome, but only if they offer something completely different.'

'And how's the final stage of the courtyard conversion looking?'

'All done,' said Flora. 'Well, apart from the final dressing. Freddie and his crew finished a couple of days ago.'

Project manager Freddie and his small team, which comprised of builders, decorators, a plumber and electrician, had undertaken all of the original work required to bring Mum's plans to life, as well as the extra flourish that I had suggested, and Dad had gone along with.

'Great,' I said, feeling relieved that it was all in hand.

'And just in time,' Dad joined in.

'I still think we would make more money renting that space separately,' I said, again picking at the thread I'd been pulling since the work to transform it began in the winter. 'Rather than piling it in with the rest, we should market it independent of the courses and for longer lengths of time.'

During the weekends from April to early October, Hollyhock Cottage opened its doors to a variety of local crafters and creators who tutored residential courses. The workshops on offer comprised opportunities to learn skills such as painting, silversmithing, sewing, linocutting, creative writing and journaling, to name a few. The guest numbers were limited to eight and they all stayed on-site in the converted stable accommodation that was situated on the other side of the garden. They also enjoyed the seasonal foodie delights cooked up by Dad. I was responsible for the general day-to-day management and the majority of the housekeeping.

The classy and exclusive set-up had been Mum's clever idea. A keen and accomplished crafter herself, she had wanted to support the local creative community in a way that offered them more than a location in which to sell their wares. There was already an exhibition space and gallery on the outskirts of Shellcombe, but nowhere for mum's artistic circle of friends to teach their skills.

Inheriting Hollyhock Cottage had initially been both a blessing and a burden, because the place needed to pay its way. Thankfully, Mum had soon come up with the clever solution that utilised the space and offered something unique to the area that was entirely bespoke. Originally, the role I now fulfilled was going to be hers and Dad had been all set to embrace the challenge of doing the cooking as well as continuing to maintain the garden.

In the early days, before Mum was taken, I hadn't been involved with any of it at all. I was at university when they inherited the cottage and while the planning part of the setup got underway and I had keenly enthused about their ideas, all the while feeling grateful that they were settled and going to be secure, living and working, in the place they loved. Conversely, I was thrilled to have escaped the confines of the cove and was all set to build myself an exciting life in another part of the world.

All our lives had been falling perfectly into place until . . .

'Ally?'

'Sorry,' I said, coming to and pushing the memory of one of my last conversations with Mum away. 'What was that?'

'The new conversion,' Dad repeated. 'I think we will have to let it out separately now anyway as this year's course and accommodation combos are all taken.'

'That's what I've been suggesting all along,' I patiently

restated. 'We have eight guests at a time and there are eight single en suite rooms. One for each. Lovely and tidy. If we start randomly offering the flat to one course member, who will have to pay much more for it because it's so much bigger and entirely self-contained, then it will leave us with an empty single, which will doubtless be impossible to consistently let.'

'I agree with Ally,' said Flora. I gave her a grateful smile. 'Her suggestion keeps it all simple and a longer let on the flat will earn a more regular income and also mean less disruption for me because there won't be a constant stream of guests moving in and out right next to my studio.'

'How are your books looking?' I asked her, before Dad came up with a counterargument.

The way I was keen to market the new space, was definitely the right way to go, but for some reason, it had proved to be an uphill struggle to get Dad to see it. I wondered if it was because it was the first thing we had done that hadn't been a part of Mum's original plan. Had she still been with us, I knew she would have come up with the idea for it herself, but as she wasn't, it was down to Dad and I to keep the business moving forward.

Perhaps that was what he found so difficult. The further we went, the further we moved away from Mum's original vision. I knew I should try to be more patient with him, but where developing the business was concerned, it was difficult sometimes and as a result we occasionally locked horns.

'My bookings are looking good.' Flora smiled. 'Opening at weekends is proving popular, especially for people who can't see me during the week because of work commitments and it's helping me spread appointments out a little more evenly, too.'

As a highly skilled practitioner, I knew how sought after appointments with my best friend were. She was proficient in both Reiki and holistic massage and had been struggling to fit clients in while balancing her own need to rest, ground and refocus between each one.

'That's really great,' I said, feeling relieved that it was working out, because I had been worrying that her desire to support so many people had been taking more of a toll on her than she had let on. 'I'm pleased it's making a difference.'

'You've got more time to ground yourself now, haven't you?' Dad expertly put in, which made me smile and Flora nod in confirmation.

'You should book yourself a session, Ally,' she pointedly said to me, which made my smile falter. 'Your aura is looking a little on the dark side.'

'Dark?' Dad questioned, looking sharply from her to me. 'She should be all red after a week in the sun having fun, surely?'

I waved my hands around my head and shoulders, trying to waft my aura away.

'You need to stop teaching him about that stuff,' I told Flora, suddenly feeling less thrilled about Dad's recently acquired knowledge and in particular his ability to apply it to me. 'It's not helpful.'

'You leave her alone,' Dad told me off. 'She realigned and unblocked a couple of my chakras while you were away and I feel fabulous.'

'Why did you need to do that?' I demanded of Flora before turning to Dad. 'What was wrong? Have you not been feeling well? You never said anything.'

I felt my throat start to tighten and my temperature rise as was always the case when I caught even a hint that something was amiss with him.

'I'm fine.' Dad frowned, quickly reaching across the table to take my hand. 'I didn't mean to panic you, love.'

'I'm not panicking,' I said, even though I was. 'I just didn't know you weren't all right. You said everything here has been fine,' I accusingly shot at Flora.

'Stop,' she sternly said. 'Everything has been fine. Everything is fine. I just got him balanced up a bit before the season starts, that's all. A little fine tuning never hurt anyone.'

Dad squeezed my hand and let it go and I tried to calm my breathing without making it obvious that's what I was doing.

'I've been spending more time on site here, too,' Flora carried on, tracking back to what we'd been saying before my mini meltdown. 'Because there's no chance of me doing any of what I need to at home. Now Freddie's left, all the stick we used to share between us is raining down on me. He feels awful, even though I've told him a hundred times that if I'd been in his position, I'd have gone, too.'

For some reason Flora and Freddie's parents had always held them both personally responsible for being twins and costing them a fortune after raising – in the loosest sense of the word – their first three sons. It didn't matter that the twins were both now adults who paid their way and contributed to the household income. Well, Freddie had until he moved out.

In fact, the older Flora and Freddie had got, the worse the abuse at home had become. Freddie coming out as bi had really set the cat among the pigeons because anything other than straight down the road in their bigoted family unit was unnatural, unwanted, unloved . . . and that was putting it mildly.

'Just what I bloody thought,' said Dad, throwing his napkin down and making us jump and Kasuku squawk in protest. 'They're arseholes, the lot of them.'

My mouth fell open and Flora's lips twitched.

'Well, I'm sorry,' said Dad, turning red. 'But they are.'

'Oh, I know that, Mr H.' Flora laughed, 'I just don't think I've ever heard you swear before.'

'Right?' I gasped. 'And two in one sentence.'

'Technically, it was two sentences,' said Flora.

'Oh yeah,' I said. 'Bloody in one and—'

'All right,' said Dad, cutting me off, 'that'll do.'

'That'll do! That'll do! That'll do!' screeched Kasuku, not wanting to be left out.

'Just think if the parrot had said—'

'Flora!' Dad warned. 'Stop right there or I'll end up regretting what I was about to suggest.'

'Which is what, Dad?' I asked.

'That Flora should move in here.' He succinctly said. 'You should move into the cottage with us, my love. You've got your business set up in the courtyard after all and we've got two empty bedrooms here in the house because Ally prefers the loft.'

Flora looked dumbstruck, but I thought Dad was really on to something.

'What do you think, Al?' He asked me. 'I had planned to talk to you about it first.'

'I think it's a brilliant idea,' I readily agreed. 'We don't have guests staying here in the house. It's family only and you're definitely family, Flo.'

If it hadn't been for her wading in and taking charge a few months after Mum had gone and goading Dad and I into picking up the plans and seeing them through, I dread to think what would have become of us. We had both been buried so deep in first our shock and then our grief, I don't think we would have ever been able to climb properly out.

Had we been left to our own devices; the garden would have become an untameable jungle and the cottage most likely fallen down around our ears. I might not have ever dreamt of a life living or working at the cottage, but had it not been for my best friend's intervention, I probably wouldn't have had any kind of life at all.

'Well . . .' Flora began, looking between us.

'That's settled then,' said Dad, clapping his hands and making Kasuku squawk again. 'If you get your act together, you could be in here before the first workshop of the season next weekend.'

# Chapter 5

Dad insisted that Flora should pick which room she wanted before she cycled back to Shellcombe that day and the pair of us spent most of the afternoon discussing the merits of the two empty bedrooms.

Originally there had been five bedrooms in the cottage, but two of those, after wrangling with the appropriate authorities, had been knocked through to give my parents' room and one of the spares en suites. There was a large family bathroom too, which I used because my space in the loft didn't have a toilet or running water.

'I think you should take this one,' I told Flora, who was finding it hard to choose.

I knew she wanted the slightly smaller room because it had a stunning sea view, but because it also had its own shower room, she was experiencing a dollop of misplaced guilt.

'I know you do,' she said, flopping down on the eiderdown-covered bed, 'but I still don't think it's fair that I get my own bathroom and you don't.'

I rolled my eyes.

'I do have my own bathroom,' I told her. 'The family one.'

'You know what I mean,' she said, chewing her lip.

'Why hasn't it occurred to you,' I pointed out, 'that if I wanted this room and the shower that goes with it, I would have taken it? I like being tucked away, right at the top of the house. It gives me a bit of distance.'

She looked at me and I could see there were tears in her eyes. Dad might not have had any idea, but Flora knew that my life in Kittiwake Cove wasn't the one I wanted to be living. Hence the need to have a bolthole that separated me from the rest of the house when I needed a little seclusion and a more private escape.

Had it not been for the welcome extra income it was going to bring in, I might have been tempted to fight for the freshly converted courtyard flat, but then as well as the lost money, I supposed I would have had Flora scrutinising my aura between clients and I would also have been in the thick of it when we had guests in residence.

'So, this is the one,' I stated, before Flora could tell me again what a hero I was for staying and taking the business on after she'd magicked Dad and I back to life after losing Mum, as opposed to helping to get it all going and then taking off. 'It really is the better choice because most of the time you're going to be on the other side of the house to that bloody parrot.'

Flora climbed off the bed to look out of the window again.

'Yes,' she happily sighed. 'This is the one.'

'We're going to practically be roomies,' I laughed.

'Your poor father.' She grinned, spinning round to look at me.

'Yep,' I laughed. 'He has no idea what he's in for, does he?'

'He must have forgotten about our legendary sleepovers,' she loudly whispered.

'No, he hasn't,' said Dad, appearing in the doorway and scaring us half to death. 'He's just hoping you've grown out of all that giggling at midnight and pinching my beers.'

'Never!' The pair of us chorused.

The following week was beyond busy as plans for the season were finalised. The cottage and courtyard rooms received a thorough spring clean and the last few things for dressing and kitting out the flat, which I was now trying to get Dad and Flora to call an apartment, as I thought it sounded more sophisticated, were delivered and set up in readiness for it being rented out.

Located slightly apart from the other rooms, I had decided to give the space a completely different feel. The aesthetic in the cottage was a mix of faded glamour and shabby chic with some quirky and eccentric accumulated additions thrown in and that look had been followed through into the single court-yard rooms.

Keeping that section of the accommodation looking similar to the cottage created a cohesive feel. When guests attended one of our unique weekends, we wanted them to enjoy the luxurious but laidback experience beyond the workshop and the meals around our kitchen table and the exquisite rooms now fitted the bill perfectly.

The apartment, however, was self-contained and, therefore, the guests who stayed there wouldn't be coming into the house and that gave me the scope to create something different. Given the location, I felt it would have been a cop out to go for the seaside theme, not to mention a bit of a cliché, so instead I linked the space to the garden, which it was set right next to.

I thought it was an amazing look, but Dad hadn't been sure about the wallpaper when it arrived.

'You don't think it's a bit dark, do you?' he'd asked, cocking his head to take in the black background, which I thought was the perfect foil to the colourful blooms it was overlaid with. 'And it's very blousy. I thought you wanted to appeal to—'

'You're not suggesting blokes can't be into flowers, are you, Mr H?' Freddie, who was kindly using his afternoon off to help me hang it, teased. 'Because you work with flowers every day.'

'No,' Dad quickly responded. 'I'm not suggesting anything like that at all. It's just not what I was expecting. It's absolutely nothing like anything else we've got.'

'Exactly,' Freddie and I said together.

Yet again, it had been Dad's resistance to doing something different to what we'd started out with that reared its head.

'Trust me, Dad,' I further said, making sure he couldn't see the invoice because the paper had been far from cheap, 'this is going to be perfect.'

And it was. Having plumped the cushions on the bed and straightened the last botanical print as I finished the final dressing, I knew I'd hit the mark. The interiors in the other rooms were simple, light and airy whereas the apartment had a decidedly darker, but sumptuous and multi-layered feel. I was immensely proud of it, which was not generally a sensation I experienced in my working life.

'Well,' said Dad, when he came to find me and looked around. 'You were right, Ally. It is beautiful. I wouldn't mind staying here myself.'

He had mostly stayed away while I had been pulling it all together.

'Yes!' I said, punching the air and feeling victorious to have succeeded in making him change his mind.

'You've definitely inherited your mum's talent for design and putting unusual pieces together, my love,' he praised as he ran his gaze over the soft furnishings.

'Thanks, Dad,' I said, leaning into him and feeling choked.

There might not have been any scope for me to utilise my language skills or passion for historical conservation at Hollyhock Cottage, but at least I could put some of my talents to good use. Not that that was enough to stop me hankering for the life I'd lost, but it was, in that moment, some compensation.

'You've done a really wonderful job,' Dad said, kissing the side of my head. 'Now all we have to do is take some photos, decide on the price and get it up on the website.'

'No rush,' I shrugged and Dad looked flabbergasted.

'But you've been going on about getting it booked practically since we started work on it.' He said, giving me a playful shove.

'I know,' I told him, 'but as you're so keen on it and it's so different to anything we've offered before, why don't you give it a test run? Try it out for a few nights and see if it works as a practical space and that everything does what it's supposed to.'

'I couldn't do that,' he laughed, looking around again.

'Flora is moving into the house tomorrow,' I reminded him. 'Are you sure you want to be in there for the first couple of nights we're together?'

He laughed at that.

'Perhaps you're right,' he grinned. 'I could stay here for a bit and give the pair of you the chance to get the silliness out of your systems, couldn't I?'

'There you go.' I laughed along with him, even though I knew he wouldn't. 'It sounds like the perfect plan to me.'

'But if I do,' he continued, 'I'm bringing my beers with me.'

With the rooms to finish airing and meticulously prepping and what Dad and I termed a 'big shop' to do on the Friday, I was up with the lark on Thursday morning – Flora's moving day – to get as much sorted as I could ahead of her and Freddie arriving with all her worldly possessions. Dad had already told her she could shift the furniture around, or even decorate the room to suit her tastes, so that was going to be interesting.

'There, that's all of it,' said Freddie, as he put down the last of the boxes that had been hurriedly and haphazardly stacked in his van.

Unusually for her, Flora was looking a little tearful. I guessed it hadn't been a happy parting from her parents, despite the fact they'd been more than hinting that they wanted her and Freddie gone for years.

'Come on, Flo,' said Freddie, giving her a brotherly bear hug. 'It's done now.'

'I know,' she sniffed into his shoulder. 'I'm okay.'

I gave her back a rub.

'Are you coming to the pub tomorrow night?' Freddie asked me. 'They've got a really great band lined up. It should be a good night.'

'I would have loved to,' I told him as Flora untangled herself but stayed close to his side, 'but with the first guests arriving on Saturday, I need to check we've got everything sorted. In my experience, how well the first weekend goes, can have a knock-on effect for the rest of the season.'

Having only been up and running for a few years, I wasn't entirely sure that was always going to be the case, but we'd had hiccups early on in the past and then bigger problems after, so I wasn't taking any risks. Starting the year off with a hangover that inevitably followed band night in The Ship wouldn't make for the easiest or most professional of starts.

'That's fair enough.' Freddie nodded. 'What about you, Flora?'

'I'll be helping out here,' she said.

'You don't have to,' I told her. 'I know you're still not comfortable that Dad's not charging you rent, but that doesn't mean you have to muck in to make up for it.'

'Joe has said he'll be there,' Freddie pitched in and I swore under my breath. 'What?' He frowned.

'Well,' I huffed, 'she definitely won't go now, will she?'

'Oh, jeez,' Freddie tutted, taking in Flora's completely pissed off expression. 'I don't know why you just can't move on.'

'Jeez yourself,' I winced, 'you're cruising for a bruising, Freddie.'

'He really is,' said Flora, punching his arm. 'We're twins remember. You're supposed to be my champion, not fighting in the opposite corner for your mate.'

'I do know that,' Freddie said, rubbing his arm. 'But I still don't get it, Flo. It happened years ago now. Getting on for a decade. Actually,' he more specifically pointed out having done the maths, '*more* than a decade.'

'So, anyway,' I said as Flora turned away looking even more annoyed. 'Thank you, man with a van. Let me show you out.'

'It's fine,' he said, taking the hint. 'I can find my own way. I'll ring you later, Flora, yeah?'

'You'd better,' she said, turning back to say goodbye. 'And thanks Freddie,' she croakily added. 'We're finally free of them, aren't we?'

'We really are!' he said, grabbing her and lifting her off her feet before spinning her around.

I didn't think I'd ever be able to keep up with the way the emotions between them swung from one extreme to the other. I guessed it was another of those mysterious twin things.

'So,' I said, once Freddie had gone, 'what do you want to sort first?'

It didn't take long to unpack everything and with the numerous strings of warm white fairy lights, bowls of crystals and lengths of silk ivy draped over every available surface, it was soon looking much more Flora style than Hollyhock Cottage aesthetic. It smelt more Flora too. Everything she owned carried a hint of incense.

'I've got you something,' I told her, once we'd flattened the last of the cardboard boxes. 'It's only small, but I thought you might like it. And I used the website you recommend to your clients, so I know it's genuine.'

I handed over a small purple velvet drawstring pouch and Flora opened it and tipped out the heart-shaped piece of selenite that was nestled inside.

'I thought after the trauma of today,' I softly said, 'that it might help.'

'It's perfect, Ally,' she said, the words catching a little. 'Thank you.'

I gave her a hug and then she told me how later she'd cleanse it and set intentions to maximise its potential.

'I feel better already,' she said, arranging it on her bedside table before throwing open the window and leaning out.

The sun was shining in a cloudless sky, but it was still chilly. That was hardly surprising though, given that we weren't even halfway through April yet. That realisation made my mood dip a bit. It was going to be months until I'd be able to get away from the cove again. I hoped my next adventure would be different to the last. Not that I was allowing myself to think about it for more than a few minutes at a time. Logan, and the memory of how I'd treated, or rather, shamefully mistreated him, were still too painful to pore over for long.

'Well, that's good,' I said, focusing back on my friend, 'and exactly what I was hoping.'

'And what about you?' she asked. 'Are you feeling better?'

'What do you mean?'

'Well,' she said, sitting on the bed and patting the space next to her. 'I could tell you weren't right when you came back from Barcelona.'

'Not right?' I frowned.

'Yes,' she nodded. 'Something didn't work out on your break this time, did it? You usually come back from one of your adventures full of it, but this time, you were almost as flat as you were before you went. And you still are, a bit.'

I hadn't realised I'd let it show quite so much. I thought I'd done a wonderful job of bluffing, but apparently not.

'Don't worry,' she reassured me, 'your dad hasn't noticed.'

'So, how come you have?' I smiled. 'What are you, some kind of mind reader?'

'You know I am,' she laughed. 'Where you and Freddie are concerned anyway. So, what is it? This Miguel guy?'

'Miguel?'

'The bloke you hooked up with.'

'Oh, him.' I swallowed. 'No, nothing to do with him.'

It was all to do with him.

'What then?'

'It's coming back to this place,' I said, trotting out the usual line I'd use whenever she picked up on a dip in my disposition and, ordinarily, what my less than buoyant mood would genuinely be all about. 'You know how I feel about the cottage and the cove. The bad memories and my concerns about Dad . . .'

Flora looked at me even more intently and my words trailed off.

'But I'll be fine,' I quickly said, purposefully sounding more perky. 'As soon as the season gets underway, my feet won't touch the ground and I won't have time to think about any of that.' She went to say something else, but I rushed on. 'And anyway, we can't talk about this stuff in here, can we? We need to be down at the rock if we're having a heart to heart, remember?'

'You're right,' she said, looking around her new room. 'We don't want to clog up the energy in here, do we?'

'Absolutely not,' I agreed, pulling her to her feet. 'So, come on. Let's get out of here and go and find out what Dad's cooking for your celebratory moving day dinner.'

# Chapter 6

Given that I'd now got my eagle-eyed, mind-reading best friend living with me, I knew it was imperative that I made even more of an effort to not think about my all too brief time with Logan and the scorching sex we'd had. I needed to pull myself together before she properly found me out, but it was hard with the consistent ache I still felt in my heart whenever memories of him flooded in.

Surely, that wasn't normal, was it? Given that we'd known each other for less than a week, I couldn't help wondering if perhaps there was more to it than mortification over how I felt about how I'd treated him. Mindful that Flora was now on my case, I threw myself into my work and focused on finishing the courtyard rooms ahead of our first open weekend of the season in the hope that the effort of doing so would finally banish all thoughts of Barcelona.

However, as I straightened the paintings – all created by local artists – and plumped the patchwork cushions – also sourced close to home – my mind refused to play along and I found myself remembering the good times in Spain and then shifting to recall my cruel final act. I hadn't slept well the night before and, predictably, Logan had walked into my dreams.

One minute we'd been hand in hand walking down a sunny Spanish street and the next, I was on my own in the same place, only in the pouring rain. I could see the back of his head in the throng of people and umbrellas ahead of me, but no matter how hard I tried to push through the wet crowd or how fast I ran, I couldn't find a way to reach him.

I had woken up drenched in sweat and opened the window, where I sat on the padded seat cushion Mum had made for the sill and watched the sea gently lapping the shore. It had been a clear night and with the moon brightly shining it should have been idyllic, but I had been too upset to consider how lucky I was to have a view like that just beyond my bed.

I had realised then, as I stared out to sea, that there could be no denying that I had started to fall in love with Logan, so it was no wonder that I couldn't really forget him, no matter how hard I worked. Our few days together had been so completely perfect, it would have been impossible for me not to have given him at least a part of my heart. I mulled over how things might have worked out if I had been honest with him, rather than playing my game of pretend. Might there have been some longevity to our romance if I'd played it straight?

'Knock, knock.'

'Come in,' I said, clearing my throat as I looked around the room I had been checking. 'Come in,' I repeated, a little louder, because the first time the words had stuck.

'Can you get the door, love?' Dad called, 'I've got my hands full.'

I rushed to let him in.

'Oh Dad,' I gasped when I saw what he was carrying. 'How pretty are these?'

'And they smell amazing, too,' he proudly said, stepping in and putting the wooden box of plants down on the tiny table. 'There's two for each room.'

Inside the crate were old-fashioned terracotta pots. One half were set with tiny narcissus and the rest with highly-scented hyacinths.

'I know you said you were growing something specific for the start of the season,' I said, sniffing deeply to draw the heady perfume further in, 'but I wasn't expecting anything like these.'

Dad looked delighted.

'I've done my best to hold them back,' he explained, even though he knew I wouldn't understand what he meant. His gardening skills and techniques were a mystery to me. The bright borders, polytunnel and veg patch were most definitely his domain. 'But these will last a while and I've got another lot about to come into bloom.'

'The vases are always wonderful, but these are even prettier. Thanks, Dad.'

Every room always had fresh flowers and we tried to make them as seasonal as possible. Dad grew tulips and daffodils in long beds also for the spring, which he cut for the cottage as well as the guest rooms, but the prettily potted moss-topped bulbs he'd thoughtfully put together were a really extra special, highly-scented touch.

In part, it was the added extras, all locally sourced, that made the finishing touches to our weekends so superior. The welcome baskets currently included locally made chocolates, wine and cordial, soap made using goats' milk from a nearby farm, as well as a notebook that incorporated locally grown pressed wildflowers in its pages.

The gifts changed as the year went on, but whatever we added was always appreciated and admired. The multiple reviews that mentioned them were testament to that and we carefully considered everything we included. Nothing was ever ordered in a hurry or with a 'that'll do' attitude.

We had agreed early on that if something was less than perfect or couldn't be traced back to the maker, then we'd do without it. It was that attention to detail that made the weekends at Hollyhock Cottage so popular. Yes, they were expensive, but the cost, in our opinion, was more than justified and the multiple five-star reviews bore that out. A stay with us was a high-end experience where guests acquired new skills, received lovely gifts, ate incredible food, had access to and enjoyed the garden and the beach and slept in superior accommodation.

'I'm pleased you like them,' said Dad, looking chuffed. 'And I've added a few more pots to the outdoor displays, too.'

There were collections of seasonally filled containers, some metal, some terracotta, dotted around the outside of the cottage and the courtyard. They were quite labour intensive, but really looked the part.

'You're a star,' I told him, dipping my head to smell the hyacinths again.

'And so are you,' he said, looking around. 'Your mum would be so proud of what you've achieved here, Ally.'

'What we've achieved,' I said, amending his kind words. 'It's all a joint effort Dad.'

'Hollyhock Cottage, forever.' He laughed, starting to take the pots out of the crate.

My smile faltered. I could admit that I was impressed with what we'd achieved, but forever was an awfully long time. But then, the last time Mum and I had walked along the beach, I had promised her I'd be here forever if she wasn't, hadn't I? She had looked as beautiful as I'd ever seen her that day, with the wind blowing her long hair wildly about her face and her bright blue eyes sparkling.

We had just spent a week together talking her ideas through and I, blissfully unaware of what was heading my way, had been thrilled about and enthused over everything. I had praised every detail, leaving her and Dad in no doubt that I was as enthusiastic about their new venture as they were.

When I later thought about my reaction to what they had shared with me, I knew part of it was the result of feeling so satisfied that they had something exciting ahead of them. Something that would soften the blow when I told them that, having fallen in love with Barcelona, I would be moving there as soon as I'd got my MA.

How I wished I'd taken the opportunity during that trip back to the cove to share my intentions after they'd told me theirs. Had I done that, the conversation Mum and I had later had on the beach might never have happened and I wouldn't have ended up stuck in the life I now found myself in.

'Promise me, Ally,' Mum had said having again listened to me praise her vision, 'promise me that if anything happens to me, you'll come to the cove and help your dad with everything.'

'What?' I swallowed, taken aback by what she was asking.

'I can tell that you're as keen as we are,' she smiled, her complexion flushed as a result of the wind. 'And having listened to what you've said about the house, I'm also certain that you love the cottage a whole lot more now than you did when you were growing up, so please say you'll move here if something happens to me and work with your dad.'

'Nothing's going to happen to you, Mum,' I said seriously, feeling it would be unfair to spring my plan to move on her then.

'I know,' she lightly responded. 'But would you do it?'

My head was shouting at me to say no, but I ignored the warning and took the lead from my heart. Most likely on the assumption that I believed it was a promise I would never have to honour. Mum had decades left to live, after all. As did Dad.

'Yes,' I therefore said. 'If anything happens to you, I promise I'll move to the cove and help Dad.'

'Thank you.' She smiled, reaching out to stroke my face. 'Now, come on,' she had then laughed, 'I told Kasuku you'd watch him take his bath.'

I took a deep breath as Dad lined up the last of the pots on the table. The memory of that conversation had haunted me ever since. Not only because it turned out to be the last time Mum and I had been together on the beach, but also because of how that rash commitment had changed the course of my life. How it had changed the course of my life *forever*, given what Dad had just said.

'There now,' he tutted, then started to put all but two of the pots back in the crate again. 'I needn't have unloaded the lot. You only need a pair for each room. What colour hyacinth would you like for in here, love?'

'Um,' I swallowed, feeling unsettled. 'Let's go for the pale pink. It will look lovely next to the Cabbages and Roses bed linen.'

'Are you all right?'

'Yes,' I said, picking the pot up. 'I'm fine.'

'Sure?'

'Sure.'

'Because I did wonder when you came back . . .'

'What did you wonder?' I asked as his words trailed off.

'Oh, nothing.' He smiled, shaking his head. 'I daresay it was just me being silly.'

So much for Flora reckoning he hadn't picked up on anything.

'I'll distribute these, then I better get back to the cottage,' he said, picking the crate up again. 'Kasuku was shouting for his bath after breakfast and I still haven't got around to it.'

The parrot might not have known it, but he had impeccable timing.

Because the spring weather could be so unpredictable, we always kicked the season off with a course that ran exclusively indoors and this year it was silversmithing with Sally Jones. Sally had been one of Mum's closest friends and the silver bangle I wore, imprinted with a rose and trailing greenery, had been gifted from her to me on the day of Mum's funeral.

'A rose for our Rose,' Sally had said, her eyes red from crying, as she slipped it on to my wrist. It was a perfect fit.

'My Rose would have loved that,' Dad sobbed, looking over my shoulder to take the exquisite detail in.

I hadn't been able to say anything. The shock of losing Mum had penetrated so deeply, it was months before I had finally got around to thanking Sally properly.

'I'll get the kettle on,' Flora helpfully said, as Sally started to set up early on the Saturday morning before the guests were due to arrive. 'My client isn't booked until one today, so I can help get the ball rolling here before I head across.'

'You are a love,' I told her, stifling a yawn. As was my habit before the first weekend launched, I had barely slept, but at least that meant Logan hadn't had the opportunity to show up in my dreams again. 'I'll ask Sally what she wants.'

Sally was in the large room to the left of the main house door, which was already propped open thanks to a sudden and most welcome warm spell. The room ran right from the front of the house to the back. The courses were mostly taught there, around another vast pine table that could easily seat ten and was positioned in front of the bay window.

The room was split in two by a huge, squishy cushion-covered sofa and beyond that there were a couple of armchairs, a fireplace with a large wood burner and a slightly battered and stained coffee table. The French doors, festooned in floor length billowing cotton curtains, opened straight into the garden and the atmosphere was light and airy in spite of the collected clutter and piles of *Country Living* and multiple gardening magazines.

'Can I get you a tea or coffee, Sally?' I asked, as she looked over her list to check she hadn't forgotten anything.

Everything was meticulously set out. There was all sorts of paraphernalia, including cushioned mats, tiny pliers, pattern stamps, an electric polisher and mandrels for ring sizing and shaping. At one end of the table there was a soldering station. I knew that was strictly a one-on-one part of the process, even for a straightforward solder.

'Peppermint tea, please,' Sally said, tying her hair up in a brightly patterned scarf. 'I've been so looking forward to today, Ally. It feels like forever since I was last here.'

'I am sorry I haven't been much of a hostess over the winter,' I apologised.

Ordinarily Dad and I would invite everyone who taught the courses to supper at least once during the closed season, but we'd been so caught up with other things, like the apartment conversion, that the time had run away with us and we hadn't got around to it.

'I don't want you feeling bad,' Sally quickly said. 'From what your dad has been telling me, you've both had your hands full.'

'We have,' I conceded, 'but I know the Zoom get together didn't have quite the same feel as a night around the kitchen table making fresh plans and finalising details.'

We'd had an online meeting to sort out the schedule for the year and other than a quick get together just before Christmas, that had been it.

'Or taste the same,' said Sally, keenly licking her lips. 'Any idea what's on the menu today? You know I'm only really in it for the free food.'

I had to smile at that. Dad's reputation as an accomplished cook was proving to be as much of a selling point as the courses these days.

'Individual gluten free goats' cheese souffles,' Dad reeled off through the open French doors, where he was deadheading some of the pots, 'with a herby dressed salad. Oh, and squidgy chocolate brownies for teatime.'

Sally groaned with pleasure.

'I wish I hadn't asked now,' she laughed. 'My tummy's rumbling already and I've only just had my breakfast.'

'There are always biscuits in the barrel,' Dad reminded her.

'Don't tempt me,' she shot back.

'Come on then, Ally,' he urged, 'the guests are starting to arrive.'

'I'll put my tea request in to Flora,' Sally kindly said. 'You go and get everyone settled in.'

By the time the guests had been shown to their rooms and a little later were seated around the table being instructed on how to size the silver they would soon be turning into stacking rings, it felt as though the winter break hadn't happened at all.

In fact, both days flew speedily by as I made endless pots of tea, loaded and emptied the dishwasher, changed a lightbulb and gave guided tours of the garden apartment. Dad was rushed off his feet too, cooking up delicious feasts both days and giving tours of his own around the garden, as well as dishing out hen keeping advice and sharing his tips and tricks for getting his superb souffles to rise every time.

I tried not to worry that it was all too much for him and knew that I should have been reassured by the happy smile he was wearing whenever I looked at him along with the sound of his laughter, which constantly met my ears through the open windows, but I couldn't help it, I did worry.

He was ten years older than Mum had been and she'd been snatched away in less time than it took me to snap my fingers, despite looking as outwardly healthy as he did. What if the same thing happened to him? The regular influx of guests at this time of year doubtless helped to banish the loneliness he'd once fleetingly mentioned, but was all the work to make everyone's experience perfect, taking a toll on his physical health?

'They're now off!' Dad called through the hall, late on the Sunday afternoon.

I rushed through from the kitchen, where I had been feeding

Kasuku pieces of dried mango, which he adored, as a treat for not shouting or swearing at anyone. He'd been respectful and reserved the whole weekend, which Dad and I had been relieved about. It wasn't always the case.

'Bye! Bye!' the old rascal shouted after me and I knew he was suddenly gearing up to shriek something worse. 'Don't f—'

I slammed the door behind me. I might have known the peace wouldn't last. I daresay he'd only been behaving to guarantee the sweet treats.

'Here, Dad,' I said, blocking out the subsequent protesting racket, 'let me help.'

As a parting gift, depending on the season, we handed out either hollyhock seeds collected from the garden in brown paper bags stamped with the cottage name on the front, or actual plants grown from the seeds. It was the finishing touch Dad was most proud of, allowing the guests to take a little piece of the cottage away with them, and even I, who so often felt a fraud for the part I played in the running of the place, had to admit that it was a wonderful memento of a weekend happily spent.

'See you again soon!' Dad called as the last car set off.

The hand which waved out of the window in response was wearing a set of silver rings that had been crafted the day before.

'What's Helen coming back to do?' I asked Dad as the car disappeared out of sight.

'The stained-glass weekend,' he told me. 'I think it's the only thing she hasn't had a go at. I always feel so proud when guests want to keep coming back.'

'And so you should,' Flora, who had come out to join us, told him. 'It's proof that this place is loved and that you've got it spot on, Geoff.'

'And, as reliable repeat visitors, the money from the likes of Helen is practically guaranteed, too,' I added.

'It's not just about the money though,' said Dad, looking at me. 'Is it?'

'Of course not,' I responded. 'But we couldn't manage to keep this place afloat without it, could we? Now, who wants that last brownie?'

'With eight beds to strip before the laundry service turns up tomorrow,' Flora cheekily said, 'I think you'd better have it, Ally, don't you?'

# Chapter 7

For the next couple of months, I further threw myself into life at Hollyhock Cottage and became the ultimate hostess with the mostess, consistently going above and beyond to tend to the guests needs. By mid-June, we'd had patchwork and painting weekends, more jewellery making, stained-glass design, decoupage and intricate embroidery techniques for those with already advanced skills.

The garden apartment had played host to two separate bookings, too. The first had been for a fortnight and the second for a week and both had gone well. I felt the original rental price Dad had insisted on was too low and knowing now that the space worked well and that the reviews had been wonderful, I suggested raising it for the rest of the summer, but he insisted it should be left as it was for the whole of the year.

It was madness really, given the setting and fabulous high-end finish, but I wasn't going to battle over it. The business profits were looking healthy now and we had paid off the biggest bills we were likely to face, namely those for the conversions and renovations. Moving forward, any money spent on the buildings would be solely for maintenance and it was a weight off my mind to have it all, finally, and so success-fully, done.

My determination to both pick my battles and further immerse myself in my role hadn't been adopted on a whim. I had set the strategies in motion with a specific purpose in mind and the results had highlighted some significant things that I was biding my time to talk to Flora about.

What had occurred with Logan in the spring had been responsible for getting the ball properly rolling and as a result, I now had to act. I had always willingly lived a lie when I was off on my infrequent adventures but my inability to fall in love with life in Kittiwake Cove, despite my recent extra effort to try to do exactly that, meant I could no longer cope with living a lie at home – for want of a better word – too. It was too much. Way too much deception for one woman to comfortably and competently endure.

I didn't yet know how I would go about rationalising my fears about leaving Dad or how I was going to instigate the change and alter things enough at the cottage to enable me to go, but I knew I had to redress the balance of truth in my life. It wasn't going to be easy, but my happiness and mental health depended on it.

'I can't believe it's this hot already,' I panted, when I met Flora at our secret rock spot on the hottest day of June so far. 'If it's like this now, can you imagine what high season's going to feel like?'

'Says the woman who loves the heat in Barcelona.' Flora smiled as she budged along to make space for me. 'Isn't it twenty-nine degrees or something there most days in July and August?'

'But that's a completely different kind of heat,' I pointed out, while wondering if, given that she'd just mentioned the place, this was the moment I should confirm that I still had my heart set on moving there. 'So, come on then, tell me what you've dragged me down here for, when we could be sitting in the shade in the garden?'

'I suggested coming here to make sure we couldn't be overheard,' she said, looking furtively around to check an eavesdropper hadn't suddenly popped out of the boulders.

'Oh,' I said, my curiosity escalating. 'What's the T?'

'There's no T,' she said adjusting the brim of the floppy sunhat she was wearing and that I hadn't seen before. 'But the topic isn't one I'd want your dad to overhear.'

'Go on.' I frowned.

Flora wasn't known for her discretion so the effort she'd gone to suggested it was a highly sensitive subject she was about to embark upon.

'Well,' she said, 'I know that as always, you're doing your best to not let it show, even more so at the moment, and I'm certain your dad still has no idea, but I can tell you don't want to be here, Ally.'

Clearly, the extra effort I'd been putting in to try to force myself to fall in love with the cove hadn't convinced either her or me that it had finally happened. There was still something missing and as hard as I had tried to find it, I had failed.

'You're right, in that I have been making more of an effort,' I told her, 'and with good reason,' I added, bracing myself to tell her what I'd decided, but she cut me off.

'Because you love your dad,' she smiled, squeezing my hand,

'and I love him, too. And I love you, Ally. Which is why I've come up with a plan.'

All the while I had been starting to strategize, apparently Flora had too.

'Before you tell me what it is,' I butted in, 'can I just tell you one thing?'

'No,' she said. 'You're going to hear me out first.'

I knew from many arguments of old that there was no point bickering, so I sat back to let her have her say. After all, she was the one who had suggested we should meet.

'Go on then,' I relented.

'I know you worry about your dad's mental health,' she said softly, 'and that the comment he made a while back about feeling lonely, really hit home.'

She still only really knew half of my worries. I hadn't specifically shared with her that I harboured deep-seated fears about losing him in the same way I'd lost Mum. I hadn't talked to anyone about the sometimes overwhelming desire I felt to practically live in his pocket and monitor his health like a hawk.

'But I'm living in the cottage now,' Flora carried on, 'so even if you weren't, he'd never be completely alone, would he? And if the pair of you employed an assistant or even a manager to take your place and help him with the business, there'd be no more work for him to take on other than what he does now.'

'So, you're saying . . .'

'I'm saying, that with someone else here to do your job, there's no reason for you to stay. Your dad has the garden and catering in hand and you've more than fulfilled the promise you made to your mum to help him. It's time you moved on, Ally.'

It seemed that I had made the decision to try to find a way

to go just as my best friend had landed on a potential solution to make it possible. We'd always worked like a well-oiled machine and Flora's idea was a good one, but I knew it was going to take a lot of thinking about before I agreed to give it a go and that my fears for Dad were going to take some untangling, too.

'I know it's time I went,' I said with a smile and Flora looked amazed. 'That's what I was going to tell you I had decided. I hadn't come up with a way to make it viable, but I decided days ago that I can't carry on living my life as it currently runs.'

'Really?' she gasped.

'Really,' I said seriously.

'You're not just saying that so you don't have to acknowledge what a genius I am?' She nudged me.

'Absolutely not.' I laughed. 'But I know I'm not going to find it easy to go. After all, I swore to Mum—'

'That you'd help your dad if anything happened to her and you have,' Flora firmly said. 'Ten times over. You've more than fulfilled that promise and I truly believe you can leave Kittiwake Cove with a completely clear conscience.'

I knew there was nothing Flora would have loved more than for me to feel as fondly about Dorset as she did, but it was impossible to live the life I wanted here and she genuinely was the best of friends to accept that and help me find a way out.

'As long as you come back for Christmas,' she quickly added.

'Dad must never find out that I've been unhappy here,' I said, having taken a moment to further process everything. 'It would break his heart if he knew that I'd been tricking him all this time.'

'You haven't been tricking him,' Flora kindly said. 'You've

been helping him and honouring your promise to your mum, but you're right, he must never find out. We need to present your desire to move on as something completely new. Maybe inspired by your last trip,' she said thoughtfully, 'something that's developed since you came back.'

'But can I really leave him?' I frowned, voicing the doubt I felt while pushing away thoughts of my previous getaway.

'In my capable hands,' Flora nodded, 'definitely.'

She made it sound so simple and in theory, it most likely was, however I knew that if something happened to him and my presence could have prevented it, then I'd never forgive myself. I had a lot of psychological unpicking and more processing to go through before I fully embraced my decision and Flora's genius idea.

'So, what do you think?' she demanded, clearly wanting me to make up my mind immediately.

'I think I'm devastated that you're suggesting I'm replaceable,' I joked.

'You've put in the groundwork,' she shrugged, playing along, 'now any fool can pick your job up and run with it.'

I gave her a shove and she yelped.

'And you'd be happy with me living on the other side of the world, would you?'

'Spain is hardly the other side of the world,' she tutted. 'Assuming that's where you'd go. That said, I'd miss you like crazy, but I'd get over it, especially knowing you were finally where you've always wanted to be.'

I again imagined myself giving tours of one of the beautiful museums in Barcelona or working to champion the spectacular Gaudí architecture Logan and I had admired. It would be amazing to use the skills I had garnered from my education and previous work experience to secure my dream job.

'So, what do you think?' Flora asked again, as I let out of wistful sigh. 'Are you going to go and start packing?'

'Given that we're in the midst of our busiest season yet,' I reminded her, 'absolutely not.' She opened her mouth to protest, but I did cut her off this time. 'But I am going to give your idea some serious thought. Like I said, I'd already decided I needed to go and now you might have found a way to make it happen. I'm in no rush though. If I'm going to do this, I want to make it happen as seamlessly as possible for Dad and that's going to take some meticulous planning.'

'That's fair.' Flora nodded.

'I still can't believe you're batting for Team Leave,' I said, shaking my head.

'I just want you to be happy,' she responded simply and I felt my heart tug.

'Please don't think I'm living my worst life here,' I said, slinging an arm around her shoulders, 'because I'm not.'

'I don't.' She smiled.

'Although,' I sighed, 'the prospect of now having to sort eight beds in this heat is a bit of a bummer.'

'I'll help,' she offered, jumping up. 'And just think, if you do leave, you'll never have to change multiple beds again.'

'That,' I said, swatting the brim of her hat so that it flopped down and covered her entire face, 'is almost reason enough to have me booking a flight today.'

Having finished remaking the beds ahead of cleaning the rooms, which I eked out over the next couple of days because it was so hot, Flora and I left Dad and Kasuku arguing over the last few grapes in the fruit bowl and walked down to the pub one evening in the sunshine.

The Ship, or to give it its full title, The Ship Inn, was a cleverly redesigned and thought-out blend of modern and traditional and a popular destination for both tourists and locals alike. It was no easy feat, trying to get the balance right to keep both happy, but Mary and Michael, the owners, had managed it with aplomb and an unexpected windfall.

The exterior was whitewashed stone, double-fronted with small paned windows and ship lanterns hanging either side of the door. The paintwork was dark grey and the creaking sign, hanging above, between the polished copper lights, sported an elaborately painted galleon in full sail.

The interior had a public bar and a small restaurant, but mine and Flora's favourite hang-out was the old-fashioned snug. It was favoured by most of the locals who frequented the place, but any patron was always made welcome.

'Two glasses of your finest Pinot Grigio, please,' Flora requested when Mary greeted us with a friendly smile in the public bar.

'Evening, Mary,' I said, before heading for the door at the far end and into the snug. 'I'll bag us a table, Flora.'

The pub had been one of the local businesses to benefit from Beatrice's will, just like Mum and Dad had with the inheritance of Hollyhock Cottage. Beatrice hadn't been a regular in the pub herself, but her father had and, aware that it was in need of updating, she had provided the means to ensure it continued to serve the cove in the way it had for centuries.

'Hey, Freddie,' I smiled, budging up on the bench seat when Flora came in with her twin in tow. 'How are you? I haven't seen you for ages now the work at the cottage is finished.'

'That's because you hardly ever come to the pub.' He pointed out.

I had been a rarer visitor than usual of late. Now that Flora was living at the cottage, we often decided to stay in rather than venture out at the end of a busy day and of course, weekends for me were all booked up. I wasn't obliged to be on site when the courses were running, but if a guest needed anything, I would rather they called on me than Dad. He had enough to contend with, keeping on top of the garden, prepping menus and cooking two meals a day. And looking after temperamental Kasuku, of course.

'I've got the taste for some dry roasted,' said Flora, the second she'd handed me my glass of wine. 'Do you want anything?'

'No, thanks,' I said. 'I'm good.'

'I'll have some,' Freddie predictably said.

Invariably the pair mirrored each other in so many ways.

'I need to tell you something,' Freddie said, inching closer, the second Flora had gone again.

'What's up?' I frowned.

He sounded serious, which was not an emotion he displayed all that often.

'It's just a rumour,' he said, biting his bottom lip.

'Well, tell me then,' I urged, knowing that his sister would be back any second and that he'd obviously waited until she was out of earshot for a reason.

He let out a long breath and looked back at the snug door.

'I saw Joe earlier and apparently ...'

'Go on,' I said, beginning to lose patience as well as the will to live.

'Tara's been spotted in Shellcombe.'

My mouth fell open and for a moment I was lost for words.

'What?' I finally gasped.

'I know.'

'Please tell me you're joking,' I eventually croaked.

He gave me a look.

'Yeah, right.' He nodded. 'Because I would joke about that, wouldn't I?'

'Shit,' I muttered. 'Shit, shit, shit.'

'What do we do,' he said urgently, 'we mustn't let Flora find out.'

He'd barely said the words before she burst into the snug and marched over to the table leaving the door swinging wildly in her wake.

'You won't believe this,' she said, throwing the bags of peanuts on to the table with a clatter. 'That bloody tart Tara has been seen in Shellcombe.'

Freddie squeezed his eyes shut and I massaged my temples.

'Did you know?' Flora demanded, jabbing her brother's arm with a pointed finger.

'Ow,' he yelped, inching away.

'Did you know?' she said again.

'If it's just a rumour—' I began, stopping when she threw me one of her most terrifying scowls.

'I did know,' Freddie confessed, rubbing his poor poked arm. 'But I literally only just heard. Joe said—'

'Oh, well,' Flora said scathingly, tearing into one of the bags and scattering some of the contents, 'if Joe said, then it must be true, mustn't it? If anyone would know, it'd be him.'

I leant into Freddie in a show of solidarity, but he mistakenly took it as his cue to go.

'I'll leave you to it, then,' he said and it was my turn to give him a look.

I hoped it conveyed the curse I was firing at him for leaving me with his twin in such an inflammatory mood. It broke my heart to think that something that had happened more than a decade ago could still have such an impact on her. But then, Flora's heart had been broken and I wasn't sure it had ever mended. Not properly anyway.

'I bet they're still in touch,' she fumed, cramming a handful of nuts into her mouth and crunching ferociously, as Freddie made a hasty exit.

'I seriously doubt that,' I soothed.

'Not that I care.' She laughed, already ripping into the second bag. 'Didn't give a shit then so I certainly don't give a shit now.'

I opened my mouth to dispute that.

'Don't,' she warned, 'say a word.'

I wanted to say that there was absolutely no reason why Tara would be back in either Shellcombe or Kittiwake Cove, so the rumour was bound to be unfounded, but I didn't dare. I picked up my wine instead and gulped down half of it in just a couple of mouthfuls.

Tara and her family had arrived in Shellcombe just as we were about to start year ten. The family had caused quite a stir, letting everyone know they had bought the biggest house in the area outright and then driving around in the most ostentatious cars imaginable. Her parents were far too glamourous for the cheap but cheerful seaside town, but it was Tara with her catwalk looks, sassy attitude and designer bags who drew the most attention in our circle.

Flora and I had no idea why she latched on to us when she swaggered into our form that balmy September morning, but our popularity had leapt from sub-zero to sizzling in a matter of seconds, so we weren't complaining. With her wild-child reputation and rumours of being expelled from her previous three schools, we revelled in her notoriety and lapped up the never before received attention.

'Two years of our lives we knew her for,' Flora said, grinding out the words. 'Two tiny bloody years. And not even full years at that, and yet the memory of her can still . . .'

'I know,' I said, reaching for her hand, but she wouldn't let me hold it. 'I know.'

'And it would be Joe who's seen her, wouldn't it? Out of everyone in the whole of Dorset, it would bloody well be him.'

I hated that she sounded so choked and that her bottom lip was trembling, but knew there was nothing I could say that would make her feel better. Flora and Joe had taken everyone by surprise when they became a rock-solid couple. They had always been friends, but were properly together for a year before Tara arrived on the scene and they had stayed that way right up until the year eleven prom.

Flora had confided in Tara and me that was going to be the night she and Joe were going all the way. They'd waited for the perfect opportunity, both wanting to be each other's first time. We were thrilled for them and promised to keep their secret. Tara even managed to wangle booking a room for them in the hotel that was hosting the prom.

In the run up to the night, we'd all had the best time. We'd picked out matching dresses, but in different colours to complement our colouring and had agreed to walk to the venue, which was right on the beach, rather than nag our parents to fork out for pretentious rides. We'd all been in complete agreement about our plan, but then . . .

'We should never have believed her about that dress or walking to prom, should we?' Flora moaned, clearly playing it all over in her head, just like I was.

'Probably not,' I sighed, 'but we had no reason not to believe her at the time, did we?'

'A Lamborghini for pity's sake,' Flora sneered. 'And a few grands' worth of designer dress to go with it.'

Tara had turned up in both. She insisted that her dad had sprung the dress and the ride on her at the last minute and that he would have been devastated if she had turned them down. So, she let us down instead. And, as if that wasn't bad enough, she later dragged a very drunk Joe, who had got completely carried away with the drinking games his mates were indulging in with contraband booze, off to the room she had booked.

'And I know,' Flora carried on, 'that she and Joe hadn't gone all the way when I found them, but that was only because I walked in on them when I did.'

Joe had spent that entire summer trying to convince Flora that nothing had happened, but having found Tara astride him with her dress hitched up, she wasn't having any of it. And as for Tara, she and her family had left the area within weeks of it happening. Their departure had nothing to do with the prom, but Tara hadn't spoken to us after it and we certainly hadn't sought her out.

'And please,' Flora said, putting up her hand, before picking up her glass, 'do not even think about telling me that I need to let it go.'

'I wasn't going to say a word,' I told her, but I did hate the fact that we'd known Joe since pre-school and still couldn't be comfortably in the same place with him even after all these years.

I knew that what had happened was all down to Tara, but had no intention of being Joe's champion and pointing that out again. Flora and I had almost fallen out over it one too many times before and I had no desire to risk it again, especially now we were living under the same roof.

'I'd love to know why the family upped and left like they did though,' Flora mused as she peered into her almost empty wine glass. 'It was practically a moonlight flit, wasn't it? I know it couldn't have been because of what Tara had done. But I do remember that her dad was a right shifty sod, wasn't he?'

'He was,' I agreed, picking up my glass and pulling hers out of her hand. 'But we didn't come out tonight to talk about the Carson family, did we?'

'No,' she said, vehemently scrunching up the second peanut packet. 'You're right. We didn't.'

'I'll get us another drink, shall I?'

'Why not?' she said, sounding happier than I knew she felt. 'Actually, get us a bottle. Each. I want to drink enough tonight to put that mare right back out of my mind.'

'Me too,' I loyally agreed.

I wasn't sure the pub had enough wine in the cellar capable of achieving that.

'Hey,' said someone else from school as I waited to get served. 'Have you heard? Tara's back and from what I've heard, she's looking as fit as—'

'Yes, Tyler,' I snapped, turning away, 'I've heard.'

Putting Tara's reappearance, fictitious or otherwise, out of our minds was definitely going to take more than a few bottles of wine.

# Chapter 8

If downing wine had been an Olympic sport, then Flora and I would have won a gold that night. I hadn't gone out with the intention of getting drunk but, given the circumstances, it would have been disloyal not to match my friend glass for glass. We somehow made it back to the cottage and into our respective beds. The next day, Flora was fine. I, however, was still nursing the very last remnants of a hangover the day after that.

'Come on, you lightweight,' Flora teasingly laughed, bouncing into my bedroom as soon as it was light that Thursday morning and whipping open the curtains. 'You can't possibly still be feeling the impact of a few glasses of wine you drunk two days ago.'

I pulled the sheet right up and over my head, blocking out the sun, which was rising earlier each day in the lead up to the solstice.

'I can,' I groaned, even though I secretly agreed with her. My muddled thoughts and banging head were more about trying to fully embrace her clever plan to replace me. I had assumed that finally making up my mind to go would be the biggest hurdle I had to cross, but apparently not. 'And I am.'

Flora grabbed the sheet and in one swift motion, yanked it completely off the bed.

'Stop!' I yelped, covering my eyes with my hands, which she then also pulled away. 'What's the matter with you?'

For someone who had so recently been floored by a rumour of the return of her arch-enemy, she was far too bouncy and buoyant.

'I'm in a good mood,' she said, flopping down on the bed next to me. 'I've got a new client coming later who I'm really looking forward to meeting, I pulled the sun card from my tarot deck this morning *and*,' she added with emphasis, reaching across to tickle me, 'it's been two days since that alleged sighting of my nemesis and there's been no mention of her since, so . . .'

'So,' I said, turning to face her and smiling, 'your good mood might be a pain in my butt, but it's completely justified.'

'I'm delighted you think so,' she said, kissing my cheek before sitting up. 'Now, come on. Your dad's made those summer fruit pastry things you love and if you don't get a shift on, I'll scoff the lot.'

Her threat was enough to get me out of bed, down the stairs and out into the garden where Dad was serving up a breakfast feast. It was an utterly idyllic setting, if a slightly eccentric one, accompanied as we were by Kasuku. Between them, Dad and Flora had carried his cage and stand outside and he was eyeing me beadily, trying to work out whether wheedling or bully-ing would secure him a few of the summer berries I'd tipped into a bowl.

As I looked around, I knew anyone else would have felt on top of the world. The sun was shining, bees were buzzing and I was breaking my fast with two of my favourite people in the whole world. And I was on top of my work too, which meant I could spend the day pottering and perfecting rather than frantically rushing about. But my head was still so stuffed full with what Flora and I had discussed at the rock, that I couldn't appreciate any of it.

'Penny for them,' said Dad, who I then realised was holding out a mug of coffee for me to take.

'Thanks, Dad,' I finally responded, as I took it from him. 'I was just thinking about the garden apartment,' I blagged. 'It's booked next week, but beyond that, the diary is still empty.'

'How can you be thinking about something like that on a morning like this?' Flora tutted, stretching her arms above her head as she looked around her, drinking in the sight of the gorgeous garden.

'I'm always thinking about things like that,' I answered, 'whatever sort of morning it is. It's my job to be thinking about things like that, remember?'

She gave me a look and I knew she was telepathically implying that it no longer had to be. I held my breath, panicking for a moment that she was going to say as much, but of course, she didn't.

'Well, you can stop worrying about that,' beamed Dad, 'because it's all in hand.'

'How so?' I frowned, turning my attention to him again.

He tapped the side of his nose.

'Just give me a bit more time and then I'll fill you in.'

I had no idea what he could be talking about because we both had access to the business booking system and I hadn't come across anything about the apartment.

'I'd rather you filled me in now.'

Dad shook his head.

'All in good time,' he calmly said. 'You worry too much. There's no need to stress.'

It was my stressing over things that I hoped stopped him feeling fractious. I had always carried as much as I could, so that he didn't have to. I looked at him again and, in that moment, it struck me that there was every possibility that he was as worried about something happening to me as I was about something happening to him. Did he think about my heart, cholesterol level and blood pressure as often as I did his?

'Me! Me! Me!' Kasuku suddenly squawked, causing all our hearts to pound.

'Damn!' I laughed, reaching for a napkin so soak up the coffee I'd spilled.

'Damn! Damn! Damn!' Kasuku cackled.

'Now you've done it,' Dad joined in, rolling his eyes.

'He'll be effing and jeffing for days,' Flora added for good measure.

After breakfast, we carried the still cursing Kasuku back into the house and went our separate ways. Dad went off to work in the garden, Flora to prepare her studio and I checked the accommodation, ahead of the watercolour course, which was running that weekend.

When I later heard the scrunch of tyres on the gravel drive, I assumed it was Flora's visitor, but when I went out to check, I found there was already a car parked on the drive with no one in it. The car I'd heard was another arrival. An unexpected one. And, as it turned out, a most unwelcome one.

With an extremely heavy heart, I watched the driver's door of the brand-new Mercedes open and Tara Carson climb gracefully out. Her blonde hair was long, glossy and expensively highlighted, her beautiful face was impeccably but subtly made up and her slender body looked toned to perfection.

'So, it is true.' She smiled, as she raised a perfectly waxed brow and closed the car door with an immaculately manicured hand. 'You've moved out of shabby Shellcombe and are now living it up in Kittiwake Cove and, even more spectacularly, Hollyhock Cottage.'

I didn't know what to say. How could she sound so composed? I wiped my hands, which were still damp from washing up some glasses, down the skirt of the wraparound apron I was wearing. Make-up free and having barely dragged a brush through my hair, I felt excessively unpolished. It was a Cinderella moment and I was definitely the one holding the broom.

In complete contrast, Tara was wearing the look I tried to adopt on my getaways – but I bet it took her a lot less effort to achieve than it did for me to pull it off. It shouldn't have mattered so much, but I hated the fact I looked the exact opposite of how I would have wished I could have appeared for this most unwelcome reunion.

'I suppose I am,' I said, then immediately felt cross with myself for not saying something to defend Shellcombe.

Had it slipped Tara's mind that she'd once lived there, too, and her family home had been far from shabby?

'It's quite the upgrade,' she said, looking around with approval.

'And Flora lives here too,' I quickly added.

'I didn't realise,' she carried on, looking delighted. 'How lucky is that?'

'Lucky, how exactly?' I frowned, thrown by her reaction.

'Because I can kill two birds with one stone, of course,' she keenly said, as if I should have known. 'I've been planning to have a catch up with the pair of you for days, and now I find you're living here together—'

'You're kidding, right?' I scathingly cut in.

'I don't understand,' she said, frowning, sounding genuinely confused and not at all like the Tara I had once been so familiar with. 'What's the problem? I thought it would be fun for us to all get together.'

'Fun?' I asked, aghast.

She took a moment to absorb my defensive stance and tone. 'But why—' she began to ask.

'Look, Tara,' I interrupted. 'I'm really busy and you need to leave.'

'Oh,' she blinked, as her cheeks flushed red. She sounded hurt even though she had no right to be. 'Okay. I'm sorry. I didn't mean to interrupt your day. Maybe we can talk when it's more convenient. I'm bound to run into you both at some point.'

That sounded worryingly like she was staying in the area. Personally, I would have much preferred to think of her packed off to the furthest reaches of the globe and not looking exactly like the woman I had spent years wishing I'd become.

Having Tara turn up on the drive and finding her utterly oblivious as to what my problem with her presence was, made me incredibly tetchy. Flora had been on a real high after meeting her client, who she had beautifully bonded with, and I hadn't the heart to kill her buzz by mentioning our unwanted visitor. Consequently, the deception, coupled with more muddled thoughts about my more than potential departure, put me in the darkest of moods and I ended up arguing with Dad.

A returning guest on the watercolour weekend had forgotten to tell us that they were vegan now, and not vegetarian as they had been on a previous visit, and Dad had turned himself inside out to accommodate them at dinner that evening.

'What are you suggesting?' he said, when I berated him about it after everyone had left the cottage for the evening. 'That I should have made them just eat the salad?'

'Not exactly,' I swallowed.

'Finishing touches,' he said, counting on his fingers, 'going the extra mile. Making the effort. All things we pride ourselves on here. Remember?'

'I do remember,' I said, and added, going over the top, 'but it was too much for you to have to sort on top of everything else, Dad!'

'A vegan dressing and souffle was not too much,' he insisted. 'I don't know what's been the matter with you today, Ally, but I suggest you go out tonight. Have a bit of a break. I can handle things here. In fact, with you in this mood, I'd much prefer to handle things here.'

I didn't need telling twice. I grabbed my bag and left without a thought as to where I was headed. Not that there were many places to head to in Kittiwake Cove. There wasn't much of anything in Kittiwake Cove.

Having worked off the worst of my temper skimming stones into the sea and paddling in the chilly shallows, I turned to look back at the few buildings at the base of the cliffs. The pub was all lit up, as were the former fisherman's cottages, and the smoky smell in the air told me the smokehouse was, or recently had been, in operation.

'I don't suppose you've got anything ready right now, have you?' I called up the beach to Joe, who I could see was working there, as I shoved my feet in my sliders.

Dad had an account with him for the cottage, but Flora and I usually steered clear of The Cove Smokehouse, as it was owned by the family of her former beau. However, as I was already feeling guilty about having not put Tara in her place and then keeping her visit to myself, I didn't think adding another crime to my list of misdemeanours would make much difference.

'Oh hey,' said Joe, turning red when he realised it was me.

He always coloured up, but I wondered if this deeper than usual flush was the result of who was back in town.

'I've got a batch of sausages ready for the pub,' he told me. 'If you help me carry them over, I'll shout you one.'

'Excellent,' I said, holding out my hands. 'Just what I fancy.'

'Is Flora not with you?' he asked, passing me a wooden crate.

'Nope, she's staying over at Freddie's and helping him decorate his flat.'

Joe nodded, but didn't say anything further. I could never be sure if he was still smitten with Flora, but I felt pretty certain he was weighed down with regret that he'd never been able to get her to believe him about what had, or hadn't, happened with Tara.

The pub was packed. I'd forgotten it was the weekend of the month when they had a live band and as soon as I'd got a drink, I thanked Joe for the smoked sausage, safely encased in a soft roll filled with fried onions and ketchup, and headed into the snug where it was marginally quieter. I had just dropped a blob of ketchup down the front of the scruffy dungarees I hadn't bothered to change out of, when someone slid into the seat opposite mine.

It was impossible not to pull a face when I looked up and saw who it was.

'Are you still too busy to talk?' Tara tentatively asked, as she handed me a serviette. 'And I wouldn't worry about that stain,' she carried on, eyeing the damp, rolled-up bottoms of my dungarees. 'It's not the only one by the looks of it and the lived-in look suits you.'

'I left the house in a rush and didn't have time to get changed,' I said defensively, as I glanced around to see if we'd been spotted. 'What are you doing here, Tara?'

'I thought I'd just pop in,' she said, scanning around. 'For old time's sake.'

'You weren't old enough to frequent this place when you lived here,' I pointed out, even though I had meant what was she doing in the area, rather than the pub.

'Didn't stop me trying though, did it?' she smiled.

That was true. Mary and Michael had turfed her out on countless occasions.

'You had more luck in Shellcombe, as I recall,' I said, taking another big bite out of the roll.

'That,' she laughingly said, 'depends on what you mean by luck. Now, I'm going to get us some drinks and then I want you to tell me all about what you've been up to since I left. To be honest, you were the last person I expected to find here.' I wondered what she meant by that. 'And I want to hear about Flora, too. *And* I want you to tell me why you physically kicked me off your property when I turned up to say hello earlier.'

'I didn't *physically kick you off* anything,' I said, imagining what it might have looked and felt like if I had.

Satisfying was the word that sprang to mind.

'I'll be back in two ticks.' She beamed as she sashayed off.

The pub was packed, so it should have taken her far longer than that to get served, but it didn't of course. I had barely started to consider which would be the best escape route for me to take before she was back.

'I got us wine,' she said, plonking a bottle and two glasses down, even though she had seen I had been drinking beer.

'I can't stay long,' I said, worrying that word had probably already reached Flora about who I was spending my Saturday night with and wishing I'd ducked out the second I'd had the chance.

'Well, it'll have to be a potted history of life since school then, won't it?' she smiled, making it sound like a cosy girl's night as she clinked her glass against mine. 'I honestly can't believe you're still living here though, even if you have gone up in the world.'

'Why is it so hard to believe?'

I might not have loved the cove, but I wouldn't put up with her, of all people, bad-mouthing it. I was still feeling guilty about not jumping to Shellcombe's defence before.

'Because all you ever used to bang on about at school was wanting to leave Dorset to travel around Europe and work in historically famous places,' she reminded me. 'You had that checklist, didn't you?'

Her response to my question took me completely by surprise. I hadn't realised she'd ever really listened to a word I'd said when we were at school. I hadn't thought about that list in a very long time, either.

'I've done my share of travelling,' I said, feeling my face flush.

'But you're living in Hollyhock Cottage,' she said, wrinkling her perfect nose. 'How did that come about? Don't your parents work for the owner?'

'They did when she was alive,' I told her. 'Beatrice left the cottage to Mum and Dad in her will a few years ago now.'

Tara whistled under her breath.

'That was quite some bequest,' she said and I couldn't argue. 'But tell me more about your travels, Ally. How many places have you ticked off that list you used to obsess over?'

'Quite a few,' I blagged, glugging down my wine. The last thing I wanted to do was let on that I wasn't particularly worldly and hadn't lived the dream I'd had at school. 'And it'll be more soon,' I enthusiastically added, the wine going straight to my head, as well as my mouth, apparently. 'I'm only really in the cove at the moment to help Dad. We lost Mum a while ago and he's needed some support to get their business up and running because it was still in the planning stage when she died.'

I then explained what had happened to Mum as well as what the business entailed, making sure Tara knew how much of a success it was. There was no need for me to exaggerate about that, but the wine I continued to knock back, on top of the beer, seemed to be encouraging me to put more of a positive spin on everything.

'I'm very sorry to hear about your mum,' Tara said sympathetically, when I finally drew breath.

'Thank you.' I swallowed.

'And I genuinely admire you for not getting so caught up with everything here that you've ended up permanently setting your own dreams aside,' she further commented.

'There was never any chance of that happening,' I said seriously, but not quite truthfully, as I drained another glass.

Did that sound heartless? I had been aiming for ambitious, but the wine . . .

'I daresay it would have been easy enough to do that though,' Tara carried on. 'Take charge of everything yourself, rather than let your dad take the reins.'

'Not really,' I said. 'The business is his baby and he's more than capable of running it without me, especially now.'

I could hear the words coming out of my mouth, but they still didn't marry up with what should have been the reality. I might not have been running the show completely on my own, but my worries about keeping Dad healthy meant I was probably still doing more than my share. More than was necessary. I needed to start backing off and let Dad step up now I was supposed to be laying the foundations for me to leave.

'With your passion for history and desire to manage important buildings from the past, I'm delighted to hear that.' Tara smiled, reminding me of my year eleven list again. 'Do you have a favourite city?'

'Barcelona.' I hiccupped. 'I lived there for a year and I loved it. That's where I'm planning to permanently move to. I might not have ticked every country off that list I had, but I know I'm going to be more than happy to settle there.'

'Wow,' she gasped, surprisingly ignoring the opportunity to goad me with a comment about unfulfilled dreams. 'You actually lived in the city, did you? You lucky thing. You won't know this, but I love Barcelona, too. I can just see you happily living there, Ally. Spanish was your strongest language, wasn't it?'

As a result of her continued interest, I found myself filling her in on the places I'd worked during my student year. She was enthralled and shared her own stories from the city, but for the first time ever didn't monopolise the conversation or twist it around until it focused solely on her.

As we drank more wine, I couldn't deny it felt good to talk to someone who was familiar with the area. My conversation with her made me believe I really did have something in common with the woman I pretended to be on my getaways. Perhaps I would be capable of finding the courage to rationalise my fears and fully embrace Flora's manager idea after all.

'You know,' Tara smiled, 'you do still fit in here, but I reckon, the moment you leave again, you'll forget all about making beds and emptying bins. I can picture you living in a beautiful Spanish apartment, working in a museum by day and enjoying the laidback nightlife and beaches in the evenings.'

'And the weekend siestas, of course.' I dreamily sighed, feeling utterly seduced and mindful of the fact that I had achieved it once already in my lifetime, so I could do it again.

'Absolutely,' she joined in. 'What could be more perfect?'

Sharing it with someone like Logan, was the first thought that entered my head, but obviously I wasn't going to tell Tara anything about the man I'd met on my last getaway. I hadn't even filled Flora in properly about the guy I'd renamed Miguel, so I wasn't going to discuss him with our enemy. Even if that adversary didn't seem quite so dastardly now.

'And what about you?' I asked. 'Are you staying put or passing through? I never thought I'd see you around here again.'

'You and me both,' she said, rolling her eyes as her phone pinged with an incoming message notification. 'Damn.' She frowned, looking at the screen. 'I'm really sorry, Ally, but I have to go.'

'Oh,' I said, 'okay. No worries.'

'I'll see you again soon though, yes?' she smiled. 'I still want to know what Flora's up to. I was so caught up in hearing about your life that I didn't get the chance to ask more about hers. I love that you're still best friends though.'

'I'll see you soon!' I called after her as I watched her walk away and every head turned in her direction.

It wasn't until she'd been gone a while, that the enchantment wore off and the guilt kicked in. I'd got so caught up talking about myself and was so surprised to discover how far she had dialled down her self-absorbed persona to give me the space to do it, that I hadn't given a second thought to setting her straight about the Flora situation. What sort of best friend did that make me?

Definitely not a very good one, but along with the knowledge that I'd just let Flora down badly, there was also an inkling that Tara had truly changed too, and if that hunch was right, did it mean we now had the opportunity to finally right the wrongs of the past?

# Chapter 9

In spite of the knackered futon she was having to sleep on and because she had been able to change some of her work appointments, Flora spent the next few days at Freddie's so, between them, they could finish decorating the flat. It was only tiny but as they had decided to blitz every room, it took a while. I would have helped out too, but with admin to sort and the cottage and rooms to clean and set up ahead of the next course, I had no free time.

I methodically worked through my tasks, kept my head down and out of Dad's way until our cross words were completely forgotten. During our brief phone chats, Flora hadn't mentioned any gossip and I was just beginning to think that I'd got away with my evening in the pub with Tara when the cottage phone rang on Friday and I was thrown right back into the thick of worrying about it.

'Would you like one egg or two?' Dad asked, at breakfast time, just as the phone in the hall started to ring.

'Two please,' I politely said, 'but I'll answer that first.'

'No, let it ring,' said Dad, which was unusual. 'If it's important, they'll leave a message. I need to get out in the veg patch and there's something I want to tell you before I go.'

'All right,' I relented, knowing that whatever he had to say must have been important because we had strict rules about answering calls to the cottage. 'I'm all ears.'

We'd just sat down, when the phone rang again.

'I can't very well leave it now, can I?' I tutted, pushing back my chair.

'No,' Dad agreed. 'Go on. That's twice in quick succession, so it might be important.'

I looked longingly at my eggs. No one poached eggs as well as Dad.

'Actually,' he said, catching where my gaze had fallen. 'I'll go.'

'No,' I said, jumping up. 'You stay there.'

I was relieved it was me who had answered when I heard who was on the other end.

'Ally, hey,' Tara breezily said, as if the ten-year gap between our calls and the rip through our friendship hadn't happened at all.

I supposed, given my willingness to talk to her in the pub, I was the one to blame for her assumption that all was well in our recently reacquainted mutual world. No more tongue loosening wine for me, I vowed. Not drunk in her presence, at least.

'Hey, Tara,' I responded quietly, closing the kitchen door. 'How did you get this number?'

'From your website, of course,' she said brightly. 'It's amazing, by the way. The business looks exactly as you described it. So pretty and welcoming, and the website is professional, too.'

'Oh,' I said, feeling an unexpected rush of pride. I had taken a long time designing the site, so it was good to know it hit the mark. Not that Tara's opinion should have mattered. 'Thank you and of course, the cottage number is listed there, isn't it?'

I tried not to think about what would have happened if Flora had been the one to pick up. I knew I was definitely going to have to tell her that I had seen Tara now and my stomach twisted at the thought.

'It is all right that I've called, isn't it?' Tara asked, picking up on my tone.

'Uh, huh,' I said feebly.

Given that we'd spent an entire evening together, I could hardly say no. I did however find myself wishing that I hadn't been quite so free and easy about telling her that I was getting ready to leave the cove.

'I wanted to call in, in person, to talk to you,' she carried on, 'but I'm working out of the area so had no choice but to ring.'

'What was it you wanted to talk about?' I swallowed, thanking my lucky stars that she hadn't turned up again, even though Flora was currently off site.

'This business with Flora,' she said, sounding incredulous now, rather than relaxed. 'I've just found out that she's still smarting over that stupid misunderstanding at prom.'

'Stupid misunderstanding?' I echoed.

'Why ever didn't you tell me?' Tara accusingly said. 'We spent the entire evening together and you never said a word about it.'

I massaged my forehead with my free hand.

'Because, I suppose, I got carried away talking about Barcelona,' I admitted. 'And to be honest, I thought you might have guessed that it wasn't all forgotten after I'd asked you to leave when you turned up here and Flora was here, too.'

'Oh,' she said. 'So, you got rid of me because you didn't want me to bump into Flora?'

'Exactly.'

'I didn't want to believe it,' she sighed, 'but I have to now, don't I? How can she not have moved on? It was more than ten years ago and nothing ever really happened in the first place.'

She sounded genuinely surprised rather than condescending.

'Flora hasn't moved on,' I succinctly said, 'because that night, you broke her heart and I don't think it has ever properly mended.'

'Fuck,' Tara gasped.

'Exactly,' I said again.

'I bet if she'd moved away,' she said crossly, 'then she would have let it go. This is what comes of living your entire life within a five-mile radius. Things get blown up out of all proportion. Take note, Ally, and expand your horizon as soon as you can.'

'You know I have every intention of doing that,' I carefully and quietly said, in case Dad was listening. 'But we're not talking about me, are we?'

'No,' she replied, sounding contrite again, 'we're not. Is it true that she still doesn't talk to Joe?'

'She does talk to him,' I corrected, 'but mostly in words of just one syllable and rarely for longer than a sentence at a time.'

'Oh God,' Tara groaned. 'So, she never did believe that nothing happened that night?'

'She did not,' I confirmed. 'And as I recall, you didn't

exactly go out of your way to convince her that it was nothing either, did you?'

'No,' she said, sounding ashamed. 'I didn't, did I? I had so much happening at home, that I didn't have the headspace to think about what had occurred at prom as well.'

'What sort of stuff?'

'It's not important now,' she said, pulling herself out of the past. 'But what is, is the two of us finding a way to fix this situation.'

'Fix it.' I laughed. 'You must be joking. Hang on. The two of us?'

'Yes,' Tara pleadingly said. 'I want you to help me, Ally. It's the least you can do given that you've seen me twice recently and never once mentioned that Flora still has an issue with me.'

'I don't see what I can do.' I swallowed, feeling terribly guilty.

'You can help me find a way to get Flora talking to Joe again,' she said, as if it should have been obvious.

'Impossible.'

'And then help me work out how to get her to forgive me.' She carried on as if I hadn't said a word. 'I want us to all be friends again. I'm truly not the same person I was when we were at school and I want Flora to see that.'

'You have no idea what you're asking,' I stammered.

'I'm asking that we work together to rid your best friend of a misunderstanding that's been allowed to moulder for far too long. Isn't that something that you'd want for her?'

It was *everything* I wanted for her. It would be amazing to get Flora and Joe talking. They might even up as friends again. Or more than friends . . .

'Of course, it is,' I began, 'but—'

I heard Dad's chair scraping over the kitchen tiles.

'Just start casually dropping me into the conversation,' Tara said, the second I'd cut my sentence off. 'Tell her that you've seen me around, that we've talked and I've changed and that you think it's time we all got together and set the record properly straight.'

'As simple as that.' I laughed, shaking my head as I imagined Flora's reaction.

'I know you can do it,' Tara cleverly said. 'And more to the point, I know you want to.'

The thought of Flora and Joe finally repairing their relationship definitely made the difficult task more tempting.

'And imagine the amazing time we'll all have as a result,' Tara wheedled as I realised her time in the area wasn't going to be fleeting and also that it might well be my last summer in Kittiwake Cove. 'Here's my number, so you can keep me up to date.'

'Are you really sure you want to do this?' I asked, as I reached for the notepad and pen we kept next to the telephone, while worrying that her plan might backfire. Mostly likely, all over me.

'One hundred per cent,' she said straight back. 'I'm not the person I was a decade ago.' The way she'd given me the opportunity to talk in the pub went some way to proving that. 'And the thought that something I did when we were barely eighteen is still having such a negative impact, is tearing me apart. I want to put it right. No, I *need* to put it right.'

'Give me your number then,' I said, resigned.

I scribbled it down and repeated it back.

'With you on the case,' she said, sounding certain, 'I reckon we'll all be the best of friends again in no time.'

Looking back, I knew we'd never really been the best of friends, but I had to admire her optimism and faith in my ability to act as mediator.

'Who was that?' Dad asked, when I went back to the kitchen, feeling flushed and carrying the slip of paper with Tara's number on.

'No one,' I said, folding the paper up and stuffing it in my pocket.

'You were a long time talking to no one.' Dad frowned. 'I wanted to be out in the garden by now.'

'What happened to my eggs?' I asked, looking down at my empty plate.

'I ate them rather than let them go to waste,' Dad confessed. 'But I've kept the water ready to poach you some fresh.'

'It's okay,' I said, waving his kind offer away. 'I'm not hungry now.' The task Tara had set me had completely taken the edge off my appetite! What was it you wanted to tell me?'

'Well,' Dad began, looking and sounding pleased with himself, 'do you remember that I mentioned, I might have something up my sleeve for the garden apartment?'

'Yes,' I said, drawing the word out.

I had searched the Hollyhock Cottage inbox, spam and junk folders for further information after his admission, despite promising to leave it in his hands, but all to no avail.

'Well,' Dad said again, 'it came off and the apartment is booked from tomorrow, right to the end of August!'

I took a moment to absorb the timeline.

'You're kidding?' I gasped. 'Are you sure?'

'Of course, I'm sure.' He laughed. 'I set it up myself. The guest will be arriving at some point in the morning and staying here for the whole of the summer. They'd already paid a deposit when I mentioned it to you before and now, they've settled up in full so we'll be handing the key over tomorrow.'

'What did you charge them?' I pounced, thinking immediately of the bottom line.

'Not the very top end of what you wanted to fix the price at, but,' said Dad, before I could moan, 'forty-five per cent on top of what we charged the previous guests.'

'Wow, Dad,' I said, feeling shocked that he'd bumped the price up that much. Perhaps he was more capable of managing without me than I'd given him credit for. 'That's amazing.'

Knowing he didn't usually have the same focus where money was concerned as I did, that was a phenomenal amount and I wondered if some of the attention I paid to the finances was transferring to him. It was perfectly timed, if it was.

'I know,' he said, sounding thrilled. 'And that money is now sitting safe in the cottage business account and providing us with a lovely little buffer.'

It really was the biggest boost to have the place booked out to the same person for the whole of the holiday season. There would be no regular handover to worry about and hopefully Flora wouldn't be too disrupted by the comings and goings, of . . .

'Did you say guest, Dad?' I asked. 'As in just one person.'

'I did,' he said. 'Don't worry, I hadn't forgotten it's not a child-friendly space. I wouldn't have let it out to a family.'

'Of course,' I said, feeling chastened. 'Sorry. I should have known you would remember. A single guest sounds perfect.'

Given the set-up of the cottage courses, we were used to solo visitors.

'They've asked for a weekly bed change,' Dad continued, 'but beyond that we shouldn't have to give the place another thought until the end of the season.'

'I'm intrigued,' I told him. 'It's a long booking, especially for someone on their own. I wonder if they're in the area for work.'

'Well, you can meet them tomorrow,' he said, heading for the door and pulling on his work boots, 'and satisfy your curiosity then.'

'I don't suppose there's any chance of those eggs now, is there?' I wheedled. 'My appetite's just come back with a vengeance.'

Dad shook his head.

'Too late,' he said, opening the door. 'Maybe it's time you had a go at poaching your own?'

'Never,' I gasped, but as I watched him head off, I thought it was a bit tragic that at almost thirty years old, my dad was still cooking my breakfast.

Flora came back from Freddie's that evening and after a fish and chip supper, eaten straight out of the paper, in the garden with Dad, we headed up to my room, rather than down to the rock because it had turned chilly, where she filled me in on how the flat had come along.

'It sounds amazing,' I said, as I turned from the window and looked at her sitting cross-legged on my bed.

'It is now,' she told me, 'but there was a point when we were up to our knees in stripped-off woodchip, and sweating with the steamer on full blast, that I wondered if it was ever going to come together.'

'But it has,' I said, flopping down next to her. 'Sometimes in life you have to break a few eggs to make an omelette, right?'

'Who said that?' She frowned, also laying down so we were facing one another.

'Lots of people, according to the internet.'

I wondered if this was the moment, I should crack a few eggs of my own and mention that I'd seen and spoken to Tara. I had been holding my breath right from the moment I heard Flora's bike on the gravel, but she was in far too good a mood for word to have reached her that I'd been drinking with Tara in the pub. In which case I decided, I'd give it a bit longer.

'Which course is it this weekend?' Flora asked, losing interest in the omelette topic.

'Patchwork,' I told her, stifling a yawn.

'I thought you liked patchwork,' she laughed.

'I do,' I told her. 'I wasn't yawning because of the course topic, I was yawning because I'm knackered. It's been a busy week.'

'I thought you would be super chilled because I hadn't been here to bug you,' she teased.

If only she knew.

'I know,' I bluffed. 'There's no justice in the world, is there?'

'Well,' she said, 'at least you haven't got to stress over getting the garden apartment booked now your dad's taken care of it.'

'That's true,' I agreed. 'I still don't know how the booking was made, though. There's no email enquiry or follow-up correspondence that I can find.'

'Maybe it was all done on the phone?'

'Perhaps.' I shrugged. 'I've seen the money sitting in the bank though, so I know it's a genuine reservation.'

'I wonder what this guest is going to be like?' Flora said, sliding off the bed and standing up again.

I looked at the clock on the bedside table.

'Me too.' I smiled. 'At least we haven't got long to wait to find out.'

We had a minor food crisis the following morning, so after welcoming Janice, the patchwork tutor and settling our weekend guests, I headed into Shellcombe to solve it.

'Are your hens off laying?' Arthur, the man who ran the nearest convenience store asked as I piled half a dozen boxes, each containing half a dozen eggs, on the counter.

'No,' I said, 'they're laying, but we only have two hens now so we buy in for when we've got guests. The delivery that comes from the farm shop was extra early this morning and by the time I went to pick it up at the gate, something had had the lot.'

It had been absolute carnage with smashed shells everywhere. Eggs seemed to be dominating my life at the moment. Both real and metaphorical ones had popped up in practically every conversation I'd had in the last twenty-four hours.

'Doubtless it was a fox,' Arthur said as he rang the cost of the replacements up.

'That's what Dad said, too,' I told him. 'I've never seen one around, but we're going to have to keep a closer eye on the hens now and maybe put a box out for the delivery.'

'And how's Kasuku?' Arthur chuckled. 'He's another bird worth watching.'

'Same as always,' I laughed. 'I wouldn't reckon much for the fox's chances if it went after him.'

I had paid and just stepped back out into the sunshine when my phone rang. It was Flora.

'Oh my God! Oh my God! Oh my God!' she shrieked the second I answered. 'Get your arse back here, quick.'

'Why?' I panicked. 'What's happened?'

I had borrowed her bike rather than driving into town as the parking wasn't great, but now regretted my choice.

'The garden apartment guest has arrived,' she squealed, 'and I just bumped into him when I was heading to the cottage from the studio.'

'And?' I asked, feeling less stressed now I knew it wasn't a Dad issue.

'And,' she giggled, 'he's bloody gorgeous. A total dreamboat.'

'Dreamboat?' I repeated, wrinkling my nose.

'I mean it,' she said. 'He's lush, Ally. You have to fall in love with him, right now. He's going to be the perfect person to get over that Miguel guy with.'

How did she know I was still dreaming about being under him?

'Flora,' I gasped, as I stowed the eggs away in the basket, but I was almost laughing too. 'Do I need to remind you that irrespective of what this person looks like, they are a guest at Hollyhock Cottage and as such, they must be treated with the utmost respect?'

'You won't say that when you see him,' she shot back. 'You'll want to rip his clothes off with your teeth.'

'Have you been drinking?' I asked, as I tucked the phone between my ear and shoulder so I could climb on her bike.

'No,' she hissed, lowering her voice but still sounding giddy. 'Sober as a judge.'

'In that case,' I smiled. 'He must be wonderful. You don't dole out praise this willingly when you're off the sauce!'

'Right?' she giggled. 'And,' she carried on, sounding more composed, 'he's got the sympathy vote, too.'

'How so?'

'Your dad told me that he's found out that the poor chap's here to come to terms with the loss of a loved one. Apparently, he stayed in Dorset a lot with them as a child and wants to revisit some of their old haunts, or the dead relative put in their will that they want him to visit some of their old haunts,' she explained and I could tell she was frowning. 'No pun intended,' she then wickedly added.

'That's really sad.' I swallowed, ignoring her attempt at humour. 'When did Dad tell you this? Not in front of the other guests, I hope?' I pushed off and started to pedal. 'I hope you were both discreet.'

'Just get your arse back here super quick,' she said bossily. 'Then we'll see how *your* discretion is going to hold up.'

# Chapter 10

Flora's quest to set me up with the new guest was frustratingly – for her – thwarted for the whole of that day because, as far as we could tell, he didn't leave the apartment. Flora had wanted me to go and knock on the door when he hadn't appeared by mid-afternoon, on the pretence of introducing myself as the Hollyhock Cottage co-owner, but I refused.

'He's entitled to his privacy,' I pointed out for the umpteenth time, having again reminded her that I wasn't co-owner. Everything was still officially in Dad's name. 'Especially given the circumstances behind his booking.'

'You won't be saying that when he heads to the pub and someone else gets their hooks in him.' She pouted. 'You'll be kicking yourself then.'

'Given that he's in mourning,' I reminded her, while trying not to picture a handsome stranger hooking up with temptress Tara, 'I can't imagine a trip to the pub is a priority for him, right now.'

She had moped over my inaction for the whole of the day and then plummeted to an even deeper depth of sulkiness when I refused to go to The Ship with her that evening. The truth was, by the time I'd cleared the dishes and tidied up after dinner, I was desperate to get out, but I couldn't face what might happen if I ran into Tara before I'd had a chance to casually, or otherwise, bring her up. She might have said that she was currently out of the area when she called, but she could have come back since then, couldn't she?

If I could have talked Flora into staying in with me at the cottage, I would have, but she wasn't in the mood for a quiet night in and given her already sulky state of mind, I knew my efforts to convince her would have been wasted.

Unfortunately, she still appeared to be moping the next morning.

'Fancy a walk?' I suggested, as she clattered her breakfast bowl in the sink. 'There's time for a stroll before you need me, isn't there Dad?'

'Loads of time,' he said. 'In fact, Janice is bringing her grandson to help out today, so there's no need for you to rush back at all. I can rope him into making the welcome drinks, if you like.'

I knew Janice's grandson Matthew was skilled at sewing and also more than capable of negotiating the kettle and cafetieres, too.

'Excellent,' I said. 'Thanks, Dad.'

'You might even bump into the new guest down on the beach,' he suggested, when Flora didn't comment. 'He did say he was looking forward to checking it out.'

'And I'm looking forward to meeting him,' I smiled at Flora, meaningfully, implying that I wanted to check him out too, but I couldn't catch her eye.

'Come on then,' was all she huffed.

I knew I couldn't put it off forever, so overnight I had come up with a plan to use a trip to the rock as the ideal opportunity to bring Tara up, but taking in Flora's tight jaw and the furrow across her usually smooth brow, I thought it would again be best left for another day.

I hoped our former friend wasn't expecting an update any time soon, because Flora wasn't the sort of woman you could rush into things, especially things of this magnitude. Getting her onside to just talk to Tara was going to take some skill on my part. Becoming acquaintances, let alone friends, might prove impossible and I knew it wasn't a topic to be broached until Flora was in anything but the best of moods.

'So,' I said, stooping to pick up a sun-bleached length of driftwood and trailing it along behind me in the sand to make wavy patterns, 'how was your evening?'

It was a stunning morning. Already warm, with a gentle breeze and the sun making the sea magically sparkle. Had I found myself in the cove in any other capacity, I might have felt content with my lot.

'Pretty shit, actually,' Flora flatly said. 'Pretty shit and pretty humiliating.'

'Oh?' I croaked, my temperature immediately soaring in spite of the breeze.

'Wanna know why?'

There was no point in feigning ignorance. There was only one thing that would make her voice sound like that.

'I think I know why,' I said, dropping the piece of wood.

'But let me just clarify it for you though,' she began to rage. 'My evening was shit because someone told me that they'd seen you drinking in the pub and laughing with Tara bloody Carson the weekend I was helping Freddie at the flat.'

'I can explain—' I feebly started to say.

'Good.' She practically shouted. 'Because that person also went to great lengths to tell me how pleased they were that we were all friends again and that everyone had been thinking it was high time I let bygones be bygones!'

We stopped walking and I turned to face her. Her hands were clenched and her whole body was rigid. Looking at her justifiably stiff stance, I was amazed she hadn't dragged me out of bed when she got back the night before and demanded an explanation there and then.

'Come on then,' she commanded. 'Let's have it. Enlighten me!'

Having not had the opportunity to smooth the way into having the conversation, I was at a loss as to how to frame what had happened in a way that wouldn't further fuel Flora's foul mood. It wouldn't be any help to mention that this was an ideal opportunity for her to hear Tara out, but infuriatingly, that seemed to be the only idea my head was capable of coming up with.

'Were you or were you not drinking in the pub with Tara Carson, the weekend I stayed at Freddie's? Yes or no?' Flora demanded when I stayed quiet.

'Yes,' I quietly croaked.

'What?' She frowned, leaning in and cupping her ears.

I cleared my throat.

'Yes,' I said, more loudly, 'yes, I was. Tara cornered me in The Ship after I'd had a bit of a row with Dad.' I didn't dare mention who had provided my supper or that I'd not walked out of the pub when I realised Tara wanted to chat. 'We had some wine and talked for a bit.'

'About what?'

'All sorts.' I swallowed. 'Mostly why I'm living in Hollyhock Cottage and how much I love Barcelona.'

'Cosy,' she scathingly said.

For a while, when we had been exchanging tales of our travels, it had been, but that was something else I needed to keep to myself.

'Did you mention me?'

'No,' I honestly said. 'Not then, no.'

She took a moment to take that in.

'But you have talked about me since?' she stated rather than asked.

I nodded.

'You've seen Tara since that night,' she said, sounding even more devastated.

'No,' I quickly said. 'I haven't seen her. She rang the cottage yesterday. I didn't give her the number. She found it on the website and called to ... well, to have a go at me actually.'

'Have a go at you about what?'

'Flora!'

We both turned around to look at whoever it was who had called her name. It was a guy I didn't recognise. He'd just closed the gate which led to the beach from the cottage garden at the bottom of the cliff and was striding quickly towards us.

'Shit,' Flora muttered. 'It's the guest who's staying in the garden apartment.'

I watched transfixed as the man got closer. Flora's words reached me from what suddenly felt like a very long way away.

'This is not over,' she hissed at me. 'Do you hear me, Ally? This is so not over.'

'Flora!' The guy called again and Flora waved.

'Hey!' she called back.

I didn't say anything, but I was silently praying that a sinkhole would open up in the sand and suck me down into it. Or maybe a freak wave would wash in and carry me off, far out to sea. But neither of those things happened and with every step the new guest took towards me, the more familiar he became. By the time he was close enough for me to register the look of intense shock in his beautiful green eyes, it was too late to turn tail and run.

'Flora,' he exhaled.

He was near enough then not to have to shout and his tone was incredulous.

'Logan.' Flora smiled. 'Hi. So, you've found the beach then.'

He looked at her for less than a second and then his eyes came back to me.

'This is—' Flora began.

'Flora,' Logan said, swallowing hard. 'Another Flora.'

'No.' The real Flora frowned, her gaze flicking to me. 'This is Ally.'

'Ally?' Logan frowned back.

'Hey,' I said, the sound catching as it got lodged somewhere between my heart and my throat on its journey out of my mouth.

'I'm Flora.' Flora reiterated, pointing at herself. 'And this is—'

'Ally,' Logan said again, his confused eyes never leaving my face. 'Not Flora, then.'

The whole interaction took less than ten seconds, but in my head, it felt like ten hours.

'Let me introduce you properly,' Flora carried on, giving herself a shake.

She sounded as muddled as Logan looked. Out of the three of us, I was the only one who was privy to all the information needed to make sense of the situation, but in that moment, knowledge felt nothing like power.

'No need,' Logan told her. 'Flora ... I mean, Ally ... and I have already met.'

'You have?' Flora questioned, looking between the two of us.

There were a million and one other things that could have happened to knock Tara out of my friend's head and I would have taken one or even all of them over what was actually playing out. It was the most surreal moment on Kittiwake Cove beach that I'd ever experienced.

'We have,' I whispered.

My throat felt completely blocked then and I was finding it an effort to even breath. Having left Logan's hotel room and guiltily not looked back, I hadn't expected to ever see him again. Tracking him down would have been impossible without more than a first name to go on and yet here he was, standing in front of me and, unless he changed his mind now because I was part of the equation, planning to spend the entire summer in Kittiwake Cove.

'In Spain,' Logan said, sounding increasingly put out now the first stab of recognition had hit him. 'Barcelona, to be precise. Back in April.'

Flora carried on looking between the two of us. Her eyes were saucer wide as they rested longer on Logan and then swung back to me. Her mouth was a perfect O. The epitome of the ultimate *no fricking way* moment.

'Miguel,' she muttered under her breath.

'Excuse me?' Logan glared.

'Yep,' I nodded.

'Wow,' Flora gasped. 'Holy crap.'

'Yep,' I said again.

Given what we had been talking about, borderline arguing over, when he found us, I thought it was highly unlikely that my friend was ever going to trust me again. Not only had I been caught drinking with the enemy, it now transpired that the guy I'd met in Spain, and had hot sex with, wasn't Spanish and he wasn't called Miguel.

He was from England; his name was Logan and he was standing just a couple of feet away looking every bit as non-plussed as my best mate.

'It's really not your day, is it?' Flora shot in my direction. 'I'm going to head back.'

'No,' I said, trying to catch her arm, but she pre-empted that and neatly stepped out of reach.

'I'll see you later.'

I watched her walk away and willed Logan to go with her, but he stayed rooted to the spot.

'I can't believe this is happening,' he said, running his hands through his lovely hair.

'Me neither,' I responded, shakily exhaling.

'When I arrived here yesterday, I thought it was a freakish coincidence that I'd come across someone else called Flora within months of meeting you,' he said crossly, firing the words squarely at me. 'But as it turns out, I haven't. I've found one Flora and one . . . liar.'

I winced at the word he'd landed on, but couldn't dispute it.

'It's ironic, isn't it?' he laughed, the sound completely at odds with his tone, 'that I'd just started to get over you. That I'd finally come to terms with the humiliation of being left hanging, convinced myself that the incredible connection I thought we had was all in my head so I could properly put you out of mind, and then I run into you here, on a random Dorset beach, where I just happen to be ...'

His angry rush of words trailed off and I shuffled uncomfortably from one foot to the other and scrunched my toes in the warm sand as I remembered why he was here. Poor Logan was going through the worst of times and now I'd magically materialised and made things a million times worse. I had no idea what to say. There were no words capable of making any of this better. Or bearable even.

'I hope you don't think it rude of me to ask,' he angrily added, 'but what the hell are you doing here and why did you tell me your name was Flora?'

I turned to face the glittering sea and pulled my plait over my shoulder. I could feel his eyes boring into me before he sat down heavily on the sand. I hesitated for a moment, then joined him a little distance away.

'I really am so, so sorry,' I told him, meaning every word. 'I'm so ashamed that I left you like that and if it's any consolation, I've regretted doing it every single day since I arrived back in the UK.'

He vehemently shook his head and it was obvious that my admission was no consolation at all. I was desperate to tell him that he hadn't been wrong about the connection, that I'd genuinely felt it too, but given my past behaviour he had no reason to believe anything that came out of my mouth now.

'Just tell me why you told me your name was Flora,' he said gruffly.

'The truth is,' I started to say and he huffed. 'The truth is,' I carried on regardless, 'that when I'm travelling alone and I meet someone, *if* I meet someone,' I quickly amended, because it wasn't by any means guaranteed that I did and I didn't want Logan thinking he was one in a long line of many, 'I always give myself a different name.'

'Why?'

'Partly because I had a bad experience the one time I told someone who I really was.' The memory of that still scared me. It had happened on my second trip and the resultant terror had almost been enough to put me off going away again. 'This guy tracked me down to the hotel where I was staying and got a bit . . . intense, and ever since then, I've pretended to be someone else.'

Logan took a moment to process that and I didn't add that I pretended I lived a different life, too.

'Do you usually go for the name of someone you know?' he asked.

'No,' I told him. 'Meeting you on the plane caught me off-guard and I said the first name that came into my head. I'd just had a message from Flora, my best friend, who you've now met, and it was her name that popped out of my mouth as a result.'

'So, you and the real Flora, who was just here with us and was also at Hollyhock Cottage yesterday, really are friends then?'

'Yes,' I nodded. 'Best friends, practically since birth. We both grew up here. Well, just up the road in Shellcombe.'

I hoped we were still friends.

'You lied to a nun,' Logan said, putting me straight back on that plane. 'I bet Sister Lucia would be disappointed about that.'

'I'm sure there are lots of things I did in Barcelona that Sister Lucia would be disappointed about,' I said in a low voice, as the memory of my and Logan's antics in the shower flashed through my mind.

'True,' he acknowledged. 'And I guess she wouldn't be all that thrilled with me, either.'

Our eyes met and I felt my breath hitch. Was he thinking of the bathroom seduction, too? He looked even lovelier than I remembered but also exactly the same and I couldn't help wondering what he thought about how I looked. I had known that I had almost returned to being plain old Ally when I caught a glimpse of myself in the mirror on the way out of his hotel room, but every last trace of the made up version of me was now gone.

I was dressed completely differently, my nails weren't painted, my hair was unravelling from the plait I kept nervously fiddling with and I had hundreds more freckles. I even had a different name, for pity's sake. Beyond my basic physical features there was nothing that Logan could have recognised about me at all. Not only had I abandoned him, I'd also left behind the version of me he thought he knew. He must despise me even more now he could see what a fraud I was.

He cleared his throat and looked away again, out across the sea.

'Anyway,' he said. 'I still don't know what you're doing here in Kittiwake Cove.'

'My dad owns Hollyhock Cottage,' I said, choosing my words with care. 'And I'm here to help him out with the business he runs from it, for a bit.'

I could have taken the opportunity to come completely clean about my getaway fantasy lives, but knowing that Logan currently had so much going on in his own life, I thought it kinder not to add more weight to his burden at this point. It took a few seconds for him to comment, and when he did, it wasn't a response I could have predicted.

'You're kidding,' he finally said, sounding stunned. 'Please tell me you're joking.'

'No.' I swallowed. 'I'm not kidding, but don't worry. I'll make sure we won't keep running into each other—'

'It's not that,' he jumped in, sounding agitated.

'I promise I'll be extra careful to make sure you're not in when I come to service the apartment.'

'It's not that,' he said again, but this time sounding angry.

'What then?' I frowned.

'For fuck's sake,' he said, thumping the sand, before running his hands through his hair again.

'What?'

'It doesn't matter.' He sighed, but I got the feeling that whatever it was, did. 'I take it you didn't get the job you interviewed for?' he then asked. 'You know, the one in Barcelona that made you forget all about me.'

'No,' I said, 'I didn't. And I know you probably won't believe this, but I didn't forget about you, Logan. In all the days that have passed since I walked out of your hotel, I haven't once forgotten about you.'

'Fuck,' he muttered after a beat had passed. 'Fuck, fuck, fuck, fuck, fuck.'

'I really can stay out of your way while you're here,' I insisted, assuming his upset was the result of my unexpected presence. 'I know the reason behind your visit and I have no intention of—'

'I'd rather not talk about that,' he cut in.

'Of course.' I exhaled. 'I'm sorry.'

I daresay he didn't want to hear about how I was feeling either, but I wished I could tell him. I wished I could tell him how bitterly I regretted not going back to him after my fake job interview. No, more than that, I wished there'd never been a fake interview. I wished I'd sat on that plane with him and Sister Lucia and told them both the truth – that I was taking a break from a life I didn't enjoy, but was still persevering with in order to honour a promise I'd made to my mum and keep my dad both physically and mentally safe. That wasn't so bad, was it? I might have been poised to make a change to that life now, but when we'd met, I'd still been right in the thick of it.

'But I do appreciate your offer to stay out of my way,' he said. 'With everything else I've got going on, I don't think I could handle constantly bumping into you, Flora. I mean, Ally.'

'I get that,' I said, feeling choked. 'I totally understand. Dad will be able to help you with anything that comes up with the apartment and I know you already know the area, but he could answer any questions you might have about the cove.'

'You must know this patch of Dorset inside out, as you grew up here,' Logan said, standing up and brushing the sand off his cargo shorts.

'Like the back of my hand.' I sighed, also standing up. 'Better than the back of my hand.'

'You make that sound like a bad thing.'

'Let's just say,' I confessed, 'this isn't my favourite place in the world.'

'Of course,' he sardonically said. 'That would be Barcelona, right?'

I watched him walk away, then turned around and headed in the opposite direction.

# Chapter 11

Ordinarily, at this point in the Hollyhock Cottage summer season, I would still have been feeling the benefit of the time I had managed to get away in the spring. The memory of those halcyon days, the escape from not constantly wishing Mum was still with us or fretting over Dad's health and wellbeing would satisfyingly occupy my mind as I remade beds, chased up orders, updated accounts and refreshed vases of flowers – but that was not the case this year. And at a time when I most needed something wonderful to recall, I felt its absence all the more keenly.

Flora still wasn't talking to me unless Dad was in earshot. The double duplicity – first Tara and then Logan/Miguel – had so far proved too much for her to move on from and, to make matters worse, Tara was calling the cottage every day wanting to know if I'd yet talked Flora into hearing her out. As a precaution, I had taken to carrying the house phone around with me, minimising the risk of Flora picking up when she was at the cottage between clients.

On top of that stress, there was the exhaustion of being constantly on tenterhooks, trying to second guess whether Logan might or might not be in the vicinity when I needed to head over to check the rooms in the courtyard. I had seen him a couple of times – once on the beach and then coming out of the apartment – and both times I'd managed to dodge out of sight, but it was all making for an even more stressful summer than usual.

And there was planning my departure from the cove to think about now, too. I was still mulling over Flora's plan to install a manager and attempting to rationalise my concerns about Dad's mental and physical health.

I knew that Flora living in the cottage would help combat any potential feeling of loneliness Dad might experience during the autumn and winter and if I could talk him into regular check-ups, I would know he was physically fit, too. The manager would take on my work and I would be able to leave the bad and sad memories I associated with both the cottage and the cove behind and launch my dream career, guilt free, stress free, home free . . . right?

I was trying to comprehend why I was finding it so difficult to accept and embrace this 'perfect plan', when the sound of laughter met my ears as I made my way through the garden to take Dad a cup of tea one afternoon towards the end of the week.

As always, once he was working in the garden, Dad completely lost track of time and that day, I discovered, he wasn't alone.

'Well, I admire you,' I heard someone say, and when I got close enough I realised it was Logan. 'It sounds like an awful lot of work to me.'

'It's a huge amount of work,' Dad confirmed, 'but I wouldn't have it any other way. Like I told you the other day, it's all turned out exactly how my wife hoped it would.'

Clearly it wasn't the first conversation the pair had had about the business and I wondered how much Dad had told Logan about Mum, and why. Perhaps they had gravitated towards discussing loved ones as a result of the reason behind Logan's booking. I hoped I hadn't come up, too.

I had told Logan that Dad owned Hollyhock Cottage and that I was here to help him out. However, I knew I had also said that I was here 'for a bit', making my presence sound like a temporary arrangement, rather than a permanent fixture. Dad would be absolutely flummoxed if Logan told him we'd met and I had said that.

'Better than she hoped actually, thanks to my daughter, Ally.' Dad carried on and my ears pricked up further, 'She's managed to find a way to enhance practically every idea her mum had and I'm so proud that there's now such a wonderful legacy to leave her.'

I felt myself turn hot in the face of potential exposure. If Logan said the wrong thing now, I was going to have a hell of a lot of explaining to do.

'Well,' said Logan, his voice closer as he moved nearer to where I was hidden, 'I'm sure you've got years before you need to start thinking about legacies, Geoff, but do bear in mind what happened to my uncle. He was literally here today, gone tomorrow.'

'That was the same with my wife,' Dad falteringly said.

'Oh, I'm sorry,' Logan apologised, sounding contrite. 'That was insensitive of me.'

'No, I'm sorry,' said Dad. 'I didn't mean to make you feel

bad. Given what happened to my Rose, I will slow down at some point. I won't stop entirely though, not even when Ally takes the reins. I might have to find someone to give me a hand with the digging, though.' He chuckled. 'I daresay that'll be a bit beyond me when I'm an old croc.'

'Your daughter's up for that, is she?' Logan asked, making me sweat all the more. 'Taking the reins full-time, I mean?'

He was just one comment away from letting slip that I'd already told him a very different story and his presence was feeling even more like a ticking time bomb.

'Oh yes,' said Dad, sounding certain, which was hardly surprising as I'd never given him cause to think otherwise. 'This is the place for her.'

'So, you won't be selling up when you retire?' Logan probed.

'No chance.' Dad chuckled again.

I held my breath, as Logan then said he'd better get on and my shoulders didn't relax until his footsteps were out of earshot. I was going to have to tell him the truth behind my getaways and the sooner the better if I didn't want Dad discovering how dissatisfied I was with my life in Kittiwake Cove because Logan had inadvertently said something he didn't know he shouldn't. For the first time, my deception felt close enough to bite me on the backside and it didn't feel good, at all.

I headed down to the beach that evening with the intention of clearing my head and getting my ducks in a row. Kasuku was cussing as I set off. He had picked up on mine and Flora's disharmony, and his language and behaviour had deteriorated as a result. If his manners hadn't improved ahead of the guests arriving the next day, he was going to find himself with me in the loft and a blanket over his cage.

Thankfully, with it being light for so long each day, Dad was outside more often than he was in and his conversation and head was so full of successive sowings and harvesting schedules, that he hadn't picked up on the prickly atmosphere.

I initially made for the rock, but then decided to sit out in the fading sun, next to the rockpools, which were teeming with life. There were no objections from any of the colourful inhabitants as I carefully slid a few bottles of beer to cool into the watery crystal-clear shallows.

It had been the solstice the day before and I usually spent the evening on the beach. I found the celebration cheering, as it meant the wheel of the year had turned again and the summer season was moving on, but the time had passed without me remembering it, such was the stress buzzing about in my head. I bet Flora hadn't forgotten. Had we been talking, we would have celebrated together.

'Mind if I join you?'

I jumped, then twisted around to find Logan nearby, barefoot and bare chested, but with a T-shirt flung over his shoulder, which he then pulled on.

'Be my guest,' I responded, trying not to watch. He was in even better shape than I remembered and I cursed the tug in my stomach the sight of him aroused. 'But I was here before you,' I pointed out, 'so you can't blame me for intruding.'

I knew I sounded put out, but his arrival was bewildering. Hadn't he previously stated that he didn't want to bump into me? That said, I supposed I could make the most of the opportunity to talk to him.

'I haven't seen you all week,' he said, sitting next to me.

'Well, that was the plan, wasn't it?' I reminded him. 'I said I would stay out of your way and you said that was what you wanted.'

He nodded and looked out towards the sea.

'And now I've ruined the effort you'd gone to by seeking you out,' he said, his forehead etched with a frown.

'Purposefully seeking me out?' I questioned, shielding my eyes so I could look at him properly. 'Is that what you've done?'

'Yep,' he confessed.

'So much for me sticking to stealth mode,' I tutted.

'Yes, I'm sorry about that.'

'It's fine,' I said, looking away. 'And you shouldn't be apologising, should you? Not when I'm the one who has been in the wrong since the moment we met. I was the one who ended up running out on you, remember?'

'Oh yes,' he said heavily, 'I remember.'

'I heard you talking to Dad in the garden earlier,' I told him, wishing I hadn't flagged my regrettable behaviour.

'I had a feeling there was someone other than us out there.'

'Impossible,' I refuted. 'I was in stealth mode, remember? Completely undetectable.'

That made him laugh and I noticed his gorgeous laughter lines. I'd bet he hadn't smiled much of late. On the plane, he had mentioned that he had a huge and complicated work project lined up for the summer and now he had grief to contend with, too. I wondered if he would be working remotely, but didn't ask given that he'd shut me down when I'd mentioned his reason for being in the cove before.

'So, why were you looking for me?' I asked. 'I didn't think you'd want to spend a second with me, unless you had to.'

'Now I know you heard my conversation with your dad earlier,' he said meaningfully, 'I'm sure you can work that out.'

'Thank you for not telling him that I'd told you I was only here for a bit when he started talking about legacies,' I said, grateful. 'And for not mentioning Barcelona, either.'

'No need to thank me,' he said, 'but I would like to know what the deal is. I was still harbouring the illusion that you were only here temporarily and living abroad until I heard what your dad had to say. Not to mention when we were together before, that you had this amazing job interview lined up . . .'

'I know,' I sighed. 'I know you were.'

'Obviously, you told me about the different name thing, but there's a lot more to it than that, isn't there? It seems to me that you're two completely different people, Ally.'

'Well,' I said, reaching into the rockpool and pulling out two beers, 'I suppose, you've hit the nail on the head, because sometimes, I am.'

'So, tell me then,' Logan said, taking the bottle I offered him and twisting off the lid. 'Who exactly are you, Ally?'

'Where to start,' I said, opening and gulping down half of my own beer.

'Well, your dad told me that your mum died before the business was established and that you didn't live here until after she passed,' Logan quietly said. 'And that told me you actually live here full-time, so why don't you start by telling me how that came about and then we can get to why you made out your life was so different in Spain, after?'

'Living here came about,' I slowly said, already dreading the second part of the explanation, 'as a result of a promise I made to my mum.'

'A promise.'

'Yes. I was here on a visit during a break from uni and she asked me to promise that if anything happened to her, I would move in and help Dad.'

'Was she ill?' Logan frowned. 'Is that why she asked you?'

'No,' I said, 'she wasn't. She was perfectly healthy, or seemed to be and, I know this sounds terrible, but that was why I promised.' I grimaced as I said it. 'I agreed to what she asked because I never thought I'd have to see it through. She and Dad were so happy and content here and I'd been so ecstatic and enthusiastic about their plans for the business, that Mum mistakenly, but understandably, assumed that if something happened to her, then I'd be happy to take on her role.'

'I see.' Logan said, frowning as he took in what I was telling him in.

'But the truth was,' I carried on, 'my excitement was born out of relief that I didn't need to worry about their future. Then, when I came back the next time with a view to sharing what my post-graduation plans were, Mum had a massive heart attack and was suddenly gone.'

'I'm so sorry,' Logan said, sounding shocked. 'That must have been terrifying.'

'It was,' I said, my breath shuddering. 'Dad and I spent an entire year in a sort of freezeframe after it happened. We were both completely numb. It was Flora, who staged an intervention, along with her brother, Freddie. They helped us turn things around. Between us all, we slowly sorted the cottage, carried on with the courtyard conversion and got the business going.'

I would always be so grateful to the pair of them for that. Other people in the community had helped, but it was initially Flora and then Freddie who had done the most.

'I can't even begin to imagine what it must have been like to lose your mum like that.' Logan frowned and I was surprised he'd said that, given that I'd heard him tell Dad that he had lost his uncle in a similar way.

'It was the worst thing I've ever had to live through.' I shivered.

'And you moved here as a result of it,' he surmised.

'That's right.' I nodded. 'I moved here and honoured the promise I'd made to Mum.'

'But you don't want to be here?' Logan perceptively asked. 'You never have?'

'There are other places I'd rather be,' I answered honestly.

'So, why don't you leave?' He frowned. 'The business is working and your dad's a good guy. I'm certain he'd understand. Your post-grad plans must still be there for the—'

'I know Dad's a good guy,' I interrupted, 'but, as far as my plans are concerned, I've never mentioned them. He has no idea what they were, because he's needed me here.'

'But he doesn't need you now, surely? Now things are working so well, you could leave and pursue them, couldn't you?'

'It's not that simple,' I said, drinking more beer – and despite the fact I was actually now working towards moving on. 'There's more to the situation than that.'

'Such as?'

Dad getting sick, Dad feeling lonely, Dad dying and me not being here to save him ... My head reeled off everything I was still working though, but I didn't say any of it out loud because

I knew it would probably sound irrational and absurd. It sometimes sounded that way to me too, but unfortunately not often enough for me to be able to dismiss it yet.

'It's complicated,' I said instead. 'I'd rather not talk about it.'

Logan looked exasperated.

'So, tell me about Barcelona then,' he said. 'When we were in Spain, you told me that you had lived and worked abroad since you graduated, but as I now know you've been here with your dad the whole time, that can't be true, can it?'

'No,' I said, briefly closing my eyes. 'That's not true.'

'So, what's the deal? What is the truth?'

I dug my fingers into the sand.

'The truth is,' I exhaled, 'that trip to Barcelona was one of a few that came about as a result of a plan Flora and I came up with to save my sanity and convince Dad that I'm happy here, even though I'm not.'

Logan looked around at the beautiful beach as if he couldn't believe his ears.

'I never liked the cottage when I was growing up and had to come during the holidays while Mum and Dad worked,' I elaborated, to help him understand. 'And now there are also my memories of what happened to Mum here to contend with.'

'Of course,' he said, acknowledging my discontent. 'So, this plan . . .'

'The plan involved me getting away a couple of times a year and while I was gone, I . . .'

'While you're gone you what?' Logan frowned.

I bit my lip, then reluctantly carried on.

'While I was gone, I would pretend I was living the life I wanted. While I was off travelling, I would pretend that

I worked in a museum, or gave tours of historic buildings, rather than being the person who actually changed beds and emptied bins.'

'So, the career you told me about in Barcelona was completely made up?'

'Yes,' I confirmed, 'and the interview wasn't real either.'

'There was no interview?'

'No,' I said, spelling it out as simply as I could. 'It was all a part of the role I was playing as were my smart clothes and chic lifestyle.'

'And your name?'

'Yes.' I nodded. 'My name, too. I know it probably sounds ridiculous, but it used to help. The memories I came back with would carry me through the rest of the year and give me something fun to think about until it was time for me to go again.'

'So,' Logan said hoarsely, 'absolutely none of our time together was real. Along with there being no interview, there really was no glamourous life abroad either. It was all a lie.'

It sounded awful, but that was the crux of it.

'Yes,' I confirmed, looking down at my T-shirt and shorts. 'None of it was real. Not even the way I looked when we first met.'

'And I just happened to be ... what?' Logan spluttered. 'A random hook-up, enlisted and tricked into scratching your itch to provide you with something to look back on while you survived another season in the cove?'

'Oh God,' I groaned. 'Yes. Yes, that's exactly what you were supposed to be, but it didn't work out like that, did it?'

'Why not?'

'Because you were different, Logan.' I couldn't believe I

finally had the chance to tell him and hoped I wasn't about to mess it up. 'That connection between us you said you felt, I felt it too and before I realised it, I'd dropped the pretence. Our time together meant every bit as much to me as it did to you. You were a million miles away from a random hook-up.'

'And yet you still left,' he said bluntly. 'You felt all that and you still ran out on me.'

'I'm so sorry,' I said, feeling ashamed all over again. 'The day I disappeared; I realised the trip had turned into something I hadn't been prepared for and I got scared, but I've regretted leaving you every day since and I've been desperately hoping you didn't feel what I felt. I haven't told anyone what happened. Not even Flora. I said I met someone, but not that I'd . . .'

I cut the words off before I went too far and said too much.

'But I did feel what you felt, Ally,' Logan said passionately. 'I felt every bit of it.'

'I know,' I said. 'I know that now.'

We sat in silence for a couple of minutes.

'So, what now?' Logan finally asked. 'You're working another season here and planning your next trip?'

'No,' I said vehemently. 'No more trips.'

'Your poor Dad,' he said, shaking his head. 'He hasn't got a clue, has he?'

'I resorted to doing this, so I didn't hurt him,' I choked, as tears started to prick my eyes. 'I've been trying to carve out a life that would keep us both happy and him safe.'

'Oh, I know,' Logan quickly said, sounding torn, 'but it's a lot for me to process. Far more than I've been imagining these last few months. I'm now trying to get my head around the fact that there's no part of the woman I spent those few incredible days with that actually exists. I don't know you, Ally, do I? I have no idea who you really are.'

'I told you, I dropped the image when we were together,' I said, standing up, 'even if I didn't find the courage to tell you the truth, I was more me then than you realise.'

He caught my hand.

'Don't go,' he begged and I looked at him, then sat back down. 'I know I sound pissed off,' he added, before letting go of my hand, 'but I really am trying to understand.'

'Are you?' I hoped he meant that.

'Of course, I am,' he said, taking a breath. 'I appreciate that your crazy plan had a well-intentioned motive behind it. You were satisfying your wanderlust by escaping the cove for a while and that enabled you to keep Geoff happy,' he said thoughtfully. 'Though how this place isn't your ultimate escape, I'll never know. If I could swap my city existence for life in the cove, I'd jump at the chance.'

'You wouldn't say that if you had my memories,' I reminded him.

'Of course,' he said, sounding apologetic.

'But I'm ditching the plan now,' I told him, suddenly and surprisingly wanting to make that crystal clear. 'I want the other life, the one I've been faking all this time. That's going to become my real life. I'm going to make it happen.'

It felt good to say it out loud and I meant it, too. Not only did I not want to live a lie any longer, but having also seen the impact my last fabricated trip had had on the man sitting next to me, as well as the toll it had taken on myself, I realised the potential to hurt that game of pretend wielded and it was time it was left in the past.

'And how are you planning to get that life?' Logan asked.

I could tell from his tone that he still thought I was mad to want to leave.

'Carefully,' I told him. 'I don't want Dad to have even an inkling that I've wanted something different all these years. As you said, he's a good guy and if he found out I'd been unhappy, not to mention, constantly worrying about him, he'd be devastated.'

'I get that.' Logan nodded. 'So, who's going to do your job?'

'Flora has suggested we bring in a manager,' I explained. 'Someone I can train up before I go.'

'And you're comfortable with that?'

'I'm still getting used to the idea,' I said honestly.

'So,' said Logan, looking around again, 'you're going to leave this place to live the life I thought you already had.'

'That's right.' I swallowed, wishing he hadn't put it quite like that. 'Not immediately of course, but perhaps by the end of the year, if the right candidate comes along.'

We both looked out to sea.

'Do you think your decision to go might make your dad consider giving it all up?' Logan asked.

'Absolutely not,' I said, puffing out my cheeks. 'He'll never stop. He's much older than he looks and should have retired already, but you've seen him in action. He's still got years of work ahead of him.'

Logan didn't say anything further and I pondered more deeply what he'd said. Dad wouldn't jack it in if I left, would he? I hoped the prospect of that wasn't something else I was going to end up fretting about. I was finally ready to rein in the worries I already had and didn't need another one to add to the list.

'And Flora's going to be here to help,' I said, more to myself than Logan.

'She'll pitch in, will she?'

'Yes,' I said. 'She's already said so.'

'Well, it sounds like between you, you've got it all worked out.'

'I think we have.' I smiled. 'Though there's bound to be the odd snag.'

'Is there anything I could do to help things along?' he offered. 'I know we don't know each other that well, but I'm sure having another friend around the place might come in useful at some point.'

'You really want to be my friend?' I swallowed, amazed that he could be so forgiving. Had I been in his position, I didn't think I could have been so magnanimous. 'Even with what you've sadly got going on and after everything I've just admitted to?'

He looked at me for a moment, as if he was weighing me up, then nodded. I wasn't sure what conclusion he had just come to or decision he had reached, but I could tell there was a lot of mental gymnastics going on.

'I can't tell you what a relief it is to have heard you out and found out the real reason why you disappeared.' He smiled. 'It's going to make all the difference.'

'It is.' I frowned. 'To what?'

'To us, of course,' he said kindly, making my heart swell with happiness. 'I want us to have a completely fresh start. I want to get to know you, the real you, properly.'

'Well, that sounds good to me.' I smiled, feeling delighted with his suggestion.

'In fact,' he said, raising an eyebrow, 'how about we make a *really* fresh start?'

'What do you have in mind?' I asked, feeling every nerve ending twitch.

'How about a swim?'

'A swim.' I objected. That wasn't what I had been hoping for. 'Are you mad? The sea is glacial!'

'Fresh,' he said, looking towards the pontoon which was anchored right at the edge of the cove. 'Not glacial.'

'Freezing!' I batted back, 'not fresh.'

'Come on,' he said, jumping up.

'We're really doing this?' I squeaked as he pulled off his T-shirt.

'We're really doing this,' he said, dropping his shorts.

It was just as well the beach was deserted. I reluctantly stood up and started removing clothes as he jogged down to the shore in his boxers.

'Fuck!' he yelped as he waded in.

'I told you,' I said, as I joined him, but only far enough for the bracing water to lap over my feet. 'Jeez, it really is freezing.'

He stuck his tongue out and then dove out of sight. I waited until he bobbed up again before reluctantly inching further in.

'Come on!' he shouted. 'Last one to the pontoon is destined to stay in the cove forever!'

'That's not fair.' I dithered, thinking there had to be warmer ways to honour our fresh start. 'You've got a head start now.'

I set off thinking that if Logan's prediction was right, I was going to be stuck in Kittiwake Cove for all of eternity because I had no chance of catching him up.

# Chapter 12

Courtesy of our time together in Barcelona, I already knew Logan had the physique for it, but he proved to be an even stronger swimmer than I could have guessed. Far ahead of me, he cut through the water like a hot knife through butter, while I trailed behind and never really warmed up, in spite of the distance we covered.

'What kept you?' he laughed, when I finally reached him and he lifted me out of the sea and on to the floating pontoon in one elegant movement, which saved me from struggling ungainly up the steps.

I pulled my T-shirt away from goose-pimpled flesh and checked my knickers were more or less still in place while I caught my breath.

'I can't remember the last time I swam out here.' I shivered, as my teeth chattered and my legs started to shake.

I felt like I'd swum the channel rather than tens of metres.

'If I lived here,' Logan grinned, looking back to the shore, 'I'd be swimming all over the cove every day.'

'If you lived here,' I responded, 'you'd be welcome to.' I bit my lip and looked towards the shore, too. It seemed a very long way away. 'I'm not sure I'm going to be able to make it back. Your friendship better be worth this fresh start you've goaded me into making.'

He laughed at that and dived into the sea again, one hand holding his boxers in place as he hit the water. I flopped down on the pontoon, my chest still heaving from the exertion, which had propelled me, reluctantly, this far out to sea. I had thought with all the work I did around the cottage, I was in pretty good shape, but clearly not.

'Come on,' said Logan, popping up like an over-enthusiastic seal. 'Look alive, Ally.' He climbed back on to the pontoon and stared down at me. I willed him to sit, but he didn't. 'Let's head back,' he swallowed, moving a little further away, 'before the tide turns.'

The tide. I hadn't even noticed what it was doing before I'd launched myself into the surf. I had lived almost my entire life having the hidden dangers of the sea drummed into me but had thrown caution and common sense to the wind to swim after a man I still had far more than friendly feelings for. It was going to be my own fault if I ended up needing rescuing.

'I'll swim back alongside you,' Logan called up to me, having jumped back in. 'Like a real friend, I'll stick with you.'

It seemed to take forever for us to get back because of my lack of stamina, but eventually we made it out of the sea and up to the piles of clothes we'd abandoned on the sand. Logan kindly offered me his dry T-shirt, which I was immensely grateful for.

'Do you think we should tell your dad that we already knew each other before I arrived here?' he asked as I turned my back

and pulled my sodden top over my head. 'It feels wrong to keep
it from him, doesn't it?'

'Oh God,' I groaned, 'I thought we were done with revealing
secrets now. Can we make this the last one?'

I turned around again and he shrugged. There was a look on
his face I couldn't fathom, but which I hoped was the result of
concern for Dad rather than another secret. He turned away as
I wriggled out of my clinging undies and pulled my dry shorts
on. It was a relief that the beach was still deserted because my
quick change was more about speed than modesty.

'I reckon we should keep things simple where Dad's concerned,' I said, rubbing my arms to get the blood flowing again.
'I'll just say I ran into you, or came to change your bed, and
couldn't believe it was you, because we'd met before, in Spain,
in the spring.'

'Flora hasn't mentioned that we'd already bumped into each
other on the beach last week?' Logan asked.

'She can't have done,' I said, biting my lip, 'because Dad
would have said something about it before now.'

'All right,' Logan agreed. 'Sounds good to me. Will you tell
him we just went skinny dipping, too?'

'Er,' I said, pointing at my wet clothes, 'I kept my modesty,
thank you very much.'

'Only just.' He grinned and I blushed.

'Logan.' I swallowed as he wrung out his soaked boxers,
which he'd now switched for his shorts. 'You are sure you
want us to be friends, aren't you? Because I know today has
been a lot.'

I was still thinking about how quickly he'd moved our relationship on.

'I do,' he said, 'and it has. But like I said before, now you've had the chance to explain things, I get it. I understand.'

'Okay,' I said.

'And if you're worried about me getting my own back, there's no need,' he joked, 'I've just made you swim in glacial seawater, so that's evened things up a bit.'

I grabbed his boxers and swatted him with them, leaving a watermark on his T-shirt.

'You said it wasn't glacial,' I reminded him.

'It was though, wasn't it?' he said, involuntarily shivering.

I decided to let the topic of him so speedily forgiving me drop. After all, he had bigger things to contend with. He was staying in Kittiwake Cove to come to terms with the loss of his uncle and even though he hadn't so far talked to me about that, I mustn't forget that it had happened. He might not have been outwardly displaying his grief, but as he'd said earlier, we didn't know each other all that well and for all I knew, he could be a really private person who didn't go in for public displays of emotion.

'In spite of the fact that you've just made me take a chilly swim, I think you're an amazing person,' I told him. 'Most people wouldn't have heard me out, especially given the circumstances which led to you coming to the cove.'

'Well,' he said, having cleared his throat, 'I'm the sort of person who likes to look at a situation from all angles, before I make up my mind about it.'

Luckily for me, I'd finally and miraculously had the opportunity to equip him with the explanation he needed to understand what I'd done and why. Had he not come to the cove, I knew I would have regretted him forever.

'I do have one question for you though, if that's okay?' he said.

'Of course.'

'If I hadn't started to become friendly with your dad, would you have told me any of what you've shared today?'

I didn't hesitate.

'Yes,' I immediately said. I might have gone back and forth over it before, but now I knew it was all better out in the open. 'I meant what I said about liking you, Logan. I might have been pretending to be someone else in Barcelona, but it was definitely me, Ally, who ... thought so much of you. I messed up and missed out on telling you that then, so I wouldn't have let this second chance pass me by. It might have taken me a little longer, but I certainly would have told you because, I mean, really, what were the odds of you turning up here?'

He smiled at that, but the expression didn't light up his eyes in the same way as it had when I'd been in his hotel bed. Perhaps it would be best if I stopped comparing everything that occurred between us now to what I'd witnessed and experienced between the sheets.

He hazarded a guess. 'More than a hundred million to one, I would have thought.'

'I'm sorry to have dumped my explanation on you at such a difficult time,' I said, wishing he'd also said something about liking me.

'It's fine.' He shrugged. 'We have no power over when fate is going to step in and wreak havoc in our lives, do we?'

'I hope I haven't ushered in too much mayhem,' I said, seriously.

'You know what I mean.' He smiled. 'Come on, you're freezing. Let's get back.'

*

I spent the longest time in the shower and while I washed the sea out of my hair, I mulled over everything Logan and I had said and every secret I had shared with him. It was the biggest relief to know that he was prepared to let what I'd done go. If I could just make amends with Flora too, then all would be well.

'Oh my God!' I squealed, when I opened the bathroom door and found her standing right outside it. 'You scared the crap out of me,' I admonished, readjusting the towel I was wrapped in that I'd almost dropped.

'You've been in there for ages,' she coughed, as a floral waft of Jo Malone scented steam billowed out of the door behind me.

'Sorry,' I said, padding towards the stairs that led to my space in the loft, 'but you've got your own bathroom. What do you need mine for?'

'I wasn't waiting to use your bathroom,' she said, following me. 'I was waiting for you.'

I turned to look at her.

'I didn't think you were talking to me,' I said, looking down at her from my slightly elevated position on the stairs.

'I'm not really,' she pouted, but with mischief in her eyes, 'but my curiosity has got the better of me and I'm dying to know what you and Logan were up to in the sea.'

'Oh my God,' I said again, this time looking over her shoulder.

'Don't worry,' she grinned. 'Your dad's still in the garden.'

'How did you even see us?' I hissed.

'I was walking on the beach.' She shrugged. 'I found your clothes piled up and then I honed in on the pair of you on the pontoon.'

'Shit,' I muttered. 'You and your bloody eagle eyes.'

There was no reason that the impromptu swim should have been a secret, but I wasn't sure what the rest of the locals would make of the little Logan and I had, or hadn't, been wearing while we took it, so I hoped no one else had spotted us. A narked neighbour moaning to Dad about inappropriate swimming apparel was the last thing I needed.

'So, are you going to tell me or what?' Flora laughed. 'I'm guessing he's got over the shock of finding you here in the cove.'

'Come on and I'll tell you,' I said, skipping up the stairs. 'We'll have to talk here because the tide's in now and we can't get to the rock.'

In spite of the date, it was chilly in the loft and I could see rain clouds rolling in. Flora closed the window and curtains while I got dry and dressed and set about the lengthy process of untangling my hair, which hadn't appreciated the earlier salt-laden soaking. My arms already ached from the unaccustomed swim, so it felt like a monumental task.

'Here,' said Flora, holding out her hand for the brush. 'I'll do it.'

'Thanks,' I said, moving to sit on the velvet-covered stool in front of the dressing table that had belonged to Mum before she and Dad were married. 'My arms are killing me.'

'So, are you knackered from the swim, or what happened before or after it?' Flora asked, looking at me in the mirror, raising her eyebrows.

'Both,' I told her, with a wry smile.

'Oh goody.' She giggled. 'So come on, spill.'

'You've changed your tune.' I pretended to huff. 'You've barely said a word to me all week.'

'And with good reason,' she said, snagging the brush.

'Ow!' I squealed.

'Sorry.' She winked. 'Now, hurry up and tell me everything.'

'I will,' I said, 'but I warn you, you're going to be disappointed.'

'I'll be the judge of that.'

'Well, my tiredness is almost entirely emotional exhaustion,' I confessed and her shoulders sagged. 'There was no love in the dunes.'

Our eyes met again and we both grinned. There had been a steamy romance novel called that on Mum's bedroom bookshelf when we were tweens and we used to sneakily read pages of it whenever we got the chance.

'Probably just as well,' Flora smiled. 'I never did work out how they got the sand out of their—'

'So,' I cut in, 'I told Logan all about my fake names and fantasy getaways—'

'You never did?' she gasped.

'I did.' I swallowed. 'Of course, I did. And,' I carried on, 'I also told him how I really feel about living and working here.'

Just as I had known they would, Flora's eyes widened even further.

'Jeez, Ally!' She gasped again, looking back across the room to make sure the door was properly closed even though we knew Dad was outside.

'I told him that I'm only here because of the promise I made to Mum and,' I carried on, 'I also shared, that I've now *definitely* made up my mind to . . .'

Flora's gaze focused intently on my face as the sentence trailed off.

'Oh my God,' she croaked. 'I honestly thought you were still dithering, but you're really going to go, aren't you?'

I nodded, but didn't say anything.

'I can't believe it.'

'Well, you should,' I said. 'You were the one who encouraged me after I said I'd made up my mind and then insisted that someone could easily take my place, remember?'

'I did say that, didn't I?' She swallowed. 'Your dad's going to kill me.'

'No, he won't,' I said, reaching for her hand. 'Not if we follow the plan I'm developing. If anything, he'll end up feeling relieved that I haven't accrued all that student debt for nothing.'

She laughed at that, but it was a shaky laugh.

'Is your decision to see it through completely down to what I suggested?' she asked astutely.

'Not entirely,' I confessed. 'Though knowing you're going to be here for Dad has made a huge difference.'

I didn't spell it out, but Tara turning up in the cove looking the epitome of everything I wanted to be had played a part, too.

'Bloody Tara,' Flora sniffed, reading my mind. 'Something else I can blame her for.'

'Well,' I said, 'there's no need to blame her just yet, because I'm not planning to do anything before the end of the season. I'll wait to start laying the foundations until then, so you can lay off the blame for a few more months and I'm sure she'll be long gone by then. The most important thing to remember is that Dad must never find out that I've been fretting over him or that I've never found a way to fall in love with this place.'

'Of course,' Flora agreed, giving my hand a squeeze then

letting it go. 'Knowing that would break his heart all over again, so we won't risk that.'

'We definitely won't.' I shuddered.

'And talking of broken hearts,' she carried on, 'you still haven't told me how you've left things with Miguel. I mean Logan. Though the fact that you were swimming in the sea together and he wasn't trying to drown you suggests things are okay between you now.'

'They are,' I said, thinking of Logan's understanding and willingness to move on.

'Why did you lie about him when you came back?' Flora dug further. 'I had him down as some Spanish lothario and he's obviously not that.'

She'd finished brushing my hair now, so we crossed the room and sat on the bed. I heard the back door slam as the rain began to drum on the windows.

'Sounds like your dad made it in just in time.' Flora smiled.

'Thank goodness.' I smiled back. 'Which reminds me, when you left Logan and me on the beach the morning he found us, did you happen to tell Dad that we were together down there?'

Flora took a moment to think about that.

'No,' she said. 'I went straight to the studio. I don't think he even knows that the two of you have met yet.'

'Perfect,' I said.

'How so?'

'Because we've agreed to keep things straightforward and tell Dad that we couldn't believe it when we ran into each other here, because we'd already met in Spain,' I explained and she nodded in agreement.

'That sounds like a good idea to me,' she said. 'Much better to have your previous acquaintance out in the open. You know how much cloak and dagger stuff stresses me out.'

'I do,' I said, my cheeks colouring as I thought of the clandestine Tara situation I was actually still immersed in.

'So come on,' Flora wheedled, picking up the thread I'd tried to pull her away from. 'Why didn't you tell me the whole story about him when you got back in the spring?'

'I suppose . . .' I puffed, trying to sound casual. 'I suppose, I didn't tell you the truth about him, because . . .'

'No fricking way,' Flora gasped, grabbing my hand as my words trailed off. I couldn't find the ones I wanted anyway. 'You did, didn't you?'

'I did, what?' I frowned, cursing the blush that suddenly burst into bloom.

'You fell in love with him.'

'What?' I squeaked, several octaves higher than before. 'No.'

'You did,' she said, sounding certain, 'you bloody well fell in love with him.'

I wished she'd stop saying that.

'Of course, I didn't,' I hotly denied, tugging my hand away from hers. 'I knew him for all of five seconds. How can you fall in love with someone after five seconds?'

'I have no idea.' She beamed. 'Why don't you tell me, because you seem to have managed it.'

'I did not fall in love with him,' I said, more calmly this time. 'I liked him. A lot. True. But there was no time for love.'

'So,' she said, eyeing me beadily, 'what happens now? Are you picking up where you left off? I know he was pissed off that morning we met on the beach, but given that you've been swimming together today, I'm guessing he has completely accepted your bare-all confession?'

'He has,' I said, mulling over what had occurred. 'I think the fact that he's currently grieving has surpassed what I'd done. He's been really gracious about the whole thing.'

'Hmm,' said Flora.

'What?'

'Perhaps,' she said, 'it's nothing to do with his grief. Have you considered that maybe he took it all so well because he wasn't as into you as you were into him?'

'Flora!' I yelped, grabbing a cushion and throwing it at her. 'Are you trying to upset me?' I scowled.

'No,' she promised, 'I'm not. It's just that, grieving or not, he's got over you pretty quickly now he knows the truth, hasn't he? And,' she mischievously added, 'if you're not and never have been in love with him, why would my suggesting that upset you so much?'

'It wouldn't,' I shot back. 'It hasn't.'

It would though and it had. It hadn't escaped my notice that the first day Logan had seen me on the beach, he'd seemed devastated about how I'd treated him, but now he was willing to forget it and be friends. Was that because he knew why I'd done it now or because he preferred the fantasy version of me to the woman I was in Kittiwake Cove?

'We're just friends now,' I told Flora, trying to sound convinced as well as convincing. 'And that's fine.'

'Eek,' Flora gasped, her tone teasing. 'He's friend-zoned you, and after all that hot sex. You must be gutted.'

'Not at all,' I said haughtily, climbing off the bed, 'with everything else I've also got going on, I'll take another friend over a lover. I honestly don't need anything even remotely complicated rocking up in my life for the foreseeable future.'

'So, where does that put Tara then?' Flora sardonically asked, also getting up.

'Right now,' I grimaced, following her to the door as Dad started shouting that supper was almost ready, 'I have absolutely no idea.'

# Chapter 13

It poured with rain for most of the night, but thankfully the next day dawned bright and sunny, which was a huge relief, as it was a watercolour weekend and, whenever possible, they were taught outside, in the garden. Bunty Babstock was the tutor and she arrived bright and early, wearing creased linen layers and a huge straw hat and looking as delicate as the blooms she loved to paint. Even though she was anything but.

'Such a relief!' she cried as she began pulling easels and canvases out of the back of her car and looked up at the cerulean sky. 'Such a relief.'

'Can I give you a hand with all that, Bunty?' I offered.

'No, no,' she said, waving me away. 'I'm stronger than I look. Just the usual fully loaded coffee will suffice, thank you my dear.'

'I'll make it,' said Flora, adding in a hissed whisper, 'You go and find Logan and give him the heads-up that the *you won't believe who I've just run into* Dad plan is on.'

I had to laugh as she put air quotes around the words.

'Where is Dad?' I asked, looking around as Bunty carried on rushing about, diving in and out of her ancient car.

The battered bodywork was testament to the narrowness of the lanes around the cove.

'In the kitchen giving Kasuku a stern talking to.' Flora grinned. 'I'll keep Geoff here so you can get into the flat and sort your random running into each other thing with Logan,' she added, speaking the words with relish.

'So much for you not liking the cloak and dagger stuff,' I teased, 'and it's an apartment, remember? Not a flat.'

'Whatever,' she shot back. 'Assuming that's where Logan is, of course. I suppose he might have taken himself off for another nearly naked swim.'

He hadn't done that and a minute later I stepped into the apartment.

'You don't mind if I come in, do you?' I asked, only realising once I was in that he hadn't actually invited me.

'No,' he said, closing the door, 'of course not. Just give me a sec.'

He rushed over to the coffee table, closed his MacBook and began piling papers together.

'I'm sorry,' I apologised. 'You're working. I didn't mean to disturb you.'

I wondered if it was the complicated project he had mentioned in the spring that he was working on. I hoped whatever it was, was distracting him from his grief. For some of the time at least. I knew only too well that it was all about balance when you were working your way through something.

'We never did get around to talking about what it is that you do, did we?' I remembered aloud.

'Oh, this isn't work,' Logan said, as he scooped the MacBook and papers up. 'It's stuff to do with my uncle's estate.'

No distraction at all, then.

'Please don't pack up on my account,' I insisted. 'I'm only going to be a minute.'

'It's fine,' he said, dumping everything in the bedroom, as his mobile, which was on the sofa, started to ring. 'I've been staring at it all for hours, so it's time I took a break.'

Looking at him closer, I noticed the dark smudges under his eyes and the state of his hair and the shorts he was still wearing suggested he hadn't showered since our impromptu swim.

His phone eventually stopped but then immediately started up again.

'Do you need to answer that?' I asked, when he still ignored it.

The ringtone was a tinny version of an Ibizan club classic, which I knew was going to be stuck in my head all day. It wasn't a track I would have guessed Logan would have picked, but that in itself was further proof that I didn't know that much about him.

I could confirm that he was a standout lover, a strong swimmer and a knockout kisser, but beyond that I was stumped. I hoped our newly formed friendship would fill in more of the blanks and I blushed as I thought how I would have loved to have had the opportunity to recheck some of the details I already knew.

'Nope,' he said, taking the phone and putting it with the rest of his things before firmly closing the door. 'It can wait.'

The music stopped and then struck up for the third time.

'Well,' I said, 'if you're sure.'

'I am,' he said, running his hands through his salt-laden hair. 'I'll put the kettle on. I could do with a coffee. Can I make you one, too?'

'No,' I said, trying to tune out the ringtone, 'no thanks. I only came over to tell you—'

Right at that moment, someone knocked on the door and Logan leapt almost as high as the ceiling. I jumped too, but he was more on edge than me. I guessed the sleep deprivation had really got to him.

'Logan?'

It was Dad. So much for Flora keeping him in the cottage.

'Shit,' Logan muttered, steering me towards the bathroom, before I had the chance to tell him that it didn't matter if Dad found me there and we could stage our 'you'll never guess what' moment straightaway. 'Wait in here.'

Their conversation only lasted a minute and then he let me out again.

'Your dad has asked me to join you all for dinner,' Logan explained. 'He said he wants me to meet his daughter.'

'We could have just dealt with that, had you not bundled me into your bathroom,' I laughed. 'Still, we can bump into each other when you come over to eat, can't we, and that'll be the end of it.'

'I can't come to dinner,' Logan regretfully said. 'I've already got plans.'

'Oh well,' I shrugged, wondering what his plans were, 'no worries. I'll just tell Dad we've been reacquainted myself. I'll explain that we shared seats next to each other on the plane and that I helped steady your nerves about flying.'

'And don't forget, that I took you out to dinner to say thank you.'

'Basically, the truth then,' I smiled. 'It sounds very romantic.'

'It was romantic.' Logan swallowed and I blushed. 'Don't tell him what happened afterwards though.'

I felt my face colour further as my libido leapt.

'I won't,' I said. 'We'll keep that to ourselves.'

'Agreed.' Logan smiled, his eyes resting on mine for heart-stopping seconds that made my stomach flip. 'We did have a good time, didn't we?' he whispered, looking at me in a way that suggested he still had more than friendship on his mind.

I was about to respond, when his phone started blaring again.

'I think you'd better get that,' I said, reluctantly dropping my gaze. 'And I should go. How are you finding staying here, by the way?' I asked, remembering my professional manners. 'Have you got everything you need?'

'It's really lovely,' he said, following me to the door. 'Everything entirely catered for.'

'Just let me know if there's anything extra, you'd like,' I said, not meaning it to sound so suggestive and blushing again because it did.

'There is one thing you might be able to help me with,' he said and my heart fluttered. 'Possibly more than one, actually.'

'Happy to,' I said, committing before I knew what to.

'In his will,' Logan explained, 'my uncle requested that he wants me to visit a few local sites while I'm here. Some are familiar, but there are others that we didn't get around to visiting when he was alive.'

'You sometimes stayed with him in the holidays, didn't you?' I said, remembering what Flora had said Dad had told her.

'That's right,' he confirmed. 'He lived in the north of the county. His house will go on the market at some point, but the legal team are dealing with that. I don't really fancy making these trips he's listed on my own, or even understand his reason for suggesting them yet, and wondered if you'd be up for coming with me?'

'I can do that,' I told him. 'I'd be happy to, if it helps.'

'It really would make my life easier.'

'It will have to be during weekdays though, if that's okay? I can't leave Dad to manage alone at weekends.'

'You won't be able to help him when you've moved,' Logan reminded me.

'No,' I said, 'but the manager will help him then, won't they?'

'True.' Logan smiled, opening the door and letting me out.

When I got back to the cottage, I found the table in the kitchen where Kasuku's cage ordinarily stood was empty and Flora was trying not to laugh, while Dad and Bunty placated one of the guests.

'It's fine, Geoff,' said Bunty, leading the shocked woman away. 'Don't look so worried. The bird adds character. Now come along, Mrs Gilding, I appreciate that the first time you meet him can be a shock, but it's over now and once we've found you a lovely spot in the garden, you'll soon forget all about it. The easels are all set up and waiting for you.'

Bunty winked at me and Dad dropped his head in his hands.

'Where is our feathered fiend?' I sighed.

'In your room,' said Dad, sounding done in and it was barely breakfast time. 'I better get on. I need to harvest some salad leaves to go with the tortilla I'm prepping for lunch.'

'Your dad fancied something Spanish.' Flora grinned at me as he collected his trug and took off along the path in the direction of the veg patch. 'And talking of Spanish delights, how did you get on with Logan?'

'He's not Spanish,' I pointed out, frowning as I watched Dad go.

'He'll always be Miguel to me,' Flora laughed.

'What exactly did Kasuku say?' I asked her.

'Do you really want to know?'

'No,' I said, changing my mind, 'not really. I know his entire repertoire, so I can pretty much guess.'

'And the look on poor Mrs Gilding's face should have given you a clue, too.'

'It was on the more offensive end of the scale, wasn't it?'

'Oh yes,' Flora confirmed. 'So, what have you and Logan agreed to tell Geoff?'

'Like I said before,' I told her, smiling at the memory of our conversation, while I started to load the dishwasher, 'everything, well other than . . .'

'That you've had super-hot sex!' She laughed. 'Or sex that *you* thought was super hot, even if Logan didn't, given that he wants to be friends now,' she teased, putting more annoying air quotes around her words and pulling a sad face.

'If anyone had sex this morning it would be super hot,' said Dad, who strode back into the kitchen and picked up his battered straw hat. 'It's already scorching out there. Who are we talking about anyway?'

Flora looked as though she was about to fall into a dead faint and I couldn't help but laugh at her.

'Serves you right for teasing,' I told her. 'And you shouldn't eavesdrop Dad. You might hear something you wished you hadn't.'

'I think I already have.' He grinned, tipping his hat to the pair of us before he walked out again. 'I'll leave you to it.'

'Well,' said Flora, throwing me the tea towel so I could dry the glasses she'd washed, 'that's my cardio done for today. I'd better get to work.'

Dinner that evening was wonderful. The lawn where we set up to eat was in the shade by then and everyone enjoyed the bowlfuls of bright dressed salad, buttered new potatoes, fresh crab and white wine until the sun had completely set.

Even though I spent most of the time on my feet, making sure everyone had everything they wanted, especially full glasses, for once it didn't feel like work.

'You need to be careful,' Flora whispered, after I'd poured the last of the wine into Dad's glass.

'About what?'

'You almost look like you've enjoyed yourself tonight,' she said impishly.

Having known me for so long, she would be able to tell.

'I have enjoyed myself,' I briskly confirmed. 'It's been a wonderful evening. It has reminded me of the lazy summer nights I enjoyed when I was a student in Spain and how I can't wait to reinstate them when I get back there again.'

'Oh,' she said, sounding disappointed. 'I thought, perhaps . . .'

'I know what you thought,' I said, dropping a kiss on her cheek, 'but the magic you reckon the cottage has is never going to rub off on me, Flo. Yes, evenings like tonight are lovely, but there's too much baggage attached to the place and not enough potential, especially now everything's established and organised.'

'Oh well.' She shrugged. 'You can't blame a gal for having one last try.'

Once we'd said goodnight to the last of the guests who had been keener than usual to linger, I pinned Dad down to have the conversation I'd been running over in my head.

'Dad,' I excitedly said, 'have you got a minute? You won't believe what's happened.'

'Oh?' he said, frowning, sounding tired as he gathered up the last of the glasses. 'Is everything okay?'

Had he noticed my upbeat tone, he would have known it was.

'Yes,' I laughed, 'more than okay. I've been wanting to tell you all evening, but I haven't had the chance.'

'Come on then,' he encouraged, once we'd carried the last few things inside. 'What is it?'

'The guest in the garden apartment.' I smiled.

'Logan?' Dad said, sounding more interested. 'What about him?'

'You never told me that was his name,' I tutted. 'If you had, I might have realised sooner.'

'Realised what?'

'That I know him,' I said, as I bagged up the napkins for the laundry service.

'You never do?' Dad gasped, his tiredness banished. 'From where?'

'Spain,' I told him. 'We met in the spring. We had seats next to each other on the flight over and I kept talking to him, because he was such a nervous passenger.'

'I can't believe it.'

'And then he took me out for dinner, to say thank you.'

'Whyever didn't you say anything the day he arrived?' Dad asked, his face an absolute picture.

I could tell from his reaction that Logan was someone he

already thought highly of. Someone who would end up as a family friend, rather than a fleeting visitor.

'I didn't see him that day because I was in town buying eggs,' I said honestly. 'But when I did eventually run into him,' I added, keeping the timing vague, 'I realised who he was straightaway.'

'Well, of course you did,' Dad chuckled. 'I would have loved to have seen the look on both your faces.'

I wouldn't.

'I bet we looked surprised.' I smiled.

'I bet you did, too,' Dad said, shaking his head. 'He's a lovely fella, Ally. And in Spain, he took you out to dinner, you say?'

'Oh, Dad,' I tutted, 'I know that tone. Don't go getting any ideas. We're happy to pick our friendship back up, but there's nothing more to it than that.'

'Yet,' he said hopefully.

'Don't forget what Logan's here for,' I primly pointed out. 'This is a difficult time for him.'

'In that case, perhaps a little summer romance is just the thing he needs.'

'Dad!' I further admonished.

'Sorry, love,' he said, sounding not quite as repentant as I would have liked. 'He's just such a lovely guy.'

'And a guy I'll be seeing more of, as I've said I'll take a few of the trips with him that his uncle has requested in his will.' Dad looked delighted. 'But if you keep looking like that, I'll change my mind, because you playing matchmaker is the last thing Logan needs.'

'I suppose you're right.'

'I am.'

'I still can't believe it though,' Dad wistfully said. 'Of all the people in all the world.'

'I know,' I said, thinking of the day Logan found me with Flora on the beach. 'I said something similar myself when I bumped into him.'

'It's fate,' said Dad, moving to close the French doors before every moth in the county made its way in. 'Fate, Ally. That's what it is.'

'Perhaps it is,' I said briskly, 'and if it is, don't you go getting any ideas about interfering with it.'

# Chapter 14

The rain returned Saturday night and lingered long into the following morning, which meant that the watercolour guests had to spread themselves around the house, rather than out in the garden. Ordinarily, having course members doing their thing in the cottage didn't impact on me all that much. Seated around the huge table or on the sofa and chairs in the room assigned the official learning space, kept everyone fairly contained, but that wasn't possible when they all needed space to paint and a different perspective.

There were easels set up in the conservatory and next to all the windows. There were even a couple on the landing and Mrs Gilding, having now seen the funny side of Kasuku's bawdy bawling, had requested he should be returned to the kitchen so she could 'capture his essence'. Eyeing her beadily from the confines of his cage, I wondered what he was intending to capture, but left the pair to it.

'I'm just popping out,' I said to Dad, who was prepping an unseasonal roast dinner, inspired by the downturn in the weather. 'Unless you need me to help?'

Peeling spuds for the masses wasn't my favourite way to

spend a Sunday morning, but obviously I'd pitch in if needs be, especially knowing what the results of my efforts would soon taste like. Dad had a knack with roast potatoes.

'I can manage, but are you sure about going out in this?' he asked, looking skywards as the rain drummed on the conservatory roof.

'Yes,' I said, looking around to make sure we couldn't be overheard. 'I need some air. It's a bit claustrophobic in here today.'

'I like it.' Dad shrugged. 'When it's like this, I can imagine your mum smiling down on our endeavours. I'm certain this is how she imagined Hollyhock Cottage would end up.'

He sounded very sure of her approval and I was pleased about that.

'In that case,' I said, pinching a handful of freshly podded peas, 'I'll leave you and Mum to enjoy it.'

It was a state of affairs he would have to acclimatise to when I'd gone and it was just him and Mum's memory in the kitchen on a Sunday morning.

'Where are you going?' he asked, looking out at the rain again.

'Just down to the garden,' I told him, popping the peas into my mouth. 'I thought I'd take a book and sit in the polytunnel. I'm sure there won't be anyone painting in there.'

'I daresay you're right,' Dad happily said. 'Though you will have some company.'

'Who?' I huffed.

I didn't want company, I wanted to be on my own for a while.

'Logan.' Dad continued to smile.

Oh well, that was different.

'What's he doing in the polytunnel?' I asked.

'Hopefully shifting the workbench for me,' Dad told me.

'Why is he doing that? He's supposed to be a guest. You can't set him to work, Dad.'

'It was his idea,' he told me with a shrug. 'I happened to mention the bench was in the wrong place and Logan said I'd most likely do myself a mischief if I tried to shift it, then he offered to move it on my behalf.'

I felt myself bristle at that, knowing Dad would have gone nuts if I'd suggested he wouldn't have been able to do it.

'And you let him?' I frowned.

'I thought it would save my back—'

'Since when has there been anything wrong with your back?'

'There isn't,' Dad cleverly said, 'but there might have been if I'd shifted that bench on my own.'

'Flora and I would have helped you with it,' I said sulkily. 'And Freddie's always dropping in, so we could have asked him, too.'

'We might still have to,' said Dad, 'because it's not the lightest bit of kit. Why don't you go and see how Logan's faring. You could take a flask and a couple of those chocolate brownies . . .'

'Dad,' I warned.

'A picnic for two, sheltering from the rain . . .' he pensively carried on.

'Dad,' I said more loudly, making Kasuku squawk.

'All right, all right.' Dad relented. 'Don't set him off again.'

As well as the paperback I now didn't think I'd get any further with, I sorted and bagged the supplies Dad had suggested and, having pulled on one of his battered wax work coats and my ancient wellies, I made a dash from the house into the garden. I hadn't got far when I heard someone walking through the courtyard.

'Hello!' I called, wondering who it could be.

I was pretty certain that everyone who was supposed to be on site – aside from Logan – was in the house, so I left the path and ducked through the gap in the wall that separated the courtyard from the garden.

'There you are,' said Tara, stepping suddenly into view.

'Oh, Tara!' I gasped. 'You made me jump.'

'I've been looking all over for you,' she said, pulling me under the protection of the vast umbrella she was carrying.

It was an action she must have regretted as I was already soaked and in such close proximity, she soon would be, too.

'Have you?' I frowned, moving a little to avoid dripping all over her.

She looked so pristine, despite being out in the deluge, and it would have been a crime to dampen her. Even her Dubarry boots didn't sport so much as a splash.

'Why didn't you come to the house?' I asked, stating the most obvious place to look.

'I did,' she insisted. 'I knocked and no one answered and then I panicked that Flora might come to the door, so I thought I'd just hang about on the off chance of spotting you.'

'It could have been Flora who spotted you, rather than me,' I logically pointed out.

'Well,' she shrugged, 'she didn't, so it's fine. This place looks fabulous by the way,' she added, looking around. 'Even better than on the website. You've done great things.'

'Thanks,' I said. 'It's all Dad out here, really. So, why were you looking for me?'

'To find out how you're getting on convincing Flora to talk to me, of course. It's been ages since I heard from you.'

'And you couldn't have rung?'

'You never sound very happy when I call,' she pouted, looking more like her old self. 'And now I'm back in the area, I thought it would be easier to talk in person. I want to get the ball rolling. I'm here for a while now, so there's no reason why we can't get together.'

Other than the fact that I still hadn't got around to telling Flora that she wanted to meet.

'I haven't talked to Flora yet,' I reluctantly and a little defensively admitted. 'I've been too busy. This place doesn't run itself, you know.'

'I can appreciate that,' Tara said, sounding surprisingly sympathetic. 'At least you won't have to worry about housekeeping on a commercial scale when you move. How about we go and find Flora together now?'

'Because she's still in bed,' I told her. 'Surely, you remember how much she loves to snooze whenever she gets the chance.'

'Oh yes.' Tara laughed. 'So, it wasn't likely she'd have answered the cottage door, was it? Do you remember when we went on that camping trip with the school?'

'God, yes.' I laughed, too. 'We were so worried about waking her too early that we dismantled the tent and packed everything up with her still crashed out in her sleeping bag.'

'I'm sure I have a photo of that somewhere.'

'Well, when you do finally see her,' I hastily suggested, 'I wouldn't mention that.'

'No, I won't,' Tara acquiesced. 'Anyway, I'd better go. I'm working from a base near here for the rest of the summer and

I'll be in the pub Friday night. I know you need to be here over the weekend, so that might be a better time to . . .'

'All right,' I said reluctantly. 'I'll do my best.'

'Excellent.' Tara smiled, patting the arm of my sodden coat. 'I'll see you then. Both of you, hopefully.'

She walked off without a backward glance and as the rain started to fall even harder, I jogged down the garden, slipping a little in my haste.

'You've got to be kidding me,' were the angry words that met my ears when I ducked inside the polytunnel.

'About what?' I asked, quickly shrugging off the coat that, given how warm it was, would soon start to steam.

Logan popped up from where he had been crouched behind Dad's trusty old bench. Dad had sown and potted up hundreds of plants on the battered thing and there were shelves and cubby holes underneath it for labels, pots, packets and the like.

'Hey.' Logan smiled.

'Who are you talking to?' I asked, as I rooted about in the bag for the flask and brownies Dad had suggested I should bring.

'Myself,' he admitted, looking sheepish. 'It's a thing I do when I'm a bit wound up.'

If that was the case, I dreaded to think what the walls of his hotel room back in Barcelona had been privy to after I'd left.

'Now, why would you be wound up . . .' I said, thoughtfully tapping my head. 'I bet you the biggest brownie in this bag, that it's something to do with the weighty task you've got roped into doing for Dad, isn't it?'

'Actually,' said Logan, making a grab for the bag, which I quickly moved out of his reach, 'I got roped into doing this for you, rather than your dad.'

'Me?' I frowned. 'It doesn't make any difference to me where the bench is.'

'I know that,' said Logan, brushing his hands down his trousers. 'But when Geoff mentioned he wanted the bench moving, I suggested he wouldn't be able to manage to do it on his own.'

'Which benefits me how, exactly?'

'Well,' he said, 'I thought it might eventually make him question whether he can manage here on his own, once you've gone.'

'But he won't be on his own, will he?' I replied. 'As well as Flora living here, I'm employing a manager, remember? I don't want Dad thinking he can't cope.'

And I didn't want to further worry about that, either.

'Do you think he won't cope?' I swallowed, unable to resist asking the question.

'Actually, I'm sure he'll be fine, with all that help,' said Logan, scratching his head. 'But I've cocked up, haven't I?'

'Yes,' I said, feeling annoyed that he'd put doubt in my head again, 'you have.'

'I'm sorry,' he said, puffing out his cheeks and looking at the bench.

He sounded so contrite, I softened a little.

'But it's okay,' I sniffed, 'because your plan has backfired. Dad knows exactly how difficult that thing is to shift, so really, the joke's on you.'

'Um,' he breathed, 'so, it is.'

'I know you meant well,' I said firmly, 'but please don't interfere again.'

'I won't,' he said, holding up his hands. 'I'm sorry, Ally.'

After a fortifying mug of Dad's strongest coffee and the

accompanying sugar hit from the brownies, Logan and I gathered our strength and managed to walk, crab-style, rather than lift, the bench into Dad's preferred position.

'Did he say why he wanted it moved?' I asked, once I'd caught my breath and we'd finished checking it was straight.

'No.' Logan shrugged as he began putting the trays, pots, catalogues and tools back in their allotted places.

I knew that some of the tools were older than Dad.

'What's that?' Logan asked, jumping back as the sound of the house gong rang out.

'Our signal that lunch is ready,' I told him. 'It's the gong Dad sounds to summon everyone to the kitchen.'

'You're kidding.'

'I'm not. Mum found it in a junk shop in Shellcombe and she used it originally. She reckoned it was just the thing for calling Dad back to the cottage when he was down here and had lost track of time.'

'Oh, I love it,' Logan grinned, 'and it clearly works. You'd have to be worlds away not to hear that.'

'Will you join us for lunch?' I asked. 'Dad always cooks enough to feed an army.'

'Thanks for asking,' Logan said, 'but I need to carry on looking through the papers I was working on yesterday. I've really enjoyed taking a break this morning though—'

'You're calling what we've just done a break?'

'Well,' he said, 'it was good to do something different. It took my mind off things, but I'm sorry I overstepped though. I'll keep out of your business from now on.'

'It's fine,' I said, 'but I appreciate that.'

I was pleased Logan had reaffirmed he was staying out of

things, but him suggesting Dad might not be able to cope had made me wonder whether he could again, too. I knew deep down that Dad had the sense to not take on more than he should and that Flora, who loved him like her own father, would try to make sure he didn't. However, it was my own mind I needed to be certain of and I would have to find a way to reassure myself that everything, in every department, was completely in order before I finally headed off.

'Ally?' Logan frowned.

'Sorry,' I blinked. 'What did you say?'

'That I'll come and find you tomorrow and we'll arrange a trip out this week, if that's still okay?'

'Oh yes,' I said, 'definitely okay. I'm looking forward to it.'

'You're still willing to be my occasional tour guide?' he asked.

'More than willing,' I told him. 'If it turns out to be the last time I see the sites, I could consider the trips an opportunity to say farewell to the area.'

'Surely it's likely that it will be the last time, isn't it?' Logan frowned. 'Or are you having second thoughts?'

'No,' I said, throwing him a smile. 'No second thoughts.'

In that moment, I wasn't sure either of us were convinced of that and I didn't have the heart to tell him that it was his fault.

# Chapter 15

The following week, the weather remembered what it was supposed to do in summer and the sun began to shine more consistently. Having raced through the familiar list of everything I needed to get done ahead of the next weekend's course and got my head straight again about leaving after Logan had planted a seed of doubt about Dad's ability to cope in my absence, I was then free to arrange the rest of my time as I wished.

Logan had been trying to tempt me back into the sea for an early morning swim, but I had only been willing to join him after Dad had dug out the wetsuit gloves and socks Mum used to wear when she and her friends partook of an early morning dip. They had been champions of wild swimming long before it became trendy.

'What on earth have you got there?' Logan asked, as he watched me pull on the gloves and boots the morning I joined him on the beach and began to add rather than shed layers.

'If you want me to swim with you,' I told him with a wry smile, 'then you have to get used to the extra apparel.'

'Fair enough.' He grinned, pulling his T-shirt over his head, which made me warm up to such a degree that I wasn't entirely convinced I was going to need to keep my extremities covered after all. 'You do you.'

'Oh, I will.' I swallowed, turning to look at Flora, who gave me an enthusiastic thumbs up, which was no help at all, given the reason I'd goaded her into getting up early, too.

I had made her promise she'd join us on the beach, because as my oldest friend and confidante, she knew I still had more than friendly feelings for Logan, even though I had initially tried to deny them. I was hoping that her presence would have a sobering impact on my libido and that talking to her while Logan stripped off, and I found myself in danger of staring too long and too intently at him, would help cool my jets. But apparently not.

'I'll play gooseberry then,' she had reluctantly agreed, when I asked her to set her alarm earlier than usual.

I had then tried to point out that she would only be playing gooseberry if Logan and I were in a romantic relationship and wanted to be alone together, but she just gave me a wry smile and I gave up. She had agreed to come and that had been my goal.

'You coming for a swim today, Flora?' Logan called over to her.

'Nah,' she said, 'I'm just the towel watcher. I'm more of a paddler than a swimmer.'

'Too cold for you, is it?' Logan laughed.

'Something like that,' she nodded.

The truth was, Flora couldn't swim. She'd tried to get to grips with improving her stroke multiple times, but the scathing words and impatience of our evil swimming teacher at school had ensured that Flora's confidence had been battered for life.

I felt certain that a kind word and some subtle nurturing and encouragement would have made all the difference, but the damage was done and I wondered how many other people had been put off as a result of the barbed words they'd been subjected to during their education. Flora hadn't been the only one who had been unkindly singled out. The title of *teacher* should never have been bestowed upon that whistle-toting menace.

'Come on then, Ally,' said Logan, with a mischievous grin. 'You look set to race across the channel today, so I'm sure you don't need a head start.'

'It's not supposed to be a race,' I reminded him, but he was already off.

I looked back at Flora.

'I can see why you went there,' she grinned. 'Shame you're stuck in the friend zone now, isn't it? You could have had a right rollicking last summer in Kittiwake Cove.'

'I'm not sure rollicking is the right word,' I said, scratching my head because my hair was tied up so tight it was making my scalp itch. 'But being his friend is better than nothing.'

'Is it though?' she called after me as I ran down to the shore and strode purposefully into the crystal blue sea.

I started to swim straight after the initial immersion and enjoyed the experience a whole lot more than I had when I'd dithered and dallied in my undies. That said, Logan was still so far ahead of me that he had been on and off the pontoon again ages before I'd reached it.

By the time I finally rejoined him on the sand, my lungs were heaving, my heart was pounding and Flora had wandered off to explore the rockpools. Some chaperone she was turning out to be.

'I've got our first trip lined up,' Logan told me as he rubbed his hair with a towel, making it stand up on end. 'Well,' he added, smoothing it down again with his hands, 'I almost have. I need to book in advance as it's a tour rather than a wander around kind of thing and I wanted to check that you fancy doing something as formal as that?'

'Of course,' I breathlessly nodded, as I pulled off Mum's gloves and appreciated how much warmer my fingers felt than they had the last time. 'Where is it?'

'Max Gate,' Logan said, the name making my heart thump even harder. 'Thomas Hardy lived there.'

'Of course,' I swallowed, my shallow breath catching. 'I know it. I've been before.'

I actually knew the place almost as well as Hollyhock Cottage because at one time I had been a very regular visitor. I had worked as a volunteer in another property in Dorchester during some holidays and had cycled further on to Max Gate as often as I could. It was a stunning home and I was fascinated by how it genuinely still felt like Hardy himself was in the next room as I wandered through it. However, my love for the house wasn't the only reason the mention of it made my heart race.

'I did wonder if you were familiar with it as you're practically a local,' said Logan, sounding disappointed. 'Are you sure you want to visit it again?'

'Absolutely,' I insisted, even though my gut reaction was to give it a miss. 'I don't mind going back. It's been a while since I was last there and like I said before, now I've decided I'm leaving the cove, you're providing me with the chance to say farewell to the few places I do like.'

Saying goodbye to Max Gate would be emotional, though.

Mum had been a huge Hardy fan and the last trip I had made to the house had been with her. She had loved his poetry even more than his novels. It was ironic that out of all the places in the area that Logan or his uncle could have picked, the first one to come up was there. Even more ironic was that I was currently reading *Far from the Madding Crowd*, even though it wasn't my usual go to.

'Well, as long as you're sure,' said Logan and I nodded to confirm that I was. 'I thought we could tour the house and then have a fancy tea somewhere afterwards. My treat.'

'That sounds perfect,' I tried to enthuse.

That had been what Mum and I used to do, too. I wondered how I was going to react to repeating the experience without her. Not too emotionally I hoped. The last thing Logan needed was me crying all over him, especially as his uncle must have had a reason for listing a trip to the house in his will and, consequently, his nephew would doubtless end up feeling something, too. I supposed we could sob together . . .

'Why don't you book it for tomorrow or Thursday?' I quickly suggested, before the thought of us crying together put me off and I backed out.

'All right,' said Logan, sounding pleased. 'I'll go and do it now. Are you coming?'

'No,' I said, looking over to where Flora practically had her nose in the water of one of the rockpools. 'I'd better go and remind Flora that she needs to get to work.'

'Fair enough,' smiled Logan. 'I'll let you know what time and which day as soon as I've booked it.'

He headed off with his towel slung over his shoulder and a spring in his step. At least one of us didn't seem to be feeling apprehensive about our impending adventure. Unlike him, I was clearly feeling more trepidation than excitement and, therefore, I came to the conclusion that his uncle's reason for suggesting Max Gate must have been a happy one and that Logan wouldn't be shedding a tear after all.

'What have you found?' I called to Flora, keen to divert my thoughts. 'Anything good?'

She beckoned me over.

'A starfish,' she said, pointing to the side of the pool. 'A really diddy one.'

It was tiny.

'That's a Cushion Starfish, isn't it?' I asked, peering closer.

'Yeah,' she said, 'I think so. How was the water?'

'Bloody freezing,' I said, tucking my towel tighter around me, 'but the gloves and socks were a huge help.'

'Hardly seductive attire though.' She grinned.

'Well,' I responded, 'that's all right, isn't it? Because the seductive part of mine and Logan's relationship is well and truly over.'

'Of course, it is,' she said, moving along to look in the next pool. 'So, are you planning on swimming every morning now? Because I won't be able to come down here every day.'

'I doubt it,' I said, patting my hair to feel how wet it had got. 'My hair can't cope with a regular soaking in salt water. It's wild enough as it is and I think a swimming cap would be the limit, don't you?'

'I didn't think it mattered how you looked.' Flora teased. 'But if I were you, I'd go the whole hog and have one of those flowery efforts. The sight of you in one of those would properly stamp out the last of the embers.'

'I think I'll pass.' I nudged her further towards the pool and she yelped. 'Besides, I don't think there are any embers now.' Not on Logan's part anyway. 'Thanks for getting up early though, just in case.'

'It wasn't really any bother.' She shrugged, looking around the cove. 'Watching the sun come up down here is hardly a hardship, is it? I mean, would you look at this place?'

With clear blue sky above us and sparkling blue sea at our backs, I supposed she did have a point. Even the cliffs looked prettier than usual with wildflowers in bloom above us spilling out of the many cracks and crevices.

'You can't deny this is a stunning spot?' Flora said, this time nudging me.

'It's beautiful all right,' I agreed. 'Just not—'

'Your cup of tea.' She smiled sadly. 'I know. Anyway, what happened to Logan? Has he gone? He didn't hang about, did he?'

'That was down to me,' I told her.

'Was it the sight of your feet in those neoprene booties?'

'No,' I snapped, 'it was not. It was because I suggested he should go and book the tickets for our trip this week.'

'Oh right,' Flora smirked, clearly pleased to have got a rise out of me. 'So, where are you off to?'

'Max Gate,' I said, the name catching in my throat. 'We're going to Max Gate.'

Flora's manner changed in an instant. She didn't say anything, but I could feel her eyes on me. She knew the significance of what I'd just said, how special my trips there with Mum had been. She also knew how the place had further fuelled my love of historic buildings, especially those that felt like they still had a strong connection with the people who had previously lived there.

'It's fine,' I said, focusing again on the crystal-clear water in the pool. 'It will be fine. In fact, I'm looking forward to it. I told Logan not to worry about suggesting anywhere I've been before, because it will give me the perfect opportunity to say goodbye. Given his uncle's wishes, our trips away from the cottage are actually going to do us both good.'

'And you meant that, did you?'

'Yes.' I swallowed. 'Absolutely. Though I admit this first one might be a bit tougher than anywhere else. Still doable though. I'll focus on Hardy and the building, rather than my memories of being there with Mum.'

Flora rested her head on my shoulder. It was both familiar and reassuring and I tried not to think about how much I was going to miss her when I'd gone.

'Okay,' she said, after a few seconds had passed. 'Any idea what the time is? I've got a client this morning and I need to get the image of that beach Adonis out of my head if I'm going to give them my full and undivided attention.'

I slapped her arm with Mum's waterproof gloves and together we walked back to the cottage.

Logan booked us tickets for an afternoon tour, which meant I had a whole morning to kill ahead of it. He had offered to drive us to Dorchester and as the town was only about half an hour away, there was no need for us to rush. As a result, I ended up getting under Dad's feet and sworn at by Kasuku.

'I'm not sure you should have agreed to go,' said Dad, as I fruitlessly wiled away the time. 'Have you told Logan that you might . . .'

His words trailed off.

'That I might what?'

'Nothing,' he said, looking into the garden. 'Here's the fella now.'

'Please don't say anything,' I begged, as Logan headed for the path to the front door.

'Don't bother with the door!' Dad called out, shooting a look in my direction, as Logan retraced his steps and ducked inside. 'You can always come in this way when the doors are open. Everyone else does.'

'Thank you, Geoff,' Logan said. 'I'll remember that.'

'Don't you look smart,' Dad commented, taking in what Logan was wearing. 'Ally's made an effort today, too.'

'Dad,' I grimaced.

'What?' he said, winking at Logan, who smiled. 'I can't remember the last time I saw you in a dress.'

'You look lovely,' said Logan. 'You wore that in Spain, didn't you?'

'Crikey,' Dad chuckled, capitalising on the moment, 'you must have made an impression, love, and you must have a good memory, Logan, because that trip to Barcelona was months ago now.'

I felt my cheeks flame as I remembered the crumpled heap of the dress on Logan's hotel room floor. It was one of my smartest and I never would have put it on had I remembered. That was proof of how jumbled my head was that morning.

'Shall we get off then?' I asked, as I noticed Logan was every bit as red in the face as I was. 'It only takes one stuck caravan on these roads and the whole place grinds to a halt.'

'I didn't think of that,' said Logan, checking a watch I hadn't seen him wear before. 'In that case, we had better go.'

'Oh wow,' said Flora, when we collided with her at the door. She looked me up and down and grinned. 'That colour really works on you, Ally.'

'The green tones bring out her eyes, don't they?' said Logan and he blushed again.

I heard Dad clear his throat behind us and Flora pinned me with a loaded look.

'Very observant,' she said to Logan, making as much of the situation as Dad just had. 'You're right. They do. You call this your lucky dress now, Ally, don't you?'

She was too far out of reach for me to pinch or stamp on so I gave her a tight-lipped scowl instead.

'Have you made up your mind about the pub tomorrow?' I asked her, changing the subject.

'Yeah,' she said. 'I'll come.'

I felt a rush of mixed emotions. Relief that she'd finally said yes, coupled with anxiety over the prospect of telling her who else was going to be there. Flora wouldn't react well to being set up, so I needed to tell her that Tara would be propping up the bar, too. And with the intention of wanting to talk to her.

'What about you, Logan?' Flora asked. 'Do you fancy a trip to the pub? Have you ventured inside our local yet?'

'I haven't,' he said and I wondered if his presence might help smooth the potentially turbulent waters. Would Flora feel less inclined to kick off if Logan was there? 'So, I'd like that, thanks.'

'You don't mind if Logan joins us, do you?' Flora asked me.

'Of course not.' I smiled. 'The more the merrier.'

Though I hoped Tara and Logan wouldn't get on *too* well.

'Right,' he said. 'We'd better get going.'

'See you later then,' said Flora, dropping the puckish behaviour and giving me a kind look, which spoke volumes.

The journey was uneventful, with no wedged caravans, and as I was a passenger for once, I was able to take in the beautiful view beyond the windows of Logan's lovely car. I didn't know much about cars, but I could tell his was top spec. By contrast, mine and Dad's was a rapidly ageing banger. I mentally added buying a newer vehicle to the list of things I needed to achieve before I left the cove.

Logan took us on the scenic route to Dorchester and I paid even more attention every time he slowed down to drive through the picturesque villages that punctuated our way.

'Just around this corner,' I said, opening the window and letting a wave of very warm air into the cool interior, 'is my favourite cottage in this entire village.'

Having checked there was nothing behind him, Logan slowed down even more and I was able to take in the thatched roof, deep set tiny windows, rickety gate and cottage garden.

'They all look pretty to me,' he said, his gaze tracking to either side of the road. 'They're chocolate box perfect, aren't they?'

'You're right,' I agreed, 'but that pink one was always the one I looked out for when we drove this route when I was younger. And Mum loved that mustard coloured one,' I said, pointing out a larger, but still cosy, abode on the opposite side. 'But obviously not as much as she loved Hollyhock Cottage,' I added, with a fond smile, while wondering if the childhood game of favourite house spotting had been the first thing to ignite my passion for old places.

'From what your dad told me the other day, it sounds as though your mum felt melded to the place,' Logan said softly, as I closed the window and sat back again. 'His description made me think of Mrs Wilcox in Howards End. Do you know who I mean?'

'Yes,' I said. As well as Hardy, Mum had loved the novels of Forster and I had read them too, so I knew how beautifully he had written of Ruth Wilcox's spiritual connection to her inherited home. 'And you're right. Mum loved the very foundations of the cottage and she knew its history far better than anyone else thanks to her years working for Beatrice.'

'She was the woman who left your parents the house?'

'That's right,' I confirmed, my gaze falling again on the view. The verges were full of wildflowers, cheerful bright, white daisies being the most prolific. 'I used to spend my school holidays trying to hide from Beatrice during the years I was considered too young to be left to fend for myself back in Shellcombe.'

'You really didn't like going to the cottage?'

I'd mentioned it before, but not elaborated.

'Not at all,' I said, wrinkling my nose. 'Mum and Dad were always busy. I used to get bored helping Dad in the garden and Beatrice used to terrify me, hence the hiding. She was a formidable woman, though an extremely generous one as it turned out. I used to stay out of her way as much as I could but now, I sometimes wonder if I'd have bonded better with the cottage and the cove if I'd got to know her better. I know I would still have the terrifying memories of what happened to Mum, but I do sometimes wonder about that.'

I knew I hadn't become attached to the cottage when I was younger because I resented having to be there, missing out on playing with Flora and Freddie, who were mostly left to their own devices, but even now, the place still sometimes felt more Beatrice's, than ours.

That was most likely down to Kasuku's lingering and loud presence, but I wondered if Beatrice herself still loitered there, too. Dad had suggested he could feel Mum's presence, so it wasn't unrealistic to think that the woman who had lived the whole of her life there was hanging about, too. I shuddered at the thought, as I imagined her drifting about the rooms and scrutinising how we had decorated and dressed them.

'Um,' Logan thoughtfully said. 'Hindsight is a mixed blessing, isn't it?'

'God, yes,' I sighed.

'So,' he said, turning the air-con up a notch, 'one way or another, you've actually had a connection to Hollyhock Cottage your whole life.'

'Yes,' I said, 'I suppose I have.'

I hadn't really considered that before, but he was right. I had as much history with the place as Mum and Dad did.

'I didn't know that,' he muttered, tapping the steering wheel.

'There's no reason why you should.' I shrugged, wondering why he was frowning so much.

'I guess not,' he said, catching my eye and turning the frown into a smile. 'So, what else can you tell me about the redoubtable Beatrice Baxter?'

It took the rest of the journey for me to fill him in and explain who else had benefited from her philanthropic bequests. Logan was amazed to hear how far-reaching her generosity had been.

'It sounds to me,' he said, pulling into a parking space, 'that even since she died, Beatrice has supported practically every local business in Kittiwake Cove.'

'She has,' I confirmed. 'And her legacy has formed a bond between the people who live and work there permanently, too.'

'You should write all that down somewhere,' he seriously suggested. 'So much of this sort of thing gets forgotten as people get older and other's leave.'

'I'm leaving myself,' I reminded him. 'I haven't got time to start writing about Beatrice Baxter.'

'Even so,' he said thoughtfully.

He took a moment to process everything I'd told him and I wondered if he was always keen to learn so much about the places he visited. His quizzing had almost tipped into interrogation, but I supposed it was nice that he was so interested. I had furnished him with all the answers I could and gone into detail in the hope that it would stop him thinking about his uncle. I had been surprised by how much I could remember.

'Come on then,' I said, prompting him when he didn't move. 'It's almost time for our tour.'

Not only had my rambling kept him engaged, but it had also stopped my nerves about visiting Max Gate taking too tight a hold. However, as we set off towards the property, a lump began to form in my throat and I carried it the entire way around the house. We had almost reached the end, when it got the better of me.

Logan seemed fine and didn't notice the rush of tears. Consequently, I was able to look, unobserved, at the writing desk and book of poetry where the tour ended and allow the treasured memory of Mum doing the same thing to wash over me. Her favourite poem was *An August Midnight* and she had been ecstatic to find the little tome open on that very page, just as it was for me then.

The words of the two short verses swam on the page as my tears continued to flow, but it didn't matter because I knew them by heart.

'*An August Midnight*,' said Logan, coming to stand next to me.

He then proceeded to read the verses aloud, which made me sniff as I wiped my eyes on the bundle of tissues I'd had the foresight to carry with me.

'How lovely,' he said, smiling at the guide who was watching us.

'I think so,' they smiled back, before nodding at me. 'And I can see your partner thinks so, too.'

'Oh Ally,' Logan gasped, when he realised the state I was in. 'Whatever is it?'

'I'm all right.' I swallowed. 'I'm fine. It's just that this was Mum's favourite poem and the desk was set up exactly like this the last time I visited with her.'

'Oh, my goodness,' he said. 'Come on.' He took my hand and led me back through the house and into the garden. 'Are you all right?' he asked, after giving me another minute to compose myself.

'Yes,' I said. 'I'm fine. Honestly.'

He tenderly kissed the back of my hand and then gently let it go.

'I hadn't realised that you'd visited here with your mum,' he said. 'I never would have suggested you come with me if I had.'

'In that case,' I sniffed, giving him a watery smile, 'I'm pleased you didn't know because I wouldn't have missed this for anything. I knew I'd feel something as we walked around, but it wasn't until I saw that poem . . .'

I had to stop talking because my bottom lip had started to wobble again.

'Sorry,' I apologised, as a few more tears made a bid for freedom and I hastily swiped them away.

'I'm the one who should be apologising,' Logan insistently said. 'I should have realised—'

'No, you shouldn't,' I cut in. 'It was obviously important to your uncle that you should come here and I'm delighted that I could accompany you. I mean it.'

Given that he was grieving over a far more recent loss than mine, I should have been the one comforting him. There must have been a reason why his uncle had wanted him to come to Max Gate, but I didn't ask if he had worked out what it was. Had Logan wanted me to know, he would have already told me.

'Come on,' I said, as my tears started to dry. 'Let's have a look around the garden and the outside of the house and you wanted to pick up some leaflets, didn't you?' I was determined to take more of the place in and let it fill up my well of love for properties of the past, which was currently running rather low. '*And*,' I reminded him, 'you promised me afternoon tea, didn't you?'

'I did,' he said, reaching for my hand again in a gesture that felt entirely natural. 'And I promise, there'll be nothing triggering about that.'

I didn't contradict him, but I knew that would depend on which tearoom he had booked.

# Chapter 16

As much as I had enjoyed spending time with Logan and as delicious as the afternoon tea, in a tearoom I hadn't visited before, had been, I found myself in the highly unusual position of being more than keen to get back to the cottage by the end of the afternoon.

The trip had been truly lovely, but the emotions it had triggered left me feeling exhausted and I just wanted to hide out in my room until I recovered. However, the sensation of overwhelm increased tenfold before I got there because when Logan dropped me off, I found Dad peacefully dozing in a deckchair with Mum's battered copy of Hardy's poems in his lap.

I didn't sleep well that night and before I went to check the courtyard rooms and refill the vases, I scribbled down a few things about Beatrice, as Logan had suggested I should. I hadn't done it because he had told me to, but because the information had been floating about in my head all night and writing it down freed me from thinking about it.

As I filled the pages of a previously unused notebook, I wondered at the wisdom of my decision to keep going out with Logan and bid a fond farewell to the county. If the day before was any sort of indicator, I would be an emotional wreck by the end of the season. However, given that I'd let him down so badly before, I felt committed to seeing the endeavour through.

'Is that what you're wearing?' Flora frowned when we collided on the landing ahead of our trip to the pub that evening. 'Why so fancy?'

'It's not fancy,' I responded, looking down at the second dress in two days that I'd picked out of my wardrobe.

She was right though. It was a bit OTT for a regular Friday night in The Ship.

'Logan's going to assume this is for his benefit,' Flora said, rolling her eyes.

'Of course, he won't,' I tutted, stuffing the lip gloss I'd been about to reapply into the dress pocket. 'Besides, he's seen me looking a whole lot fancier than this.'

Compared to the sleek look I had initially adopted in Barcelona, my current outfit was definitely dress down Friday.

'That's as maybe,' Flora shrugged, setting off downstairs, 'but you should make him aware that the effort you've gone to is to impress Tara, not him.'

I stopped dead behind her and she spun around to look at me.

'What?' she demanded. 'It's obvious she's going to be there tonight.'

'How is it obvious?' I gasped. 'I haven't mentioned her name once.'

'Exactly,' Flora said wisely. 'Radio silence is your most unique tell and the look of relief on your face when I said I'd come tonight was a dead giveaway, too.'

'And you're still coming, knowing she'll be there?'

'Hell yeah. I want to get this reunion over with. And I'm coming to keep an eye on you, too,' she said.

'Me?' I frowned. 'What have I done that requires you keeping an eye on me?'

'Fallen under Tara's spell, that's what,' Flora said crossly. 'I've no idea why, but you're clearly in awe of her again.'

'I am not,' I hotly denied.

'Yes, you are,' she batted back, looking almost amused. 'Why else would you go to the bother of dressing up to go for a drink? She's cast a spell on you, just like she did to both of us when she first arrived, wearing all the right labels and saying all the cool things.'

'I'm not sixteen,' I huffed, but I knew I sounded it.

And Flora was right of course. Tara looked exactly like the woman I wanted to be and I had made an effort to try to impress her, just like I had in high school. I felt a bit pathetic and wanted to go and get changed, but Flora wasn't done with me yet.

'No,' Flora said, 'you're not a teenager and neither am I. You haven't forgotten how things ended between us and Tara when we were, have you?'

'Of course, I haven't—' I started, but she cut me off.

'Good,' she said, running down the last few steps and grabbing her bag. 'Let's go and find Logan then. You can warn him about Tara on the way. Give him the chance to erect an anti-bitch barrier. That's assuming he'll want to ward her off, once he's met her.'

The thought of him not wanting to ward her off made my stomach churn. I abandoned the decision to change outfits and went to say goodnight to Dad instead.

\*

The pub was busy by the time Flora, Logan and I arrived, but thankfully not so packed that you couldn't make yourself heard. I was relieved because the last thing the sensitive situation called for was raised voices.

There was no sign of Tara. Something else I was pleased about because it gave Flora the chance to have a drink and chill. Had she been bombarded the second we crossed the threshold; she most likely would have walked straight out again.

'I'll get these,' Logan offered, as we made our way to the bar.

He pulled out his wallet and dropped it and I picked it up for him.

'Are you all right?' I asked, as his eyes scanned the bar.

His gaze swung back to me.

'You've got me feeling jittery,' he laughed, taking the wallet from me. 'Now you've explained the reason for tonight's trip, I'm thinking it's going to be more pistols at dawn than a laid-back pint.'

'Sorry,' I apologised. 'I suppose I did ramp the drama up a bit.'

'Or maybe,' said Flora, 'you didn't ramp it up enough. I'm not beyond resorting to pistols if the situation requires it.'

'She's joking,' I said, giving her a shove, as Logan looked like he was getting ready to leave. 'Why don't you go and find us a table, Flora?'

She winked at Logan and sauntered off. To the casual observer, her swagger suggested she didn't have a care in the world, but I knew what was really going on beneath the surface.

'Right,' I said to Logan, hoping that a beer might take the edge off. 'Let's get some drinks.'

An hour later, there was still no sign of Tara and I was feeling less fond of her again. She'd been practically hounding me to set things up and now she'd stood us up. I checked my phone, but there was nothing. No message, text or missed call. She really was the limit.

'No word from the great one?' Flora sardonically asked. 'Maybe she's engrossed in breaking hearts somewhere else further along the coast. Or perhaps, not turning up was part of her plan to further piss me off, all along.'

Logan was standing next to the pool table, where Flora had just thrashed him for the third time. I felt bad that I hadn't paid him much attention, but I had been distracted waiting for the bad penny to turn up.

'Fancy another game?' Flora asked him, nodding at the table.

He checked his phone then put it away again.

'No, thanks,' he said, shoving his cue back in the old oak barrel next to the fireplace. 'I've had enough humiliation for one night.'

'You and me both,' I muttered.

'I'll go and get another round in,' he said. 'Same again?'

'Yes, please,' said Flora, setting the table up for another game.

'Yeah, I'll have a pint,' I said, standing up. 'But I'll get these.'

'I don't mind,' he said. He was already on his way to the door. 'I don't want Flora goading me into playing again.'

'That was you, actually playing, was it?' she teased and he shook his head.

'You'll be fine,' I said, steering him away from the door. 'This round is on me.'

'Here,' said Flora, handing the poor guy a different cue. 'See if this one brings you more luck.'

Logan winced as Flora broke with all the force of a piston.

The balls scattered across the baize, two rolling into pockets at the furthest end of the table. Logan groaned and I laughed and left them to it.

The laughter died on my lips however, as I pushed my way into the bar at the exact moment that Tara walked in. She looked livid, but her expression changed the second she spotted me.

'Oh my God,' she gasped, rushing over. 'I bet you thought I wasn't coming, didn't you?' She didn't give me a chance to answer. 'Of course you did and I daresay this has done nothing to raise me in Flora's estimation. I know I'm late, but I've had *such* a bad day.'

'Well,' I lied, 'I'm sure Flora will understand. Especially if you were stuck at work.'

'I was,' she said, pulling me in for a hug and enveloping me in her perfume. 'And you are sweet, Ally, but I know I've burned my bridges. Again.'

'You might have done,' I grimaced. 'Shall we go and find out? Flora's playing pool in the snug with a friend.'

'I bet she's thrashing them.' Tara tentatively smiled.

'Of course she is.' I smiled back.

'Come on then,' she said. 'Let's get a drink and go and watch. I'm sorry I haven't had a chance to get changed. I've literally come straight from a meeting. You by the way,' she added, looking me up and down, 'look gorgeous. I bet that fabric's vintage, isn't it?'

'It is,' I confirmed, as she spun me around. 'And you look fabulous, too.' I reciprocated. 'So sleek and smart.'

She put her hands on her slender waist.

'Hardly appropriate for a Friday night in the pub,' she smiled, her hair swinging forward as she looked down at her shoes. 'But what my job requires, and what yours will soon, too,' she added with a wink.

I quickly looked around, hoping no one I knew was in earshot.

'Yes, well,' I said quietly, 'we're not supposed to be talking about that, are we?'

'Sorry,' she whispered, tapping the side of her pretty nose. 'Inner circle only. Now come on, I'll get these.'

As usual, it took Tara no time to get served, but given the time we'd taken to chat, I'd been gone a while before we returned to the snug. I walked in ahead of Tara, who was carrying the tray of glasses, and with a smile plastered across my face.

'I was just about to send out a search party,' tutted Flora. 'You've been gone forever.'

'My fault I'm afraid,' said Tara, stepping out from behind me.

'Most things are,' Flora sighed, narrowing her eyes.

'Hello, Flora.' Tara smiled, ignoring the barbed comment. 'Long time, no see.'

Flora nodded but didn't return the greeting.

'I'm afraid I waylaid Ally, just as she was about to get served,' Tara carried on.

'It's packed out there now,' I joined in, wondering where Logan had disappeared to.

'And I'm really sorry I'm so late,' Tara apologised as she set down the tray. 'I got held up at work and then I couldn't get hold of a colleague I needed to talk to. Flora, I know that spending time with me is the last thing you want to do, but I'm so pleased you're here.'

Flora still didn't say anything, so I moved towards the table and gave her a look.

'Well,' she finally said, standing up, 'you only just caught me. I was about to head home.'

'You'll stay a bit longer now though, won't you?' I said and she shrugged.

'Look, I know you have no reason to believe me, Flora,' Tara said, rushing straight to the heart of the matter. 'But I honestly had no idea that you were still living with this hatred of me. And worse than that, that you still weren't talking to Joe.'

Flora's eyes flicked to me.

'And I had a go at Ally about that,' Tara added, dragging me into it. 'Because she never mentioned it. I found out from someone else and I was so upset—'

'You were upset . . .' Flora echoed.

'Yes.' Tara nodded, ignoring the even more sarcastic tone. 'I was. I know I was a total bitch in school, but when my parents and I left Shellcombe in a rush that summer, I had so much more on my mind than thinking about the stupid prank I'd pulled on you at prom.'

'Well, it's nice to know it meant so much to you.' Flora scowled.

I resisted the urge to ask why they had left in such a rush.

'Fuck,' said Tara, dropping into a chair. 'Why am I making such a mess of this when I've been rehearsing what I'm going to say for days?'

'No idea,' said Flora, folding her arms.

Tara gulped down half of her wine and I picked my glass up.

'I thought you were on pints.' Flora frowned at me.

'I was earlier,' I said.

'Oh shit,' said Tara, looking at the empty glasses. 'Were you? Sorry. I ordered this and as Ally and I had enjoyed the wine the other week, I just got the same again.'

Tara was digging herself into the deepest hole and Flora looked ready to fill it right back over the top of her.

'Come on,' I said, pulling Flora's sleeve. 'Let's sit down.'

'Okay,' Tara bracingly said, once we were settled. 'I'm going to start again and this time, stick to what I've been planning to say.'

'Where's Logan?' I asked, when she didn't then say anything.

'He had to make a call,' Flora told me. 'He's been gone ages. Go on then,' she nodded at Tara. 'Let's hear it.'

'Okay,' Tara said, taking a deep breath and fiddling with the stem of her glass. 'Okay,' she repeated as she pushed her wine away. 'Firstly, the situation with Joe at prom, Flora, that was all me. I could see he'd had more than plenty to drink that night. You know his mates had smuggled in bottles of spirits?'

'I remember that.' I nodded.

Freddie had had a mammoth hangover which bore that part of her story out.

'I took Joe up to your room on the promise that you were already waiting for him,' Tara continued, sounding mortified. 'He said he was feeling tired and sat down and I jumped on his lap when I heard you in the corridor. He was pretty gone by that point and had no idea what was happening until you burst in and started shouting at him. And me, obviously.'

Flora didn't say anything.

'That is what Joe has always said,' I pointed out.

'I know that,' Flora snapped, then turned on Tara. 'So, why did you do it?'

Tara looked sorrier than I'd ever seen anyone look.

'Because I was a bitch,' she said. 'And I was so jealous of what you and Joe had going on, I decided to ruin it. And as I'm truth-telling, I should tell you I never had any intention of wearing the dress we'd picked out together or walking to prom. Dad did get me the gown and ride, but only because I'd asked him to.'

'We'd already guessed that,' I told her. 'We might have been gullible, but we weren't completely stupid.'

Hearing her clarify what she'd done made some of her polish and shine dim in my eyes, but at least Flora had heard the truth from the horse's mouth. I just hoped she believed it.

'Of course, you weren't stupid,' she sighed. 'But I was self-ish and spiteful, though I'm not anymore. Had I known the repercussions of that night were still echoing around the cove, I would have come back years ago. I can't believe you and Joe still aren't talking, Flora.'

'Yeah, well.' Flora shrugged, sounding less pissed off than I had expected her to.

'I really am so sorry,' Tara sniffed, her eyes filling with tears. 'You could have been married with half a dozen kids by now.'

'I don't think so,' Flora gasped, looking horrified. 'I'm not my mother.'

'But you know what I mean,' said Tara, dabbing her eyes with a serviette. 'Your life could have been completely different if it hadn't been for my stupidity.'

'My life's pretty great, in spite of your meddling,' Flora said forthrightly. 'And your life turns out how it's supposed to, you know. There's only so much you have a hand in.'

That was as close to an acceptance of what she had said as Tara was likely to get. I could see that Flora believed her version of events and hoped she would be able to find it in her heart to tell Joe that.

'Sorry,' Tara tutted as her phone sprang to life, filling the snug with a catchy dance classic. 'I'll put it on silent,' she added, quickly.

'What if it's the person you were trying to get hold of earlier?' I reminded her.

'They can wait,' she smiled. 'No more work for me until Monday now.'

'You still haven't told me what your work is,' I said.

'No work chat tonight either,' she responded, raising her glass. 'Tonight, I just want to hang out with friends. Can we be friends again now I've cleared the air, Flora?'

'You know as well as I do, that we've never been friends,' Flora bluntly said. 'Not real ones. However,' she relented, 'you do seem to be a better version of yourself these days, so maybe we can move on.'

I could hardly believe my ears. I had expected her to put up more resistance than that.

'I am,' Tara vehemently said, as she shrugged off her Joseph jacket. 'So much better. Good things only is my mantra and I've done a good thing tonight, haven't I?'

Flora looked at me and I smiled.

'I suppose you have,' she said. 'And you can do another good thing now by getting more drinks in.'

Tara grabbed her bag and jumped up.

'Come with me then,' she said to Flora. 'Beer or wine for you, Ally?'

'Um,' I dithered, feeling like I was picking more than a drink. 'You know what, with it being a work day tomorrow, I think I'll have a Coke.'

'Don't worry,' Tara said, patting me on the shoulder, 'the end is in sight.'

'The end of what?' Flora frowned.

'Ally having to spend her time keeping other people happy, of course,' Tara declared as my face flushed red. 'When she leaves Kittiwake Cove, she'll be able to do what she likes at the weekend, won't she?'

Flora's eyes bored into mine.

'Shit,' said Tara, looking between us, 'please tell me you knew, Flora.'

'Of course, I knew,' she tightly responded. 'I just didn't realise the rest of the world did. Wasn't this supposed to be a secret?' she demanded of me.

'I shouldn't have said anything,' said Tara, sounding tearful again.

'Oh, don't worry,' said Flora. 'It's not your fault, Tara. Ally's the one who can't seem to keep her stories straight these days.'

The pair went off and I found myself wondering if I was going to be shoved out of our newly formed fragile friendship.

'All right?' asked Logan, appearing as if by magic and slipping into the seat next to mine.

'You've been gone ages,' I said accusingly.

'Sorry,' he apologised. 'Has your other friend turned up yet?'

'Yes,' I said, 'and everything seems okay, but time will tell. She's just gone with Flora to get another round in.'

'Are you really all right?' Logan frowned. 'You don't sound it.'

'I'm okay,' I said, suddenly feeling the full weight of the last few days land squarely on my shoulders. 'Just tired, you know.'

'The trip to Max Gate was a lot, wasn't it?' Logan said sympathetically.

'It really was,' I agreed. 'But I loved going back.'

'And saying goodbye,' he said wistfully. 'I suppose, this is just the start of it all for you, isn't it?'

'All off what?'

'The influx of emotions you're going to experience as you get ready to leave the cottage and the cove. And your dad.'

'I daresay you're right,' I said, 'but I'll get through it.'

I was about to tell him that seeing more of Tara would help because she was the epitome of the woman I wanted to be, but she and Flora walked in right at that moment.

Given that Logan then couldn't take his eyes off Tara, I concluded that she was the sort of woman he liked the look of, too. He might have seemed happy enough with the Ally he'd found in Kittiwake Cove, but if the way he stared at Tara was anything to go by, I think he might really have preferred the sleek Spanish version called Flora.

'And who are you?' Tara practically purred when she spotted him. 'Another new local?'

Flora looked at me and raised her eyebrows but I pretended I hadn't seen.

'He is for the next couple of months,' Flora said, nudging Logan along the seat so she could sit next to him. 'Budge up.'

'I'm Logan,' he said to Tara, as he moved closer to where she had sat down. 'I'm staying at Hollyhock Cottage for the summer.'

'Oh my.' Tara smiled, first at Flora and then me, before looking back at Logan. 'Kittiwake Cove just got interesting.'

'His uncle has just died,' I stupidly blurted out. 'Sorry,' I gasped, turning to Logan. 'I shouldn't have said that.'

'I'm very sorry for your loss, Logan,' Tara smoothly responded, before he could say anything. 'I hope being in this beautiful part of the country proves to be a balm to your grief. Though perhaps you haven't seen much of it yet?'

'Him and Ally have been taking trips out, ' Flora revealed, even though that wasn't entirely accurate. We'd only been out once so far. 'So, he's seen some of it.'

'Is that right?' Tara asked, her eyes widening. 'That sounds ... cosy.'

'And my uncle lived in the north of the county,' Logan added, 'so I'm already familiar with certain parts of it.'

'Accompanying Logan is giving me the opportunity to say goodbye to the area,' I chimed in, for some reason feeling I had to explain why I was going out with him.

'So, Logan knows you're planning to leave the cove, too, does he?' Tara frowned.

'Oh, yes,' I said. 'He does.'

'The list is growing by the day,' Flora said and Tara nodded.

'No, it isn't,' I shot back, feeling flustered. 'It's just us four and that's how it's going to stay.'

'Are they always like this?' Tara laughed; the question directed at Logan as she laid a proprietorial hand on his arm.

'I honestly couldn't say,' he laughed, sounding nervous.

'Well, I think it's wonderful.' Tara smiled at me. 'How lovely to have the opportunity to say a fond farewell, in such wonderful company. It's so much lovelier than going it alone and feeling more inclined to say, good riddance.'

# Chapter 17

The walk back to the cottage from the pub was mostly silent. There were plenty of things I wanted to say and I daresay Flora had a whole lot she wanted to get off her chest too, but with Logan walking between us, it hardly felt like the moment.

Logan had been the perfect gent when we decided to leave The Ship, offering to see Tara home, but as she had her car, it wasn't deemed necessary. The gentlemanly gesture did however give Flora the opportunity to throw me another of her best *I told you so* looks, implying the pair might be a match, which I determinedly pretended I hadn't seen.

'So,' said Logan, when the silence started to stretch beyond the bounds of what was comfortable, 'would you say tonight was a success? Are the three of you friends again now?'

Flora had mostly ignored me after I had snapped at her after her comment about how many people now knew I was planning to leave, but she had talked to Tara a bit, so I supposed that was a success, of sorts.

'Given that stupid prom prank, we've already established that we never really were friends,' Flora light-heartedly reminded him, 'and thinking more about it, I wouldn't say we're going to be bosom buddies now, either. Ally and Tara might be, but not me. However, the evening did go some way to clearing up a few things.'

'I don't think we'll get that close,' I was quick to say, 'but I'm pleased we now know for certain that it was Tara behind the whole set-up and that Joe played no part in it. Reciprocating or otherwise.'

'The only thing he sounds guilty of is drinking too much and believing what Tara told him about you waiting for him in the room,' Logan said reasonably. 'Will you talk to him now, Flora?'

She let out a long breath.

'Maybe.' She shrugged. 'I guess. Though he really should have known better than to drink so much on that of all nights. And I daresay, given her motives, Tara didn't do anything to discourage him, so . . .'

'Oh, Flora,' I groaned.

'What?'

'Just let it go,' I said, rounding on her. 'Even your own brother thinks it's time you moved on, so why don't you? What Tara said tonight puts Joe completely in the clear as far as getting off with her is concerned, but you're still looking for something to throw at him.'

Logan cleared his throat, clearly uncomfortable to hear my harsh words.

'We're ten years away from it now,' I continued. 'It's time to grow up and move on.'

Flora looked floored. Out of the two of us, she was the one who usually told it straight. Hating conflict, I had always had a tendency to skirt around things and soften the edges of whatever it was that I wanted to say, but I'd hit my limit.

'Well,' she said, swallowing hard, 'that's me told, isn't it? Congratulations Ally, on finding your backbone at last.'

'I thought you could do with a dose of your own medicine,' I shot back.

'So,' she said, nudging Logan, 'what did you think of Tara? Is she someone you could imagine being *friends* with?'

'Yes,' I said, ignoring the emphasis Flora put on the word and hating the fact that I desperately wanted to know. 'As impartial observer, what did you make of her, Logan?'

He didn't answer straightaway and I wondered if he felt like a condemned man. He was going to struggle to find an answer that would please both Flora and me, but then perhaps he didn't think he had to and would say exactly what he felt.

'It's not really my place to comment, is it?' he said evasively, 'and I don't know about me being friends with her, but I'm surprised that you two to are. Were. Whatever.'

'Weren't,' Flora corrected. 'But why do you say that?'

'Well,' he said, 'guessing what she was like at school—'

'Mouthy, trouble, annoyingly cool and a huge fan of labels,' Flora succinctly described. 'Much the same as she is now, based on what I've seen tonight.'

Everything Tara wore was a designer brand and I hadn't been able to stop staring at the bag I knew was a Birkin. However, I didn't think she had been mouthy. Or not intentionally gobby, anyway.

'Exactly,' said Logan. 'Nothing like either of you.'

'Er,' Flora loudly said. 'I think I'm pretty cool.'

'And I don't mind labels,' I shrugged, though I was surprised to realise that I wasn't feeling quite as determined to own as many of them now as I previously had been.

I knew I wouldn't feel comfortable spending tens of thousands of pounds on something to carry my phone in, like Tara obviously had. Especially my phone, which was now so ancient it had an imprint of the keyboard burnt into its screen.

'You know what I mean,' laughed Logan. 'I don't have either of you pinned as mouthy or trouble. Well, maybe you a little bit, Flora.'

'Hey!' She yelped, giving him a shove.

'You didn't feel that way the day you spotted me on the beach,' I reminded him.

'That's true,' he agreed, 'but as soon as you'd explained everything, I forgave you.'

'But, had I not happened to be here,' I pointed out, 'you'd still be hating me.'

'That's a horrible thought.' He shuddered. 'But yes, I suppose I would, but you were here and it's all water under the bridge now. Just like you told me before, you really are much like the person I got to know in Barcelona and as far as the labels are concerned, Ally, you look wonderful just the way you are. You don't need expensive brands to look good.'

I thought of my carefully curated getaway wardrobe. TK Maxx had been a huge help when I put that together.

'So,' I tentatively said, 'the clothes I wore in Spain . . .'

'What I remember most about your clothes,' he grinned, 'was that they were generally in a heap on my hotel room floor.'

'Guys!' shouted Flora, rushing to cover her ears. 'I don't need to hear this.'

I ducked around Logan and pulled Flora's hands away from her ears.

'What do you think about my getaway clothes?' I asked her.

'Let's see.' She frowned. 'Well, they looked a bit out of place in your bedroom, which I suppose confirms that they fitted the image you wanted to portray. You look every inch the successful professional woman in them.'

'You did look like that,' Logan agreed. 'But I think you look lovelier now.'

I looked down at the dress, I was wearing, trying to process my thoughts.

'Have I said the wrong thing?' He winced when I didn't say anything.

'Yes,' said Flora, linking her arm through his. 'Because Ally doesn't want to look like Kittiwake Cove, Ally. She wants to look like Tara.'

'Really?' Logan asked, wrinkling his nose.

'Between you and me,' Flora loudly continued in a singsong voice, 'I think Ally has a crush on Tara.'

'As I recall,' I snapped, harking back to a time when Flora had been questioning her sexuality, 'you were the one with the crush.'

I regretted the words the second I'd said them. Had she not been teasing me, I never would have come out with something like that.

'Flora.' I sighed, but she had already dropped Logan's arm and was striding away. 'Flo!' I called again.

She didn't look back and by the time we reached the cottage there was no sign of her. Logan said a hasty goodnight and headed off to the courtyard and I slipped into the house, keen to avoid waking Kasuku. The irony wasn't lost on me that this was the first evening in years that Flora, Tara and I had spent together and it had ended with a row. Only this time, it was all my fault.

Not surprisingly, I didn't sleep well, so I took advantage of the fact that I was awake hours before the first guests were due to arrive. I checked the tide times and headed down to the beach for a swim. I hadn't expected to want to dive in again after that first icy plunge, but Mum had been right, swimming in the sea was both invigorating and addictive. I couldn't help wishing that I had given it a go when she was alive, rather than make excuses every time she had asked me to join her.

It was a warm, sunny morning and I made a point of mindfully breathing in the fresh sea air and admiring the wildflowers that lined the path beyond the garden and led down to the beach. I tuned in to the sounds, too. The call of the kittiwakes, after which the cove was named, wasn't everyone's cup of tea, but I realised I'd grown to like the cacophony.

There was no one else on the beach and I quickly undressed, pulled on Mum's neoprene gloves and booties and walked down to the shore. It was only then that I noticed someone climbing up the steps and on to the pontoon. I could tell it was Logan from the way he dived back into the sea and I quickly waded in to the water, feeling pleased that I'd made the effort to make the most of the early start.

I was more than halfway across when I realised he wasn't alone. The person with him had been out of sight behind the pontoon but as I approached, they appeared and climbed out using the steps. I began to tread water, wondering if I could turn back unnoticed, but then Logan jumped up and pointed me out and the person with him waved.

I could see then that it was Tara and she looked stunning. Her classically cut one-piece showed off her perfect figure and there wasn't a neoprene glove or booty in sight. I reluctantly began to swim towards them, wishing I'd braved the cold and left the accessories at home.

'Ally,' said Logan. 'What with it being a Saturday, I didn't think you'd be swimming today.'

With the pair of them watching, it had seemed to take forever to cover the distance and I held on to the steps to catch my breath before climbing out.

'Our guests aren't due until later,' I puffed, as I joined them. 'But I still can't be too long because I'll need to get showered before they arrive. Hey, Tara,' I added.

'Hey yourself,' she smiled. Her face looked as beautiful devoid of cosmetics as it was made up. 'What are you wearing?' She frowned, her eyes tracking down.

I looked at my feet and wiggled my toes.

'They were Mum's,' I said, pulling the gloves off before sitting down and tucking my feet under me. 'They keep my extremities warm.'

'What a brilliant idea,' she said, picking up one of the gloves. 'I should have thought of that. A pair of these might have saved my nails.'

Her toenails were the same shade of cerise as her fingernails and the colour looked great against her tan.

'Clever you,' she said, handing the glove back.

The old Tara would have jumped at the chance to make fun of me.

'My hands are actually freezing,' she said, rubbing them together. 'Can you warm me up, Logan?' she wheedlingly added.

She held out her hands and he took them between his own.

'Heaven,' she purred, winking at me. 'And don't forget my feet.'

'Er no,' said Logan, dropping her hands. 'I'd rather not.'

'Fair enough,' she laughed. 'Folk can be funny about feet, can't they?'

'Yes,' he said, grinning at me, 'especially strangers' feet.'

I had to look away. The memory of the attention he'd once paid my feet was almost too exquisite to recall. Tara twisted around to look at him and when I dared to look again, he was staring out to sea. The picture of innocence.

So,' I said, the smile evident in my tone, 'how come you decided to swim out here this morning, Tara?'

'Oh,' she said, turning back to me, 'Logan mentioned last night that he's taken to coming for an early dip and that you sometimes join him, so I thought it would be fun to come along. It's been ages since I've had a swim in the sea. Usually, I stick to fifty laps in the pool at my gym.'

'Wow,' I said. 'Fifty laps.'

'Every day,' she said, looking at her toned legs. 'It keeps me trim. Unfortunately, there's no pool around here, but the sea will suffice. As long as my hair can handle it.'

'So, you are staying in the cove for work then?' I asked, wanting to clarify her current living arrangements.

'Reasonably close to it.' She nodded, but didn't elaborate.

I was keen to know more about the career that justified the expense of a Birkin, but was mindful of the time.

'I'd better go,' I said reluctantly, wishing I'd had Logan to myself. 'Are you two coming in yet?'

I knew I wasn't going to like the answer, whatever it was.

A yes, would doubtless see me trailing after them on the swim back, but a no would mean leaving them alone together. I wasn't usually prone to jealousy, but I felt a stab of it then.

'I didn't see your stuff on the beach,' I said, suddenly realising. 'Did you not bring towels?'

'Tara showed me this little nook called the rock and we put our stuff there,' Logan said, diving back into the water. 'Do you know it?' he asked, when he bobbed up again.

'Yes,' I said, 'I know it.'

I was surprised Tara had remembered it, but I wouldn't be telling Flora that she had shown it to Logan.

'Right,' I said, pulling my gloves back on as I stood up again. 'Anyone coming then?'

'Not me,' said Tara, laying back and closing her eyes against the glare of the sun. 'I'll stay a bit longer.'

'Me too,' said Logan, climbing out.

Tara squealed then laughed as he shook his head and sprayed us both with droplets of chilly seawater.

'See you later then,' I said, climbing down the steps.

'Pub tonight?' Tara asked, leaning up on her elbows.

'Not for me,' I said. 'I'll be helping Dad with dinner until quite late.'

'What a way to spend Saturday night,' she tutted. 'You'll come Logan, won't you?'

He gave a non-committal shrug.

'You pair are no fun at all,' she said, laying down again. 'But don't worry, Ally. You're on a countdown now. This time next year, there'll be someone else here to wash the pots.'

Neither of them said anything further and I made my slow way back to the shore. For some reason, Tara's words hadn't elicited the level of excitement I usually felt when I imagined summer weekends left to my own devices and doing as little or as much as I fancied. I resisted the urge to look back at the pontoon when I reached the shore.

Dad was up and getting ahead with prepping meals by the time I arrived at the cottage.

'I thought you were still in bed,' he smiled, when I padded in, barefoot and damp. 'Have you been for another swim?'

'I have,' I told him. 'I'm getting used to the cold now.'

'Your mum would be proud,' he beamed. 'I know I am. It's a pleasure to see you embracing one of the best things about living in the cove. All that sea,' he said, gesturing roughly in the right direction, 'and you hardly ever use it. You'll be paddleboarding next.' He chuckled. 'It does wonders for the abs, so I've been told.'

'What does?' asked Flora, as she entered the kitchen.

'Paddleboarding,' Dad and I said together.

'I'd love to have a go at that,' she said wistfully and I felt relieved that she hadn't walked out when she spotted me.

'You should give swimming another go then,' said Dad. He knew that Flora had been through hell in the pool at school. 'Don't let that old cow bag hold you back.'

'It's a bit late for that.' Flora smiled regretfully.

'No,' Dad said stoically. 'If I've learnt anything since I lost my Rose, it's that it's never too late to do anything.'

I was inclined to agree with him, but I wasn't sure Flora would be climbing back into blue water anytime soon.

'And there's another thing these last few years have taught me,' Dad carried on, imparting further wisdom, 'which is that you should never be afraid to pursue your dreams and you should always, always follow your heart.'

'That's two things,' said Flora, checking them off on her fingers.

Dad tutted and she grinned at me. I was off the hook then. My mean comment had been forgotten. Or set aside for now, at least. Flora had really struggled with her sexuality for a while during her teens and I knew it had been low of me to allude to it.

'Isn't that right, Ally?' Dad asked, looking to see if I agreed.

'Absolutely.' I swallowed. 'You're right, Dad.'

The part about following your heart was crucial as far as I was concerned, but that presented me with a problem now, because all of a sudden and, for the first time in a long time, after my walk down to the beach and subsequent swim, I wasn't one hundred per cent sure what it was that mine wanted . . .

# Chapter 18

As a result of Dad's words of wisdom, and the desire I felt to keep adding notes to what I had already written about what I could remember of Beatrice, I felt thoroughly discombobulated for the entire weekend and found myself going through the hostess motions entirely on autopilot. I hadn't seen much of Flora, as she had two days full of reiki and tarot reading bookings and I didn't see anything of Logan or Tara at all.

The solitude would have once been welcome and I would have greedily embraced the opportunity to recall and embellish thoughts of the fantasy dream life I could soon be turning into reality, but the feeling I'd had after Dad had imparted his 'it's never too late' and 'follow your heart' speech, had thrown me completely off course.

Thankfully, a bottle of wine, drunk alone in my room on Sunday evening after the guests had all left, accompanied by some phone holiday-photo scrolling, set me back on track and gifted me the insight to see that my wobbly weekend hadn't been the result of my heart doubting its main goal at all.

Rather, it was the Saturday morning swim and the sight of Tara and Logan looking so good together in their swimwear that had knocked my ducks out of their formerly regimented row. It was still a matter of the heart, just not the one I had previously assumed.

If I shoved the thought of Tara and Logan getting together out of the equation, and set my own feelings for Logan aside, then I found all was still right in my world. I reminded myself that Dad had also once said 'if you can dream it, you can do it', and my dreams that Sunday night were all about me living my best life in Barcelona and that settled it. I *could* dream it and I *would* do it and the two newest arrivals in Kittiwake Cove could get on with doing whatever they liked.

'Kasuku,' I swallowed, closing my eyes for a moment as I set out the breakfast things on Monday morning, 'be a love and do that a little more quietly, would you?'

His response to my tenderly asked suggestion that he should bash his metal food bowl against the bars of his cage at a quieter level was met with a squawk and an ear-splitting increase in decibels.

'You arse,' I muttered.

A bottle of red wouldn't usually induce a headache of such mammoth proportions and it was far from an ideal start to the week, especially when I had all the beds to strip at top speed. I hadn't done any the evening before, even though I knew I had booked an early laundry collection.

'Look at him!' Flora loudly laughed, as she pointed at the pesky parrot, who was now hanging upside down, the bowl clasped in his beak. 'He looks like he's rattling the bars in a prison cell.'

'Feed him, would you?' I pleaded. 'I can't cope with the racket.'

'No chance. I like my fingers too much to risk doing that.'

'Bribe him to drop the bowl with a bit of mango or something, then.'

'You do it,' she refused. 'Your pet, your problem.'

'He's hardly that.' I grimaced as Dad walked in and Kasuku dropped the bowl and stood to attention as if he was the best, loveliest and most obedient parrot in the world.

'Little sod.' Flora tutted.

'And it's too late,' Dad told his feathered friend, wagging a finger at him, 'because I could hear you all the way down the garden.'

Kasuku picked the bowl up again.

'I think I'll skip breakfast,' I said.

'What's up with you?' Flora frowned. 'You look hungover. You weren't in the pub, so what happened?'

'Doesn't matter,' I said croakily.

'I'll tell you who was in the pub, though,' she carried on. 'Tara and Logan. They were sharing a bowl of chips and had their heads together for ages.'

The visual made my stomach twist.

'So?' I snapped.

'Well,' Flora said, 'maybe they're hooking up—'

'Don't gossip, Flora,' I said, wanting to shut her up in spite of my earlier resolution to not care. 'You'd hate it if they were talking about you behind your back.'

'I wasn't gossiping,' she said, turning red. 'More like stating a fact.'

'Well, don't do that, then,' I said, shoving my feet in my sliders and ramping the tension between us back up again.

Suddenly, I was spoiling for a row. Dad looked at me and shook his head.

'What?' I shrugged.

'It's like living with a couple of teenagers,' he tutted, sounding cross.

Flora looked worried and I felt bad then. I daresay she was concerned that Dad was regretting inviting her to live with us when the truth was, I was the one acting like a child and causing an issue. Perhaps I should start to flag Flora up as the 'golden girl' so my departure would come as a blessed relief and the two of them could live in mutual peace and harmony . . .

'I'm sorry,' I said. 'I know you weren't gossiping, Flora. I'm just in a bad mood this morning. I'm going to sort the rooms.'

She didn't offer to help, like she usually would, but I could hardly blame her.

'See you later,' I sighed.

I had opened the windows, stripped the beds and picked up the towels in just three of the rooms when a shadow fell across the open door.

'Please don't tell me they're here already,' I yelped, picking up the pace.

'Please don't tell you who are here, already?' asked Logan. 'Are you all right?' he added, when I turned around.

'Hungover,' I admitted, feeling like a stressed out, sweaty mess. And not a hot one. 'And I'm really behind this morning. The laundry is due to be collected and I've got at least another hundred rooms to do.'

'Here,' said Logan, stepping further in, grabbing a pillow and efficiently pulling off the case. 'I can help.'

'No,' I said, 'you mustn't. You're a guest. Dad will be cross if I let you help.'

'Your dad's singing along to the radio in the polytunnel,' he smiled. 'So, he won't know, will he? And besides, I've helped him since I've been here, haven't I?'

'In that case,' I gratefully accepted, 'thank you. I usually start this as soon as the guests have left, but I wasn't in the mood yesterday and had wine and an early night instead.'

'You weren't in the pub then?'

'You were there,' I said, wrestling with a duvet. 'So, you know I wasn't.'

'Well,' he said, 'I didn't think I'd spotted you, but I didn't stay late so you could have gone in after I'd left.'

'And what about, Tara?' I asked, unable to resist. 'Did she linger, do you think?'

'No idea.' He shrugged. 'She was still there when I left though.'

'And how did you find the chips? They're usually really good.'

Logan looked at me and raised his eyebrows.

'It's a small place,' I shrugged. 'Nothing goes unnoticed. It's one of the things that drives me nuts about living here. Well,' I amended, 'it used to. Now the thought of everyone being in each other's business is a comfort because I know Dad will be well looked after when I go.'

'That's definitely still happening then?'

'Of course it is.' I frowned. 'Why wouldn't it be?'

Logan shrugged.

'Flora told me,' I carried on, 'about the chips. She wasn't with Joe, was she?'

'She was with a few people. I think her brother was there, but I don't know what Joe looks like, so I couldn't say.'

I hoped Flora had seen him. If I hadn't snapped at her, she might have told me.

'So, what did you and Tara talk about?' I nosily asked, as we switched rooms. 'Did she mention her work or what she's doing back in the cove?'

'Er,' said Logan, cocking his head, 'no and no. We did talk about early morning swims though.'

I thrust a pillow at him, almost catching him where you should never catch a man.

'And did you swim together today?' I asked tersely.

I knew I was in danger of letting him know that I was jealous, but it was harder shoving the pair of them out of the equation than I had thought it would be.

'No,' he said. 'I told her I would, but then decided to give it a miss.'

'You stood her up?' I smiled, feeling pettily thrilled. 'She won't like that.'

I couldn't believe it was something she'd experienced before, but I could imagine her not showing up. I gave myself a mental ticking off as that uncharitable thought reared its ugly head. Tara had so far proved that she was a changed person, so she didn't deserve my scepticism. I ignored the fact that I hadn't doubted her sincerity before she'd been introduced to Logan.

'It wasn't a date,' he said. 'I don't want swimming with her to become a habit.'

Oh, happy days!

'So why did you say you'd be there?'

'No idea,' he said, running a hand through his hair.

'Probably the Tara Effect.'

'The what?'

'The Tara Effect,' I repeated. 'This thing she has that makes her irresistible to all men.'

'She's not irresistible to me,' he hastily said and I threw him a sceptical look.

'You sure about that?'

'Absolutely,' he said, resolute. 'She's not my type at all.'

I could feel myself starting to glow.

'There's only one woman around here who I want to spend time with every day.'

'And who might that be?' I swallowed, not wanting to presume, but hoping nonetheless.

My heart thumped then fluttered and given how the brightness of the room completely contradicted the size of Logan's pupils, I would have bet my next plane ticket on him experiencing a similar sensation, too.

'You know exactly who that might be,' he said huskily, taking a step towards me.

I matched his move and my breath caught as I wondered if I was about to seduced in room five. I hoped I was.

'It's you, Ally,' Logan breathed, my name heavy on his lips as I felt my body being drawn to his like a magnet. 'There's only you.'

'Ally!'

I closed my eyes in expectation of the welcome pressure of his lips on mine.

'Ally!'

Wait. That wasn't Logan's voice. I opened my eyes and found him on the other side of the room.

'In here, Dad!' I shouted, the words catching on their way out of my mouth.

'The laundry guy's here,' he said, appearing in the doorway and sounding out of puff. 'Hey, Logan. What are you doing in here?'

'Are you all right, Dad?' I frowned. 'You look a bit flushed.'

'Of course, I'm flushed,' he tutted. 'And out of breath too, given I've just jogged here from the cottage.'

'Jogged?' I frowned.

'I offered to help when I realised my talking to Ally was holding her up,' said Logan, matching the action to the words.

'All hands on deck,' said Flora, suddenly appearing in the doorway and manoeuvring around Dad. 'The collection guy wants to get on. What are you two up to in here?' she added suggestively, breaking into a grin.

'Nothing,' we said together and my face flushed as brightly as Dad's.

'I'll go and get the stuff from my room,' said Logan, slipping out. 'I got it ready earlier, to save you a bit of time.'

'What a gent,' Flora said, giving me a wink and, having provided her with an opportunity to tease, I knew my earlier faux pas was forgotten.

Dad and I were enjoying a cup of tea in the garden that afternoon when Logan came to find us. Kasuku was with us too, but thankfully in a quieter mood. He muttered softly to himself as he cracked sunflower seeds, scattering the shells far and wide.

'Logan, my lad,' said Dad as if he was greeting a long-lost relative. 'Pull up a chair and I'll pour you a cup of tea.'

'No, no,' Logan insisted, 'I don't want to interrupt.'

'You're not,' I said, squinting up at him. 'But you've missed all the cake.'

'Well, as long as you're sure.'

Dad held out an already filled cup which Logan accepted.

'That you've missed all the cake?' I teased. 'Definitely. It was spiced carrot cake today and that never lasts more than a minute.'

Logan laughed and then tried to open a deckchair one handed. I sat properly up and relieved him of the teacup.

'Thank you,' he said, taking it back again once he'd got the chair up and sat gingerly in it.

'You can never tell if you're going to end up flat on your back with a deck chair, can you?' Dad laughed.

I had a fondness for Logan in that position and since our nearly but not quite something in room five earlier, I'd fallen to thinking about him in that state a lot.

'How are you settling in?' Dad asked, then clarified with a chuckle, 'to life at Hollyhock Cottage, not in that chair.'

Logan smiled at both of us.

'Really well,' he sighed happily. 'It's so beautiful here. The perfect escape from my hectic life and work in the city. At this rate I'm never going to want to leave.'

It was a shame he wasn't visiting under happier circumstances. He'd barely mentioned his uncle to me, but his loss must have been having an impact on Logan's time in the cove, which he seemed to be falling in love with. His uncle was the reason he was here, I remembered, so I sent up a grateful thought, thanking him for pushing his nephew my way.

'That's good to hear,' said Dad, sounding satisfied. 'The apartment is still available beyond your allotted time if you'd like to extend your booking,' he added, with a twinkle.

'I'll keep that in mind,' Logan said.

'Are you thinking of renting it beyond when the courses run, in general, Dad?' I asked. 'Or are you just offering it to Logan because, well, it's Logan?'

There was no denying he had a soft spot for my friend and, as was becoming increasingly obvious, I still did too.

'As it's not connected to the courses, I don't see why it couldn't be made available all year round,' Dad said thoughtfully. 'The extra income wouldn't hurt, would it? And as it's just one unit, we could do the towels and linen in the cottage easily enough.'

'I guess,' I said, biting my lip and thinking it over.

I would have preferred to keep things as they currently ran so Dad wasn't left to take on more than he needed to out of season. He was right about the extra income, but where would extending the apartment booking calendar leave us manager-wise? I had been thinking about offering a spring to autumn contract, but if there was going to be work beyond those times, would that need to change?

Mulling over the potential change to my plan made me realise just how much freedom and free time I had during the closed season. I daresay I'd never find that level of flexibility in my working life again, but then fulfilling my passion would make the sacrifice worth it. Wouldn't it?

'But on this occasion,' Dad smiled, tracking back to what I'd originally asked, 'I'm offering because it's Logan.'

I wondered if he was still playing matchmaker. He might give it up if he happened to glimpse Logan and Tara together and saw how well suited they seemed to be despite Logan telling me he wasn't interested and . . . talk of the devil.

'Here you all are,' Tara beamed as she came into view. 'I knocked at the house, but it was deserted. I hope you don't mind that I've . . .'

Her words trailed off as Kasuku began to squawk and cuss.

'Whatever's the matter with that bird?' she gasped above the din as her hand flew to her chest.

'You made him jump,' Dad harumphed. 'You made me jump, too.'

'So, what's all this?' Tara asked, as if Dad hadn't huffed. 'Pimm's on the lawn.'

'It's tea,' said Dad, standing up. 'And the pot's empty.'

He was unusually unwelcoming and I guessed Flora had filled him in about Tara's surprising return, before I'd got around to doing it myself. He hadn't been a fan of hers a decade ago and he clearly still wasn't willing to forget the fallout she had inflicted.

'I just wanted a quick word with Ally,' she said, sounding a little less sure of herself.

'And ventured uninvited into the garden to make sure you got it,' Dad replied pointedly.

'Well, it's a stunning garden,' she praised, 'and I couldn't resist taking a look, so I hope you'll forgive me. And from what I can remember, you had an open house policy when you lived in Shellcombe, didn't you?'

'We did,' Dad smoothly responded, 'and we have here in Kittiwake Cove, too. Our door is always open to friends. I think I'll take Kasuku back to the house. He doesn't seem all that struck on your perfume.'

Tara opened her mouth to say something further, but changed her mind and stayed silent until Dad and the trolley he was pushing Kasuku's cage on, disappeared out of sight. Logan stood up again and gave me a smile, suggesting he'd enjoyed the lively exchange.

'What did you want to talk to me about, Tara?' I asked.

'I wondered if you might fancy a trip out?' she asked me. 'Logan and I were chatting Saturday night about a restaurant that's opened in Bournemouth and I realised it's right up your street. It's usually packed out, but I've managed to secure a lunch booking for two, tomorrow.'

'Oh, that sounds—' I began to say, but Logan cut me off.

'Ally can't do tomorrow,' he promptly said, on my behalf. 'She's already got plans.'

He held out a hand, which I took, and pulled me to my feet.

'She's coming with me to see the Cerne Giant and Durdle Door,' he said, filling me in on what my plans were and giving my hand a significant squeeze before letting it go.

'That's a rather touristy thing to do, isn't it?' Tara said, wrinkling her nose and sounding annoyed. 'And besides, both sites will still be there the day after tomorrow and millennia after that, whereas this booking is like gold dust.'

'But I can only take tomorrow off,' I said, playing along with Logan. 'And I have already promised I'll go.'

'And as I told you on Saturday, I am something of a tourist, Tara,' Logan reminded her. 'I'm only really familiar with the north of the county courtesy of the childhood holidays I spent with my uncle and both these landmarks are on his list of places for me to visit. We talked about it all in the pub, remember?'

I couldn't help wishing the landmarks hadn't been listed. Mum loved both and given how I had reacted to visiting Max Gate, I was potentially in for another tearful trip. Assuming the day out was really happening and Logan hadn't just made it up to get me out of having lunch with Tara. Though why he would have done that, I had no idea.

'Oh well,' Tara gave in. 'Fair enough. I can hardly top trump a deceased relative's wishes, can I?'

I thought that was further proof that she'd changed. The old Tara would have sulked until she got her own way, dead relative or not.

'Shame though,' she said temptingly. 'This is a truly authentic tapas place with rumour of a pending Michelin star. I wanted to give you a reminder of the taste of the good things to come, Ally.'

'That does sound good,' I commented, thinking that a taste of the future while I waited to grasp it would have been a wonderful treat. 'But a promise is a promise.'

'Perhaps I'll see if Flora's free to come with me instead,' she pondered.

'I'm certain she's working tomorrow,' I said, knowing it wouldn't be her scene at all.

'No harm in asking though.' Tara flashed a winning smile. 'Remind me again, which way is her studio?'

'I'll take you,' I offered.

'No, no,' she said. 'You stay. Just point me in the right direction.'

Logan and I watched her walk away.

'You better have a good reason for costing me a lovely lunch,' I said, giving him a nudge. 'You know how much I love tapas.'

'Indeed, I do,' he said seductively. I blushed.

'So, tell me then.'

'Oh,' he said, looking surprised. 'I thought it would be obvious. I didn't think you'd want to go with her and further fuel what Flora had previously said about being in thrall to Tara. I thought I was doing you a favour. And,' he carried on, 'I genuinely was going to ask you to come out with me, just before she turned up. I know it's selfish, but I want you to myself tomorrow, Ally.'

His words, combined with the memory of our near miss moment in room five, made me tingle all over.

'In that case,' I smiled at him, 'how can I resist?'

# Chapter 19

As I lay in bed, I mulled over the events of the day. I had been as astonished to hear Flora say she had taken up Tara's offer to eat tapas as I was to discover that Tara had actually gone ahead and asked her, but that wasn't the only focus of my midnight musings.

Later in the day, Logan had come to the cottage and dropped off a large envelope for me. I hadn't seen him and he had asked Dad to pass it on. Inside I discovered a guidebook for Max Gate and postcards, as well as a leaflet from the local Historical Society, which was asking for volunteers who could give tours of landmarks in the area as well as at a couple of prestigious properties in the county that were now in their care.

I had done some work for the Society before and looking through the leaflet elicited some very happy memories of the summers I'd spent with them and which the trauma of losing Mum and becoming the self-appointed caretaker of Dad, had tamped down.

It felt surprisingly good to think about those times again and they weren't the only memories I enjoyed reliving.

'I want you to myself tomorrow,' Logan had said.

I want you to myself . . . I want you to myself. I quietly chanted the words until they began to meld together. Had we not earlier shared that delicious, almost but not quite something moment, I wouldn't have paid them half as much attention, but we had shared that moment and it had tipped the scales in favour of us being more than friends again. Or at least, it had in my head.

As I couldn't be sure what was going on in Logan's, whether his choice of words had been innocently expressed or not, I decided I would play it cool on our trip to see the Giant and then Durdle Door. To avoid potentially making a fool of myself, I would keep us strictly in the friend zone that Flora had already pointed out he had placed us in. If there was any further move to be made to push us into a different one, then it would have to come exclusively from him.

'Are you heading to the beach for a dip?' Flora asked, as I poured us all coffee the next morning and Dad set up Kasuku's bath.

'No, not today,' I said. 'I won't have time to do anything with my hair ahead of spending the day with Logan if I do.'

'Does a day with Logan require you to do something with your hair?' Dad asked meaningfully, as Kasuku dived in to the tray of warm water and began to splash, fluff up his feathers and cluck in appreciation.

'Dad,' I warned. 'I'm just helping Logan out, remember? I've told you a hundred times now, we're just friends.'

'I know,' he grinned, 'but that doesn't mean I have to believe you, does it?'

I knew he was angling to find out if there had been something more between Logan and I than adjoining plane seats and a meal out in Barcelona.

'Hear, hear.' Flora, who knew for certain that there had been, enthusiastically agreed. 'Even with Tara now on the scene, I'm sticking with Team Ally and Logan.'

'That,' I said, giving her a stern look and wondering if she and Dad had been conferring in private, 'is no help at all.'

I wanted to remind her that she'd been the one to flag Logan and I up as friends, so according to her, there was no such thing as Team Ally and Logan, but I couldn't say anything without Dad overhearing.

'As if there could ever be Team Tara and Logan,' Dad said, sounding appalled. 'Logan wouldn't look twice at a woman like that.'

'You don't think smart, successful and confident are the sort of traits he looks for in a woman then, Dad?' I asked, feeling mildly offended.

'Of course, I do,' he responded, 'and you're all of those things,' he loyally added. 'But if you think that's what Tara is, you're wrong. She's smart though; I'll give you that. Though probably not in the way you meant it.'

'How do you mean it then?' I frowned.

'You might think she's changed,' Dad started.

'I *know* she's changed,' I interrupted. 'You only have to acknowledge how she's set things straight with Flora to know that. Right, Flo?'

'Right,' she said succinctly.

'If you won't take my word for it, Dad, surely you have to accept Flora's? She'd hardly be having lunch with her otherwise, would she?'

Dad looked between the two of us.

'I suppose not,' he begrudgingly conceded.

He still didn't sound convinced and I wondered what he was going to think of me when I started to dress like Tara. During future trips back to Kittiwake Cove I wouldn't be turning back into the current version of myself. If I was moving on, then I was moving on in every sense. Although, I did love my baggy dungarees . . .

'Tara looks smart enough,' Dad then said, 'but she's all style and zero substance.'

'That's a bit harsh,' I tutted, while Flora laughed.

'I know Logan would much rather be with someone like you, Ally.' Dad smiled. 'There's more to life than eye-wateringly expensive Birkin bags and Louboutin shoes. What?' He shrugged, as mine and Flora's mouths fell open. 'I clocked those red soles a mile off.'

'You know what, Dad,' I smiled, 'you never cease to amaze me.'

'Good,' he said. 'And I feel exactly the same about you. It drives me nuts that you don't appreciate the value of what you've created here. You're an astonishing business woman, Ally, with amazing talent.'

It was kind of him to big me up, even though all I'd really done was pick up and put into practice what Mum had already come up with. However, his praise and acknowledgement of what he assumed was my commitment to the business and the cottage was doubtless going to make explaining to him that the things in life he thought so much of weren't the things for me, all the harder. I hoped he would buy my story that moving on was a plan I'd only just come up with, rather than one I'd been harbouring for years.

'And you can further utilise that talent soon,' he happily carried on.

'How so?' I tentatively asked.

'By talking to the journalist representing one of those popular county mags, who has been in touch. *Dearest Dorset*, I think it is,' he said, scratching his head. 'Or something like that. They want to feature the cottage and the courses in their spring issue and I said they could come out and talk to you.'

'No way, Dad!' I protested. 'You know I hate doing that sort of thing.'

The launch of the business had received quite a lot of local press attention and I had struggled to smile through all of it, even though I knew we needed it.

'Just as much as I do,' Dad reminded me. 'But you're a million times better at it and you'll look far more appealing in the photos than me, too.'

'But we don't need the publicity now,' I reminded him, dreading the thought of seeing myself so on display. 'The courses for next season are practically full already. We won't have room to take on more guests who might come our way as a result of the feature.'

Though I had to concede, it could be the nudge I needed to get on with setting up the waiting list I'd been thinking about since we'd lost two attendees in one weekend during the previous season. I'd cursed the fact that we hadn't kept the details of the other people who'd wanted to join and been told there were no spaces left. I bet a couple of those disappointed folk would have snapped my hand off. It really was remiss of us not to already have a system in place.

'If you sort out that waiting list you've been on about,' Dad said shrewdly, 'we'd have no problem keeping track of further enquiries for courses that are currently fully booked, would we?'

'You're right,' I had no choice but to agree. 'I'll set it up this week.'

'And the offer of a glossy magazine feature is a gift,' Flora chimed in. 'If the journalist is freelance, then the article might even pop up in other county publications, too.'

'Flora's right,' said Dad, sounding thrilled. 'I hadn't thought of that. We can't start resting on our laurels just because business is currently brisk.'

I knew they were both right, but the last thing I wanted was Dad having to deal with more work once I'd left. I knew the majority of it would fall to the new manager, but Dad would still have to be involved.

'And it would be the perfect way to showcase the garden apartment,' he carried on, with a twinkle in his eye, 'which brings us neatly back to its current resident . . .'

'Unbelievable,' I tutted, but I couldn't suppress a smile.

All the lovely things I had been thinking about Logan while in bed had flown out of my head after my conversation with Flora and Dad, and I was still feeling stressed about the magazine interview and potential accompanying photo shoot when I met him at the cottage door.

'Morning Ally,' he beamed. 'Wow, you look great.'

I wasn't sure I did, as I had opted for a practical rather than pretty outfit, but it was kind of him to say. I knew the terrain we were going to be traversing required sensible footwear and the weather forecast suggested long sleeves would be best for someone with my kind of skin, so I was wearing a light cotton shirt teamed with shorts and Mum's sturdy walking boots.

Nonetheless, I smiled. 'Thank you,' I said as I picked up my bag and hat. 'This belonged to Mum,' I said, indicating the hat. 'It's supposed to have factor fifty protection, which is ideal for today. Have you got headgear?'

'In the car,' he said, opening the passenger door for me. 'And I'm already smothered in factor fifty sunblock, too.'

'Same,' I said, climbing in. 'Always best to play it safe. Not that there's room for any more freckles on my face now.'

'Or on your body.' Logan grinned. 'I noticed when we were swimming. Not that I was staring.' He blushed. 'I just happened to notice.'

'How could you not?' I laughed as he closed my door. 'I still can't believe you said you like them,' I commented as he settled into the driver's seat.

'I didn't,' he corrected, making me beam. 'I said I love them.'

'Did you go a for a swim this morning?' I asked, remembering I was supposed to be playing it cool.

'No,' he said. 'Not today, so if Tara turned up, she would have been on her lonesome again. Perhaps you and I will have to pick a different time to go if we want to carry on, so we can guarantee avoiding her.'

'Um,' I said, deciding not to gloat over that suggestion. 'So, where are we heading first?'

'Shellcombe to fill the car,' he told me. 'And then Cerne Abbas to see potentially the largest phallus in the entire world.'

'A fuel stop and a giant phallus it is then,' I laughed.

There were lots of cars parked by the time we arrived in Cerne Abbas and a few hundred steps into the walk, I was feeling further pleased that I had had the sense to wear Mum's boots. The practical lace-ups were a far cry from the red soled beauties Dad had surprised me by identifying on Tara's feet, but there was a time and a place for practicality over sex appeal and the Dorset hillside was it.

'Crikey,' gasped Logan, when he got his first glimpse of the giant we had come to admire. 'It's even bigger than I thought it would be.'

'Quite disconcerting, isn't it?' laughed a guy who was pushing a buggy with a toddler in, next to us. 'Does nothing for the male ego at all.'

'You're right,' Logan laughed along.

I felt a bit sorry for the giant. Over the years he'd been etched into the chalk, his nakedness must have been subjected to every sort of comment and innuendo imaginable. His club was impressive too, but how many people speculated about the size of that, I wondered?

'Given your reaction and what you said when we were talking to Tara in the garden,' I said to Logan, as we walked around the outline of the figure, 'I'm guessing you haven't been here before?'

'Er, no,' he said, sounding momentarily unsure but I didn't know why. This wasn't a trip you'd be likely to forget. 'And I have no idea why it was on my uncle's list, either.'

I was about to try to delve further into that. All I knew about this deceased relative so far, was that he'd lived in the north of the county and for some reason wanted Logan to visit some familiar, and unfamiliar, landmarks and sites. And given that Logan had just said he had no idea why, about this particular one at least, it was all beginning to feel a little ... well, odd. However, his next words gave me the opportunity to share some remembered local knowledge, which I relished.

'I wonder how tall the giant is?' he asked.

'One hundred and eighty feet,' I readily reeled off from memory. 'And the area is full of rare plants and invertebrates thanks to the chalky soil.'

'Someone genned up last night,' Logan said, looking impressed.

'I didn't need to,' I told him. 'Mum loved this place. She reckoned there was magic here and we visited every year, so I already had that info locked in the memory bank.'

My eyes prickled with tears when I thought of Mum standing where I currently stood, just like they had at Max Gate. Thankfully, they were cut off by the arrival of the guy with the buggy and a woman who I guessed was his partner.

'We used to come here when it was just the two of us.' She smiled at us. 'And I know the figure isn't really anything to do with fertility rites, but I fell pregnant the month after our last visit, so watch out.'

As one, Logan and I took a step away from the giant and then laughed.

'Excuse the overshare,' grinned the guy.

'Just a heads-up,' the woman laughed, as she looked fondly at the toddler. 'Would you two like me to take your photo? You won't get the giant in if you try to take a selfie.'

I was about to overshare myself and tell her that we weren't a couple so there was no need to worry about an unexpected nine months later gift, but Logan spoke first.

'A photo would be great,' he said, handing her his phone. 'Thanks. Come on, Ally.'

He pulled me to his side and flung an arm around my shoulder.

'Say cheese!' instructed the woman.

'Cheese!' Bellowed the toddler, which made us laugh and the snaps, which I saw later, looked wonderful as a result.

'Tune,' the woman laughed, as Logan's phone began to blare and she handed it back. 'We had many a night raving to this in Ibiza, didn't we love?'

'That we did,' said her partner, stifling a yawn, 'but not for a while now.'

I thanked the woman while Logan declined the call and put his phone away again.

'Thanks!' he called after them and they waved in response.

'Didn't you need to answer that?' I asked.

'No,' he smiled, 'it can wait.'

'I don't mind chatting to the giant if you need to call back,' I further said. 'I've been dying to ask him about his club.'

I thought Logan might laugh at that, but he didn't.

'What is it?' I frowned and he took a step closer.

'I need to tell you something, Ally,' he said earnestly. 'The thing is—'

Whatever he had been about to say was lost because the guy with the buggy was back again.

'It's here!' he shouted to the woman, bending down to pick up a tiny sock. 'Follow the trail of abandoned socks and you'll soon find my son,' he said to us, rolling his eyes.

'I'm like that with gloves in the winter,' Logan responded. 'Come on, Ally. Let's head back.'

'Oh,' I said, setting off just a step behind him. 'Okay.'

I wondered what he had been about to say. Whatever it was, it had wiped the smile off his face and had nothing to do with socks or gloves, but he seemed to have forgotten it as quickly as he'd been about to spring it on me.

'Do you want kids?' he asked, as we left the site ahead of the couple who were still trying to wrangle their rigid toddler into his car seat.

I was pretty certain that wasn't anything to do with what he had been going to say on the hillside, but for some reason, I wasn't inclined to remind him about that.

'At some point,' I said, 'sure. Not for a long time yet, though.'

'Would you come back to the UK to have the baby?'

'I can't say I've given it any thought,' I said, looking out of the window. 'I still need to grow up myself before I think about bringing another human into the world.'

'You don't think you're grown up?'

'Er, no,' I said, looking at him again. 'I mean, I still live at home, I work with my dad and up until recently, I pretended to be someone else for a couple of weeks every year. Things might be set to change, but right now, I'm playing at life, Logan, not living it.'

He shook his head at that and looked more put out than I thought he should.

'The way I see it,' he said, 'is that you run a hugely successful business with your dad, who happens to be your business partner, and you used to travel to Europe a couple of times a year to have your needs met.'

'Excuse me?'

'Your needs, as in your desire to embrace European culture,' he hastily amended.

'Well,' I frowned, 'no matter what kind of spin you try to put on it, I'm still a fraud.'

'I don't think you are.'

'I am,' I said bluntly. 'But I won't be for much longer. By this time next year, I'll be full-time living the life I currently only get to play at less than part-time.'

'And you're still certain you want to do that?'

'One hundred per cent,' I said, resolute, ignoring the fact that for some reason my head was disconcertingly shouting that it was more like eighty-five.

By the time we arrived at the car park that led to Durdle Door, the sky had been enveloped in a blanket of wispy white cloud. It was fairly insubstantial, but it knocked the edge off the intense heat, which I was grateful for.

Logan hadn't commented on the change in the weather, so I didn't know how he felt about it, but then he hadn't commented on anything. I got the impression that he still couldn't get his head around the fact that I didn't see Hollyhock Cottage and Kittiwake Cove as the idyllic escape that he did. I had thought he had accepted my desire to leave Dorset, even understood it after my explanation about never bonding with the house and what had happened to Mum, but perhaps not.

'I know it's probably a stupid thing to ask,' he said, finally breaking the silence, 'but this place is open, isn't it? I know it's not the school holidays, but I expected it to be busier than this.'

'Did you check the website?' I asked, unlocking my phone as I noticed there were just a few vans parked up. 'Sometimes it's shut for—'

I practically jumped out of my skin as someone knocked on the driver side window.

'The site has been shut for filming,' a woman wearing head-phones and carrying a clipboard told us. 'There's supposed to be someone at the entrance to stop anyone coming in.'

'Oh no,' I said, although I was intrigued to know what was being filmed.

I knew the site was often used as a location, but I hadn't given any thought to the possibility of the landmark being out of bounds when Logan had said we were coming here.

'Recording for a film, you mean?' he asked, sounding impressed.

'I'm not allowed to say what we've been shooting,' the woman said mysteriously, 'but this cloud has scuppered us, so we're packing up for the day. If you can hang around, I'll give you the all-clear when we're done and then you can walk down to the beach. Assuming that's where you were heading.'

'Yes,' I said, 'we were. Thank you, that would be great.'

'Do you think this means we're going to get the place to ourselves?' Logan grinned, the moment she'd gone.

'Unless anyone else turns up,' I said, smiling at his excitement, 'I think we might.'

'That would be amazing,' he said, as he scanned the road for cars. 'I'm almost tempted to go and stand there and turn anyone else away myself.'

'That would be a bit mean,' I laughed. 'Why don't you grab the picnic instead? It's a bit of a walk down to the beach, and uphill on the way back, so it would be good if we didn't have to take too much stuff with us.'

By the time we'd eaten the picnic, the woman was back and we had the all-clear.

'Come on,' said Logan, racing ahead. 'Hurry up.'

His former quiet mood was forgotten and feeling relieved, I rushed to catch him up.

'Oh, Ally,' he gasped when we reached the point in the path

where the stunning landmark came fully into view. 'Would you look at that?'

The sweeping curve of beach was deserted and the sea shimmered blue, green and every shade in between. I had visited numerous times before, but I'd never had the place to myself. It was perfect and the rapt expression on Logan's face told me he thought it was, too. Given his reaction, I guessed this was another new recommendation on his uncle's list.

'Come on,' he said, holding out his hand.

My heart raced as I took it and we rushed down the steps to the beach hand in hand. Our entwined fingers felt every bit the flawless fit that they had been in Barcelona. It made me wonder if other parts of us would still be the ultimate match, too.

'Crikey.' Logan swallowed as we crossed the sand, his voice choked with emotion. 'I had no idea a lump of limestone could make me feel like this.'

'It's spectacular, isn't it?' I wistfully sighed, the depth of my own feelings matching his, though mine wasn't solely the result of the view.

'Let's take some photos,' he suggested, 'quickly before anyone else comes along.'

He let go of my hand and while he zipped about, snapping the view, I pulled my shoes and socks off. There was still no one in sight and we were utterly alone.

'Oh, come on,' he said, when he noticed me paddling, 'we can do better than that.'

He began to strip off, just as he had in Kittiwake Cove.

'Come on,' he said again, as he scanned the clifftop.

'We're really doing this?' I laughed, thinking those were the words I'd uttered before.

'Looks like it.' He beamed back.

I followed him into the water wearing just my knickers and bra. The water didn't feel anywhere near as bracing as it had the first time, when I'd experienced it back in Kittiwake Cove. Whether that was because it was genuinely warmer or because I was becoming more acclimatised, I had no idea.

Rather than swim about, Logan reached for me and, treading water, pulled me into his arms. I felt my breath catch, as my determination to play it cool took flight.

I tried to look everywhere other than at him, but it was difficult in such close proximity, so I tipped my head back to look at the sky. The action was supposed to save me, but the moment I felt Logan's lips on my throat and his fingers brush my back and then move around to caress my breasts, I knew I was sunk.

'Logan,' I gasped, as his lips met mine. 'Oh God,' I groaned, kissing him hard and leaving him in no doubt that this was a path I was more than happy to be back on.

Whether it was the setting and being in the sea or the build-up of unquenched desire I'd experienced since he'd reappeared in my life, or a combination of both, I had no idea, but one thing I did know was that I had never wanted anyone more. And as we became further entwined and our kisses more urgent, I could feel how badly Logan wanted me, too. He was looking right into my eyes and with the slightest pressure in just the right place, I felt deep waves of pleasure pulse through me.

'Logan,' I said again, shifting to wrap my legs even more tightly around him.

I could feel myself falling headlong back in love, as well as lust, with him. I had tried so hard to fight the feeling because I knew what I had done in Barcelona made me unworthy of him, but the truth was, right from the moment he'd miraculously appeared in Kittiwake Cove, I had been fighting a losing battle.

'Ally,' he swallowed, his voice like treacle, 'we have to stop.'

'I don't think I can,' I told him, my legs gripping tighter.

'You have to,' he said, easing himself away a little.

For a moment I thought he was rejecting me, but then I noticed his eyes were focused on the clifftop.

'There are people on the path,' he said regretfully. 'We should get dressed.'

Giggling, we splashed out of the water and I rushed to pull off my knickers and bra and struggle back into the shorts and shirt. I looked decent enough on the bottom, but the clinging cotton shirt didn't leave a lot to the imagination.

'That,' said Logan, his bare chest rising and falling as he flopped down on the sand next to me, 'was without doubt, the best sex I've never had.'

'Me, too,' I agreed, pulling the damp shirt away from my skin. 'Though I'm pretty sure I had more sex than you did.'

He grinned at that.

'Only just though,' he said. 'Had I not caught sight of those walkers, we would have been neck and neck.'

Within a minute, the group passed by. I drew my knees up to my chest, trying to retain a little modesty. We were subjected to looks of both amusement and disapproval and I guessed we hadn't quite got away with our love in the sea. Though, was it love or sex for Logan? Or both? Whatever it turned out to be, it was definitely more than friendly . . .

'Afternoon.' Logan waved as the last of the group looked back at us.

'Don't,' I said, turning my face away.

'What?' he laughed. 'We've done nothing to be ashamed of.'

'You can be the one to tell my dad that when we're in court for indecent exposure,' I laughed, giving him a shove.

Logan shoved me back and within seconds we were entwined, kissing again and my hair was full of sand as well as sea.

'But thinking about it,' I said, when we eventually drew breath, 'Dad would be thrilled. He's been trying to nudge us together ever since he found out we'd already met.'

'Has he now?' Logan said thoughtfully. 'Is that really what you were thinking about while I was kissing you?'

'It did cross my mind,' I confessed and Logan shook his head. 'I reckon Dad thinks that you coming to the cove is fate or something.'

Mum had been the great believer in fate, but I now had the feeling that some of her thinking had rubbed off on Dad, too.

'But don't worry,' I carried on, when Logan didn't say anything, 'I'm not going to mention, or even hint at, any of what's just happened.'

'Okay,' he said, running a hand through his hair and sitting up. 'So much for sticking to friendship.'

'This trip has rather scuppered that, hasn't it?' I said, biting my lip and also sitting up.

'I think our nearly kiss in room five did that.' He grinned and I felt my insides fizz again.

'So,' I ventured, 'what happens now?'

'I know what I want to happen,' he said meaningfully.

'You do?' I whispered.

'Yes,' he said, reaching for my hand and kissing the back of it, 'of course, I do. But I still have some things to work through. Would you be happy to hold off going public until I've got a few more things to do with my uncle sorted? It shouldn't take too much longer and then my head will be completely clear again.'

'You mean . . .' I couldn't bring myself to ask outright, in case I'd misinterpreted what I thought he was implying.

Given how I had treated him in the past, I had no right to hope for a continued romantic relationship with him, but I thought that was what he was hinting at.

'I mean,' he said, exactly spelling it out, 'I want to be with you, Ally. In every sense. It's more than obvious that we can't be just friends, isn't it?'

'But I do want to be your friend,' I told him, feeling so happy I thought I was going to burst. *And I desperately want to combine that with what we had in Barcelona, too,* I thought, but didn't add, for fear of ruining the moment.

'And I want to be yours, too,' he said keenly. 'And we can be, we can have all of it, but just in private to begin with, if that's okay with you?'

'In private suits me just fine,' I told him, thinking a clandestine love affair sounded super sexy. 'But we'll have to be extra, extra careful around Flora, because she's the queen of sniffing out secrets.'

'And if your dad really is hellbent on getting us together, he might turn out to be the king,' Logan wisely added, 'so we'll need to watch ourselves around him, too.'

'Good point,' I agreed.

'On guard then, Ally,' he said, pretending to hold a sword aloft.

'On guard,' I said back, mimicking the gesture and laughing.

# Chapter 20

On the journey back to Hollyhock Cottage, I decided I would head straight upstairs to shower, rather than risk Flora spotting my still-damp hair and asking me how I'd managed to swim without the bathing costume, my only costume, which was currently hanging on the washing line.

I didn't want her getting the wrong idea – namely the right one – and then saying something and getting Dad fired up too. Logan and I had agreed to keep the shift in our relationship under wraps and I was determined not to fall at the first hurdle by getting caught out in a lie about skinny dipping. Or almost skinny dipping . . .

'Bugger,' I grumbled, when I spotted Tara's car on the drive. 'What's she doing here?'

I felt unaccountably reluctant to see her again, but then I didn't much want to see anyone in that moment. If I couldn't be with Logan, I wanted to hide out in my room and relive certain significant moments from our memorable day out instead.

'Dropping Flora off, I should think,' Logan sensibly said. 'They had lunch together, remember?'

Just as he said that, my tummy gave the loudest rumble.

'Sounds like you need feeding, too.' He chuckled.

'It's the sea air.' I blushed. 'It always makes me hungry.'

Which was often inconvenient, given where I currently lived.

'Me too,' he said sexily, lightly running his fingers up the inside of my arm and grinning. 'Hungry for you.'

'Oh stop,' I said, feeling half crazed with desire, even though we both knew the line had been as corny as hell. 'We're under wraps, remember? But God, I wish I could sneak over to your place tonight.'

'Why can't you?'

Given that Logan was the one who had initially set the boundary, he really shouldn't have been encouraging me to step over it – but if he wanted me as badly as I wanted him, I supposed I could appreciate why he'd suggested it. I ached with longing at the thought of spending an entire night with him again.

'I have admin I can't put off,' I hastily told him, reminding myself in the process, 'and I need to ask Dad when this journalist he was on about earlier is likely to turn up. I hope it's not too soon because I don't think I can cope with much more being loaded on to my plate right now.'

'Of course you can,' Logan said rousingly. 'Remember what Flora says . . . the universe never gives you—'

'More than you can handle,' I recited, finishing off my best friend's most quoted mantra. 'How did you know that's what she says?'

'It's cropped up in conversation,' he said, turning red. 'Do you think she's right?'

'Probably,' I reluctantly conceded. 'Annoyingly, she nearly always is. I suppose I could come over on the pretence of dropping off some towels though, couldn't I?'

'Oh God, Ally,' he laughed, 'if that's the best excuse for calling in that you can come up with, we're going to be outed in a heartbeat.'

'Especially if I'm not carrying any towels.' I laughed, picturing the scene.

'Exactly!'

The turn the conversation had taken might have been humorous, but it raised a serious question. How were Logan and I going to secure some private time with Flora working right next door to the garden apartment?

'Well,' I said, 'I'll have to come up with something else, won't I? Otherwise, I'm going to burst.'

'Me too,' Logan agreed. 'Don't forget, you've had more sex than I have today.'

That made us both laugh again.

'God, I want to kiss you,' he said, his eyes on my mouth.

'Likewise,' I swallowed as I quickly undid my seatbelt, 'which is why I'm going to go.'

Having made it into the cottage unnoticed, I took my time in the shower, then slipped on a floaty tea dress and went down to the kitchen. Kasuku's cage was covered, so I knew he had disgraced himself at some point. I didn't peep under it for fear of setting him off again and, having poured myself a cold glass of water, I went into the garden.

'Here she is.' Dad smiled when I found him, Flora and Tara sitting on the lawn.

Dad went to stand up, but then thought better of it because he was in one of the deckchairs. I was surprised to find them all together, looking and sounding so relaxed. The tableau didn't marry up with our earlier conversation, but then I spotted a couple of empty bottles of wine and guessed that might have helped smooth the way and get the words flowing. I hoped they hadn't been about me . . .

'What have you been doing?' Flora asked, looking up at me. 'We heard Logan drive round to the courtyard ages ago.'

'I wanted to have a shower,' I lightly said. 'It was hot, doing all that walking, so I wanted to freshen up ahead of dinner. I haven't missed it, have I?'

The kitchen was devoid of yummy smells and there were no pans on the hob or in the oven.

'I'm having a night off.' Dad smiled and my heart sank.

'How was your lunch?' I asked Flora and Tara, my tummy rumbling again, that time because of the thought of plates loaded with flavoursome tapas.

'Give me ten minutes,' said Dad, holding out his hand for me to pull him up, 'and you'll find out.'

Once he was on his feet, he took a second to gain his balance and then headed back to the cottage.

'It's supposed to be your night off, Geoff,' said Flora, jumping up and rushing after him. 'I'll give you a hand.'

'Lunch was divine,' said Tara, pouring me a glass of wine. 'As you're about to find out, because we came back with at least half the menu.'

'Really?' I gratefully gasped, taking the glass.

'Yep.'

'Oh, that's amazing because I'm literally famished. Thank you.'

'It's not a doggy bag kind of place,' she further said, pouring iced water from a jug for herself, 'so I got them to make us up a hamper. I told you I wanted to give you a reminder of what you've got to look forward to and I knew I'd find a way.'

She'd always had a knack for bending people to her will and she sounded very pleased with herself. Which was fine, because on this occasion, I was very pleased about it, too.

'Because right now, I think you need that reminder, don't you?' she said.

I glanced back at the cottage but there was no sign of Flora or Dad.

'What do you mean?' I asked, lowering my voice.

'Well,' she said, sipping her water and crossing her legs as the ice cubes clinked together in the glass. How could she look elegant in a deckchair? 'I know you told me how you're making plans with a view to leaving the cove—'

'Shhh,' I said, putting a finger to my lips.

'Oh, don't panic,' she tutted, also looking towards the cottage, 'no one can hear. The point I'm getting at is that ever since you told me you were off, you've looked nothing but settled.'

'Settled?' I hoarsely whispered.

'Yes,' she said, 'you know. Settled, cosy, at home, here for the duration. The classic Kittiwake Cove resident. If you're faking it, it's quite a façade.'

'Of course I'm faking it,' I told her. 'I've been faking it for so long, I've forgotten how not to and you know I'm being extra careful about making sure that Dad doesn't get an inkling as to what's on the horizon.'

'So, your departure really is still happening then?' She didn't sound convinced.

'Yes,' I insisted.

'You're not having any doubts?'

'None.'

'Oh well, in that case,' she said, as she raised her glass to mine, 'cheers to you. You're quite the performer. You had me fooled. I honestly thought you were having second, maybe even third, thoughts.'

'Even if I had been,' I said, still with one eye on the house, 'I can't see why it should matter to you so much.'

'Because I want to see you fulfil your potential,' she said kindly. 'And I have a friend who works in a museum in Barcelona,' she added, 'and I've being going to mention you to them, but wanted to be completely sure you were still up for making the move.'

'Really?' I said, my eyes flicking back to her and my heart racing at the prospect of her knowing someone who might be able to point me in the right direction job-wise.

The kind of position I was going to be looking for was like gold dust, so a recommendation would be a huge help.

'Really,' she smiled.

'Well, yes,' I confirmed again, 'I'm still up for it, but with the season in full swing, I need to be focused on that. I can't afford to get carried away thinking about what comes next when I need to keep things on an even keel and play the long game with Dad.'

'You won't want to sample the food Flora and I have brought back with us then?' she said mischievously.

'After all the effort you went to to get it, of course I'm going to eat it,' I told her and she laughed. 'I mean it though, Tara,' I said seriously, 'nothing's changed. I'm still set on turning my dreams into reality and the trips I'm accompanying Logan on are doing nothing more than helping him out and giving me the opportunity to make some memories. Assuming that's what you're referring to.'

It was the only thing I could think of that she might know about that could have made her doubt my conviction to leave Kittiwake Cove.

'Making memories with Logan?' She winked.

'No,' I said, 'more like taking a mental snapshot of the Dorset landscape.'

'Oh right.' Tara beamed. 'Though I daresay you're spending as much time admiring him as you are the view, aren't you?'

'Well,' I said, feeling an unfortunate blush begin to bloom. 'Logan is . . .'

'I'm very interested to hear how you're going to finish that sentence,' came Logan's voice nearby.

I jumped so high I sloshed half of my wine on to the grass.

'Logan,' I said, as he walked through the gate that separated the garden from the courtyard. 'Join us, why don't you?'

The little path was intentionally left to get overgrown during the summer, affording us some privacy and a separation between work and home, which was why, neither Tara nor I had spotted Logan or heard his approach.

'Sorry,' he said, but not looking it. 'I didn't mean to make you jump.'

'And we didn't mean for you to catch us talking about you.' Tara smiled at him.

'All good, I hope?' he fished.

'Of course,' Tara practically purred. 'Oh, I see you've had a shower, too.'

'I needed it,' he said. 'It was so hot on the beach, wasn't it, Ally?'

'Sweltering,' I choked and Tara gave me a look.

'And where the giant is,' Logan casually carried on, 'it was boiling there, too.'

'I wasn't expecting to see you again today,' I said to Logan. 'Is everything okay?'

'Flora messaged and asked if I'd like to join you all for dinner and I couldn't resist.'

'Well, I'm pleased you couldn't,' said Tara. 'Because there's loads. Flora and I came back with practically half of what was on offer.'

Right on cue, Flora and Dad appeared carrying two huge platters.

'There's another one of these to come,' said Flora, 'and more wine, too.'

'I'll get it,' Logan offered.

'And you go with him, Ally, to get the plates and cutlery,' Dad directed. 'Tara can help me move this table.'

We all did as instructed, but I could feel Tara's eyes on us as we walked away.

'So,' said Logan, picking up the platter, 'what were you and Tara talking about? I know my name cropped up, but what else?'

I stopped and looked at him. I was a little taken aback that he'd so bluntly asked, but then he had caught us talking about him.

'Sorry,' he said, noticing my reaction. 'It's none of my business, is it?'

'It's all right,' I said, reasoning his curiosity away. 'She wanted to make sure I still wanted to leave, mostly. For some reason, she'd got it in her head that I'd had, or was about to have, a change of heart.'

'Oh.' Logan frowned. 'Right. But you're not though, are you?'

'Absolutely not,' I stated firmly, wishing he wouldn't keep asking. 'You should know that better than anyone.'

'Of course.' He nodded. 'I do.'

'Come on then,' I said, 'let's get back down there because, left to her own devices, I wouldn't put it past Tara to accidentally tell Dad that this time next year, I'll be living off tapas while living in Barcelona.'

'She wouldn't do that,' said Logan, sounding horrified, 'would she?'

We hurried back to make sure she didn't get the chance.

'So,' said Dad, sitting with his hands resting on his belly after he'd eaten his fill, 'what did you think of that little lot, Ally?'

I was still making the most of the moreish croquetas, but every dish had been to die for.

'Delicious,' I said, having swallowed another mouthful. 'Absolutely divine.'

'My favourite was the patatas bravas,' said Flora, who reckoned she'd eaten as much again for dinner as she'd had for lunch, and Tara had eaten another plateful, too.

'What about you Logan?' Dad asked. 'Authentic enough for you?'

'Absolutely,' he said, as he picked up his glass and held it up to Tara. 'Entirely authentic. Thank you for bringing it all back. It is, as Ally said, delicious.'

Tara beamed when he said that and I wished she wouldn't.

'As good as the real thing.' Dad nodded. 'That's quite a commendation, isn't it? Is this the sort of meal Logan took you out for in Barcelona, Ally?'

I felt Logan stiffen by my side and saw Tara's eyes widen.

'What's this?' she asked.

'Oh,' said Dad. 'It's not a secret, is it?'

His words had a slight slur to them and Flora, raised her eyebrows in amusement.

'Had you two met before Logan arrived in Kittiwake Cove?' Tara practically demanded.

She sounded remarkably pissed off and I could only assume that she had set her sights on Logan and was now trying to suss out the potentially shifted parameters of our relationship.

'You knew each other before?' she asked again, her voice an octave higher.

'Well,' said Logan, looking flushed, 'it's a funny story actually.'

'Oh goody.' She smiled, but sounded disgruntled. 'I love an amusing anecdote.'

'It was a total fluke—' Logan began.

'No, lad,' said Dad, going to tap his nose, but missing. 'It was fate.'

'Fluke or fate,' I said, 'Logan and I were assigned seats next to each other on the same flight out to Barcelona back in the spring. Obviously, we were total strangers then, but we got talking and—'

'It was meant to be.' Dad smiled. 'They got talking and then went out to dinner.'

'And Ally also took me on a Gaudí tour,' Logan unnecessarily said, furnishing Dad with more details.

'And the rest,' Flora then mouthed at me and I turned as red as Logan.

'It was all down to Sister Lucia,' Logan carried on.

'Ah,' said Dad. 'It was divine intervention, then. Wait ... what?'

'There was a nun next to us on the plane,' I told him,

deciding to elaborate myself before Logan literally bared all the details. 'She encouraged us to see each other again once we left the airport.'

'And then what?' Tara asked, sounding amazed. 'Logan turned up here and you had an unexpected reunion on the beach?'

'That,' said Flora, clearly enjoying the revelations, sounding thrilled as she poured more wine, 'is *exactly* what happened.'

'We hadn't been in touch since Spain,' Logan carried on, thankfully omitting the part where we'd had mind-blowing sex and I'd then left him high and dry, 'and I had no idea Ally lived here when I made the booking, or even on the day I arrived.'

'He spotted us on the beach one day, ' Flora said, 'arguing about you actually, Tara, and . . .'

'Why didn't you say anything?' Tara said, jumping up. She looked first at Logan, then at me. 'Why didn't either of you mention it before?'

'Probably because it was none of your business,' said Dad, sounding suddenly sober.

I could only assume that she'd reacted like that because she actually had set her heart on bagging Logan and now realised I'd probably snagged him first. I can't deny it felt nice to be the one with the upper hand for a change.

'Sorry,' said Tara, shaking her head. 'Of course, it isn't my business.' She flopped back down again, the deckchair thankfully not collapsing. 'It's just that . . . I thought we really were all friends again.'

'We are,' said Flora.

'But,' she sulkily sniffed, 'friends don't keep secrets. I feel a total fool that everyone other than me knew.'

I didn't know what to say. I hadn't kept it from her in the hope that it would upset her if she did find out.

'Well, well, well.' Dad chuckled. 'I'm beginning to think you might have a heart, after all, Tara.'

'Of course, I have.' She pouted, then laughed. 'But don't tell everyone.'

'Secrets can be tricky things,' Dad added, looking at me. 'You have to keep track of them, otherwise they're bound to catch you out when you least expect them to.'

We raised our glasses to Tara's heart and, trying not to think too deeply about what, if anything, Dad might have meant, I wondered at the wisdom of keeping mine and Logan's now rekindled romance under wraps. If Tara thought we were nothing more than reacquainted travel companions, was she now going to try to go for it with him? I wouldn't want to witness that, and more to the point, how would Logan handle it if she did?

# Chapter 21

'So,' I said, once Logan and Tara had left, Dad had gone to bed and it was just Flora and me sorting the crockery and leftover food in the kitchen, 'how was your lunch? And I don't mean what did you make of the menu.'

What I really wanted to talk about was Tara's reaction to finding out that Logan and I had met before he arrived in Kittiwake Cove, but I knew Flora would make more of my feelings for him if I started the conversation with that.

'It was actually really good.' Flora smiled.

'You sound surprised,' I observed.

'I was,' she laughed. 'I still am. I didn't expect to actually enjoy it. I only accepted the invitation because I wanted to do a bit of digging and potentially catch her out.'

'Catch her out?' I frowned. 'I don't understand.'

Flora wiped her hands on a towel and fixed me with a level stare.

'In case you haven't noticed,' she carried on, 'I've been struggling to accept Tara's Little Miss Goody Two Shoes act.' I had caught a vague whiff of disbelief, but nothing that suggested she had genuinely deep doubts. 'However, having spent most of the day with her, I don't think it is an act.'

'So,' I surmised, 'in all the time she's been back this summer, you haven't truly believed in her transformation?' Flora shrugged. 'Please don't tell me you still have doubts about what happened at prom?'

'No, I do believe what she's told us about that. It's been the rest of it. I wasn't convinced that such a catty leopard could really change its spots.'

'So, are you convinced now?' I asked. 'Did you catch her out about anything?'

'Yes I am and no I didn't,' I was relieved to hear her say. 'We talked a little about her work. She does something in property, but only has one project on the go at the moment, which isn't tied to the office. Hence her turning up here.'

'I wonder what she's working on.' I frowned. 'Is she self-employed? She must be good at her job, whether she's her own boss or not, to have bagged herself such a laidback summer.'

Flora smirked.

'What?'

'You're even nosier than I am.' She laughed.

'I'm just curious.' I pouted. 'I haven't had the opportunity to talk to her about her career.' Given Tara's love of labels, I guessed it paid well, but beyond that I only knew what Flora had just told me. 'What did you tell her about yourself?'

Having discovered for myself that Tara now had the ability to listen and share, rather than dominate a conversation, I knew that Flora would have had the chance to talk.

'I told her how I'd left the home from hell behind after Geoff generously gifted me a room here and that, along with Freddie, you and him and Hollyhock Cottage are my everything.'

'Oh, Flo.' I sniffed.

'Well, it's true.' She smiled. 'I live here, I work here and I love you both.'

'And we love you, too,' I said, pulling her to me for a hug.

'Good,' she said, from the depth of my embrace, 'because you're stuck with me now.'

'And did you talk about Logan?' I asked as I let her go.

I thought I'd left it long enough before dropping him into the conversation, but Flora still gave me a knowing look.

'No,' she said, with a smile. 'We didn't, but given her reaction to finding out that the pair of you met in Barcelona, I reckon you've got yourself some stiff competition.'

'There's no competition,' I said, trying to coolly waft her suggestion away.

'Oh really?' she teased. 'So, you're not interested in pulling Logan out of the friend's zone again now? Shall I let Tara know the path is clear for her to snag him?'

'No,' I said immediately, 'you should not.'

'I knew it!' Flora grinned.

'But not because of me,' I said, as I focused on wiping down the worktops. 'The poor guy is grieving, remember? He doesn't need women squabbling over him.'

'Who would be squabbling?' Flora shrugged. 'You've just declared you're not even in the arena, so surely Tara would have an uncontested win?'

'There is no arena,' I said, throwing the dishcloth in the sink.

'But you're right,' Flora continued, 'Logan is having a tough time, so I won't interfere. I've read his cards though and seen love on his horizon. Among other things.'

'What other things?' I demanded, trying not to become too

distracted by the thought of Logan in love. 'And did he ask you to read his cards?'

'I told him I would send him some healing,' Flora said vaguely. 'Now, come on. You'd better get to bed, otherwise you'll be in no fit state to talk to this journalist tomorrow.'

'What?' I gasped, as someone knocked quietly on the back door, making me jump.

Flora hadn't jumped, I noticed, so she must have been expecting whoever it was. She went to the door and opened it just a couple of inches.

'Two secs,' she mysteriously said, then closed it again.

'Who's that?' I asked.

'Never you mind,' she tutted, physically turning me away. 'Now, the interview for the magazine your dad was talking about this morning is tomorrow at ten thirty—'

'You're kidding?'

'No,' she patiently said, 'I'm not kidding. He must have told you.'

'He did not.'

'Well, now you know. And don't forget we're starting to plan mine and Freddie's birthday party tomorrow, too.'

'I haven't forgotten,' I stoutly said, even though her mentioning seeing love on Logan's horizon had pretty much made me forget everything.

'Of course, you hadn't.' She grinned, picking up her keys. 'You can lock up, because I don't know how long I'll be.'

'Where did you say you were going?' I asked.

'You know I didn't,' she said, slipping out of the tiniest crack in the door. 'Mind your beeswax.'

I rushed to look through the window and just spotted sight

of her walking down the garden with a guy. From the back, he looked remarkably like Joe.

I was up extra early the next morning, keen to make sure that the cottage and courtyard rooms were looking their best for the arrival of the journalist I hadn't known was coming until Flora mentioned them. I might have been reluctant to do the interview and nowhere near as invested in the business as I was about to make out, but I still wanted to present myself and mine and Dad's work in the best possible light.

I had been tempted to knock at the garden apartment when I was checking the other rooms, but the curtains were still closed and I walked away knowing it wouldn't have been sensible to become further distracted ahead of the interview. A clear head was what I needed, one that wasn't full of the image of Flora's card representing the lovers in her tarot pack, so I left Logan to his late start.

'Vanessa Fielding,' stated the woman, who arrived at exactly ten thirty.

She was wearing a slightly crumpled linen shirt dress and leather sandals, and carried a notebook and phone as well as a large canvas tote. Her greying dark hair was haphazardly pinned up and I felt myself instantly warming to her. I couldn't accurately age her, but somewhere in her sixties would have seemed about right, though which end of the decade, I couldn't have said.

'Hi.' I smiled back. 'I'm Ally. Come in.'

'Thank you, Ally,' she responded, stepping inside.

'Can I take your bag?' I offered. 'I thought we'd start with coffee in the kitchen.'

While I made us drinks and plated up some of Dad's chewy almond biscuits, Vanessa, at my invitation, took herself off on a tour of the ground floor. I was keeping an eye on Kasuku but so far, he hadn't commented on Vanessa's arrival. He was watching her closely, but displaying none of the traits that would suggest he was about to throw an insult her way. That was an excellent start in itself.

'Wow,' Vanessa beamed, when she came back into the kitchen. 'This place is truly stunning, Ally.'

I felt a rush of pride and offered her a seat at the table.

'Thank you,' I said. 'I'm delighted you like it.'

'A friend of mine came on a jewellery making course last year and has done nothing but rave about it,' she flatteringly carried on. 'I've been wanting to offer you a feature spread ever since, but I've only recently had a spot come up.'

'It's always a thrill to receive positive feedback.' I flushed, feeling peacock proud.

The depth of the sensation was a surprise. I hadn't realised I actually cared so much about what people said when they went away. Of course, I wanted the business to continue to be a success, but the genuine sense of pride I felt was unexpected.

'Everything posted on the review sites is glowing,' Vanessa said, as she reached for a biscuit. 'Even the one negative comment I found was a positive.'

'A negative comment?' I questioned.

'Someone,' she said, 'suggested their waistbands were always a little snug as a result of your dad feeding them.' She took a bite of the biscuit. 'And now I know why!' She laughed as she chewed. 'Now,' she said once she'd finished, and as she flicked open her notebook, 'tell me everything.'

I gave her the lowdown on how the business had come about, what my role in it was (basically filling in where Mum should have been), the part Dad played and how everything was organised, and then I took her over to the courtyard. I noticed Logan's car had gone, but stayed focused on Vanessa as she fell into raptures over the rooms.

'And what are these little baskets for?' she asked, picking up a hamper.

I explained about the locally sourced gifts and seasonal vases of flowers that accompanied them, as well as the hollyhock seeds or plants every attendee went away with.

'It's all divine,' she said, scribbling frantically. 'Simply divine.'

'Mum certainly had a wonderful vision.' I smiled at Vanessa's continued praise. 'And I'm simply carrying her wishes out.'

'Your mum came up with all these extra touches?' Vanessa asked, looking at me over the top of her on-trend glasses, while pointing at the hamper, which she had just put down, with her pen.

'Well, no,' I conceded, 'those were my idea, but she would have done ...'

'And the conversion of the garden apartment?' she further enquired. 'Was that part of your mum's original plan, too?'

'No,' I said, 'I came up with that. It felt such a waste to have the building just sitting empty when we could utilise it.'

'Right,' Vanessa said thoughtfully. 'Remind me again of the months the courses run.'

While I gave the dates and further details, we walked from the courtyard into the garden, where I could see Dad working on the veg patch.

'I'd rather you didn't put it in your article,' I said, as he looked up and waved, 'because I haven't mentioned it to Dad yet, but I am now wondering about opening the cottage up in the winter to run some festive themed day classes. Making wreaths and decorations, that sort of thing.'

When I had previously thought about extending the garden apartment availability, I had been worried about making more work for Dad, but now I was thinking that if a manager was going to end up being employed for the whole of the year, then I might as well come up with more for them to do. They could take responsibility for anything new and leave Dad to peruse his seed catalogues and plant lists much as he always did throughout the 'ber' months.

'Oh yes,' Vanessa encouraged. 'I won't include it, but it does sound wonderful. Can I have first dibs on the wreath making workshop?'

'Of course.' I laughed. 'If it comes off, you'll go straight to the top of the list. And with autumn decorating becoming so popular now,' I rushed on, getting properly in the swing and rather carried away, 'that might be another residential weekend we could offer, tacked on to the end of the season.'

Vanessa rested her hand on my arm.

'Ally,' she gently said.

'Umm . . .' I was miles away, imagining the log burner crackling, the table set with felt toadstools and dried leaves, the smell of pumpkin spiced latte and sweet, freshly baked leaf-shaped iced biscuits wafting through from the kitchen.

'I hope you don't mind me flagging this,' she said tentatively, as I refocused, 'but when we started this interview, you went to great lengths to tell me that all you've been doing here is seeing through your mum's vision.'

'That's right,' I confirmed. 'It is.'

'It might have been at the very beginning,' she carried on, 'but this place is you now, Ally. It's all you.'

I opened my mouth to deny that, but pre-empting what I was going to say, she didn't give me the chance.

'I have no idea why you're so reluctant to own it,' she said tenderly, 'but you've listed so many clever touches and suggested plenty of new concepts, both large and small, that you must be able to see that you're every bit as invested as your mum would have been, had she been here to see the initial idea through.'

I didn't know what to say to that.

'Have I offended you?' She frowned. 'Because that wasn't my intention.'

'No,' I croaked, trying to smile. 'Not at all.'

'My guess is, then,' she carried on, 'that you're holding back from claiming what you've done because you don't want your dad to think you're taking over, but having spent just a short while with you, I can see that you have the drive and ambition to take this business even further, and I'm sure he would wholeheartedly welcome and support that.'

I should have been feeling thrilled that I had done such a good job of making Vanessa believe that I was so invested in the business, but the emotion that reared its head was a shock. She had pointed out that I was the person who had moved Mum's vision along, it was also me who had come up with the added extras and the conversion, and I was now the one who was suddenly buzzing with ideas about a new seasonal direction.

I knew I wasn't holding back from claiming any of it for Dad's sake, as she had suggested, so what was going on?

'And talking of Dad,' I said, buying myself some time to regroup, 'let me introduce you. But again, please don't mention my new ideas.'

'Mum's the word.' Vanessa winked.

'Dad!' I called, the wobble in my voice indicative of how my entire body felt.

I left the pair of them chatting and headed back to the cottage to prepare lunch.

'What the hell just happened?' I muttered to myself. 'What the hell is going on?'

By the time Dad and Vanessa arrived in the kitchen, they looked and sounded like the best of friends and I had mulled over what Vanessa had said and was feeling much better about it.

I had put the influx of new ideas down to my desire to leave Dad with some exciting new additions to the business. Focused on them, I could rest assured knowing he wouldn't be thinking about the empty loft. That was doubtless why I was so excited about them and the pang I felt knowing I wouldn't be here to see it all so seasonally set up, was more about my love of autumn than the thought of missing out.

'Now,' I said, while Dad washed his hands at the sink, 'I can't take the credit for lunch, because as you know, this is Dad's department, but I can tell you that the salad and dressing are both delicious. You will join us, Vanessa, won't you?

'I suppose I could send a message to say I'm going to be slightly later for my next appointment, couldn't I?' she said, checking her watch.

'I'd love it if you did,' said Dad, his cheeks looking a little flushed.

'In that case,' she smiled at the pair of us, 'how can I refuse?'

I directed her to the hall, which was the best place in the cottage to get a mobile signal.

'There,' fondly clucked Kasuku, watching her go. 'How lovely.'

Given the look still lighting up Dad's face, I could tell he thought Vanessa was very lovely indeed.

# Chapter 22

Having been in no rush to leave, it was just as well that Vanessa had called ahead and rearranged her next appointment. She had been as fascinated to hear about Beatrice Baxter and her generous bequests as she had about the cottage and the courses.

I think I had taken Dad by surprise when I started talking about Beatrice too, my memory jogged courtesy of the things I had been noting down since mine and Logan's trip to Max Gate. I realised I would have to be careful about that sort of thing where Dad was concerned.

Though perhaps, I could tell him that my memories of Beatrice and her legendary legacy had further sparked my interest in history and, in turn, my desire to depart. It would be a little underhand, but potentially very helpful when the time came to tell him I was leaving the cove for historical pastures new. As it were.

When Dad came back inside, having eventually waved Vanessa off, I could tell from the fact that he was grinning like the Cheshire Cat that he had enjoyed her visit as much as she had.

'Well,' he said, sounding relaxed, 'that seemed to go well.'

'More than well.' I smiled in response. 'I wonder when the feature will be published.'

'Vanessa said she'd keep me informed about that.'

'Did she now?' I beamed.

'She did. And she's going to email us copies of the photos, too.'

Dad had taken Vanessa, along with her camera on a second tour so she could take some photos that didn't include me, while I cleared away the lunch things. I had been relieved that she was the one taking the shots and hadn't turned up with a photographer in tow. I hoped the fact that I was so relaxed in her company would come through in the images.

'And she's asked me to meet her for a drink in Shellcombe,' Dad hesitantly continued. 'She's staying in the area for a few days. I said I might go, but I won't if you don't think I should—'

'Of course, you should,' I cut in, feeling delighted. 'Vanessa is wonderful. I think it would be great if the two of you went out.'

'It's only a drink,' he said shyly, but I knew it was more than that. It was a milestone. Dad hadn't so much as looked at another woman since we'd lost Mum and he'd never got back in the habit of going down to the pub either. 'As long as you're sure.'

'It's nothing to do with me,' I was eager to point out, 'but yes, I'm very sure.'

With perfect timing, Kasuku hopped from one perch to another and wolf whistled.

'There you are.' I laughed. 'It's Kasuku approved. You have to go.'

I left Dad mulling over which shirt he should wear on his *just a drink* trip out and walked down to the beach. Flora was still working and I knew I had time to see if Logan was back before we started planning the birthday bash, but what I suddenly craved more than anything else, was a little solitude and peace and quiet.

I headed straight for the rock and squeezed myself out of sight of the kayakers and families with little ones building sandcastles. I sat on the cool, covered ledge and took a few deep breaths.

Had it just been Vanessa's words about my personal investment in the business which had taken me by surprise, I could have properly set my feelings aside. The theory I had come up with – feeling excited about wanting to leave Dad with something to keep him engrossed when I left – was valid, but really, I couldn't now shake off the feeling that there was more to it than that.

The trips out with Logan and subsequent note taking had triggered something new in me. We had visited places and seen things I hadn't bothered with for years and they'd all sparked a reaction. A shockingly affectionate one. I might not have wanted to feel connected to Kittiwake Cove or the surrounding area, but clearly, I was. I was, just like Dad and Flora, somehow melded to the place and its past. All of a sudden, I could appreciate how I had got so caught up with the history of the other countries and cities I visited, that I had completely overlooked what was right on my doorstep.

And then there was the cottage itself. Until very recently, I had viewed it solely as my parents' domain, the place where I had sulked my way through school holidays and then it became the house I had to move into because devastation had struck. My room had been a stopgap to sleep in until I left for somewhere better, but was there anywhere better? The autumn image I had so easily conjured while talking to Vanessa had truly tugged at my heart. No longer filled with heartbreak, the cottage was finally beginning to feel like my home.

I blamed Logan for the shocking change. Had he not talked to me and taken me out, I most likely wouldn't have been experiencing this tumultuous turnaround. My blinkers would still have been in place and my head would have been full of the sights and sounds of the life I had convinced myself I still wanted. Now I discovered, I couldn't be sure what I wanted ...

'Ally!'

I didn't know how long I had been sitting there, but my bum felt numb when I shifted while Flora squeezed her way in next to me.

'Here you are,' she said. 'I've been all over the cottage and garden looking for you. Are you all right?'

'Yes.' I swallowed. 'Just needed some time out.'

'I didn't mean to interrupt,' she apologised.

'You haven't,' I told her. 'Honestly, I'm fine.'

'Your dad said the interview went well.'

'So well, he got a date out of it,' I said, sounding better than I felt.

'I know,' she laughed. 'How cool is that? That's two of us in two days.'

'What?' I frowned.

'Nothing.' She grinned. 'That's not what you're upset about, is it? Your dad and the journalist?'

'No,' I rushed to say, my desire to reassure her of that making me forget her cryptic comment. 'I'm thrilled about that and actually, I'm not upset about anything. I really did just want to chill for a bit.'

'Fair enough,' she said. 'Why don't we head to the pub to talk about the party now if you've finished chilling? Freddie has finished work and can meet us down there, are you up for that?'

'Absolutely,' I enthusiastically agreed. Party planning would be the perfect distraction from my muddled thoughts. 'I just need to go and grab my purse.'

'No, you don't,' Flora smiled, holding up her beloved Lucy and Yak bag. 'I've got mine and I can just about run to buying you a lemonade.'

'Crikey,' I laughed, 'it's my lucky day.'

There was no sign of Freddie at the pub, but when I opened the door to the snug, my heart leapt at the sight of Logan sitting at a table. It then plummeted when I saw the expression he was wearing as he stared morosely at the pint in front of him.

'Ally,' he said, looking up as the door swung shut behind me. I was pleased to see a smile replace his frown. 'I was hoping I'd see you today.'

'You can always come and find me at the cottage,' I reminded him. 'You don't need an invitation to come over, especially now . . .'

My words trailed off as I realised Flora was in earshot and I also noticed that there was another glass on the table.

'Hey Tara,' Flora said brightly as the door opened again and I realised who Logan's drinking companion was. 'I'm going to treat Ally to a lemonade. Can I get you one, too?'

'You are a love.' Tara smiled. 'Thanks, but no. I'm all good. Logan got me a wine. I wouldn't normally be drinking at this time of day, but he looked like he needed some company.'

'Oh,' I said, 'what's up?'

Tara squeezed my arm as she reclaimed the seat opposite him.

'What's up with you more like?' she asked, forgetting whatever Logan's current woes were when she looked at me. 'You look all in.'

'Nice of you to point that out,' said Flora, rolling her eyes.

Sorry,' Tara apologised. 'You just look so knackered, Ally.'

'I am,' I said, flopping down. 'I didn't sleep well and I had an interview with a journalist that has set me thinking.'

'About what?' Flora frowned, sitting next to me. 'Why didn't you say before?'

'Oh, all sorts,' I said, as I ineffectively rolled my shoulders to try to relieve some of the tension that had built up, and feeling guilty for not filling her in before when I was talking about it now.

'Such as?' Logan also asked, sounding world-weary himself.

'Work stuff mostly,' I shrugged, 'and,' I added, looking at him and feeling that familiar tug of desire, 'I've been thinking about the trips out with you, too.'

'The memory makers, you mean,' said Tara, giving me a nudge and pulling my attention away from Logan's luscious face.

'Yes,' I confirmed, 'those . . .'

'Well, what about them?' Tara insisted. 'They're serving their purpose, aren't they?'

Flora looked at me and I wondered if she had an inkling as to what was going on in my head. I didn't think I'd said or done anything to suggest I was having second thoughts about leaving, but Tara had already wondered and Flora was the most intuitive person I'd ever met. And besides, labelling my musings as second thoughts was a bit much. It was just a wobble, nothing more. I was still Team Leave. Definitely Team Leave.

'They're certainly serving a purpose.' I nodded. If I chanted

Team Leave often enough, would I reclaim my position in the squad?

'Something tells me you're not feeling as averse to Dorset as you thought you were, Ally,' Logan said perceptively.

'And something tells me,' Flora added, 'there's something that journalist said that's made you realise that you have a connection to Hollyhock Cottage and the cove, after all.'

'Jeez, you two,' I said as I exhaled, my gaze purposefully avoiding Tara's. 'Would anyone like to apply their sleuthing skills to guessing what new idea for the business I've come up with, too?'

'A new idea?' Flora asked, sounding excited as she bobbed up and down in her seat.

'Oh Ally,' Tara admonished, looking first at Logan and then me, 'you need to keep your eye on the prize. Your dream life is within your grasp. A good word from me and it could be even closer than that.'

'I know,' I said, running a hand through my hair and feeling further conflicted, 'and I appreciate that, Tara, I really do—'

'Life in beautiful Barcelona,' she dreamily carried on, 'a life that your friends who love you and want you to be happy, have helped you to finally embrace.'

'I know I came up with the manager idea,' Flora said, looking intently at me, 'but if you've changed your mind—'

'She hasn't changed her mind.' Tara laughed. 'She's just got a bit distracted this summer, that's all. The handsome guest has thrown her a curveball.'

Could Logan's presence alone really explain away what I was currently feeling?

'Oh, don't blame, Logan,' I said, rushing to his defence and realising that we still hadn't talked about why Tara had thought he needed company. 'I'm the one who has started talking myself in and out of this decision.'

'You need to talk yourself squarely back in,' Tara said firmly.

'You're very keen to see Ally take on this new life, Tara,' said Flora. 'Why is that?'

'Because,' she said, sincerely, 'largely as a result of what happened the year we left school, I hate to see wasted potential and dreams cast aside. No one else knows this, but when my family left Shellcombe, my father was a broken man. His business had folded and he'd been declared bankrupt. I honestly thought the stress of it was going to give him a stroke or a heart attack.'

'Oh Tara,' Flora gasped.

'We were left with nothing.' She sniffed. 'And it took Dad years to start again, but now he's a huge success. I suppose, seeing him go through that and overcoming the odds has left me wanting to see everyone succeed. Whether we have big dreams or small ones, we should all be striving to make them come true.'

I could understand that and given the sympathetic look on Flora's face, I could tell that she got it, too.

'Your dreams are pretty straightforward Ally,' Tara said to me, clearly not wanting to elaborate on what her family had gone through, 'and achievable too. So don't give up on them. Your dad's a good man.' Little did she know it, but she was echoing exactly what Logan had said. 'He'll understand why you have to go. He'd most likely hate it if you didn't. You can't give up now.'

'You're right,' I said, as the original pattern in my kaleidoscope of dreams shifted back into its familiar place. 'I need to get back on track.'

'Yes,' said Tara. 'That's more like it. And quash the "I heart Dorset" vibes, too, otherwise your dad will be in for an even bigger shock when you tell him you're leaving.'

Having seen his reaction to my talking to Vanessa about Beatrice and the history of the cove, I'd already picked up on that, so I knew she was right.

'I know.' I agreed, then turned to Logan. 'I'm sorry Logan, but I think we'd better stop going on our trips. For a little while at least.'

It would make seeing him without anyone catching on difficult, but needs must if I didn't want to become further muddled.

'Well, that won't be an issue now, will it?' Tara said, her head sympathetically tilted to one side.

'No,' he gruffly said. 'I guess not.'

'Why?' I frowned. 'What's going on?'

'I've got to leave the cove for a bit,' he said devastatingly.

No wonder he'd looked glum when we arrived and had been in need of company.

'But why?' I swallowed, hating the thought of him not being around.

'There's a complication with my uncle's estate,' he sighed, 'and I need to be on hand in person to fix it. Being available will hopefully get it sorted sooner. Unfortunately, the solicitor dealing with it isn't local, which is nonsensical, really.'

'You're right,' I agreed. 'That is ridiculous. So, when will you be back?'

'I can't say for certain.' He shrugged. 'But I'll keep you posted.'

'When will you be leaving?' Flora asked, her eyes on me.

'Tonight,' he said. 'I should be packing now, really.'

'Tonight,' I echoed.

'I hope you'll be back for my party,' Flora said kindly.

'Our party,' said Freddie, making me jump.

'I was wondering where you'd got to,' said Flora, hitching her chair over to make room for her twin.

'I got caught up,' he said. 'Can I get anyone a drink? Aren't you and Flora drinking?'

'I was going to get us lemonade,' said Flora, 'but I got sidetracked.'

'Pints then?' Freddie offered.

'Yes, please,' I said. 'But I've come out without my purse, so I won't be able to reciprocate.'

'You can be in my debt.' He winked. 'Anyone else?'

'Not me,' said Logan, pushing away his drink and standing up. 'But thanks. I need to get off. Duty calls.'

'I'll see you off,' I said.

'No,' he said, giving me a sad smile. 'You stay. I'll have a quick word with your dad at the cottage, then I'll message you when I know more.'

'We can make plans for the party later,' I said. 'I don't mind walking back with you.'

'It's fine.' He nodded. 'I'll see you all soon.'

'You better,' added Flora, as he left.

I couldn't think of anything else to say.

I knew I wasn't the best company after Logan left and Flora had filled her brother in about his departure, and the looks Tara kept throwing my way were doing nothing to lift my spirits.

'Don't worry,' she said conspiratorially, when Freddie had gone to the bar again. 'Logan will be back soon and, in the meantime, use his absence as an opportunity to refocus.'

'I don't know why you think I have an issue with him going,' I snapped, as I began to wonder at the wisdom of embracing her return to the county. 'I'm fine.'

'Are you and Logan an item, Ally?' asked Freddie, who had just returned from the bar with uncanny timing.

'No,' Flora and I said in unison, making him flinch.

'Oh,' he said, realising he'd hit a nerve. 'Sorry. I just came back to ask what you wanted again. I'd forgotten. Was it wine or a pint?'

'It was a pint,' I said, more calmly. 'Thank you.'

When he came back from the bar, he wasn't alone.

'Mind if I join you?' Joe asked.

'I've no objection,' said Tara.

'And you won't hear any complaints from me,' I commented, pleased to have everyone's attention diverted elsewhere.

Flora didn't say anything, but budged along the bench she was now sitting on, so Joe could sit next to her. I willed her to look at me, but she wouldn't.

'Hey Ally, Freddie mentioned that you might need something to take your mind off . . .' Joe began and Freddie, sitting on his other side, dug him sharply in the ribs. 'That is to say, if you've got a bit of spare time on your hands, Mary could do with another volunteer on the carnival committee.'

The Kittiwake Cove carnival was small fry compared with the summer celebration in Shellcombe. The large town went all out and had a procession of sea-themed floats and fancy-dress competitions, crabbing contests and even a firework finale. The cove opted for a more cultured itinerary, but I knew it still took quite a lot of organising.

'Nothing too time consuming,' Freddie elaborated, taking up the cause, 'but enough to stop you pining for . . .'

Flora leant forward, threw him a look and his words trailed off.

'With the business to run and this birthday party to organise,' Tara reeled off, looking at the twins, 'I think Ally has enough to do, don't you?'

'Er, thanks, Tara,' I said, 'but I can speak and decide for myself. I don't need you accounting for the little free time I have. I'm more than capable of organising that.'

Given how everyone stared at their drinks and no one said a word, I knew I'd been a bit blunt, but I was getting fed up with her bossiness. Wanting to see me fulfil my potential and offering to put in a good word with her friend in Barcelona was one thing, but taking over my itinerary was a step too far.

'Let's have a look at this party list then,' I said, holding out my hand for the piece of paper Flora was fiddling with. 'This doesn't look too tricky. It won't take long to sort out.'

'As long as the weather behaves,' said Flora, absent-mindedly chewing the end of the pen she'd been writing with. 'It won't be much of a garden party if it's pissing down.'

'It won't rain,' I declared, with as much authority as I could muster. 'It wouldn't dare. You know, we've got a lot of this planned out already.'

'I'm looking forward to helping Geoff with the catering,' Joe smiled. 'The food is going to be fantastic.'

I had been amazed that Flora had given the green light for that coalition to go ahead, but looking at the pair of them now,

I realised that they were on a far friendlier footing than they had been for years. In which case, I supposed I should stop snapping at Tara. Given that she was the one who'd paved the way for the reconciliation, I should rein my sudden impatience with her in a bit.

'I'm still not sure we'll fit a bouncy castle on the back lawn though,' Freddie said thoughtfully and Tara looked shocked.

Clearly, her idea of a garden party didn't match the twins', who were still both definitely kids at heart. I made a mental note to get her on the castle, if only for a couple of bounces and the mischievous look Flora gave me, suggested she was thinking the same thing.

'Have you found Mary a new recruit then, Joe?' Michael, the landlord, asked as he did a quick sweep of the snug and collected a few glasses.

'New recruit or victim?' Flora asked, waggling her eyebrows.

'Potato, potahto.' Michael grinned, clanking the empty glasses together.

'Yes, he has,' I said, throwing my hat in the ring. 'It's me, if that's all right.'

Volunteering would hopefully serve a double purpose. It would be distracting to have something else to think about while Logan was away and helping out would doubtless drive me so crazy, I would be itching to leave the cove by the end of the season.

'Oh right,' said Michael, sounding gobsmacked. 'Cheers, Ally. She'll be made up.'

Everyone else looked surprised, too.

'I didn't really expect you to say yes,' said Freddie, as he got up and headed back to the bar with Joe.

'I hope you won't end up regretting that decision,' Tara said warily.

'I won't.' I told her. 'Getting caught up in the squabbles of the carnival committee will drive me crackers, but as a result, I'll be packing my bags at the first available opportunity.'

Flora nodded in agreement.

'That's as may be,' Tara said lightly, 'but I would imagine your dad will have a different take on it, won't he?'

'He will?'

'Yes,' she said. 'Going from carnival champion to cove deserter is bound to be a blow, isn't it?' she shrugged. 'I thought you were going to wind in this potential new love for the place you seem to think you're feeling?'

'Oh, bugger,' Flora muttered.

Tara was right. In trying to find a way to stop myself from clock watching until Logan's return, I'd just steamrollered right over my previous conviction, and Tara's suggestion, to play down my sudden fond feelings for Kittiwake Cove.

'Bugger indeed,' I echoed, but with no desire to rush off and tell Michael I'd changed my mind.

# Chapter 23

I was feeling genuinely gutted that Logan had been called away just as we had nudged our relationship from friends back to almost lovers and went out of my way to fill what little spare time I had in the hope of supressing the upset. However, even though I was keeping busy with the intention of occupying my mind, my call to action ended up being responsible for a whole lot more than that.

Having offered to help with the carnival planning and, as I had pointed out in the pub, I fully expected to feel frustrated by the endless lists and petty details, but the sensation of irritation hadn't landed.

The meetings had come thick and fast, but none lasted long and they were surprisingly fun. A few times, I had been assigned the role of gofer and had to visit other parts of the county to collect supplies and equipment. I was also tasked with running off the posters and flyers at the print shop in Shellcombe and untangling metres and metres of jumbled bunting.

As a result, I ended up feeling further connected to the area, rather than desperate to leave it behind and I had also added notes about the history of the celebration to those I'd already made about Beatrice. The notebook that I had taken up after Logan had suggested I write things down was filling up fast. The countryside and villages I drove through were beautiful and the trips gave me the opportunity to admire the age of some of the cottages. Ultimately, my good deeds made me feel more a part of the cove community than I ever had.

The fact that the carnival meetings were held in the pub was no hardship either. A walk down to The Ship was an evening better spent than moping about at home, pining, as Freddie had so annoyingly put it, for my absent and frustratingly silent beau.

My involvement with everything had gone some way to stop me missing Logan, who hadn't called in the two weeks he'd been gone or responded to any of my messages, but it had further confused my thoughts about whether I now wanted to leave and, as Tara had warned it might, it also looked to Dad like I was immersed in the Kittiwake Cove summer events calendar and loving it. I could see it was a disaster for the Team Leave project.

As the days passed and Logan's continued silence lengthened, I began to wonder if he had prescribed me a dose of my own medicine. I could appreciate that he needed to focus on the issue with his uncle's estate, but a message would only take seconds to type and send. I had taken him at his word when he said he had forgiven me for abandoning him in Barcelona, but had I been naïve to do so? Was his treatment of me some kind of revenge, or was entertaining that idea doing him a disservice?

Comparing his absence to my disappearance over a pint in the pub one evening, I finally came to the conclusion that his actions were actually worse. When I had left him, we had barely known one another, but since his arrival in the cove, our relationship had both strengthened and deepened. Or so I had thought. We'd shared our stories and secrets, but none of that seemed to make a difference when it came to him keeping me in his life's loop.

The summer that had so recently been gearing up to be the best ever was practically now beyond saving. Not only had I fallen in love with the cottage and the cove right when I wasn't supposed to want either, I was also ironically in love with a man I wanted very much, but who had completely disappeared.

'Any messages?' I asked Dad when I returned from my swim early on the Saturday morning the weekend of Flora and Freddie's party.

I had carried on with the daily dip Logan and I had briefly got going, but funnily enough, Tara hadn't turned up once and I guessed that Flora had been right about her motives.

'We've had a couple of cancellations,' Dad told me, sounding disappointed.

'What, for this weekend?' I asked, echoing his tone.

The two-day workshop was seaside-themed embroidery and appliqué and always one of the quickest to sell out.

'Yes,' said Dad. 'Angela Price and her daughter, Alice.'

'Oh no,' I said, instantly recognising the names because they were regular guests. 'I hope they're okay.'

'Alice's toddler has chicken pox,' Dad informed me, 'and as Angela doesn't drive, she can't get here.'

'That's such a shame. Have you tried anyone on the waiting list?'

I had set it up soon after we'd discussed it and all the workshops had at least a couple of people hoping to fill any spots that might become available.

'It's too short notice for most of the people I've tried so far,' said Dad, holding up the notepad he was jotting responses on. 'There's one woman who can get here this afternoon, but I said I'd talk to Meredith and everyone else on the list first and then get back to her.'

Meredith was the tutor and I wasn't sure how she'd feel about someone joining partway through the day. If she was teaching basics and the guest was a beginner, she'd ideally need to be present from the off to get the most out of it.

'What about Vanessa?' I suggested, as another off-season idea for the business unexpectedly popped into my head. 'She's still nearby, isn't she? She must be if she's coming to the party tomorrow.'

Vanessa and Dad had been out a few times since that first drink and Flora had been keen for Dad to invite her to the birthday party. I had tried to ask him how things were going with her, but he was playing his cards close to his chest. I hoped it wasn't because he felt awkward talking to me about the new woman in his life, because I genuinely didn't mind. If anything, it was a comfort and if Mum could have communicated from beyond the grave, I know she would have felt the same.

'Yes,' said Dad. 'She is. I'm not sure if embroidery is her thing, but if no one else on the list can make it, I suppose I could ask her, couldn't I?'

'Definitely,' I said. 'And if she says yes, I'll set up the spare bedroom so she can stay in the cottage rather than the court-yard. I could nab the flowers and welcome basket from the room over there to make it extra special for her.'

I didn't know if she had already submitted the feature about us, but if she hadn't, some firsthand experience of one of the courses could only enhance what she had to say and I hoped my suggestion that she should stay in the cottage would help Dad to realise that I already considered her to be a part of our family.

'That would be lovely,' said Dad, sounding pleased. 'I'll get on with ringing around.'

By the time I'd showered, everything was arranged. Vanessa was on her way, so I could get on with preparing her room, but sadly the other spot was unfilled. The woman, who had considered taking it just for the afternoon, had called to say she had changed her mind before Dad had spoken to Meredith and no one else was available.

'Why don't you do it?' Dad suggested, having checked again that there was no one else available.

'Me?' I laughed as I got the kitchen ready to receive the guests for coffee and pastries after I'd shown them to their rooms.

'Why not?' He smiled. 'You never get the chance to take part.'

'Because I haven't got a creative bone in my body,' I reminded him. 'Not for crafts, anyway. I'd most likely sew my work to my skirt.'

'That's exactly what Vanessa said she'll end up doing.' Dad chuckled. 'She's not a skilled sewer either. It might be nice if the two of you had more time to talk.' I stopped arranging the mugs and looked at him. 'I'd like you to get to know each other better.'

His words suggested that he had started to take on board what I had been discreetly trying to get across and I was delighted. The flush on his face confirmed that there was a burgeoning romance poised to blossom right under my nose. At least one of us was going to enjoy a summer of love!

'In that case,' I smiled, thinking what a wonderful turn Dad's life had taken since Vanessa had offered us the interview, 'sign me up.'

Dad gave me a hug and I felt a lump form in my throat as my spirits lifted and a deep rush of relief coursed through me. Until that moment, I hadn't really taken on board that I still hadn't got my fears about him being lonely as under control as I had previously thought, and when I thought about it further, I was still harbouring the same anxiety about his physical health, too. Even though I hadn't realised it, I had been surreptitiously concerned about both.

Knowing he now had Vanessa in his life was a huge boost to Team Leave and I felt the pendulum once again swing away from Kittiwake Cove and towards Barcelona. Given my recently increased attachment to both the cottage and the county, it was a surprise to feel excited about going again, but I suddenly did. My new found passion for the area would make it even more of a treat to come back to, rather than to live with every day, wouldn't it? Yes, of course, it would ...

'Perfect,' said Dad, looking a little misty-eyed himself as he let me go. 'Now, let's get on. The guests will be arriving any minute.'

By the time I had welcomed everyone and filled Meredith in on the attendance changes, I was feeling more excited about taking part, even if I was going to show myself up as an incompetent crafter. Experiencing the workshop as a participant rather than organiser was going to be interesting and I hoped the newest idea I'd dreamt up was going to prove as popular as the regular events, too.

So many of the local attendees, and even the tutors

themselves, said how wonderful it was to come together to sew and make and that it was a shame there was little opportunity to find a venue to do it in on a regular basis with their own projects, especially during the winter months.

What I was considering was a weekly creative supper club where those who lived close enough to make it practical, could bring their projects and enjoy a communal meal during the darker months. Ultimately, it would be down to Dad to decide whether it should happen as he would be the one cooking the suppers, but I had a feeling he'd be on board. With less to do outside from late autumn onwards, he often turned to the kitchen during the evenings when he'd exhausted his seed catalogues and cooked and baked far more than we could sensibly eat.

'Come in, come in,' I said to Vanessa, who I found lingering on the doorstep. 'You should know to just walk in by now.'

She looked a little apprehensive, but whether that was because she was about to try her hand at a new skill or because she was staying overnight in the cottage, I couldn't tell.

'Are you sure you don't mind me staying?' she asked. 'It seems a bit of an imposition, especially as I'll be in the house rather than the courtyard.'

It was the sleepover.

'Not at all,' I told her. 'It was actually my idea and to be honest, you're making my life easier because the spare bedroom will take me less time to turnaround than the courtyard room.'

I wasn't sure the part about the turnaround time was strictly true, but it seemed to make her feel better and that was what I had been aiming for.

'Oh well,' she smiled, 'in that case.'

With just a couple of minutes to spare, I showed her to the

room, which she loved, and poured her a coffee while she selected a pastry from the few that were left. I then took my seat at the table and tried to supress a smile while she and Dad exchanged a chaste and speedy kiss hello.

'Mine still looks like a phallus,' sighed Vanessa, leaning across to see if I was making any better progress later that day.

The woman on her other side laughed.

'And mine is still a bit Leaning Tower of Pisa,' I acknowledged, turning the fabric so the lighthouse I was attempting to create stood straight. It didn't work though because that made the rocks it was perched on all the wrong angle.

'I can see what you mean,' said Meredith, looking at Vanessa's attempt, 'it's because you've made the top so round, that's what's done it.'

Vanessa held her work up so everyone around the table could have a giggle and I liked her all the more for that.

'That reminds me of my Simon,' said the woman opposite, making us laugh all the harder.

Ordinarily I would have helped with setting up and serving lunch, but Vanessa insisted she would do it that day. I was inclined to protest, but as I watched her and Dad working effortlessly around each other, I held back. They had the makings of a well-oiled machine and Kasuku's manners, whenever Vanessa was around, were impeccable, which was a wonderful bonus.

'I told you there was enough room, didn't I?' Flora shouted to her brother who was standing with his hands on his hips at the other end of the lawn late on Sunday afternoon.

I was pleased the course guests had left because the dynamic

duo were already hyped up and very vocal and the party's official start time was still a way off yet.

'I thought we'd decided on the blue one!' Freddie loudly
shouted back.

'Had we?' Flora shrugged, looking up at the pink and silver
turreted creation with a look of love in her eyes. 'You coming
on?' she asked me as she kicked off her shoes.

'Not yet,' I said, trying to instil a modicum of calm. 'I'm
still helping Dad.'

'I don't think he needs your help,' she said, jumping on and
immediately starting to bounce. 'Between him and Vanessa,
they've got it all covered, haven't they?'

'Probably,' I said happily, 'but I will just check. Tara's on her
way. I'm sure she'll bounce with you.'

'Yeah right,' Flora laughed, then stopped to hiccup.

'Don't you throw up on there,' I warned her as I walked
away. 'The clean-up fees are astronomical.'

As well as baking a ginormous cake, the buffet and hire of
the castle had been mine and Dad's gift, so having read through
the small print; I knew what I was talking about.

'Ally,' called Vanessa, beckoning me towards the kitchen.
'Can I have a word?'

I hoped she'd found something for me to do. Keeping busy
with the food prep and blowing up balloons had helped to keep
my mind off the fact that Logan was a no-show. It wasn't until
that morning that I realised I'd been pinning my hopes on him
turning up for the party, in spite of the fact that I had no reason
to believe he would.

'What's wrong?' I asked Vanessa when I was close enough to
see that she looked worried.

'Nothing, I hope,' she said, screwing a tea towel tightly up in her hands. 'I just . . . well, I just wanted to ask if you think I'm overstepping?' She sounded wretched. 'This was your mum's home and I know how much she loved it and now I suddenly seem to be installed in it. It's just dawned on me how quickly it all seems to be happening.'

'It is happening fast—' I began to say, but she rushed on, looking even more concerned.

'And during our interview you talked so much about the influence your mum had on this place and how it still really feels like *her* home—'

'And *you* pointed out that given my colossal input since Mum's death, the cottage is *my* home, too,' I reminded her, as I gently removed the tea towel from her suffocating grasp. 'And you're extremely welcome in it, Vanessa. I haven't seen Dad looking this happy in years. You're not overstepping at all.'

'So, you really don't mind?'

'I really don't mind,' I said, giving her a hug. 'You fit here.'

'I do?'

'You definitely do.'

Vanessa and Mum were very different, but I knew Vanessa was a woman Mum would have been friends with.

'Okay,' Vanessa said, letting out a long breath and sounding reassured. 'Thank you, Ally. Thank you so much.'

'Thank *you*,' I echoed, with emphasis.

Vanessa's presence was going to help smooth the ripples my departure would leave in its wake, and I was, perhaps selfishly, grateful for that. It was another win for Team Leave, and for Dad too, because Vanessa was truly wonderful.

After her dire warnings, I couldn't wait to tell Tara that

everything was back on track. She would be as thrilled as I was and she'd have no further excuse to try to boss me around. Not that she had overstepped since I'd bitten back in the pub. She wasn't exactly as meek as a lamb, but my standing up to her had definitely made an impression.

'Well, you've made my day.' Vanessa beamed. 'I feel the need to celebrate. A turn on the bouncy castle should do it. Is Flora on there yet?'

'She is.'

'Good,' she said. 'I couldn't beat the birthday girl to it, but I've been dying to have a go. Are you coming?'

'In a bit,' I promised.

I watched her go, then checked again that there was enough food to feed the hungry hoards.

'Where's Vanessa gone?' asked Dad, who rushed in from the pantry carrying the huge cake in a box.

'To join Flora on the bouncy castle,' I took pleasure in telling him.

'That woman,' he laughed.

'That woman indeed,' I agreed. 'She's a breath of fresh air, isn't she?'

Dad put the box down.

'She is,' he said. 'I don't think I realised how much I needed someone to come along and help me blow the cobwebs away until she turned up.'

'You and me both,' I said, thinking of my own experience when it was at its happiest, as well as his.

'I'm sorry about Logan,' Dad said, sounding upset as he reached for a packet of brightly coloured candles.

'It's fine.' I shrugged, playing it cool. 'Friends come and go, don't they? And besides, I'm sure he'll be back soon. If only to collect his stuff.'

Dad fiddled about with the candle box and tutted when he tore the lid.

'What is it?' I asked, knowing there was something more than torn cardboard on his mind. 'Has he been in touch?'

'No.'

'What then?'

He let out a long breath, clearly regretting bringing Logan up.

'Dad,' I warned.

'I daresay it's nothing,' he mumbled, 'but I thought I'd see if I could get a message to him via the solicitor's firm he told me was dealing with his uncle's estate . . .'

'And?'

'And,' he said, putting down the box, 'it's the oddest thing, but the firm doesn't seem to exist. I guess I must have misheard the name or something.'

A clanking of bottles in the hall cut the conversation off before I had time to comment.

'Any chance of a hand?' Tara shouted.

'I'll go,' I offered, thinking it would be the ideal opportunity to tell her I was back on the Team Leave path. 'We'll talk more about this later, Dad.'

The thought that Logan might have lied about the name of the solicitor he was working with wasn't a pleasant one, but then, as Dad had said, he might have misheard. For the moment, I resolved to forget all about it. It was my best friend's birthday party and I wasn't going to let anything spoil that.

*

Half a flute from each of the bottles of champagne Tara had turned up with to celebrate Flora and Freddie's birthday helped to dull the ache that Logan's non-appearance and potential deception had caused, despite my determination to ignore it.

'Are you having a good party?' I asked Freddie, over the sound of the Spotify playlist that was currently pumping out 'Delilah' by Fred Again.

'The best!' he shouted, as we watched everyone on the castle bouncing in time with the music, our heads also bobbing along.

I would have gone on again myself, but having told Flora about the cost of sanitising the inflatable party palace, I didn't want to show myself up. Or land myself with a bill.

'Where's Flora?' I asked. I was supposed to be rounding them both up so Dad could present them with his confectionary creation while we all sang happy birthday.

'I'm not sure.' Freddie frowned. 'She was leaping about on there like a loon a minute ago.'

We looked around and the sound of raised voices near the cottage, during a brief lull in the music, met our ears.

'What the hell?' Freddie muttered.

We rushed along the path, but both stopped dead when faced with the sight in front of us.

'They definitely weren't invited, were they?' I said to Freddie.

'No,' he said, his fists balling at the sight of Joe trying to hold back not only Freddie and Flora's parents, but their three thuggish brothers as well.

'I'm not going to keep asking you nicely,' Joe said, his usual good humour sounding strained. 'You need to leave. You're not ruining this for Freddie or Flora.'

'Come on,' I said, grabbing Freddie's sleeve. 'They look set to pummel him.'

I had to admire Joe's bravery. He wasn't a small guy by any means, but each of the brothers were easily as wide as the proverbial brick restroom.

'What are you doing here?' Freddie shouted at his family, his jaw clenched.

'We heard about the party and wanted to celebrate with you and Flora,' said his mum.

'Well, that's a first,' Freddie snarled.

'Our invitation must have got lost in the post,' said his dad.

'Or has she forgotten us now she's fallen on her feet,' one of the brothers said nastily, as they all looked around. He then pointed at Freddie. 'Just like you have now you've moved out, too.'

'Flora and Freddie were both trying to forget you lot long before they moved out,' I said, taking an instant step back as they all took one closer to me.

Freddie and Joe moved to stand in front of me.

'You need to leave,' Joe said again, sounding even fiercer than before. 'You've made Flora's life a misery in the past and I love her too much to let it keep happening now.'

Freddie turned and looked at me, wide-eyed, and his parents looked shocked, too. The brothers, however, sneered and jeered.

'You made her pretty miserable yourself, Joe,' one of them taunted, 'or have you forgotten that?'

'That's all sorted now,' said Joe, pulling his shoulders back and squaring up to the mouthiest of the trio.

'So, how do you propose to stop us joining in?' shouted

another, rolling his shoulders and sticking out his elbows in an attempt to look even wider.

I was starting to think things were about to take an even nastier turn than just a bit of back and forth baiting banter.

'With this,' announced Flora, who suddenly appeared from around the side of the cottage with Dad's power hose in her hands.

'You moron!' shouted one of the brothers.

'She wouldn't, would she?' I gasped at Freddie.

'I think she might.' He grinned.

'You wouldn't dare,' their mother said bolshily, as she rolled her eyes. 'Not if you know what's good for you. You haven't got the—'

'Turn it on, Geoff!' Flora yelled and Dad obliged.

There was a heart-stopping second of silence and stillness and then an arc of freezing water burst out of the end of the hose, instantly soaking all five of the uninvited guests.

'Turn it off!' they all yelled as the rest of us cheered and laughed, but Flora was relentless. 'Pack it in!'

Drenched to the skin they turned tail and fled with everyone assembled still cheering and making sure they'd captured the hilarious moment on their phones.

'Right,' said Flora, dropping the hose Dad had turned off again. 'Where's my man?'

She grabbed Joe by the hand and they ran back down the lawn and jumped onto the bouncy castle while the rest of us rushed along in their wake.

'At bloody last!' shouted Freddie, punching the air as his twin sister and his best friend started to kiss with total abandon and without a care that the rest of us could see them. 'At bloody last.'

Just as he said that, the pulsating playlist moved on, 'Loving Arms' struck up and practically everyone else jumped back on to the castle. Flora and Joe stopped kissing and when Flora looked down at me, her expression was rapturous. Years of hurt had just been healed, and not all of them were about teenage heartbreak.

'You did this,' said Freddie, pointing at Tara.

'I did some of it,' she conceded, clapping her hands. 'Geoff was the one with the hose.'

We all laughed at that. I still couldn't really believe what had just happened and wondered if it was Joe's chivalry in defending her honour and long-desired birthday party that had pulled down Flora's final defences or had he already broken through the barricade before that?

'It's brilliant,' said Freddie. 'I need another drink. Where's the rest of that champagne?'

'Come with me,' said Tara, beckoning him away.

'I think I'll go and help Dad with the cake,' I said, but they couldn't hear me above the music.

When I got to the kitchen, I quickly realised that Dad and Vanessa were kissing in the pantry. Thankfully, neither of them noticed me and I backed away and out of the room undetected. Suddenly it felt like everyone around me was falling in love or, if not in love, then having a romantic moment and, rather than forgetting about Logan's absence and prolonged silence, it was in that moment all I could think about.

I went up to my room and rang his mobile. It was turned off and yet again, the call didn't connect. Had Dad been able to track down the solicitor, I would have given Logan the benefit of the doubt, but as he hadn't, I felt angry and hurt and was left wondering what the hell was going on.

Back in the garden, I discovered Tara had thrown off her former insistence that castles were for kids and was jumping up and down, hanging on to Freddie's arms as if her life depended on it. Freddie had never been her biggest fan and I knew he would regret the extra champagne he'd guzzled in the morning, but in that moment he looked ecstatic.

'Come on!' Joe shouted when he spotted me, but I pretended I hadn't heard.

'I thought they'd be wanting the cake by now,' Dad, who was holding Vanessa's hand, commented as they wandered up.

'They've got more staying power than I have,' Vanessa laughed.

I wasn't sure I believed that. She looked pretty sprightly to me.

'I reckon they're starting to slow down,' I said, looking at Flora who seemed to be starting to flag. 'I'll go and finish getting set up.'

Third time had to be a charm.

'Need a hand?' Vanessa offered.

'No,' I smiled. 'I'm good, but thanks.'

Dad had put the hose away again now it had served its hilarious purpose and the kitchen table was soon crammed with the kind of buffet that would keep kids wired for days. Sickly confectionery, ice cream and jelly, sausages on sticks, bowls of crisps, white bread ham sandwiches and even cheese and pickle tinfoil hedgehogs and it was all going to be washed down with very grown-up cocktails.

'I don't get this,' said Tara, who was the first to join me and look over the packed platters. 'This is all kids stuff.'

'It's supposed to be,' I explained. 'Flora and Freddie asked for the kind of party they'd always dreamed of having when they were growing up.'

'Oh, I see,' she said, looking at the table with fresh eyes. 'Now it makes sense. No wonder Flora was so determined the family weren't going to ruin her and Freddie's big day.'

'And Joe helped, too,' I reminded her, as I shifted piles of paper plates and bowls.

Joe had been braver than the rest of us put together, warding them off single-handed and with nothing but his own bare hands. It had made me see the mild-mannered guy in a fresh light. Not only did I now have the comfort of knowing Dad was going to be in safe hands when I left, Flora was too. Not that she couldn't look after herself, the hose escapade was proof enough of that, but it felt good knowing Joe also had her back.

'That he did,' Tara smiled, before helping herself to a mini sausage on a stick. 'Well, this isn't the kind of party I had when I was a kid, but I was a guest at a few and I can see you've done them proud. So, cheer up,' she added. 'He's not worth moping over, you know.'

'I'm not moping,' I said, frustrated that she'd tugged the conversation around to Logan.

'Believe me,' she continued, 'the last thing you need right now is to be tethered to someone at this monumental point in your life. You're bound to meet loads of new people when you move and if you're already tied to someone else, then you won't feel you can . . . explore all your new options.'

'You do know that Logan and I are just friends, don't you?' I tried to casually say as I surreptitiously checked no one was listening in the doorway. It wasn't strictly true, but we hadn't got much further than that so it wasn't a total lie. 'I'm not tied to anyone.'

'That's all right then,' she said, as I tuned into the sound of people heading up the path. 'Fresh start, clean slate. Just give me the word and I'll contact my pal in Barcelona.'

'Food!' Flora yelled the second she appeared and the throng fell on the spread like a plague of locusts.

'And pass the parcel straight after,' shouted Dad. 'No one's allowed back on the inflatable for at least an hour after eating.'

'Good plan,' said Vanessa, as she soaked up the first spill.

'This is the best party ever,' said Flora, the words slurring as she draped an arm heavily around my shoulder.

'Well,' I couldn't help but laugh, 'you've provided most of the entertainment.'

'They had it coming,' she giggled, then turned serious, 'but I've hardly seen anything of you, Ally. Where have you been?'

Given that she'd been glued to Joe for a lot of the time it was hardly surprising she hadn't spotted me, but I didn't flag that.

'She's been playing hostess, of course,' said Tara. 'But she's ready for some fun now, aren't you, Ally?'

'Oh yes,' I said, downing one of the super-strength cocktails and grimacing. 'I'm ready now.'

# Chapter 24

Everyone came through their post-party hangovers unscathed and the bouncy castle was deflated in as clean a state as it had arrived. During the week that followed, the fabulous celebration and the soaking Flora had gifted her family was all anyone could talk about. Well, almost all anyone could talk about.

The fact that she and Joe were again very much an item after a decade-long hiatus was the hottest topic and the news that Dad and Vanessa had been seen holding hands in the pub came in close behind.

Still, no one had heard from Logan and Dad was all for bagging up the things he had left behind and advertising the apartment as available again. Fortunately, he stood down when Flora reminded him that Logan had already paid to stay the whole summer and there'd be trouble if he turned up and someone else had taken up residence. Not that any of us really believed that he would turn up again now.

'So,' said Tara, when I met her on the beach one evening, 'how long are you expecting the meeting to go on tonight? I'm sick of playing gooseberry to Flora and Joe.'

'No more than an hour,' I told her. 'And as you were the

one who instigated their reconciliation, you only have yourself to blame.'

'I know,' she smiled, 'and I am pleased, really. It's just that now with Logan gone, there's no one else to play with when you're not around. I don't suppose you've heard from him, have you?'

'Nope,' I said, bending to pick up a piece of sea glass. 'Not a word.'

It was a soft green piece and beautifully smooth. I added it to my pocket where it ground against the other pieces I'd stowed there. I kept meaning to add them to the bowlful I had in my room, but I always forgot until I picked the next piece up. As my fingers ran through the collection, I wondered if there might be someone local who would be interested in running a course based around creatively using sea glass. The ideas to extend the business were still coming thick and fast now the dam had been breached.

'Oh well.' Tara shrugged. 'Never mind. At least now, you can focus solely on your departure plans.'

That was proving easier said than done when I was still dreaming up new ideas for the cottage. They weren't filling the entire gap Logan had left, but they were going some way to achieving it. I had hoped communicating with Tara's Spanish contact would help that too, but she'd had trouble getting hold of them, which felt about right, given my current run of luck.

'Hurry this meeting along if you can,' Tara sighed, 'I really do get bored on my lonesome.'

'You could always talk to Freddie,' I suggested.

'I still don't know why you signed up to help with the carnival,' she said, blanking the idea, and I guessed their ease with one another at the party had been alcohol–fuelled and had subsequently worn off. 'It's taking up practically all of your free time now.'

That had been the point, but to pee me off, rather than pull me in. It was still a very fine line.

'Well,' I said, trying to placate her before she turned too bossy again, 'now I know this is going to be my last proper summer in the cove, I want to give something back and it will give me something to think about, should I find myself missing the place.'

Tara harumphed at that.

'There'll be no chance of that, but you should still be careful,' she warned. 'Don't forget how those memory-making trips with Logan turned out. You almost changed your mind about leaving because of them, didn't you?'

'I know what I'm doing, Tara,' I said firmly, even though half the time I felt like Miley on the wrecking ball, swinging between one option and the other. 'I'm counting down the days until the end of the season and looking forward to getting everything underway, so you can back off.'

The more direct approach seemed to finally do the trick and she stood down.

'It's going to be your very own *Eat, Pray, Love* experience,' she said lightly, linking her arm through mine.

'I don't know about that,' I said, releasing myself as we reached the pub and I opened the door. I could get on board with the food and spiritual enlightenment, but I'd had enough of love now to last me a lifetime. 'I'm no Julia Roberts.'

'Who is?' Tara sighed wistfully.

As I had predicted, the meeting was finished within the

hour and it was mostly a repeat of everything we'd discussed in the last one.

'Have you heard there's a storm heading this way?' asked Noah, the oldest and one of the last few fishermen in the cove. 'It's supposed to hit at the weekend.'

I hadn't heard, but given the reactions of everyone else, I guessed they had.

'It won't have any impact on us,' Mary said forthrightly as she closed the meeting. 'Shellcombe maybe, but we're protected by the sweep of the cove, aren't we?'

'That's right,' agreed another committee member. 'We haven't been touched in living memory and this latest threat won't come to anything either.'

Noah jutted out his chin.

'We'll see about that,' he belligerently said. 'I've got a bad feeling.'

'That bit of seaweed hanging outside your back door been having words, has it?' someone else teased.

'All right,' Noah said truculently, standing up. 'We'll see who's laughing this time next week, won't we?'

I watched him stomp away and hoped his morbid foretelling wouldn't amount to anything. Dad would be devastated if the hollyhocks got a battering just as they were reaching their peak.

'All done?' Flora asked, when I joined her, Joe and Tara in the snug.

'Yep,' I said, slapping down the notebook I hadn't added anything to. Unless you counted the sea glass workshop idea I'd been mulling over while everyone else argued over whether two rival ice cream vendors could operate at opposite ends of the cove without falling out. 'All done.'

'Thank God,' said Tara theatrically. 'There's only so much tonsil tennis I can stand being exposed to and this pair have pushed the limit.'

'Hey,' laughed Joe. 'You can't call it tonsil tennis. We're not at school now.'

'Sometimes I wish we were.' Flora said, kissing his whiskery cheek. 'I'd do a few things *very* differently.'

'Me too,' Joe reciprocated, kissing her back.

Tara and I gave each other a look.

'Well,' she said, 'I wouldn't go back. Not for all the Birkin bags in the world.'

That was quite a declaration, but given that she had shared the circumstances surrounding her family's departure from Shellcombe, I shouldn't have been surprised.

'More drinks?' she offered, standing up.

'Yes, please,' Joe and Flora chorused.

'I'll get these,' I offered. 'It must be my turn.'

'I'll come with you,' Tara said, 'anything to get me away from this pair for a minute.'

The bar was packed and for once we had to wait to get served. I wondered if some of Tara's star quality was wearing off now she was practically a regular.

'I know we haven't really talked about it,' I said, while we waited, 'but I am sorry about everything that happened with your dad's business when you lived here.'

'It's all water under the bridge now.' She shrugged. 'He still became a huge success in the end and having made his fortune, he's now ready to retire.'

'Will he sell his business?'

'He better not,' she laughed, running a hand through her

smooth curtain of hair. 'Because I'm hoping he's going to hand it on to me.'

'To you?' I frowned and she turned red. 'Do you work for your dad, Tara?'

'Sort of.' She stalled. 'I'm sure I told you that.'

'No, you didn't,' I said, thinking it was hardly fair that she'd been sniffy about me working with mine when she was doing the same thing, though probably on a vastly different financial scale. 'You said that you worked in property, but not who with. I guess that makes us the same, doesn't it?'

'No,' she said touchily, obviously not liking the comparison. 'It does not. You change beds and empty bins; I deal with properties that are worth millions.'

'Oh right,' I snapped. 'Well, I actually do a hell of a lot more than that, but that's me put in my place, isn't it?'

'Sorry,' she said, pulling on my arm, like a wheedling child. 'I don't know why I put it like that.'

I looked at my arm and she let it go.

'Oh well,' I said, turning back to the bar, 'at least you've just further proved that you really have changed.'

'I have?' she blinked.

'Yes,' I told her. 'You never apologised for anything in the past.'

'That's true,' she said, with a cautious smile. 'And I really am sorry. To be honest, I envy you a bit. There's so much stress involved with my job and if I mess up, there's so much money at stake, too, whereas you—'

'Make beds and empty bins.'

'I do know you do more than that.' She blushed. 'Tonnes more.'

While we waited for Michael to pour our drinks, I mulled over what Tara had said. She'd mentioned stress and high stakes but she didn't look under pressure to me. As far as I could tell she was spending the summer swanning about and had barely mentioned work.

'You heard about this storm?' someone next to me said.

'Yeah, yeah,' said their neighbour. 'I'll believe it when I see it.'

The impending storm – or non-storm depending on your point of view – overtook the birthday party and the twins' family baptism as the hot topic and, as Dad hadn't mentioned it, I thought I would tell him about it when I got back. He could batten down the hatches in the garden then, just in case. I hoped the weather wouldn't impact the weekend. We'd never had to cancel before and even though we had a non-refundable clause, I knew having to instigate it might cause a few issues.

'You coming?' I asked Flora at the end of the night.

Tara had long left. She'd said she was fine, but she'd seemed a bit off since our conversation at the bar.

'Nah,' said Flora. 'Joe wants to check on the smokehouse and I said I'd go with him.'

'Will you be okay walking back on your own?' Joe asked me.

'Yes,' I said, 'I'll be fine, but thanks for asking. I'll see you in the morning, Flora.'

'Night.' She grinned.

It was wonderful to see her so happy and I wondered what might have happened between her and Joe if Tara hadn't messed things up for them at prom.

'Night, Ally,' said Joe.

The cottage was in darkness and I jumped almost as high as

the sitting room ceiling when I went to check the French doors were locked and found Dad sitting in his armchair.

'What are you doing in the dark?' I gasped.

'I hadn't realised it had got dark,' he said, sounding a bit glum, especially considering the romantic upturn his life had recently taken. 'I was just having a bit of a think.'

'Can I put a light on?'

He leaned to the side and turned on the table lamp that was next to his chair. We both blinked while our eyes adjusted to the change in light level.

'What were you thinking about?' I asked him.

There was a glass on the table and a bottle of single malt, which was highly unusual.

'You, mostly, my love,' he said mildly, taking me by surprise.

'Me,' I said, sitting on the sofa. 'Why? What have I done?'

'Done?' Dad smiled. 'Why are you assuming you've done something?'

'Well, have I?'

I was suddenly feeling like a caught-out teenager. I'd never been particularly unruly during those hormone-fuelled years, but I'd had moments of rebellion and they'd all been found out.

'The only thing I've discovered tonight that you've done, Ally, is try to do everything in your power to make me happy,' Dad contemplated, 'and I have to admit, I had wondered on occasion in the past if that might have been the case . . .'

'I don't understand.' I frowned as his words trailed off.

'I thought I was mistaken,' he elaborated, 'but now I know for certain, that you have secured my happiness in this cottage and in the cove at the expense of your own.'

I began to feel light-headed.

'But how can you possibly know that?' I asked, not denying it.

The only people who had known of my discontent were Flora and Tara and I was certain neither of them would have said anything. Then I remembered, Logan knew too.

'Was it Logan?' I therefore asked. 'Has he been in touch and said something?'

'No,' Dad softly said. 'Not Logan. How I found out is irrelevant.'

'Not to me.' I swallowed.

'Nonetheless,' Dad carried on, 'I would like to know the reasons behind your well-intentioned deception, if you feel able to tell me. As well as why my life here in the cottage and the cove is working, but yours isn't.'

Given the shock I had just experienced, I wasn't sure I was capable, but the moment had come and I had to face it, even though it was entirely unexpected and delivered by an unknown hand.

'Well,' I croaked, as I looked around the lovely room Dad and I had created together, 'I suppose the crux of it stems from the complicated relationship I've always had with this place. You know how much I hated coming here during the school holidays when I was growing up.'

Dad nodded at the memory.

'Yes,' he said, 'we went to battle about that a few times, didn't we?'

'And then moving in after the trauma of losing Mum ...' I carried on, but my words faltered and it was some seconds before I could go on. 'Let's just say that, to me, the cottage has always felt like *your* home, yours and Mum's. It's never been the right fit for me and it holds so many difficult and painful memories.'

I realised I was making it sound as though I still felt this way and yet, even though a part of me did, especially where the memories were concerned, I knew there had recently been a positive shift in the cottage's favour.

'I see,' Dad said mildly, entirely without judgement, annoyance or upset.

He was being the good man that Logan and Tara had so recently said he would be when this moment came. It was on the very tip of my tongue to tell him that my feelings had changed, but I stopped myself, knowing that if I did end up leaving, there would be no point.

'And the business plan felt completely like yours and Mum's, too,' I continued instead, 'because it was. But I believed in it and wanted to help you get it up and successfully running, so then I would be able to . . .'

'So then you would be able to what?'

In all the times I'd recently imagined sitting my father down and explaining to him that I wanted to leave the cottage and the cove, I had never once imagined it happening like this. My plan had been to tell him that my decision was a new one, rather than something I'd been biding my time to put into action for years.

I took the deepest breath.

'Leave here and look for a job abroad,' I blurted out in a rush, 'most likely in Barcelona. The sort of job that my time at university and my year working in Spain prepared me for.'

As I said the words, images of the leaflet from the local Historical Society and the notebook I had been filling about Beatrice, the cottage and the carnival, raced through my mind and, in a flash, my brain slid the pieces into a completely perfect new pattern. There was the potential for me to do the same sort of work here, I realised, *and* combine it with all the new plans I'd come up with for the business.

'Well, that sounds like a good idea to me,' Dad said stoically, before I had the chance to say any of what I'd just worked out. 'I've often wondered if you've felt those years studying for qualifications you weren't now using were wasted.'

'Perhaps, but now I think about it, Dad—' I started to say, but he didn't seem to hear me.

'You always gave the appearance of someone who was so content,' he wistfully carried on, 'which is why I set my suspicions aside and never asked if you were truly happy. I regret that, but now things are going to change,' he added briskly, slapping his hands on his knees. 'We'll take on a manager to fill your place,' he declared, really getting into his stride. Obviously, it won't be the same as having you here, but we'll make it work.'

'But, Dad—'

'With Flora here,' he rushed on, 'and Vanessa now, too, you won't need to worry about me. I might have felt a twinge of loneliness in the past, but not now. Winter might be a little on the quiet side, but I'll cope.'

He sounded both determined and delighted that he had come up with the perfect idea to give me exactly what I had let him believe, and what I had thought I wanted.

'What do you think, love?' he asked eagerly.

I desperately wanted to tell him about the festive day courses and the sea glass weekend, the creative supper club and all the other things I'd recently dreamt up, which would help him through the winter, but I didn't because I couldn't bear the thought of me not being the person running them alongside him.

'I think,' I said, not wanting to further disrupt things, given how graciously he'd accepted the situation and come up with an idea, just like Flora had, to allow me to leave, 'that I wish I'd talked to you about my feelings much sooner and that I'm very sorry if you feel deceived.'

'I don't feel deceived,' said Dad, making me cry, 'I feel lucky. Blessed to have a daughter who loves me so much that she's been willing to sacrifice her own happiness in order to secure mine. But now it's time for you to go and find what makes you happy, my darling, and don't even think of trying to say anything different or come up with some excuse not to go, because I won't hear of it.'

'Oh, Dad,' I sobbed as I flew into his arms.

As I clung to him and he held on to me, I realised that it wouldn't matter how I put my change of heart now, he was never going to believe it. He would say I'd come up with it because I thought it was what he wanted to hear and that it wasn't my true heart's desire. Ironically, I could finally see that what I actually wanted was everything I already had, everything, that in just a few brief minutes I'd now given up, and which I had no idea how to get back.

# Chapter 25

After a night spent fruitlessly tossing and turning, I woke to discover that the storm that had been discussed in the pub now looked likely to strike the cove, just as Noah had predicted. Given the swirling maelstrom that already occupied my head and my heart, I took it as a personal affront that the world in which I lived and was trying to anchor myself to, might now be assaulted too.

I desperately wanted to find the words that would enable me to convince Dad that I had had a genuine change of heart and that I hadn't made the turnaround up because I was fretting over leaving him, but the speech just wouldn't form. Therefore, the fact that he wasn't around to talk to was probably no bad thing and Flora wasn't about either.

With the storm warnings now coming thick and fast and sounding more dire by the minute, Dad was out in the garden moving, securing, covering and protecting what he could, and Flora had sent a text to say that she and Joe were heading off for a weekend far inland, where the wind and waves wouldn't reach.

The trip was totally last minute and the result of Flora having no work booked and Joe knowing it would drive him nuts to be in viewing distance of the smokehouse, which was practically on the beach, but unable to do anything to protect it. Tara had also messaged to say that she had taken off, so I was feeling thoroughly abandoned and had no one to talk through what Dad had confronted me with by the time Sebastian, who was tutoring the course that weekend, called.

'Ally, hi,' he said, sounding downhearted, 'it's Seb.'

I knew why he was ringing, because I had just been about to ring him.

'Hey Sebastian,' I said, as I flicked into business mode. 'I was literally just getting ready to call you.'

'We have to cancel, don't we?' he said glumly.

'Yes,' I said. 'Looking at the forecast, we definitely do.'

If the storm landed with the force Noah and now the meteorological society were suggesting, I wasn't going to want the stress of being responsible for the safety of our guests, their cars and belongings. Seeing Dad, Kasuku and myself safely through it was going to be enough to contend with and that was why I had stayed indoors to sort it out.

'Is there any chance we could reschedule?' Sebastian asked hopefully. 'This weekend is such a great earner for me and I nearly always get commissions on the back of it, so it's the kind of gift that keeps on giving throughout the rest of the year.'

'Every weekend until the end of our season is booked,' I told him, having sympathised over the loss of extra income and reminded him that he'd still get his teaching fee thanks to our non-refundable policy. 'But if the guests from this weekend would be willing to rebook, or we could find other attendees from the waiting list, then perhaps we could add it on to the end. I'd have to talk to Dad though,' I hastily added.

Given what had occurred the evening before, I could hardly now carry on making plans and decisions for the business on Dad's behalf. Only if he wanted us to host an extra weekend to accommodate the cancelled course, would we go ahead.

'I'll leave it with you,' Seb gratefully said. 'And you'll let the guests for this weekend know what's happening, won't you?'

'I'm printing off the spreadsheet with their details on as we speak.' I told him, as I clicked the icon on my laptop screen. 'I'll start ringing round right away.'

'I'll let you get on, then. What a nightmare.'

'It's that all right.' I sighed. On a personal level, it couldn't have come at a worse time. I could have done with no storm and the weekend running as planned, purely to occupy my mind. 'Let's catch up again next week,' I suggested, not wanting to end the call on such a miserable note.

'Assuming we're all still here,' Seb groaned, sounding even more maudlin.

'We will be,' I said determinedly. 'We'll be safe as houses.'

Having quickly rushed out to tell Dad that the course was now officially cancelled, I then spent a long morning trying to get hold of everyone who had booked.

A few people had been expecting the call and completely understood, a couple more, who were travelling the furthest, had no idea what was in the offing because they hadn't seen the storm warnings, and one woman was downright rude.

I was almost tempted to hang up on her when she accused me of being a snowflake who was making something out of nothing, but I dug deep and kept my professional persona until she cut the call off and then I had a good swear and moan. Thankfully, guests like her rarely came along.

'Just goes to show,' I said, fiercely striking her name off the list as Dad came in looking grubby and exhausted, 'you can never tell what someone's really like, can you? They might show themselves in one light on the outside, but have something completely different going on underneath . . .'

My words trailed off and my face flushed red. To all intents and purposes, I could have been describing myself. If Dad was thinking the same thing, he thankfully didn't let on.

'Don't tell me,' he said thoughtfully, as he kicked off his boots. 'It was Margo.'

'Yes,' I gasped. 'How did you know that?'

Margo had already attended a couple of weekends with us and I couldn't recall her ever complaining about anything or giving the tutors any grief.

'Just a feeling,' Dad said sagely, as he ran a bowlful of hot water to wash his hands in. 'I've always thought she had a bit of an edge. You ask Flora. She'll say the same.'

It smarted a little that the two of them shared the same opinion when I hadn't picked up on it, but I supposed I should have been delighted that they were on the same wavelength given that they were going to be living together. But what if Flora moved in with Joe, I suddenly panicked. What would happen then? Dad would be left with no one in the cottage. Unless the manager moved in. Perhaps they should be permanently on-site given the courses were residential, but which room would they have? Would they live in the cottage or would the garden apartment be a better option . . .

The room started to shift and I gripped the sides of the table to steady myself as a wave of nausea and anxiety swept over me, making my heart thump. I hated the thought of all the changes that were going to happen if I kept my mouth shut and went along with Flora, and now Dad's plan, which would enable me to leave.

'Look out!' squawked Kasuku, who had seen me starting to list. 'Look out!'

'Ally, love,' said Dad, rushing to dry his hands, 'what is it?'

'I'm okay,' I said, giving him a wobbly smile. 'I'm all right. I've probably just been staring at this screen for too long and didn't eat enough for breakfast,' I blagged, pointing at the laptop I'd barely looked at. 'And I didn't sleep particularly well.'

He put a hand on my shoulder and gave it a squeeze.

'We really need to talk, Dad.'

'I know.' He nodded. 'Because there's so much to organise and we will talk about it, but not now, love. With this storm on the way, it's all I can think about. Shut that thing down,' he said pointing at the laptop, 'and we'll get some lunch and then I want to have one last check outside together to make sure I've done as much as I can to protect the garden.'

He looked worn out already, and I knew I had no choice but to let the Team Leave topic drop. For now, we both needed to focus on the situation directly in front of us.

'It won't be that bad, will it?' I swallowed, the potential impact the storm might have, finally sinking in.

'I daresay it'll be a storm in a teacup,' Dad said with a smile, but I couldn't help thinking he'd gone to a lot of trouble if he really believed that.

The storm hit earlier than predicted as a result of the rapidly strengthening wind that rushed it along. I had thought the siege mentality Dad had started to display might have been a bit over the top, but when the phone line cut out just as I had been about to answer it and then the power gave out, too, I was grateful for the stock of candles and matches, the Thermos and the picnic food that would hopefully see us through.

'I don't think we're in Kansas,' Kasuku muttered, edging first one way along his perch and then the other. 'I don't think we're in Kansas.'

He had been impossible to quieten a good hour before the wind really started to howl and I wondered if he'd got some kind of sixth sense. I knew animals had the ability to sense earthquakes and other natural phenomena and wondered if birds were the same. For all his annoying habits, Kasuku was a clever parrot really.

'I don't think we are either, my old friend,' Dad grimaced as something clattered outside and the rain dashed against the window with such force it sounded as though someone had lobbed a handful of gravel at the glass.

'What do you suppose that was?' I asked, only just resisting the urge to start biting my nails.

'God knows,' said Dad, shaking his head. 'There was nothing left untethered or laying about out there, but given how rough it's starting to sound, I suppose it could have been something blown in from somewhere else.'

'But we're a good distance from anywhere else,' I unnecessarily pointed out.

'I don't think this storm is going to respect boundaries or care about how far it throws things, do you?' He had to raise his voice when he said that as the noise of the wind cranked up a notch and I began to fear for the roof.

A flash of lighting elicited a screech from me and the way

everything lit up I realised just how dark it had turned. It wasn't even close to evening and it was so dark inside the cottage, it felt almost like bedtime. Something else began to rhythmically bang and Dad looked at me and shook his head. After a minute, the sound stopped and I began to feel properly scared.

'Whatever that was has gone for a burton,' Dad commented.

'I wish we had metal shutters like you see on the windows of shops in American films,' I said, sitting in a chair and drawing my knees up to my chest.

'I wish I had a superhero dome of protection around the whole place,' Dad said with a wry smile, 'around the entire cove, but especially over the polytunnel. There won't be anything of it left at this rate.' It started to hail and he groaned. 'What the wind hasn't already shredded, this hail will tear right through.'

'The cover is made of thick stuff though, isn't it?' I said, trying to find an atom of hope for him to cling to, but then the hail began to hammer all the harder.

'Not thick enough to withstand this.' He had to practically shout as he raised his hands and then let them resignedly fall.

'I don't think I'll sleep in the loft tonight,' I said, pulling a fleecy throw around my shoulders.

'Sleep?' Dad laughed. 'I don't think there's going to be much chance of that wherever you lay your head.'

'I suppose not,' I said, as another flash lit up the room and Kasuku squawked and cussed.

He quietened a little when Dad filled his bowl with dried mango pieces and then covered his cage with an extra thick blanket. The sensory reduction of his world seemed to sooth him and Dad and I smiled as we listened to him clucking over his good fortune. The mango was usually strictly rationed.

'We need a distraction too, Ally,' Dad said wisely. 'How about a game of cards?'

'I wouldn't be able to concentrate.'

'Something else then.'

'How about,' I suggested, thinking I might as well grasp the nettle as our options for alternative entertainment were so limited, 'I tell you about some of the new ideas I've had for the business.'

Dad looked surprised.

'New ideas?' he asked. 'You are still thinking about this place then?'

'Of course I am.' I swallowed. 'I'm still invested, Dad.'

More than ever, I wanted to add but didn't, for fear of having to listen to him refute it.

'Well,' he said, looking choked. 'That's grand. Let's hear what you've come up with then.'

I blinked back the tears I could feel prickling my eyes. What I wanted to hear was him telling me how he'd had his former suspicions about my unhappiness confirmed, but that was something else that was going to have to wait. I knew that if I pushed him, he'd shut down completely and I wanted to keep the channel of communication about the cottage and business as open as I could.

'And perhaps you could tell me more about what you have in mind to do when you leave?' he then proposed.

I waved that suggestion away.

'Let's just focus on what I've been thinking about for the

cottage,' I said, hopefully adding, 'If the storm hears what I have to say, it might leave it intact so we can see it through.'

Dad chuckled at that but didn't pick up on the fact that I had said *we* could see it through, rather than him organising it.

'You sound like Flora.' He smiled. 'That's the sort of talk about the universe that I expect her to come out with.'

'Perhaps I've caught a dose of whatever she's got,' I laughed.

'She had the right idea, heading off with Joe, didn't she?' Dad said, pouring coffee from the flask he'd made up earlier as the wind rattled the rafters again.

'Yes,' I agreed, warming my hands around the mug he handed me. I needed the comforting feel of it, more than the heat. 'I hope the smokehouse is still standing. It's been in Joe's family for generations, hasn't it?'

It was another landmark I could add to my notes about the cove.

'It has,' Dad confirmed, as an ominous rumble of thunder began to roll around.

We stopped to listen. It sounded as though it was moving in slow motion and making its way around the entire curve of the cove. The cove, I remembered that someone in the pub had said, never bore the brunt of bad weather. All I could assume now was that this motherload was intent on making up for what the area had missed out on in the past.

'Come on then,' said Dad, when the noise finally petered out. 'Tell me what you've been dreaming up.'

I took my time, stopping when it was impossible to make myself heard above the rumbling din and lashing rain, to fill Dad in on every one of my new ideas. There were the autumn and festive one-day workshops to explain, as well as the weekly creative supper club, the sea glass weekend (assuming we could find someone local to run it) and finally, the possibility of lengthening the season this year to fit in Seb's cancelled course at the end.

Dad didn't interrupt, but listened intently as he took it all in.

'My goodness,' he said, leaning forward and lacing his fingers together on the table in front of him once I'd finished, 'that brain of yours has been in overdrive, Ally.'

'I know.' I smiled, thinking how ironic that was. 'It's taken me by surprise. I didn't think there was anything else we could do here, but then all these new ideas started clamouring for my attention.'

'There's certainly a lot to consider.'

'I don't think any of it would take too much setting up,' I explained. 'The workshops would only last a day and the creative supper club just a few hours, so it should still feel like we've had a proper off-season break.'

'Like *I've* had a proper break, you mean,' Dad corrected, finally picking up on the fact that I was still going we, we, we all the way home. 'And anyway, the new manager could take on most of the planning, couldn't they?'

'Yes.' I swallowed, the words sticking. 'I suppose they could.'

'Well, I think it all sounds wonderful.' Dad beamed, making my chest swell with pride, even though I hated the thought of someone else taking it on. 'And I've been having a bit of a think about some new ideas myself.'

'You have?' I asked, feeling excitement override envy. 'Tell me.'

'I've been wondering if there might be something that I could offer connected to the garden. Perhaps a container planting course as the guests are always commenting on the ones we've got here, or maybe seasonal grow and cook days.'

'Oh Dad,' I gasped, feeling thrilled, 'they both sound wonderful! You've never suggested anything like this before.'

'It was Vanessa who sowed the seed.' He blushed. 'When I gave her the tour the day of the interview, she said I was so enthusiastic about the garden that I'd be a natural, should I ever want to teach about it.'

'Well,' I smiled, 'she's right about that.'

'It would be good to get more out of the garden.' He smiled, then grimaced as the wind picked up and ripped apart something else before sending it flying. 'Assuming there's any garden left after the storm has had its way with it.'

All the time he had been talking about his potential plans, I hadn't noticed the noise of the wind, but now I honed back in and it didn't sound any calmer.

'What's that?' Dad frowned as he picked up another sound, and I cocked my ear to listen.

'I think it's a car,' I shouted, as I rushed into the hall and a flash of headlights momentarily lit up the wall. 'Yes, it is.'

'What, on the drive?' Dad gasped.

'Of course, on the drive,' I called back, although in the air Harry Potter style, wasn't beyond the bounds of possibility, given the circumstances.

I peered out of the window, but the combination of shrubs and climbers blowing wildly from side to side and the rain streaming down the glass made it impossible to make out what the vehicle was or who was in it.

'I think they've gone now,' I called again.

'You come back in here then,' Dad demanded.

The kitchen did feel slightly safer as it was the most central space in the cottage. With the conservatory behind, the sitting room to the left and utility and boot room to the right, the area felt cocooned, but not at all cosy.

'If the wind wasn't blowing straight down the flue, I'd suggest lighting the wood-burner,' said Dad, rubbing his arms.

'It is chilly,' I agreed. 'I'll go and grab us a couple of jumpers.'

'All right, but be quick.'

The noise was worse upstairs, so I grabbed duvets and pillows too, so we could sleep, or at least try to, on the sofas. A quick glance out of the window in my bedroom, which felt as though it was going to be ripped out at any moment, revealed a swirling tempest.

The sea churned and the waves crashed and I shuddered to think that I had been swimming out there just the day before. I wondered what was happening to the pontoon. Another bolt of lightning ripped across the sky, momentarily blinding me, and I rushed back towards the stairs, determined to close all the curtains and block out the terrible sight. We'd just have to endure the noise.

# Chapter 26

It took me a minute the following morning to work out where I was and what had happened. The only noise I could hear was a buzzing in my ears and Kasuku climbing about in his cage. Then I remembered the storm and held my breath waiting for the dreadful cacophony to start again, but it didn't.

The sun was shining and the sitting room, where I was curled up on the sofa, was bathed in the comfortingly familiar summer's morning glow. It was impossible to believe what Hollyhock Cottage had previously been subjected to when everything was now so peaceful and calm.

I closed my eyes and let out a long breath, feeling relieved that it was all over. I had no idea what time I had fallen asleep, so was clueless as to how long it had taken the storm to blow itself out. I twisted around to look at the chair where Dad had finally settled after relentlessly pacing, and found it empty.

'Dad!' I shouted, as I kicked off the duvet I was tangled up in. 'Dad!'

When the storm was raging, I had made him promise that he wouldn't go out without me once it was all over, but he'd obviously broken his word and gone to assess the damage unchaperoned. Still wearing my summer pyjamas, I thrust my feet into my trainers and opened the front door.

'Oh my God,' I gasped, overcome by the sight that greeted me.

The usually clear path around the cottage was blocked and hindered by horticultural carnage. There were smashed hollyhocks, small branches and shredded leaves everywhere. I carefully made my way around the perimeter of the house and miraculously finding nothing more amiss with the cottage than a couple of slipped rooftiles, I set my sights on the garden, which was doubtless where Dad had headed.

It was immediately obvious that the main garden hadn't got off as lightly as the battered plants and pots around the house. There were shredded and ripped up shrubs, their roots exposed, torn larger tree branches and snapped and broken blooms wherever I looked. The beautiful herbaceous border, Dad's newest project, which had this year just come into its own for the first time, was all but flattened. He'd warned me that the damage would be worse than a winter storm would inflict because everything was in full leaf, but I hadn't expected it to be quite so appalling. He would be devastated.

Just as I reached the point where the path forked, I heard a noise in the courtyard and decided I should make a quick detour to check the rest of the buildings. It was a stalling tactic really because the thought of seeing the look on Dad's face was too much. The garden had helped to heal him at a time when little else could reach him and I wasn't sure I could cope with seeing him experience the loss of so much of it.

Trying and failing to swallow away the lump in my throat,

I ducked under the climber-covered, and now part collapsed, arched walkway, and stopped dead in my tracks.

'Logan,' I gasped, as he walked from the garden apartment to his car.

I took a step back and watched as he walked around, taking in the scratches and dents his formerly pristine vehicle was now covered in.

Like so many other moments that had happened this summer, I had played out the occasion of his return dozens of times in my head. I had imagined berating him for not keeping in touch and, since Dad still hadn't been able to track down the solicitor he had said was working for him, angrily demanding to know if he really was in the cove to grieve a dead uncle. A story which now seemed more like fairytale than fact.

However, none of my increasingly accusatory mental confrontations made allowances for my heart to excitedly race, my palms to sweat or my knees to turn weak, so why was I experiencing each and every one of those physical reactions now? He forgave you; my brain annoyingly reminded me, which was no help at all.

'Hey,' was all I could say, once I'd forced my feet to take a step forward again.

Logan jumped and spun around.

'Ally!' he cried. 'Oh, thank God, you're all right. Where's Geoff?'

'I don't know.' I shrugged. 'I haven't seen him yet this morning.'

Logan made a move towards me and I stepped back again.

'I need to go and find him,' I said quickly.

Now I had alerted him to my presence, I wished I hadn't.

I wasn't ready to deal with his unexpected return on top of everything else.

'Just wait,' he pleaded, running a hand through his hair. 'Please, Ally. I have to talk to you. There's something important I need to tell you.'

'I think I've already guessed some of it,' I said sadly, his desire to impart something important the very moment he saw me again, convincing me there was some sort of treachery behind his stay in the cove. 'And the rest will have to wait. You can see for yourself what we're dealing with here this morning.'

'What do you mean you've guessed some it?' Logan frowned, ignoring my reference to the chaos that surrounded us.

I let out a groan and wished I'd carried on looking for Dad rather than taken this detour.

'I've, that is, Dad and I, have worked out that you're not who you have been saying you are,' I told Logan, feeling like a hypocrite because he'd only recently said the same thing to me.

It was Dad's sleuthing that had flagged his trickery up, so Logan needed to know that I hadn't been the only one who had become suspicious.

'And although I still have no idea why you needed to make up a backstory ahead of arriving in Kittiwake Cove,' I further said, 'I'm assuming your dead uncle has never existed, let alone lived in the north of the county.'

Logan's mouth opened and closed, but he didn't refute what I'd deduced and any miniscule lingering doubt that I might have been wrong was carried away on the breeze.

'Your backstory is as much a fabrication as mine was in Barcelona,' I said, aware that the admission meant I couldn't claim the high ground. 'And now, I need to find Dad.'

I marched off thinking that I wasn't sure I would be able to forgive Logan whatever he'd done as readily as he'd previously absolved me, even if he had battled the worst weather Dorset had seen in decades to get here and was now looking full of remorse.

'I'll come with you,' he said. 'I have to talk to both of you.'

'You're going to have to wait—' I started to say, but then I heard Dad shouting and rushed off in the direction his voice had come from, with Logan right behind me.

'Oh Dad!' I gasped at the sight that met us. 'What are you doing in there?'

He was standing in the remains of his treasured polytunnel and looking angrier than I'd ever seen him. His shouting was born of pure frustration and I couldn't blame him. The plastic was shredded and the plants and vegetables were submerged in what looked like a quagmire. There were broken pots everywhere and I could see his trusty old work bench had been smashed, too. There were pieces of it scattered as far as the other side of the garden.

'I shouldn't have skimped on this,' he thundered, throwing up his hands. 'I should have got a proper team in. Had a decent set-up, rather than this Heath-bloody-Robinson monstrosity.'

The tunnel had been constructed by him and a couple of friends from scaffold poles and waterpipes and he had been thrilled with it, but I wasn't about to say that now. Nor was I going to mention the fact that it had kept us fed for years and therefore paid for itself many times over, until the storm to end all others had blown in. I couldn't imagine there was a tunnel on the market, homemade or otherwise, that could have coped with the ferocity of the winds that had ripped through our garden.

'I think you should come out of there, Geoff,' said Logan, as he looked about.

Dad let go of the pole he had been shaking, to prove how unstable the few bits left standing now were.

'Where did you spring from?' he barked, sounding even more annoyed.

'He blew in with the storm last night,' I said, acknowledging it had been Logan's car I had fleetingly seen on the drive. 'Please come out of there, Dad. There's nothing you can do.'

'I'm not sure you're welcome——' Dad started to say, but Logan cut him off.

'I don't care what she's told you,' he desperately said. 'I want you to hear my side of it. I want you both to know everything.'

'You're talking in riddles,' I snapped, rounding on him. 'And I'm nowhere near capable of solving them now. I'll talk to you later, okay?'

'But, Ally——'

'But nothing,' I snarled, really beginning to lose it, as Dad moved further away. 'I was falling in love with you Logan and you left. And that would have been okay if you'd left for the reason you said you had to go for, but you didn't, did you? And then you didn't call or message or anything. How do you think that made me feel?'

'I know exactly how that made you feel,' he shot back.

'Really?' I choked. 'You're going there?'

'Look, I'm sorry,' he said, holding up his hands. 'I told myself a million times that I would never do that.'

'You should have made it a million and one.'

'Fuck, Ally,' he cursed, sounding aggrieved. 'If you knew what it has cost me to come back here . . .'

'A few dents in your car.'

'You're way off,' he said, trying to reach for me. 'And I was falling back in love with you, too, you know.'

'I can't do this now,' I told him again. All I wanted was for him to leave me to deal with one disaster at a time, but he wouldn't let up. 'For pity's sake, Dad,' I yelled, 'will you just get out of there?'

What was it with the men in my life?

'Fine,' Dad shouted and marched back through what remained of the tunnel.

Everything would have been fine if his right foot hadn't snagged on something as he slipped in the mud. Unbalanced, he twisted to right himself, but ended up falling heavily and with a sickening crunch. He let out a scream of pain and Logan and I rushed to reach him.

'Shit,' I said, looking at the angle of Dad's ankle and leg.

'That's putting it mildly.' Dad grimaced, the colour draining from his face.

'Should we move him?' Logan asked me.

'With a potentially broken ankle or leg,' I huffed. 'Hardly.'

'It'll just be a sprain,' said Dad, making to move.

'Stay where you are,' I said loudly, as a shot of pain contorted his features. 'Logan, can you please go back to the cottage where there's usually a mobile signal in the hall and phone for an ambulance?'

'An ambulance?' Dad baulked.

'Yes, Dad,' I said, trying to stay calm. 'You need to go to the hospital and I'm not going to risk moving you. You came down really hard, so you could have hurt more than just your leg.'

Thankfully, there happened to be a paramedic crew in the

area who could attend and by a huge stroke of luck, the lane to the cottage had just been miraculously cleared of the trees that had come down sometime after Logan's arrival. It was a relief to have someone on our side during such a catastrophic morning.

'I'll take you to the hospital,' Logan offered once Dad had been lifted into the ambulance.

The crew had been wonderful, even pretending to moan about the mess the mud Dad was covered in was going to make of their ambulance, to keep his spirits up. He tried to joke along with them, but I could see he was in agony and worse than that, he looked scared, too.

'I can manage,' I told Logan, but I couldn't seem to stop shaking.

'You can't drive like this, can you?' he said sensibly, looking at my hands. 'Please, let me help.'

I quickly showered off the mud and gathered a few things together while Logan fetched his car. The thought of seeing Dad in a hospital bed made me quake, but I knew he would be thinking about everything we'd gone through after Mum died and that galvanised me into action. He was going to need me to be strong. This was not the moment to fall apart, and whatever Logan had to tell us would have to wait.

# Chapter 27

When Flora and Joe arrived back at the cottage Sunday evening, Flora held me tightly in her arms for the longest time and I was grateful for the opportunity to completely let go and succumb to the emotion the events the last few days had triggered.

Dad somehow discovering how unhappy I'd previously been at Hollyhock Cottage had proved traumatic enough, but the storm, the unexpected reappearance of Logan and then Dad's accident, had all but tipped me over an emotional edge I hadn't been on the brink of since losing Mum. Perhaps, it wasn't quite that bad, but it wasn't far off.

'Oh my God, Ally,' Flora cried, when I blurted out what had happened to Dad, the moment she walked through the door. 'Whyever didn't you ring us?'

'I didn't think,' I sobbed, my own tears, which had been so near the surface all day, finally flowing. 'I just focused on deal-ing with what was right in front of me and at the time, that was Dad falling and then looking like death warmed up.'

'Of course,' Flora said, as she tore off reams of kitchen towel and handed me half. 'Thank goodness you were with him and your first aid training kicked in. What exactly has he done?'

I was grateful for that, too. I undertook regular sessions and, in light of the day's events, would be checking my certificate was still up to date.

'Broken his fibula,' I explained, as I took a shuddering breath. My part in the drama had ended hours ago, but having subsequently spent so long at the hospital subjecting myself to all sorts of dark thoughts, I felt exhausted. 'It's a clean break, which is something to be grateful for.'

'That's a sports break, that is,' said Joe, with a wry smile. 'He'll be chuffed about that. He can tell everyone he did it playing football.'

Flora threw him a look.

'It was his stubbornness that caused it,' I corrected and Joe looked contrite. 'And he's lucky he didn't break anything else. He's pretty bruised down his right side, which took the main impact, and his ankle is horribly swollen. He's going to ache all over.'

'I suppose the one small mercy was that he didn't go over on a path,' said Flora. 'The mud might have absorbed some of the impact.'

'The ambulance took quite a lot of the mud, too,' I said, shaking my head, 'and you should see the state of the polytunnel, which is what he was ranting over. The whole thing is a right off and Dad reckons the loss is his own fault because he should have had a professional team in to put one up.'

'Looking at the carnage as we drove back along the coast,' Joe said sensibly, and I wished Dad was with us to hear him, 'a more expensive tunnel wouldn't have fared any better. Is there any damage to the cottage?'

'I've spotted a couple of slipped roof tiles,' I explained, 'but I think that's it. I still need to have a really detailed look around, and in the courtyard, too. The garden and veg patch are completely trashed though and that's what's killing Dad.'

'I know someone who will be able to put the roof tiles back,' Joe said helpfully. 'And I'll go and have a proper scout about outside now to save you having to do it and then I'd better head off. I think Mum and Dad might need a hand at their place. Thankfully nothing major though. They got off lightly compared to some.'

'Thank you, Joe,' I said gratefully, as Flora gave him a kiss. 'As long as you're sure you can spare the time, I'd really appreciate that.'

It was such a relief to pass that responsibility on and to be honest, I was so tired, I probably wouldn't have made a competent job of the recce, should I have had to do it myself. I should also have been feeling relieved that the hospital was keeping Dad in overnight, which meant I didn't have to immediately look after him, but the fact that they were making him stay because they weren't happy with his blood pressure was no comfort at all.

'There's no point doing that, Flora,' I said, as she went to fill the kettle. 'We've still got no power. And no phone line, either.'

'Oh bugger,' she muttered.

'My thoughts exactly,' I agreed.

I wished then that I'd thought to charge my phone at the hospital. The battery was low and without the landline, I was going to be relying on my mobile to check up on Dad.

'Was the smokehouse all right?' I asked Joe, just as he was about to set off and begin his inspection. 'Sorry, I didn't think to ask before.'

'By some miracle,' he said, sounding amazed, 'it was completely untouched.'

Given its proximity to the beach, that was a marvel. Perhaps the storm gods had a fondness for smoked food and had granted the place a pardon.

'Which is more than can be said for pretty much everywhere else we saw on the drive back,' Flora said, as Joe kissed her again and then purposefully strode off. 'I had no idea it was going to be so bad. I never would have left if I had.'

'No one could have predicted what was really going to happen,' I said, slumping down into a chair and shoving my hands into my hair, which I discovered was a total tangle. 'The weather forecast gave us a clue, but what actually occurred was unprecedented.'

'Noah knew,' Flora reminded me, and I dredged up a smile. 'So, what are we going to drink then?' She asked, looking around the kitchen and opening and closing cupboards.

'I've got some bottles of Coke,' said Tara, appearing in the doorway, 'and barbecued seafood skewers, burgers and salad. The power is off for literally miles, but Michael and Mary are cooking up a storm at the pub. No pun intended. They're emptying their fridges to feed the masses and giving everything away.'

Tara's sudden arrival set Kasuku squawking and she stuck her tongue out at him. But I felt a rush of affection for the old bird who, until then, hadn't made the slightest fuss, even though he had been abandoned practically all day.

'Tara,' I said, feeling shaky as I stood up and went over to the cupboard where Kasuku's treats were hidden, 'you're a lifesaver.'

'I try my best,' she beamed, 'you should know that by now.'

Once I'd fed my feathered friend and Flora had filled the table with bread rolls, plates and cutlery, I positively fell on the food. My last square meal felt like days ago and by the time I'd wolfed down more than my share, Flora had filled Tara in on what had happened to Dad. Touchingly, the news seemed to have knocked the wind out of her sails.

'Your poor Dad,' she said, looking genuinely upset.

'And poor me,' I sniffed, while Flora cleared the plates and Tara opened more bottles. 'This has made a total mockery of one of the things I've spent the last few years here trying to avoid.'

'Which is?' Tara asked, handing me a bottle.

I knew there was wine in the pantry and even though I felt more inclined to dive into that, rather than drink more Coke, I didn't succumb, because I wouldn't be able to drive to the hospital should I need to.

'I've never outright told anyone this,' I said, having swigged a mouthful and supressed a burp, 'but one of my biggest reasons for staying here was to . . .'

'Go on,' Flora coaxed, as she sat back down.

'To protect Dad,' I quietly confessed as my cheeks turned pink. 'After losing Mum, I foolishly thought that I could be his guardian angel and that if I was always on-hand to look out for him, then nothing bad could happen.'

'Oh Ally,' Flora sighed, and I wondered if she'd guessed.

'But,' I said emotionally, 'as today has proved, I'm a crap guardian angel, as well as a crap daughter. I was practically standing next to him when he fell and I didn't catch him.'

Had I not been so distracted by Logan's presence, I might have reacted and averted the disaster, but I was too exhausted to bring up his untimely return. Having driven me home, he had dropped me at the cottage and then gone straight on to the courtyard, correctly sensing that I was in no fit state to talk.

'I wasn't here for Mum,' I said, my bottom lip quivering, 'and now I've let Dad down, too. For so long, I've been so scared of losing him in the same way I lost Mum, but this stupid accident has proved to me that even if I'm in his pocket, it won't make any difference as far as keeping him safe is concerned.'

'You can't control everything, Ally,' Flora said kindly. 'The world and the universe aren't set up that way.'

'I know.' I nodded. 'I might just as well have been on the other side of the world, mightn't I? Which reminds me,' I swallowed, looking at them both, 'Dad has given me his blessing to leave Kittiwake Cove.'

'He's what?' Flora frowned as Tara's eyes widened. 'What are you talking about?'

'It's true.' I nodded. 'A couple of nights ago he told me that over the years, he'd had the odd suspicion that I wasn't happy here and then someone confirmed it for him and he said I should go and find whatever it is that will make me happy.'

Flora looked more shocked with every word I uttered and I began to wonder if her blood pressure was any more stable than Dad's.

'He said the same thing as you, Flora,' I carried on. 'That we should take on a manager.'

'I don't believe it,' she muttered.

'And I've suggested a couple of things to do during the closed season, which will help offset the cost of having to pay someone more than the wages I draw,' I further explained.

'But how did he find out?' Flora demanded. 'He didn't get the manager idea from me.'

Her face was flushed and I could tell from her tone how angry she was and how defensive she felt, but she needn't have worried. I'd never for one second thought it had been her who had filled Dad in.

'It was me,' Tara said simply, after a beat. 'I was the person who told your dad how you really feel. And if it's any help, he said he has the best daughter in the world. Not a crap one, Ally, as you just said.'

'What the hell were you thinking?' I gasped, rounding on her. 'What made you think you had the right to say a word to him about any of it?'

'I said it,' she said, looking directly at me, 'because I believe you *both* deserve the right to be happy. I know you told me that you'd made up your mind to go when I first arrived here, but when Logan showed up . . .'

'When Logan showed up what?' Flora joined in.

'He'd barely been here five minutes before Ally was wavering. I could tell you'd all but changed your mind about going after that first trip out with him,' she said to me, 'but I knew that you'd be settling if you stayed. Your dad deserves so much better than that. And so do you. You both deserve to live lives that make you happy.'

I put my hand over my mouth to supress the invective I could feel building.

'So, you genuinely had Ally's best interests at heart?' Flora more calmly asked.

'Of course I did,' Tara responded.

'You weren't trying to drive a wedge between her and Geoff?'

'No.' Tara flushed. 'What the hell?'

'So,' Flora turned to me, 'you are going to leave?'

'I always said I would.' I shrugged, the words catching. 'And having proved I'm no guardian angel, I might as well, mightn't I?'

No one said anything else. Kasuku clucked over his food bowl and the clock on the wall carried on ticking, as I imagined Dad cooking at the stove and the courses carrying on at the cottage without me watching over them. They were painful images.

'Oh my God, Ally,' said Tara having interpreted the look of anguish on my face. 'You really have changed your mind, haven't you?'

Flora's gaze darted between the pair of us.

'Yes,' I said, swallowing over the lump in my throat. 'Yes, I have.'

'But Geoff has said he's happy for you to go,' Tara reminded me. 'That was the whole point of me telling him how miserable you are. He wants you to find your happy.'

'But that's the thing,' I said, looking around. 'I have. All the time I was committed to searching for an escape, meant I missed the moment when the cottage and the cove started to feel like home. I had been so convinced that this place would *never* be for me because of what I had felt for it in the past, that I didn't notice when things started to change.'

It was Logan's arrival that had properly opened my eyes. Though I realised now that I had experienced a slight shift on the journey back from Barcelona. On the drive into the cove, I had assumed my desire to arrive was to block out what I had done, but I could see it for what it really was now. A proper homecoming.

'So, you're not going then?' Flora asked tentatively, looking confused.

'I don't want to,' I told her. 'I really don't. So, no, I'm not.'

I had no idea how I was going to convince Dad that my change of heart was for all the right reasons and not a sop, but I was determined to find a way. At least with his leg in a boot or cast, he'd be a captive audience and would have to listen to what I had to say, once I'd worked out what that was . . .

'Oh, Ally!' Flora gasped, then raced around the table to give me another hug.

I knew she would have been happy for me to go had it been the right thing, but she was more ecstatic to see me stay. Tara watched us, but didn't join in with the celebration.

'Well, you can lead a horse to water,' she said with a sigh. 'This place really means something to you now, doesn't it?'

'It does,' I confirmed. 'The time I spent with Logan, coupled with getting more involved with the community and working out how I can still do the work I love, has helped everything click into place. Not to mention the torture I felt imagining someone else seeing through my new ideas, too.'

We all jumped as the lights came on, the cooker started to bleep and Kasuku screeched.

'Let there be light!' Flora commanded, throwing up her hands as though she was the one responsible for the timely reconnection.

'Oh, thank goodness,' I said happily. 'I can have a shower.'

The one earlier had been purely to wash the mud away.

'Good,' said Flora, 'because you stink.'

'Hey,' I protested. 'It's no wonder. I've had a really stressful day.'

'I have to go,' said Tara.

'Because Ally stinks?' Flora giggled.

'No,' she tutted. 'Because there's something I have to do.'

Flora sat on the bathroom floor while I had my shower.

'What do you reckon Tara's hasty exit was about?' she asked, as I lathered my hair.

'My lack of personal hygiene,' I suggested.

Tara's mood had taken the weirdest of turns once she'd realised I'd found my happy in the cove and she'd ended up leaving practically straightaway and looking rather anguished herself.

'My pungent unwashed odour?' I tried again, when Flora didn't respond.

She didn't laugh and when I looked around the screen, I found her deep in thought.

'What are you thinking?' I asked.

'Probably nothing.'

I didn't comment, knowing she wouldn't be able to bear the silence for long.

'Do you think she's still in touch with Logan?' she soon said, falling for my trick.

I hadn't expected her to say that, though.

'Did you notice which way she drove off?' I asked.

'What?'

'Did she go down the drive or around to the courtyard?'

'Down the drive.'

'In that case,' I said, reaching for the conditioner, 'she probably isn't in touch with him.'

'How do you work that out?'

'Because he's back and if they were in touch, she would have most likely gone to see him in the garden apartment, wouldn't she?'

'He's what?' Flora gasped. 'Since when?'

'He arrived during the storm,' I filled her in, 'but I didn't see him until this morning. You should see the state of his car.'

'Bugger his car,' she tutted. 'I don't believe it. Why didn't you say anything before?'

'Because I was a bit preoccupied with what happened to Dad.'

'Fair enough,' she conceded. 'What did Logan say when you saw him? Did you give him a rocket for the radio silence?'

'He said,' I told her, 'that he has something important he wants to tell me and Dad, but I'm not sure I want to hear it.'

Flora waited for me to fill the silence then.

'But, I suppose, given that he forgave me for running out on him and heard me out when I explained why I had done it, I probably should.'

'It's very generous of you to give him a second chance.'

'Well,' I said, as I turned the shower off and reached for my towel, 'I'm following your example, aren't I? You gave Tara a second chance and look how well that's worked out.'

Flora didn't respond to that.

# Chapter 28

The next few days were hectic, with numerous visits to see Dad, who was having a much longer than usual stay in the hospital because the staff still wanted to keep an eye on his blood pressure, which I had been informed was erratic. He seemed to have accepted the situation but wasn't happy about it, whereas I felt relieved to know he was in the best hands and was feeling proud of myself for not having spun into a decline over the situation.

I supposed that could have been because the hospital staff were looking after him, rather than me, but I was so busy, splitting my time between hospital visits, the cottage and what to do about the next course, I didn't have time to worry, dissect or think too deeply.

Listening to what Logan had to say was still on the backburner, as when I'd briefly seen him, he had insisted that he still wanted to talk to Dad and I together. I refused to have the risk of further destabilising Dad's currently fluctuating blood pressure on my conscience and Logan was on board with that, even though it meant he was going to have to wait a bit longer to have his say.

Much to the tutor and attendees' relief, I decided that the

next course should go ahead. Due to the previous cancellation, there was little I needed to do by way of preparing the court-yard rooms. The lack of fresh flowers was more than justified given the state of the garden. However, what I was going to feed everyone on both days was still to be decided.

Dad's homegrown fare was a wonderful selling point, so I emailed the guests explaining that what would usually be on offer wasn't currently available. No one had grumbled, but I knew that could change when they were faced with my limited culinary skills. Something tinned on toast was a far cry from what we usually served up.

'So,' I said, when I arrived at the hospital the evening before Dad was due to be discharged, 'how are you feeling today, Dad?'

'I'm perfectly all right,' he huffed, having clearly become more fed up about the situation since the last time I'd see him. 'No idea what I'm still doing in here.'

'Well,' I said, 'you'll be home tomorrow, so don't get worked up about it now. If you bugger your blood pressure again, the consultant will make you stay even longer.'

He sniffed at that.

'The roof tiles were sorted today,' I told him, trying to change the subject.

'You mean, they've been off all this time?' He frowned.

'Not off,' I reminded him, 'just slipped a bit. Joe's friend who righted them had lots of other locals to help first. People who came off a whole lot worse during the storm than we did.'

'I can't imagine there's anyone who has lost more in their garden.' Dad swallowed, looking heartbroken.

I knew his leg and the bruising, which was now in full bloom all over him, was paining him, but it was the loss of the garden that was the real root cause behind his mental anguish. The devastation had truly taken a toll and I needed to be watchful of that in case his already descending mood dipped further.

'I know it all looked bad the morning after—' I began to say, but he cut me off.

'Can we talk about something else?' he asked. 'What have you decided to do about this weekend?'

I explained that the course was going ahead, but I wished he would let me talk about the garden because Freddie, Joe and a few others had been working tirelessly on the clear-up and they were convinced the polytunnel wasn't as beyond repair as it had first looked.

'I suppose it's a blessing this happened while you were still here,' Dad said mulishly. 'Otherwise, I would have been in a right pickle, wouldn't I?'

'Now Dad, about that,' I started to say, but an alarm further along the busy ward started blaring and it was impossible to carry on.

It was slow going the next day, getting Dad home and up the stairs. He had refused to acknowledge the replanted containers that flanked the front door and bypassed Kasuku and the kitchen in favour of his bed. He barely had a civil word for Flora either, who looked at me worriedly while Freddie helped him negotiate the stairs. I hadn't seen him so low since Mum had died and it made me feel both sad and sick.

'He doesn't seem right, does he?' Flora said to me.

'I daresay he's just tired,' I said hopefully. 'He'll be fine now he's back on his own turf and in his own bed. He'll be himself again in no time.'

Thankfully, my hunch was right and after a couple of decent night's sleep Dad was feeling much better, demanding breakfast in bed and a chaperone to help him down the stairs so he could hold court from an armchair Flora and I had moved into the kitchen. He was still eschewing talk of the garden, but I tried not to fret over that or force the issue.

'You have to keep that leg elevated when you're off it,' I reminded him as he wriggled to get comfy.

It was only early in the day, but I was already feeling run off my feet.

'It is elevated,' he said, pointing at the cumbersome boot.

'Not high enough,' I tutted.

'There's the phone,' Flora said, as she carefully repositioned the cushions for him. 'You answer it, Ally, and I'll get your dad settled.'

I left her to it.

'Hollyhock Cottage,' I said, pasting on a smile in the hope that it would come across in my voice.

'Hey, Ally.' It was Tara. 'Are you okay? You sound done in.'

'I am done in,' I said, taking the phone into the sitting room and closing the door. 'It's been one hell of a week. Which you would know, if you'd been around.'

I knew I sounded accusatory, but she was the second person to recently disappear from my life without keeping in touch and it grated a bit, even though the first one was now back. Not that his arrival had simplified anything.

'I'm sorry,' she apologised. 'I'm still caught up with a work thing, but I have been checking in with Flora. She's been keeping me up to speed.'

I hadn't realised that. I wondered if she'd mentioned that Logan had returned.

'She told me you've decided to run the course this weekend.'

'I have to,' I said. 'I need to keep things going, otherwise we'll end the season with disgruntled customers. And tutors. I've no idea how I'll manage with the cooking now we've no produce and my lack of culinary skills, but—'

'That's actually what I'm ringing about,' she interrupted. 'You can do breakfasts and lunches, can't you?'

'Just about,' I said. 'The bakery in Shellcombe is going to deliver pastries and bread and I can throw together a salad and dressing for lunch with some of Joe's smoked fish and meat, but it's the evening meal on Saturday and then the Sunday lunch that I'm going to struggle with. They're the big ones.'

'That's what Flora thought,' Tara said, sounding thrilled. 'So, I'm going to send prepped gourmet meals from a restaurant chum who grows all his own veg and raises the meat he cooks, too. I've arranged it for this weekend and the next. Hopefully Geoff will be back on his feet and able to do a bit after that, but if he isn't we'll carry on with the set-up.'

I didn't know what to say.

'It won't be the same obviously,' Tara continued when I didn't comment, 'but I thought it would be a weight off your mind while you get sorted. It will still be seasonal and sort of local. As long as you keep the wine flowing, everyone will be happy enough and it's my treat. I'm footing the bill and don't even bother arguing about that.'

'Oh, Tara,' I said, feeling relieved, 'thank you so much.'

It hadn't even entered my head to try to source something like that.

'I know your dad won't be impressed that someone else's

meals are being served in his kitchen,' she chuckled, 'but I'm hoping he won't be too upset.'

'Given the alternative,' I smiled, picturing myself making a mess of the simplest dish, 'I'm sure he won't be upset at all.'

'Well, that's all right then,' she said. 'The delivery is scheduled for Saturday morning and I'll see you soon.'

She hung up before I could thank her again.

Dad had graciously accepted Tara's generous offer but still refused to so much as glimpse at the garden, which was a shame given the headway the team, who had given up so much time to tackle it, had made. He had also opted to go back upstairs out of sight once the weekend guests were due to arrive.

'I don't want a fuss,' he said, when I tried to get him to change his mind, 'and they're all bound to make one.'

I knew he was right, but it was going to be a nuisance for me, traipsing up and down all day to check on him and keeping an ear out every time I heard him on his feet and hobbling to the en suite.

'But Dad,' I said, giving it one last go, 'I don't like the thought of you upstairs all weekend on your own. You're bound to get fed up.'

'I won't be on my own,' he said, a twinkle in his eye appearing, 'or fed up. I've spoken to Vanessa and she's coming to stay.'

I knew the pair had been messaging since Dad's accident as she was out of the area and the news of this second sleepover was music to my ears. Vanessa could take on Dad while I handled everything else.

'In that case,' I said, feeling thrilled, 'I'd better check the spare room.'

'Assuming it's needed,' Flora said cheekily, which I ignored.

Having warmly welcomed Vanessa back, I left her and Dad to it and the day ran much as a Saturday always did, though without Dad in the kitchen the vibe felt very different. Kasuku was inclined to sulk and it was brought home to me just what a good team we all were when we were pulling together.

I couldn't wait to tell Dad about my change of plan and that I would be the one setting up and running all the new ideas I'd come up with for later in the year. I still wasn't sure how best to frame it to make him believe I was staying put for all the right reasons, but I didn't want to put it off much longer.

'So,' I said, when I went to collect his and Vanessa's dinner tray on Saturday evening, 'what did you think?'

A vast delivery of prepared meals from Tara's chef friend had arrived just as she had said it would. All I had to do was heat and serve them. I had explained to the guests where the food came from, as well as reminding them as to why, and they all enjoyed it, but were sorry to have missed out on Dad's wonderful home cooking.

'I enjoyed it,' Vanessa said brightly, helping me stack the tray. 'And you liked the sauce, didn't you, Geoff?'

She gave me a wink and I grinned.

'It was all pretty good,' he said, taking me by surprise. 'The lamb was very tender.'

I didn't push him to comment further, knowing that it would have taken a lot for him to say something positive even if he had savoured every mouthful and wiped his plate clean.

'We thought we might come down for a little while later, Geoff, didn't we?' Vanessa said, taking me further by surprise.

'Yes,' said Dad, 'I mustn't stay in the same spot for too long and there's only so much room to manoeuvre up here, so it'll be good to have a stretch.'

Vanessa looked at me and smiled. What a wonderful influence this woman was.

By early Sunday evening, I had stripped all of the beds, with Flora and Joe's help, and felt exhausted. I didn't think the weekend had been one of our best, but I'd done as much as I could. I hoped the next one would be easier and Dad would be even more involved. That said, he had ended up downstairs for most of Sunday and actually soaked up the fuss made of him, practically revelled in it, in fact.

'Right,' said Flora, linking her arm through mine, once we'd filled the bags with the laundry ready for collection, 'pub.'

'You must be kidding,' I said. 'All I want is a hot bath and my bed.'

'There's a carnival meeting tonight,' she carried on as if I hadn't spoken. 'And it will do you good to have a change of scenery.'

'I can't really leave Dad, can I?' I pointed out.

'In Vanessa's capable hands,' Flora laughed. 'I'd say so, yes.'

'And I thought I'd pop in to the cottage,' said Joe. 'I know Geoff won't talk to you about the garden, Ally, but he might listen to me. There's nothing wrong with the tunnel now we've fixed the frame. It just needs re-covering.'

Even despite Vanessa's best efforts, Dad was still being stubborn where the garden was concerned. The trauma of what had happened to it had cut deep and I thought it would be good for him to hear what Joe had to say. I hoped Dad would be less likely to dismiss him than he had Vanessa and me.

'All right,' I agreed. 'Thanks, Joe. Pub it is then.'

'I haven't seen Logan,' Flora said, when we reached the beach on our way to The Ship and slid off our sandals. 'Have you?'

'No,' I said, as I pushed my toes into the warm sand and looked towards the pontoon. 'I haven't.'

I knew, now that Dad was properly on the mend and things at the cottage were feeling almost back to normal, I should make more of an effort to see him, but there was a part of me that was reluctant to. Whatever it was that Logan had to say was bound to upset the apple cart again and I didn't have enough energy to cope with that on top of everything else.

I know Logan had once echoed Flora's words, that the universe wouldn't give me more than I could carry, but it currently felt like a motherload. Not to mention a father-load . . .

'And I never thought I'd feel this way,' I added, 'but I'm actually missing the early morning swims.'

'Well, now Geoff can negotiate the stairs unaided,' Flora smiled, 'there's no reason why you can't start going again, is there? Especially now the pontoon is back.'

'Where has it been?' I asked, having not realised it had broken free.

'Halfway to France, according to talk in the pub,' Flora laughed.

I wasn't sure if she was joking, but I knew a lot of things had happened both during and after the storm that I hadn't heard about until recently because I had been so caught up with Dad and the cottage. I did, however, know that in classic cove style, the community had pulled together, just like the guys in the garden, and things were being mended as quickly as possible. I'd have to write about the storm in my cove and cottage notebook, before too much of what had happened was forgotten.

'Even that fella staying up at your place has pitched in,' said Noah, when we fell to talking about it in the pub. 'Joe told me he worked more hours than anyone else helping to clear and tidy the cottage garden last week.'

I hadn't realised that.

'And this weekend he's been going around with some of the others, doing whatever he's been asked further afield,' Noah further said, sounding impressed.

'That probably explains why we haven't seen him,' Flora said to me.

'He's a good lad,' chipped in Michael.

'The best,' added Mary. 'Now, let's go and get down to carnival business.'

As I drank my pint and listened to the latest planning update, I promised myself that I would now seek Logan out so he could tell Dad and I whatever it was he wanted to impart. I wasn't sure he was either *a good lad* or *the best*, as Michael and Mary had put it, but further putting off hearing him out wasn't going to help me decide, was it?

'Have you told Tara that Logan is back?' I whispered to Flora.

'No.' She shrugged.

I went to say something else, but a stern look from Mary stopped me.

'Now,' said Michael, rubbing his hands together, 'who fancies putting their name down for a stint on the ducking stool?'

We didn't volunteer or stay late and Joe was looking tense when we got back to the cottage.

'Where's Dad?' I asked, noticing the kitchen armchair was empty.

'Him and Vanessa have gone up,' Joe told me. 'He still thinks the tunnel should come down, rather than be repaired.'

'What?' I frowned.

'He reckons it's a death trap.'

Flora rolled her eyes.

'See if you can talk him around if Vanessa can't, will you?' Joe asked me. 'It would be such a waste to scrap it.'

'I'll try,' I promised, but I didn't fancy my chances.

'You need to tell him that you're staying too,' Flora said.

'Staying?' asked Joe. 'What are you talking about?'

'Nothing for you to worry about,' she said, kissing his cheek.

'You women and your secrets,' he laughed.

I felt a warm glow, knowing that Flora had been true to her word and kept mine.

'Do you mind if I stay with Joe tonight?' she asked me.

'Not at all,' I said. 'You get off and I'll talk to Dad in the morning.'

However, I was just making myself a camomile tea when I heard him bumping down the stairs.

'You're getting the hang of that,' I smiled when he appeared in the kitchen far sooner than I had expected to see him.

'This boot is driving me nuts, already,' he said, sounding frustrated, as he made for his chair and flopped down into it before hoisting his leg up onto the pile of cushions. 'Vanessa's in the bath, so I thought I'd come and talk to you.'

'Oh,' I said, opening the cupboard and taking out another mug. 'About anything in particular?'

I didn't expect there would be and wondered if this was the moment I would finally find the words and the way to tell him I had changed my mind about leaving.

'There is actually,' he said, looking a little flushed.

I made him a tea too and then sat at the table, facing him.

'Are you remembering to take your painkillers?' I asked.

I had been making the biggest effort not to fuss, but was finding it hard.

'I haven't needed any today,' he told me. 'But I might before I go to bed.'

'So,' I said, 'what is it you wanted to talk to me about?'

He looked at me for a moment and then said, without any preamble whatsoever –

'I've had an offer on the cottage.'

It took a moment for me to take in what he'd said.

'What sort of offer?' I frowned. 'You mean someone wanting to buy it?'

'That's it,' he said, blowing on his tea. 'An offer to buy the house, garden, outbuildings, the lot.'

'Oh, right,' I said. 'That's a bit odd, isn't it?'

'It was certainly unexpected,' he agreed. 'But it's a good offer, Ally. Very good, according to the current market.'

'Not that it matters . . .' I started to say, but there was something about his expression that stopped me.

'Might be too good to turn down,' he said, shocking the life out of me.

'You can't be serious,' I gabbled. 'You can't sell this place!'

'I didn't say I was selling it,' he calmly responded, 'but I have decided that I am going to think about it.'

'But why would you even want to?' I gasped. 'Everything

here is perfect. It's taken us years to get to this point. What does Vanessa have to say about it?'

My hands were shaking so much, I had to put my mug down for fear of sloshing the camomile contents, which I was definitely going to need, all over the table and myself.

'She doesn't know anything about it,' said Dad. 'Give me some credit, Ally. I wasn't going to mention it to anyone else until I'd talked to you and actually, I'd like to keep this just between us while I make up my mind.'

I'd rather he hadn't mentioned it at all and especially to me.

'But why are you even thinking about it?' I demanded. 'Why on earth would you want to sell? I thought you were happy here, Dad!'

'Don't get me wrong,' he said, 'I love what we've done here. Adore it. And your mum would be so proud, but with the garden in ruins and you leaving—'

I shook my head.

'But I don't want to leave now,' I blurted out. 'I've been putting off telling you, but I've changed my mind.'

Dad shook his head in response.

'Well, of course you're going to say that—'

'No,' I cut in. 'I mean it. I'm not saying it because of what you've just said. Ask Flora. Ask Tara. They both know I've had a change of heart.'

'I see,' Dad said sceptically.

'It's true,' I told him, frustration causing a rush of tears.

'You are entitled to leave,' he said with a smile, which made me want to throttle him, 'as am I, if that's what I decide.'

'No,' I said. 'This is all wrong. This can't be happening.'

'I've only said I'm thinking about it,' Dad reiterated, as my world fell apart.

How could he sound so calm?

'But what about Kasuku?' I said, clutching at straws. 'He can't leave here, remember? Beatrice made that part of the terms of her will, didn't she?'

Dad didn't have an answer for that.

'We're going nowhere,' I said, forthrightly . 'That parrot and me, and you, we're staying put in Kittiwake Cove.'

# Chapter 29

Predictably, that was another night I didn't get much sleep and early the following morning, I pulled on a vest and a pair of shorts and headed down to the beach to think. I was too wound up to swim safely, so headed for the sanctuary of the rock instead. That secluded, secret place had helped clear my head many times in the past and I hoped it still held some of the magic that would enable me to make sense of the crazy situation I was currently facing.

'Jeez,' I gasped, when I found the ledge already occupied. 'You scared me.'

Logan had jumped too. Sitting bent over, with his head in his hands, he hadn't spotted me until I had squeezed my way right into the confined space.

'What are you doing down here?' I asked harshly.

I felt annoyed to have my plan for some private time thwarted.

'I actually came down here to think about you,' Logan smiled sadly, 'and here you are.'

'Yes,' I said, as I tried to convince myself that the extra fast beat of my heart was down to the shock it had just received, rather than the sight of him. I didn't have either the time or headspace for my own rocky romance right now. 'Here I am.'

'I've been going out of my mind waiting to talk to you and Geoff, Ally,' he continued. 'It's been ages. Far too long really.'

I could understand why he felt that way because it had been a long time, however with everything else that had been happening in the wake of the storm, he knew I'd had to prioritise where I focused my energy and what was best for Dad. His blood pressure had only recently stabilised and I still wasn't about to agree to the pair of us listening to Logan if it was likely to send it haywire again.

'Joe has been keeping me up to date with how your dad's getting on and I was wondering if today might be a good time to come to the cottage to talk to you both?' Logan then predictably asked.

I took a deep breath.

'I know it isn't what you wanted, Logan, but would you consider talking to me without Dad,' I requested. 'He's got a lot going on at the moment.' Even more than I had realised until our conversation the previous evening. 'And I'm trying to limit his stress as much as I can. I'm guessing what you have to tell us might cause some?'

'You're right,' Logan sighed, sounding upset. 'It will, and given the circumstances, I am willing to talk to just you, rather than the two of you. Heaven knows,' he said, running a hand through his hair, 'I can't put it off any longer.'

'Okay,' I said, 'let's move out of here then.' I didn't want my not-so-secret hideaway tainted with whatever it was he was about to say. 'And there's something I want to say to you first. Will you listen?'

'All right,' Logan agreed as he followed me back to the beach.

'I'll listen, but only if you promise to hear me out afterwards, without storming off.'

That sounded ominous.

'I promise,' I reluctantly vowed.

There was space in front of the rock where we could sit relatively hidden from view so we settled ourselves there. It was too early to be hot, but it was warm and the breeze had a softness to it that was a stark contrast to the sharpness of the wind that had blown in during the storm.

'So,' I said, kicking the conversation properly off. 'I have a favour to ask.'

'A favour?' Logan frowned. 'Well, if I can help, I will.'

I faltered for a moment, wondering if I was doing this the right way around. If Logan had something devastating to say, I might not want him doing me the favour I was about to request, but I supposed I was in it now.

'You love Kittiwake Cove, don't you?' I tentatively carried on, picking up a warm handful of sand and letting it trickle through my fingers.

'You know I do,' he said, looking out over the sea. 'In spite of what it's cost me, I love it very much.'

I hadn't realised it had cost him anything and refused to get sidetracked by asking.

'Well, that's good.' I nodded, brushing my hands together, 'because, depending on whether or not I'm still talking to you after you've said your bit, I might need you to use your enthusiasm for the area to help Dad reignite his.'

'I don't understand.' Logan frowned.

'Neither do I really,' I told him.

I still didn't think I'd properly got my head around what

Dad had said. Having received an offer on the cottage was one thing. It was a desirable and much coveted location, but actually considering whether he should accept it was madness.

'What's going on?' Logan frowned. 'Your dad loves the cove more than anyone else I know. He's melded to this place as seamlessly as the sand is to the sea.'

I adored that description and hoped he would repeat it to Dad if necessary.

'That's what I thought, too.' I swallowed, sharing what Dad had asked me to keep between us. 'But now, I'm not so sure. He's had an offer on the cottage and he told me last night that he's considering accepting it.'

Logan looked horrified.

'I think, on top of feeling so distressed about what's happened to the garden, the accident has unsettled him,' I said, trying to pin my understanding on something tangible. 'And he won't listen to reason. Or at least, he won't listen to me.'

'No,' said Logan, plunging his hands into his hair. 'No, no, no, no, no.'

I was shocked by his reaction.

'This can't be,' he said, sounding desperate. 'This isn't right.'

'I'm aware of that,' I said back. 'And I've tried to tell him that I've changed my mind about leaving now, too—'

Logan's mouth fell open.

'You've changed your mind?' he gasped. 'You've really changed your mind?'

I knew I'd been back and forth a bit, but his shocked tone surely wasn't justified.

'Yes,' I told him, 'but Dad won't accept it. He reckons I'm only saying it to please him and to stop him considering this out of the blue offer, but that's not it at all. I genuinely want to stay. I've come up with a way to make my life and career aspirations properly work here, but shockingly too late to save Hollyhock Cottage.'

Logan let out a shout of frustration and I flinched. Whatever was the matter with him?

'This is all my fault,' he said, unfathomably, repeatedly thumping the sand.

'How could it be your fault?' I glared. 'Dad has had a random offer on the place.'

Mum had died without a will, but she'd always told me that her share of the cottage would one day be mine. At the time it hadn't been something I had been comfortable to even contemplate, but now I found myself wishing it was the case. If I had a legal share in the property, I could have put a stop to Dad even considering that wretched offer.

'A random offer,' Logan said, jabbing a finger at his chest, 'that has been made because of me.'

'I don't understand . . .'

Logan took another breath and the previously wild look in his eye changed to one of utter anguish.

'Of course you don't,' he said, more calmly now. 'How could you?'

'Tell me then,' I said, beginning to feel desperate. 'Tell me.'

Logan closed his eyes and when he opened them again, he began to fill me in.

'Thanks to your dad's search for the solicitor who doesn't exist, you've worked out that I don't have a dead uncle,' was the first thing he said. 'The uncle and the requests in his will were just a story to cover my actual reasons for being here.'

'Which are?' I demanded.

'Oh, Ally,' he groaned. 'I came here to talk your dad into selling Hollyhock Cottage,' he said shamefully, 'and to keep you focused on leaving the cove.'

'What?' I struggled to say.

'I was sent here by my employer with the intention of buying the cottage on their behalf,' he said devastatingly.

'You mean ...' I stammered, the suggestion sounding unlikely, but if what Logan had just said was true, then correct nonetheless, 'you were a plant?'

He looked everywhere but at me.

'Yes,' he confirmed, 'that's exactly what I was.'

'I don't believe it,' I mumbled.

I went to stand up, but my legs felt like lead and I couldn't move.

'When I was tasked with this job, I had no idea that I was going to find you here,' he carried on, still sounding wretched. 'I thought I'd died and gone to hell when I realised this place was connected to you. I knew I was in trouble from the moment I first saw you.'

'Why? Because you thought you were going to be found out before your dirty work was done?' I sneered. 'You said on the plane to Barcelona that you had a challenging summer ahead. I wish I'd known then that it was going to involve me.'

'I wasn't worried about being found out,' he said, shaking his head.

'What then?'

'I knew I was in trouble,' he said, faltering, 'because I was still in love with you, Ally.' I felt my breath hitch. 'I still *am* in love with you.'

'You can't possibly say this to me now—' I started to say, but he cut me off.

'I have to,' he bowled on. 'I knew straightaway that I wasn't going to be able to see the job through. I love you and have developed such a fondness for your father, too. And then I fell in love with the cottage and the way you run it *and* the cove—'

'If that's the truth,' I somehow managed to say, 'then why didn't you tell me about all of this weeks ago?'

'Initially, I was scared of losing my job,' he admitted, sounding uncomfortable. 'But when I stopped caring about that and planned to tell you, I realised the CEO would pin my failure on my manager and they'd end up losing far more than what I stood to sacrifice.'

'So, you kept quiet . . .' I said, feeling shocked by what had been playing out during the last few months and which I had been blind to.

'Yes,' Logan admitted, 'but I turned double agent. I came up with a plan to act in your best interests, while keeping my manager convinced that I was still looking after theirs.'

'How?'

'I had a feeling you weren't as convinced about leaving as you thought you were,' he explained, 'which is why I took you to places that I thought would tug at your heartstrings. It was no coincidence that we ended up at Max Gate after your dad told me your mum loved Hardy's poetry.'

'And the trips to Cerne Abbas and Durdle Door . . .'

'All carefully orchestrated,' he said. 'Even making sure you got the Historical Society leaflet was done with the hope that you would further think your decision through. I thought that if you changed your mind about leaving, then by the time the offer landed, you and Geoff would simply dismiss it. Then, once you'd turned it down, I could convince the CEO there was nothing further to be done and my manager wouldn't be blamed.'

'So why did you leave in the middle of this elaborate ruse you say you created?' I asked suspiciously. 'Why did you disappear and risk your plan not coming to fruition?'

'My manager guessed some of what I was up to and forced me to leave,' he told me.

'The manager you've been trying to protect?'

'That's the one,' he confirmed.

'It doesn't sound like they were worthy of your protection and concern, does it?'

'Maybe not.' He shrugged. 'And by that point, they'd decided they wanted to get rid of me and have a shot at securing the sale themselves.'

'If they were so keen to buy the place,' I said, 'then why didn't they do that right from the start? And how come you've come back when you've supposedly been banished?'

'I've come back because after I told the CEO I wasn't going to see the job through and they fired me, there was no reason for me to stay away.'

'You've been sacked?' I gulped. 'You lost your job to save my home?'

'Yes,' Logan said. 'Even before I came to Hollyhock Cottage, the role I had been assigned in the dodgy plan to buy it didn't sit well with me. Good riddance to the job,' he said seriously, 'especially if it saves my relationship with you.'

'Oh, Logan.'

'But all of this hasn't saved your home, has it?' he said sadly, 'because an offer has been made anyway and your dad is now considering accepting it.'

I'd momentarily forgotten that.

'So, who is it who wants the cottage?' I asked. 'Who sent you here to turn my world upside down so they didn't have to get their hands dirty?'

'It's Tara,' he said devastatingly. 'Tara wants to buy Hollyhock Cottage.'

# Chapter 30

I knew Logan had carried on talking after he had confessed his shocking revelation, but I had no idea what he said because all I could think about was Tara. Tara was the person who was set to tear mine and Dad's lives apart. It was Tara who had taken me in with her effortless style, her seemingly sincere encouragement and her desperate desire to make amends for the sins of her past. It was Tara who had spoon-fed me her bullshit . . . and I had stupidly lapped it up.

'I have to go,' I blurted out, as my legs came back to life and I jumped up.

My stomach rolled from the sudden movement and I tasted bile in the back of my throat.

'Ally!' Logan called after me as I set off.

'I'll come and find you later!' I shouted back. 'I need to think.'

What I really needed to do was rip Tara's head off.

'Where have you been?' Flora frowned when I rushed into the kitchen. 'I thought you were still in bed.'

'And I thought you'd still be at Joe's.'

'He's already at the smokehouse, so I thought I might as well come back early,' she explained. 'Are you okay?'

'I'm fine,' I said, slowing down so I didn't inadvertently give anything away. 'I just needed a bit of fresh air, so I went down to the beach.'

'You look flushed,' she observed. 'Was Logan down there, by any chance?'

'He was actually,' I said, filling a glass with water, 'but he's not the reason I'm feeling hot. It's really warm out there already. Are you working this morning?'

'No,' she said, pouring muesli into a bowl. 'I've no one booked until this afternoon. Why? Do you want to do something? Maybe we could try to get your dad in the garden as it's so nice.'

Kasuku eyed Flora's choice of cereal with intense interest. If he spotted an almond there'd be no shutting him up.

'No,' I succinctly said. 'Let's leave Dad to Vanessa's ministrations for now. I need to pop out again. Would you be able to hang around and keep an ear out for him if she has to leave before I get back?'

'Of course.' She smiled. 'Are you sure you're, okay?'

'And maybe listen out for the laundry collection person, too?' I requested, already heading towards the door again.

'Sure,' she said.

She was beginning to look more suspicious than concerned, so I grabbed my phone and left.

'I'll see you later then!' she called after me and Kasuku squawked.

I headed along the beach towards the pub. I still had no idea where Tara was staying in the cove, or even if she was staying in the cove, but I had to start my search for her somewhere.

As I strode along, I realised that she'd given very little away about her current circumstances, but I remembered she had said she worked for her dad. That must make him the CEO who had fired Logan. Was it him who wanted my home and if so, why? Had I been capable of listening to more of what Logan had said, I might have already known the answer to that.

'Ally!'

I spun around and was shocked to fortuitously find my adversary jogging along the beach towards me. Clad in designer running gear, she looked radiant and her smile revealed nothing of the serpent that lurked beneath the surface, poised and ready to strike.

'I was going to come and see you this morning.' She beamed, her glossy, high ponytail jauntily swinging.

She wasn't even out of breath and I was hard pushed to resist the urge to trip her up and squish her face into the sand.

'Were you?' I glared.

Her smile faltered and her pace slackened to a walk.

'Oh God,' she said, her shoulders dropping. 'You know, don't you?'

'About you *still* being the lying, scheming cow you always were?' I said, my head cocked and my tone saccharine sweet. 'Yeah. I know.'

'Can we talk?' she begged, her cheeks flushed in the face of my accusation.

'I don't think so,' I snapped back.

Now she was in front of me, I felt too angry to listen to her. I should have given Logan's confession time to settle before I rushed to find her.

'Please,' she pleaded, but I wasn't taken in. Once bitten and all that. Or in my case, twice. 'Please just listen to what I need to say and then I'll be out of your life if you want me to be. And for good this time.'

'Is that a promise?' I seethed.

'Yes,' she said. 'Not that you have any reason to believe I'd honour it, but it is. It's a promise.'

I jerked my head towards the pub. Michael was outside checking a delivery. The really big curtain-sided brewery lorries couldn't make it down the twisty road that led to the cove, so everything had to come in twice as often by van.

'Hey Michael,' I said, 'I know you're not open, but is there any chance I could borrow the snug for five minutes?'

I wouldn't be giving Tara longer than that.

'Afraid not,' he said. 'The cleaner will be wanting to get in there any second.'

'It's literally just for five minutes,' I tried again. 'Tara has a confession to make.'

Michael raised his eyebrows.

'Another one?' he commented. 'I thought you were done with all that.'

'So did I,' I said, shooting daggers in her direction while she stared at her feet.

Michael caved. 'Go on then. Five minutes.'

It felt odd being in the pub when it wasn't open. A bit like being at school after hours or in the holidays. The pumps were covered in towels and there was no music or chatter. The only noise I could make out was the distant drone of a vacuum cleaner.

'Right,' I said, marching into the snug, 'let's hear it. We're on a clock and we've probably lost half a minute already.'

Tara sat in the seat opposite the one I flopped down into. She remained frustratingly silent as she fiddled with the bent edge of a menu. I was tempted to rip it out of her hands.

'I'll start then,' I snapped. 'It has come to my attention that Logan was sent here to worm his way into mine and Dad's affections and to talk Dad into selling the cottage, while you used your considerable charm to convince me that moving to Barcelona was the right thing to do and, as a result, make Dad's decision to leave here easier. Am I right so far?'

I was rather proud, given the emotional maelstrom I was being tossed about in, to have summed the situation up so succinctly.

'Yes,' she said quietly.

'Okay,' I nodded, 'now, it's your turn. You're going to tell me why you've gone to such lengths to buy my home. Why do you want it?'

'I didn't want it for myself,' she told me nervously. 'I was buying it for my dad.'

'Your dad,' I repeated. 'Your dad, who you work for? Your dad wants to live in Hollyhock Cottage?'

'He doesn't want to live in it,' she confusingly carried on.

'So . . .'

'He's retiring,' she said, and I remembered that she'd previously mentioned that. 'And he hasn't been able to decide who he wants to hand his business on to. It's been a toss-up between me, his only child, and a bloke called Guy Simonds. He's like the son Dad has always wished he'd had.' She swallowed, sounding upset. 'Workwise, Dad has always pitted us against one another, forcing us to prove ourselves and this last challenge he threw down was to be rewarded with the ultimate prize.'

'His business,' I surmised. 'The prize was his business and the purchase of my home was going to be your means of securing it.'

'Yes.' Tara nodded. She looked tired all of a sudden. 'I stupidly told Dad that I would secure the sale of whichever property he set his sights on, no matter how unachievable it seemed, in order to ensure that it was me who would carry his business on.'

'And out of every house in the world, he picked Hollyhock Cottage?'

It sounded unlikely to me.

'He did,' Tara nonetheless confirmed. 'He gave me until the end of the summer to do it and said I could use my assistant, Logan, to help me achieve it, in any way I saw fit.'

Logan being the man I'd fallen in love with in Barcelona. What were the odds of that?

'But why Hollyhock Cottage?' I frowned.

Her father's choice made no sense to me at all.

'Because he had tried to buy it in the past,' Tara said, shocking me, 'and failed. He offered Beatrice Baxter an extortionate amount for it, but she wouldn't sell.'

I had had no idea that had happened, and I bet Dad didn't know either.

'I can't say I'm surprised,' I said, 'about Beatrice I mean. She loved that cottage. It had been in her family forever and she had been born there, but why did your dad want it?'

'Purely as a status symbol,' Tara said disparagingly. 'It's the biggest property in the cove, so he had to have it. He's never got over being turned down all those years ago and tasked me with finishing the job. He never got over Kasuku's reaction to him either,' she added, biting her lip. 'Apparently, he used to go ballistic whenever Dad turned up.'

I didn't like the thought of Tara's dad trying to bully Beatrice into selling and was pleased Kasuku had made his feelings known.

'Kasuku's not all that keen on you either,' I pointed out.

I thought it was dogs who had the best instincts about people, but maybe parrots could pick up genetic connections and sly motives, too.

'He hates me,' Tara said sadly. 'I reckon he can tell who I'm related to.'

We stopped talking as Michael reversed through the door carrying two coffees.

'Sorry, Michael,' I said, starting to stand up. 'Our time must be up.'

'It is,' he said, 'but when I told Mary you were in here, she said to bring you these and tell you to stay as long as you need to.'

'Thank her for us,' Tara said softly.

'I will,' he said, giving her a look I couldn't fathom.

'Mary has become a bit of a confidante during the last few days,' Tara told me once he had gone. 'She's been so kind.'

'You mean, you've told her what you've been up to?'

I felt rather put out that Mary hadn't warned me of the danger Dad and I were in.

'I have,' Tara confirmed. 'And she was all set to tell you, but when she heard what I'd subsequently worked out, she changed her mind.'

'What have you worked out?' I asked, wondering if her calculations justified Mary's silence.

Logan's confession on the beach had made me think of Tara as a hard-faced business woman who was every bit as ruthless as her dad, but her manner of speaking, as she explained about his cruel competition, coupled with her generosity over sorting the meals for the recent course, didn't marry with that. To me, she still looked more like the person she'd been all summer.

'That I don't want to buy the cottage for Dad and that I don't want to work for him or have anything to do with his business going forward either,' she said compellingly, her smile from earlier almost back in place.

'You mean, you don't want your dad to pick you over Guy to take over his empire?'

'I don't,' she confirmed, 'and given that I told him I was leaving the company with immediate effect within minutes of you telling Flora and me that you'd changed your mind about leaving the cove, he's not very likely to, is he?'

'Oh,' I said, feeling taken aback. 'You really told him that?'

'I did,' she said. 'I've genuinely hated the trickery and treachery and your revelation was the final straw.'

'Crikey,' I said, puffing out my cheeks. 'So, it was my decision to stay, and your hatred of the whole deceitful affair, that made you decide to leave.'

'In part,' she said, picking up her cup. 'I've learned a lot these last few weeks, too.'

'Such as?'

'Seeing you and Geoff together,' she told me. 'Knowing the lengths that you were willing to go to, to make your dad happy, taught me that was what a real father–daughter relationship should be about. I was supposedly making my dad happy too, but at a terrible cost. So many people were destined to be made miserable as a result of my actions and that's not something a relationship should be based on.'

'It's not the healthiest model for family life, is it?' I said, wrinkling my nose.

'Definitely not,' she said. 'You and Geoff have shown me the true meaning of family this summer. And the birthday party you held for Flora and Freddie played a part, too. It was such a wonderful occasion and everyone was so happy to be there and central to it all was that beautiful house. The very house that now accommodates your best friend, too. It's so much more than bricks and mortar, isn't it? It's the perfect home.'

I couldn't argue with that.

'So,' I said, thinking back to the time of the party, 'were you wavering in your mission all those weeks ago?'

'I was,' she said. 'I was all over the place. Banishing Logan was the lowest point and I ended up hating myself for doing that. It was my last-ditch attempt to drive a wedge between the two of you and try to see buying the cottage through myself.'

That tallied with what Logan had told me.

'Logan has just told me he's no longer working for your dad,' I said.

Tara looked at me sharply.

'Is he back?' she gasped.

'Yes,' I said. 'And he has been for a while. He's staying in the garden apartment again. I'm surprised you haven't run into each other.'

'He's most likely been avoiding me,' she said shrewdly. 'I owe him the biggest apology. I never should have roped him into all of this. I can't tell you how much of a shock it was when I found out that the pair of you had been together in Barcelona.'

'Having experienced quite the surprise that first day when he found me on the beach,' I told her with a wry smile, 'I've got a bit of an idea.'

'He really loves you, you know.'

I wasn't ready to think about that yet.

'So,' I said, trying to change the subject, 'you've both lost your jobs this summer.'

'And Logan has lost his heart, too.' Tara smiled. 'And I've found something far more valuable than my pay check.'

'What's that?'

'My self-respect,' she said happily. 'I can sleep easy now, knowing that I've done the right thing.'

I raised my cup to her when she said that and wondered how Flora was going to react when she found out that her former distrust of Tara was far from misplaced.

'And you and Logan can pick up where you left off before I interfered,' she carried on, 'and you and your dad can carry on living the life you both love in Hollyhock Cottage.'

'If only,' I said, putting the cup down again.

'What's happened?' she asked, her own cup clattering on its saucer.

'Dad's seriously thinking about your offer, Tara,' I told her, with a heavy sigh. 'I really think he's going to sell the place.'

'But I didn't make the offer,' she said, sounding puzzled. 'I never got that far and even if I had, I would have withdrawn it by now.'

'So, if it wasn't you,' I asked, 'who was it?'

Having said a hasty thank you to Michael and the waiting cleaner, Tara and I raced back to Hollyhock Cottage. Flora was just carrying Dad's empty breakfast tray into the kitchen when we burst in, causing Kasuku to screech and her to nearly drop the tray.

'You idiots,' she gasped, setting it down. 'What are you playing at?'

I bent double in an attempt to sooth the stitch in my side.

'I need to talk to Dad,' I panted.

'We both do,' Tara added.

She didn't sound out of breath at all.

'No,' I said, as I straightened up again, 'it will be better if it's just me.'

'What's going on?' Flora frowned.

'I'll fill you in later,' I promised. 'Is Vanessa up there with him?'

'No,' she said, 'you've just missed her. He's on his own and he's in a weird mood.'

'What do you mean weird?'

'Thoughtful like,' she said. 'He wanted me to find the number for his solicitor. Is everything all right?'

'Fine,' I squeaked.

I didn't want her panicking as much as I was.

'Clearly, not fine,' she said, brandishing a sticky spoon. 'Someone better fill me in, right now.'

'Oh, all right,' I caved, pointing at Tara. 'You tell her what's been going on and I'll talk to Dad.'

'Oh God.' Tara grimaced. 'Do I have to?'

'Yes,' I said, pulling the spoon from Flora's grasp and throwing it in the sink before crossing the room in three strides, 'you do.'

Dad was still in bed when I went into his room, and I again wished he'd let me escort him into the garden. If he would take just a minute to look at the progress and recovery his beloved outdoor space had made since the storm, I felt certain he'd feel far less inclined to consider selling up.

'Morning love,' he smiled, when he saw me. 'That was quick. Have you got it?'

'Got what?'

'The number for the solicitor,' he said, inching further up the bed. 'I just asked Flora for it.'

'Oh no,' I said, as if I hadn't known about it. 'She didn't mention it. I've come up to talk to you about something else.'

'Oh right,' he said, 'go on, but make it quick. I've got a lot to do today.'

I hoped it didn't involve accepting the offer on the cottage.

'I was wondering,' I said, heading straight to the heart of the matter, 'if you could tell me who has made the offer on the cottage that you told me about?'

'I can't remember the company name,' he said, thinking, 'but I can tell you it's a fancy business though. I've checked them out online and they're legit.'

'Um,' I said, 'I know they're legit.'

'Oh?' He frowned. 'How do you know that?'

'Because I've just discovered who the people behind the company are,' I told him, hoping his blood pressure wasn't about to go through the roof again. 'And when I tell you who it is, you're not going to want to consider selling to them a second longer.'

# Chapter 31

While Tara filled Flora in on what had really been happening over the summer, downstairs, I relayed the details to Dad, upstairs. Flora's reaction had initially been wild and I later discovered that Logan's timely arrival was the only thing that saved Tara from death by extremely stern ticking off. Luckily for Tara, the fact that she'd learnt from the experience and acted on it, saved her from the worst of Flora's wrath.

Conversely, my explanation of events didn't seem to have an impact on Dad's current train of thought at all. I hadn't wanted to go into too much detail for fear of escalating his blood pressure again, so stuck to a speedy run down of Logan and Tara's involvement and a brief explanation of how, many years ago, Tara's father had tried to get Beatrice to sell and why he still wanted the cottage – namely as a status symbol, not a home.

'I see,' was all Dad said, pensively, as his head slowly nodded up and down and he took it all in. 'Well, this is all a turn up for the books, isn't it?'

I was stunned that he could remain so calm, but grateful that his blood pressure wasn't going to be compromised. Unless of course, he was fizzing on the inside and not letting it outwardly show.

'Is there anything you'd like to ask me about it all?' I asked.

'No,' he said. 'I don't think so. Though I will want to have a word with Logan at some point.'

'Of course.'

'Not today though,' he said, as he turned his head away.

'I'll leave you to it, then,' I said, walking to the door.

I hadn't really known what to expect when I told him, but it wasn't this.

'Ally,' he said, as he looked at me again.

'Yes, Dad.'

'I'm still going to need the number for the solicitor.'

I was almost in tears by the time I went back down to the kitchen and Flora leapt to her feet and pulled me in for a hug. I spotted Tara agitatedly pacing about on her phone on the terrace outside and Logan was standing closer than was safe next to Kasuku's cage. The old bird eyed him beadily, but surprisingly made no attempt to take a chunk out of him, which he easily could have done.

During my retelling of events to Dad, I had further concluded that Logan really had been trying to make the best of the horrible situation he found himself in and the decent behaviour of the family parrot further confirmed that my forgiving thoughts were justified.

Whilst trying to subtly open my eyes to the wonders of my life and the landscape I currently had on my doorstep, as well as offering me an opportunity to fulfil my historical work aspirations via the local society I had previously volunteered with, Logan had also been trying to protect Tara from her father's cruel game playing and bolshy business tactics. For as long as he could bear to, anyway.

Watching her gesticulating and walking tirelessly up and down, I could tell it was her dad she was talking to and the gloves were off. She was smiling when she eventually came back inside though, which was a surprise. As was the fact that Kasuku had watched her stride in, but this time ignored her.

'What's going on?' I asked, disentangling myself from Flora's embrace, but keeping hold of her hand.

'Well,' Tara swallowed, banishing her smile, 'I don't know if any of what your dad has told you confirms this, Ally, but mine has just told me that it was him who put the offer in on the cottage. He did it himself.'

'Fuck,' said Logan, voicing the reaction Flora and I were thinking.

'Fuck,' Kasuku repeated.

That was a new one. I hoped he hadn't already committed it to memory.

'Dad didn't tell me much at all,' I told Tara, 'but I'd already guessed that was the case.'

'And has Geoff now dismissed the offer?' she asked. 'Now he knows where it's come from, has he given it up?'

'I don't know,' I tearfully said. 'He barely reacted when I told him everything and he's still asking for the solicitor's number, so I don't know what he's thinking.'

I probably should have just outright asked him, but he hadn't been in the most communicative of moods.

'This is all my fault,' Logan groaned, sounding devastated. 'I thought I was doing the right thing, but I should have just come clean from the start, shouldn't I?'

'Yes,' Flora said gruffly, before I could answer, 'you should have.' Poor Flora. If the sale happened, she was set to lose her business premises as well as the roof over head. 'But,' she added generously, 'hindsight is a wonderful thing and it's obvious your heart was in the right place. I know you were trying to protect more than one person through all of this.'

I couldn't argue with that.

'Go to him,' Flora said, giving me a gentle shove in Logan's direction. 'Heaven knows we need some good to come out of this situation.'

'Yes,' Tara agreed, looking between us, 'give the man a hug for pity's sake. I couldn't see it at the time, Logan, but I can see now that you were looking out for me as well as trying to protect Ally and Geoff.'

'I just wanted to find a way through this that meant no one got hurt.' He sighed. 'Though I wouldn't have minded your dad's over-large ego taking a battering, Tara.'

He opened his arms to me and I walked into them and settled comfortably against his chest. I'd fantasised about meeting him again many, many times since I'd left his hotel room in Barcelona in the spring, but I'd never once imagined that our reunion would involve anything as complicated as the few weeks we'd just gone through. At least we'd found our way back to each other now, though. Whatever happened next, knowing we would face it together, was a huge comfort.

And Flora had found her way back to Joe this summer, too. I supposed Logan and I should consider ourselves lucky that we hadn't had to wait a decade to have our muddle unravelled. The only one out of us who hadn't been lucky in love was Tara and thinking about it, she hadn't been all that lucky anywhere, had she?

'What are you going to do, Tara?' I asked her. 'I'm guessing that phone call to your dad wasn't of the reconciliation kind.'

'Damn right,' she laughed and I had to admire her buoyancy. 'It definitely wasn't a patching up kind of call, but he did say the nicest thing he's ever said to me. Not that he realised it.'

I wondered if that accounted for the smile she had ended the call with.

'Which was?' Flora asked.

'He told me that having thought more about the cottage, since I'd suggested I could get my hands on it, he'd realised he did still want it, more than anything, and that was why he bypassed me and put in the offer to Geoff himself.'

'I don't see how that was nice.' I frowned. 'It sounds like he thought you couldn't do your job.'

'Exactly!' She clapped, making me jump. 'He didn't think I had it in me to do his dirty work, which is a *huge* compliment when you think about it, *and* he also said he thought I'd get too emotionally involved to see it through.'

'Oh.' I smiled, though still wishing it wasn't Hollyhock Cottage which was at stake. 'Now I get it.'

Flora walked around the table and gave Tara one of her trademark hugs.

'You get why that made me so happy, don't you?' Tara said to her and Flora nodded.

'Just like Geoff did the other week, he was suggesting you have a heart.' Flora grinned.

'Exactly,' Tara said, with tears in her eyes. 'I do have a heart and I do care. Dad sees both of those things as faults, but I don't.

I think they're blessings. I can't remember the last time I felt this happy and it's all as a result of letting go of a situation that stressed me out and made me miserable. When I was caught up in it all and determined to prove myself as more than a spoilt brat who'd had life handed to her on a plate, I couldn't see my role in the business for what it really was, but I can now.'

'I'm going to book you in for some Reiki,' Flora said, sounding proud of Tara's wisdom and insight as she kissed her cheek. 'Get your chakras unblocked and realigned and send you back into the world fresh as a daisy.'

'Oh, yes please,' Tara said, even more tearfully. 'I'd love that.'

'You can book me in, too,' Logan put in. 'I feel like I need a fresh start. I started out really enjoying working for your dad, Tara, but this cruel competition he set up between you and Guy showed him to me in a completely different light. I know this summer has taken a toll on both of us and we're better off without him. Just like you, I'm feeling a hundred times happier, even if I have no idea what I'm going to do next and am obviously still worried about the future of the cottage.'

I looked up at him and planted a soft kiss on his lips. I wouldn't mind what he ended up doing as long as it didn't take him away from the cove. We mightn't be together at the cottage, but we'd end up somewhere hereabouts. Just a few weeks ago I couldn't wait to leave and now all I wanted was for us all to stay. It was a shocking turnaround, but not as shocking as the thought that Dad was still thinking about selling.

'If it's any consolation,' Tara said to Logan, 'I have no idea what I'm going to do either and I won't be able to even think about it until we've sorted out the mess here. What are we going to do about this horrible situation, Ally?'

'The only thing we can do,' I said, feeling resigned to wait it out, 'bide our time.'

'What if I talked to your dad?' Logan offered, obviously not liking my idea.

'Dad did say he wants to talk to you,' I told Logan and I felt him tense up, 'but not today.' I knew better than to push for that. If Dad's stubborn streak was provoked, we'd have an even harder job on our hands. 'But thank you for suggesting it. I want to keep what's going on between the four of us and give Dad time to come to his senses.'

'But what if he doesn't?' Flora asked, sounding desperate. 'What if Geoff doesn't come to his senses?'

'That,' I sighed, thinking there might be something subtle I could do to help things along, 'is a risk we're just going to have to take.'

'Are you sure, Ally?' Logan frowned, clearly still not convinced. 'It's a big risk.'

'I'm as sure as I can be.' I swallowed. 'Business as normal, for now at least. Okay?'

'Okay,' they all reluctantly agreed.

'What's going on here then?' asked Joe, who walked in having found the front door open and made us all jump. 'Has no one got any work to do?'

'I could ask the same of you,' said Flora. 'I thought you were going to be at the smokehouse all day.'

'I'm just having a bit of a break,' he told her.

'Good.' I smiled at him as I let Logan go. 'Because you're just the man I was hoping to see.'

'Always nice to hear.' He laughed.

'I have a favour to ask of you,' I said further.

'I knew there'd be a catch.' He tutted, but he was still smiling. 'Go on, then.'

'If I give you the money for it, could you order the cover for the polytunnel?'

'Is there any point?' Logan asked.

'I thought your dad wanted to do away with it.' Joe frowned.

'He did.' I nodded. 'He does, but I think he's wrong and we should fix it.'

'Me too,' Joe agreed.

'So, can you do it?'

'I'd be happy to,' he said, 'and I'll get a crew together to get it in place, too.'

'Excellent.' I smiled. 'Thanks, Joe.'

Later that day I caved and gave Dad the number of the solicitor he had been turning our office upside down trying to find. I couldn't give it up without a comment though in spite of what I'd said to Logan, Flora and Tara about waiting it out.

'Are you sure you need it, Dad?' I asked, handing over the old address book I'd previously hidden away until he started to try to google the number.

'I am,' he resolutely said, 'now more than ever.'

That didn't sound good, even to my ears, which were trying their best to put a positive spin on things.

'With any luck,' he carried on, flicking through to find the right page, 'I'll catch the fella I need before the end of the day and get the ball rolling.'

'Are you sure you've thought this through?' I said, my heart sinking in my chest on the assumption that he'd now definitely decided to sell.

'I've thought of little else,' he said, ushering me out of the door.

Determined not to let the realisation of what was happening overwhelm me, and knowing there was a lot that could happen between deciding to sell a property and it actually happening, I turned my attention to doing something I could enjoy and embrace with an open heart – further rekindling mine and Logan's romance.

We'd gone from boiling hot to oh, so not and with everything now out in the open, I was hellbent on both recharging our passion and thanking him for instigating my change of heart and helping me find a potential new career path. I knew that path might again change if the cottage was lost to me, but for this one evening, I was going to carry on regardless.

A supper picnic for two on the beach felt like as good a place to start as any.

'Wow,' said Logan, when he joined me. 'What's all this?'

'A date,' I said, taking a step away and looking down at the blanket I'd filled with fine food and drink. 'A proper, romantic date to draw a line under everything that's gone on between us before. I want us to pretend we're meeting for the first time after a tearful parting on our flight back from Barcelona.'

He cocked his head to one side and looked from me to the picnic and back again.

'I don't think I can do that,' he said.

'Oh,' I choked, feeling my stomach drop.

'We've had some really good times since I arrived in the cove and swapped city life for coastal living, Ally.' He then grinned. 'And I don't want to forget any of that, even if there has been some muddle and mayhem going on, too.'

My stomach unclenched as I took a step towards him.

'That's fair,' I agreed, smiling up at him. 'How about we do a bit of editing and stick to just remembering the best bits?'

'Like our time in the sea at Durdle Door?' he suggested.

'Exactly like that,' I sighed happily, my libido further leaping into life.

'That sounds like a far better plan,' he said, pulling me close and kicking this new phase of our relationship off with the longest kiss.

By the time we'd eaten our fill of the delicious food I'd cobbled together via the pub, Joe's smokehouse and the cottage stores, I was feeling replete and far more relaxed than the single glass of Prosecco, and the situation with Dad, warranted.

'I'm going to have to watch my alcohol intake around you, Logan,' I hiccupped, laughing.

'Oh,' he said, tracing a finger down my spine and making me tingle all over. 'Why's that then?'

'Because,' I said dreamily, 'being with you all of the time is going to make me feel drunk on a permanent basis.'

'I'm not sure if that's a good thing or a bad thing.' He smiled, sitting up. 'I associate being drunk with making bad decisions and suffering regrettable hangovers.'

'Tipsy then,' I amended, leaning into him. 'Just on the right side of tipsy.'

'That's better,' he said, softly kissing my neck. 'That's a far more pleasant state to be in. And I know I'm going to have to watch myself around you, too.'

'You are?' I gasped, in response to the touch of his lips.

'Yes, I am,' he said, punctuating each word with another tantalising kiss, before drawing away so he could look at me again. 'I know there was a time, not all that long ago, when you couldn't wait to escape the cove—'

'You do know I genuinely don't want to leave now though, right?' I cut in.

'I do know that.' He nodded. 'And the thing is, I don't want to leave, either. I'm every bit as invested as you are, Ally. I used to love life in the city but now I love living by the sea. More specifically in the cove.'

'Kittiwake Cove?' I asked, knowing he couldn't possibly mean anywhere else.

'That's the one.' He laughed, then turned serious. 'I can't bear the thought of leaving, but my time in the apartment is coming to an end and I have no idea what I'm going to do beyond that.'

On top of everything else I had going on, I couldn't allow myself to picture him packing up his car and driving away.

'Sorry,' he said, noticing my changed expression, 'I shouldn't have mentioned having to leave, not tonight. I didn't mean to bring the mood down.'

'It's fine,' I said, this time kissing him, 'we just need to come up with a way to keep you in the cove. There's still time. I'm adding you to my list of things to sort.'

If Dad has his way, we were both going to need a new home as well as new jobs, so I added those to the list, too.

'Your increasingly lengthy list.' Logan frowned.

'That's the one,' I said, puffing out my cheeks.

I didn't want our mood to dip further. Not when we'd been having such a wonderful time, so I pulled him in for another kiss.

'You're vibrating,' Logan suddenly said, mid-kiss.

'It's my phone.' I laughed, pulling it out of my pocket.

I realised then that the dance anthem Logan used as his mobile ringtone was the same one as I'd heard belting out of Tara's phone. I wondered what would have happened had I made the connection sooner. Would I have worked out what they were up to? I supposed, there was no point dwelling on that now.

'It's a message from Flora.' I grinned, when I read what she had typed. 'Dad's already gone to bed and she doesn't think he'd notice if I didn't make it home tonight.'

'In that case,' said Logan, leaping up and gathering the remains of the picnic together, 'I'd be more than happy to offer you a bed for the night.'

'Now that,' I said, holding out my hand so he could pull me up, 'is an offer I'm not going to refuse!'

It felt amazing to be properly back in Logan's life, not to mention in his bed, with no secrets and no pretence. The next course ran like clockwork and I'd even cooked a simple dish on the Saturday. The whole week would have been perfect, had it not been for the fact that Dad was in almost constant touch with his solicitor and I was still none the wiser as to why.

'I thought I might spend some time in the garden today, Dad,' I told him, the morning the polytunnel cover was due to go up. 'Will you come out with me?'

'I can't,' he said, 'I'm expecting a phone call and Vanessa is going to drop in at some point, so I need to be here to let her in.'

I had been hard pushed not to fill Vanessa in on what was happening, but as everyone else had been carrying on as normal, as I'd requested, I had gritted my teeth and stuck to that course of action, too.

'I'm sure she can find her own way in,' I pointed out.

'I might join you later,' Dad conceded, but I didn't hold out much hope. 'After I've taken this call, I'm waiting for. And I'm going to talk to Logan today, too.'

'Fair enough,' I said, thinking it was about time he did talk to him. Logan had been on tenterhooks waiting to be summoned. 'I'll leave you to it.'

'Is he coming?' Flora asked eagerly, as she looked over my shoulder when I joined her and the others outside.

I was still amazed by how much the garden had recovered after the ravages of the storm. It was living proof of the resilience of nature and I wished Dad would take a look at it. I knew he had been heartbroken by the aftermath, but if he could just see the improved state of things now, I was sure he'd feel differently about wanting to leave.

'He said he might,' I told her. 'He's waiting on a phone call.'

'From the solicitor?' she asked, biting her lip.

'Most likely,' I said, although he hadn't said as much. 'It's been like a hotline between the cottage and the office for days now. Come on,' I added, not wanting to dwell on it, 'let's go and see if we can help Joe and the others.'

I was truly touched to see that so many people had come to help. All they knew about the polytunnel's path to recovery was that Geoff needed a hand with it and they had turned up to pitch in, much like they had in the aftermath of the storm. Even Tara was in civvies and gloves and willing to help.

Joe talked us through what he thought would be the best way to get the vast cover up and over and we all moved into the positions he assigned us.

'Right, come on,' he then shouted. 'Let's get this done!'

It took almost an hour to reach the point where we had the sheet laid out and ready to heave up and over and my arms were already beginning to ache.

'On three!' Joe bellowed. 'One, Two—'

'Wait!' shouted a voice behind us. 'Wait! You need more people on this side.'

I dropped the piece of cover I was holding and spun around to find Dad speedily approaching on his crutches with Vanessa close behind.

'Well, about time!' shouted Michael from the pub, who had no idea just how significant Dad's appearance was.

'Dad,' I said, rushing over as he looked around the garden.

'Would you look at this?' he said, his eyes taking it all in. 'This isn't half as bad as it was after the storm, is it?'

'It's not.' I swallowed, a lump forming in my throat.

'I had no idea . . .'

'Everyone's been working so hard to clear and tidy it, Dad,' I told him. 'And mother nature has been lending a hand,' I added, thinking how things were beginning to grow and green up again. 'And I know Tara's dad will most likely pull the polytunnel down, but for now, I wanted to be able to use it again. For you to be able to use it again.'

'Tara's dad?' Dad frowned, sounding genuinely confused.

'What did I tell you, Geoff?' Vanessa groaned, sounding annoyed. 'I knew this would happen if you didn't spell things out. I'll take your place, Ally,' she insisted. 'You carry on talking to your dad.'

'What did Vanessa tell you?' I frowned, as she rushed to take my place in the line up just as Joe moved a couple of people and shouted for everyone to start pulling again.

Dad took a few steps back so we were further out of earshot and I stuck close to his side.

'She told me that I hadn't made my intentions clear,' he said, his eyes bright and his cheeks flushed pink, 'and that confusion would arise as a result.'

'Your intentions to sell the cottage.' I swallowed. 'She needn't have worried about that. I've got the message. I only wish it was the wrong one.'

'It is,' said Dad, shaking his head. 'I'm not selling Hollyhock Cottage.'

'What?' I gasped. 'You're not?'

'Of course, I'm not,' Dad rushed on. 'I can't possibly leave here. I only ever said I was considering that offer, didn't I? And the second you told me who was behind it, and how they'd gone about making it, I dismissed it without another thought.'

'But the solicitor,' I blurted out. 'You've been talking to them every day. I thought it was to sort the sale.'

'No,' Dad said vehemently. 'I was sorting out my will. Something I should have done a long time ago and I instructed them to write a strongly worded letter to Tara's father, rejecting his offer, too.'

'Oh, Dad,' I said, flinging my arms around him and almost unbalancing him. 'I've been out of my mind with worry.'

'I'm sorry, love,' he said, hugging me back as best he could with his crutches in his hands. 'But if you were so concerned, and as I hadn't made the situation clear like Vanessa said I should have done, why on earth didn't you just ask me about it?'

'Because I didn't want to aggravate the situation,' I admitted. 'And I didn't want to unsettle your blood pressure again, either. I'm sorry,' I said, shaking my head and thinking this whole thing could have been resolved days ago. 'From now on, if there's something bugging me, I'll bring it up.'

'Good,' said Dad, hugging me again. 'And while we're doling out apologies, I'm sorry, too.'

'What about?'

'Not believing you when you said you wanted to stay in Kittiwake Cove for all the right reasons,' he said, making my heart race.

'But you believe that now?' I laughed, thinking all my Christmases had come at once.

'I do.' He nodded. 'Vanessa has just made it very clear to me.'

I was going to be throwing my arms around her, too.

'So,' I said, my vision blurring with tears, 'we're staying in Kittiwake Cove.'

'Of course we are.' Dad beamed. 'The cottage is your legacy, love. One you wouldn't have wanted in the past, but I know you feel differently now.'

'Oh, I do,' I said, wiping my eyes. 'Yes, I do.'

'Now come on,' he said, nudging me out of the way with one of his crutches. 'Let the dog see the rabbit, because Joe will never get the cover on at this rate and I need to clear the air with Logan, too.'

I stood back and happily watched him take charge. Logan looked over at me and grinned and I felt my heart kick in my chest. Everything was falling properly into place and I had finally found the place in the world that I wanted to call my home, forever.

# Chapter 32

The morning of the first day of the Kittiwake Cove carnival dawned bright and sunny and with a day of helping out ahead, I didn't need distractions of any kind, but when Flora came bursting into the kitchen after an extra early trip to the beach to meet Joe, I knew I was in for the first delay of the day. Dad and I gave Kasuku a cautionary look, but thankfully the old parrot seemed willing to let her sudden arrival pass without squawk or comment.

'Do you have to run everywhere?' asked Joe, who came panting in behind her.

'I'm making up for lost time.' She beamed at him, her face aglow. 'Remember?'

Vanessa, who was almost permanently in residence now, and I exchanged a look but she appeared to be as clueless as I felt.

'What's going on?' yawned Logan, who hadn't been keen to make such an early start and had only just padded down the stairs to join us.

When I looked over at him, I had to battle to resist the urge to drag him straight back up the stairs again. I fancied him the most when he was all mussed up and now that, with

Dad's blessing after their heart to heart, he'd moved out of the garden apartment and into the house, I saw him in that state, a lot.

His time staying in the courtyard wasn't strictly up, but as Tara was currently not working, had no income and no desire to return to living under the same roof as her dad, she'd packed up her room in her parents' home and moved into the apartment. She and Logan had fledgling plans to set up a business together and Dad and I had decided to forgo the rent on the apartment for the rest of the season so they could get their ducks in a row. We had all commented on how ironic it was that she was living rent-free on site at Hollyhock Cottage when the original plan was for her to buy it outright, but not live there at all.

'Where's the fire?' Tara then asked as she too rushed in through the same door where Flora and Joe had just appeared. 'Freddie said you looked like you'd got the wind behind you when you ran back from the beach, Flora. Is everything okay?'

'Where is my brother?' Flora frowned.

'Here!' Freddie wheezed. 'I gave Tara a head start today.'

'Yeah, right.' Tara guffawed, clapping him on the back. 'You keep telling yourself that, my friend.'

While Logan and I had carried on with our chilly morning swims, Tara and Freddie had taken to running together.

'So,' said Flora, happily looking about her, 'here we all are then and that couldn't be better, actually.'

I looked around and realised she was right. Everyone I cared most about in the whole world was now assembled in the kitchen and they had all played a part in helping me fall in love with both the cottage and the cove and find a new way of fulfilling my ambitions there. Apart from Kasuku perhaps, although he was now far better behaved than he had been even just a few weeks ago, so I supposed I should give him some credit.

'Why's that then, Flora?' Dad asked.

She reached for Joe's hand and the pair stood side by side.

'Because,' said Joe, breathlessly answering on her behalf, 'Flora is desperate for you all to know that I've just asked her to marry me . . .'

'And I said, yes!' Flora squealed.

It took some minutes for the shouts, whoops and inevitable avian squawks to die down and then when the pair said they were planning for the wedding to happen in the autumn, which was just a few weeks away, it all kicked off again.

'We've wasted enough time,' said Flora, as she and I hugged. 'And Geoff,' she said, releasing me and turning to Dad who had jumped up in spite of the weighty boot on his leg and was shaking hands with Joe. 'We're not having a traditional cere- mony, but nonetheless, I was wondering if you would do me the honour of giving me away? You've always been more of a father to me than my own dad.'

'I would be honoured,' Dad told her, the words catching in his throat and there wasn't a dry eye in the house after that.

I was going to be at Flora's beck and call as the non- traditional equivalent maid of honour, while Freddie would be best man, and Tara and Logan offered to be on-hand to help with anything we couldn't manage. For a low-key, alternative wedding, it was already getting out of hand! I hoped Kasuku didn't fancy himself as ringbearer . . .

*

It was unusual to see the cove bustling and so busy. Usually, it was the town of Shellcombe that was swamped with sunseekers, but the Kittiwake Cove carnival was a very special celebration of a different kind of life beside the sea in Dorset. I couldn't help thinking that it was a shame this was the first year I'd taken that on board, but then I decided I should embrace Flora's mindset, throw myself into it and make up for lost time.

Once I'd checked the festival marquee was up and running and that the various tutors who came to teach at the cottage had everything they needed to make plenty of sales on their stalls, I discovered I wasn't the only one throwing myself into the occasion.

'Did you know?' I gasped, my eyes on stalks. 'Did she tell you?'

'Nope,' Logan laughed. 'I didn't have a clue.'

Sitting above a huge pool of water on a ducking stool was Tara. She was soaked and shivering, so someone had already hit the target and sent her plummeting. She caught sight of us and waved, just as another contender struck lucky and she dropped like a stone, with a dramatic squeal and splash, which made everyone laugh.

'Do you want a go?' Logan asked me.

As tempted as I was, I passed on the opportunity.

'No,' I smiled, clapping along as Tara, as elegantly as she could, retook her spot and was hoisted up again. 'I'd only be disappointed if I missed.'

Logan tickled me when I said that.

'You meanie.' He laughed. 'You've forgiven her now, haven't you?'

'Of course I have.' I grinned wickedly. 'But when she's set herself up like that, it is tempting, isn't it?'

'I was the first one to knock her in,' said Flora, who happened to walk by, carrying a tray of bread rolls down to the smokehouse.

'From what I know about your shared history,' Logan said, taking the tray from her as we all fell into step, 'I'm not at all surprised to hear that.'

'Come and try these scallops Joe's smoked,' Flora said, neatly changing the subject. 'They're selling like hotcakes, but I asked him to save you some.'

Dad and Vanessa were sampling them too and the four of us set up a makeshift picnic near the rocks, away from the main hustle and bustle and as far as Dad could comfortably get.

'Divine,' he said, wiping his mouth with a paper napkin and we all agreed. 'I hope they'll be on the wedding feast menu.'

'Oh yes,' I said. 'They'll be properly in season by then, won't they?'

Dad nodded and popped another one into his mouth.

'I'm going to offer to do the catering,' he said, once he'd savoured and swallowed.

'And I know a photographer who I can rope in to help,' said Vanessa.

'Flora will love having everyone involved,' I said. 'Maybe she and Joe would consider having the ceremony at the cottage, Dad,' I suggested.

'I noticed some of the hollyhocks are already starting to flower again,' said Logan, which I could tell made Dad's day. 'And I thought we could have a go at fixing up your potting bench next week Geoff and get some more salad going.'

'Sounds good to me,' said Dad. 'If we're lucky it'll be ready to harvest in no time. You've got yourself a keeper here,

Ally,' he added, nodding at Logan. 'Don't let him go again, will you?'

I felt my face flush.

'Leave them alone, Geoff,' tutted Vanessa good-naturedly.

'No, Dad.' I smiled, as I thought how wonderful it felt to have Vanessa in my corner. 'I won't. I'm keeping everything here in the cove close to my heart from now on. Logan, you, Vanessa, my friends, our home and our business *and* my new role with the Historical Society.'

'I'm thrilled to hear it,' said Dad leaning over and kissing my cheek. 'I can't begin to tell you how much I'm looking forward to seeing where you take us next, with these wonderful new plans you've got.'

'I did wonder if you'd forgotten about those.'

'Absolutely not,' he said. 'But first, when the season comes to an end, and if you can manage to squeeze it in, I want to send you and Logan back to Barcelona for a week or two.'

'Oh Dad,' I gasped, thinking how wonderful that would be and feeling grateful that the Society were willing to be flexible about my start date. 'Really?'

'It's practically arranged already,' said Logan, beaming. He was clearly in cahoots with Dad and I didn't think I could love him more.

'And when you get back,' Vanessa brightly said, giving me a nudge, 'your dad and I are going away somewhere, too.'

'Really?' I was shocked, but delighted to hear that.

I didn't think it would do Dad any harm to take a break with the new woman in his life. Sticking to the old but also embracing the new felt like a fine way forward for him and me.

'Really,' said Dad. 'I've worked out there's a life beyond the cove.'

'While I've worked out my best life is in it.' I laughed.

Having later taken my final turn on the carnival committee duty rota, I was released from my role in time for Logan and me to head out to the pontoon to watch the fireworks that were being launched from the cliffs above the village.

Rather than swim, he'd booked us a couple of paddle-boards so we could enjoy the spectacle in dry clothes and thankfully we'd both kept our balance and not fallen off on the trip across.

'Where had you hidden this?' I asked, as he uncorked and poured Champagne into two flutes.

'Didn't you notice I had a rucksack?' He grinned, producing a container filled with croquetas and another containing a dip.

'I was too busy trying to stay upright.' I laughed, sitting on the blanket he had spread out. 'You must have better balance than me. And where did you get this food from?'

I knew it wasn't Dad's.

'From the restaurant Tara took Flora to,' Logan said, sitting next to me. 'I wanted us to enjoy a sort of Dorset and Spanish fusion tonight.'

'Where we started,' I sighed happily, 'combined with where we've ended up.'

'Exactly,' he said, as I leaned into his arms and he kissed me softly on the lips. 'And who knows where we'll go next.'

We kissed until the first fireworks sent up showers of spark-ling gold and silver stars high into the evening sky.

'If it's all right with you,' I smiled, having mulled over what he'd said once the first wave of the display was over and after he had kissed me again, 'once we're back from Barcelona, I'd very much like to stay here for a while.'

'In Kittiwake Cove?' He smiled.

'Right here in Kittiwake Cove.' I smiled back. 'It's now by far, my favourite place in the whole world.'

# Acknowledgements

What a pleasure it has been to write a second standalone title and whisk you away to another UK county I love, Dorset. I had the pleasure of living there for a couple of years during the mid to late nineties and my son was born there, so I have very fond memories of Wimborne and the surrounding countryside and coast.

As always, I have multiple people to thank for their support, both in the creation of this book and beyond.

First up my fabulous agent, Amanda Preston, and editor extraordinaire, Clare Hey. What a dream team you are! Thank you and the entire Books and The City Team for your continued enthusiasm for my words. Thanks also to the fabulous rights department at S&S, who are sending those words further around the globe year on year. You're all amazing!

My Famous Five have played a larger than usual part in keeping me on track during the last few months and our inaugural getaway last autumn was an absolute highlight and a hilarious one, too! Thank you, my loves. Here's to many, many more.

Thanks also to my non-writing but still essential chums Claire Howard (constantly referred to as Jewellery Claire now) and Sue Baker. This book is for you, Sue. I can't tell you how much I appreciate my 24/7 hotline to you and the fact that, more often that not, you know that I need you before I do, something I'm very grateful for!

A huge thank you to all of the event organisers, librarians, newsletter subscribers and bloggers who so kindly continue to be stalwart champions of my books and an extra thank you to librarian Louise at Dereham Library who has been instrumental in broadening my reading horizons in the Second Sunday Book Club. If you're local, do come along.

And last, but never least, the hugest of all hugs has been reserved for my wonderful readers. Whether this is your first book by me, or your eighteenth (yep, I've just counted and, amazingly, it is eighteen), please know that you are always welcome in my fictional worlds. With so many books to choose from, I'm both honoured and delighted that you've picked up mine. Thank you.

So, until next time, my loves, may your bookshelves – be they virtual or real – always be filled with fabulous fiction.

With love

H x

# About the Author

Heidi Swain lives in Norfolk. She is passionate about gardening and the countryside, and collects vintage paraphernalia. *The Holiday Escape* is her eighteenth novel. You can follow Heidi on Twitter @Heidi_Swain or visit her website: heidiswain.co.uk

# The Book-Lovers' Retreat

Novel *Hope Falls* is friends Emily, Rachel and Tori's favourite book. So, when they get the chance to spend summer at the cottage in Lakeside where the film adaptation was located, they know it is going to be the holiday of a lifetime.

Six weeks away will give them a chance to re-evaluate their life choices. For Emily to make career plans and for Rachel to decide whether to move in with her partner Jeremy. Then Tori has to drop out at the last moment, and her space is offered to another *Hope Falls* afficionado, Alex.

Alex turns out not to be who they expected. But as the summer develops, so does their friendship. Could this be where their lives will change course forever . . . ?

AVAILABLE IN PAPERBACK AND EBOOK NOW

# The Summer Fair

Beth loves her job working in a care home, looking
after its elderly residents, but she doesn't love
the cramped and dirty houseshare she currently
lives in. So, when she gets the opportunity to
move to Nightingale Square, sharing a house
with the lovely Eli, she jumps at the chance.

The community at Nightingale Square welcomes
Beth with open arms, and when she needs help
to organise a fundraiser for the care home they
rally round. Then she discovers The Arches,
a local creative arts centre, has closed and the
venture to replace it needs their help too – but
this opens old wounds and past secrets for Beth.

Music was always an important part of her life, but now
she has closed the door on all that. Will her friends at
the care home and the people of Nightingale Square
help her find a way to learn to love it once more . . . ?

AVAILABLE IN PAPERBACK AND EBOOK NOW

# That Festive Feeling

Holly has the place to herself this Christmas, house-sitting for friends who live on Nightingale Square. Newly single and finding herself unsure about next steps for her career, she plans to hunker down and make some life decisions.

On early morning walks around a nearby lake she bumps into May, who is also new to the area, and her dapper Dachshund Monty. Quickly, a firm friendship blossoms. Then when Holly meets Bear, a rather large and rather attractive man, and his rescue dog Queenie, her stay suddenly feels even more appealing.

As the community comes together for the season's festivities, Holly must start thinking about where life will take her next. But distractions close to home make thinking about the future more tricky than ever ...

Will she get that festive feeling this Christmas?

AVAILABLE IN PAPERBACK AND EBOOK NOW

# A Christmas Celebration

When Paige turns up unannounced at Wynthorpe Hall, she discovers the place she knew when she was growing up has changed beyond all recognition.

One night while driving home after delivering library books and shopping to residents she stumbles across an isolated cottage and meets Albert, its elderly and rather grumpy owner. She quickly realises there's more to Albert than meets the eye and the same can be said for the other man she can't seem to help running into, handsome but brooding Brodie.

Each of them has a secret and a desire to hide away from the world, but with Christmas on the horizon, is that really the best way to celebrate the season?

AVAILABLE IN PAPERBACK AND EBOOK NOW

# A Taste of Home

Fliss Brown has grown up living with her mother on the Rossi family's Italian fruit farm. But when her mother dies, Fliss finds out she has a family of her own, and heads back to England with Nonna Rossi's recipe for cherry and almond tart and a piece of advice: connect with your family before it is too late ...

Fliss discovers that her estranged grandfather owns a fruit farm himself, on the outskirts of Wynbridge, and she arrives to find a farm that has fallen into disrepair. Using her knowledge gleaned from working on the Rossi farm and her desire to find out more about her past, Fliss rolls her sleeves up and gets stuck in. But what will she discover, and can she resurrect the farm's glory days and find a taste of home?

AVAILABLE IN PAPERBACK AND EBOOK NOW